WICKED Betrayal

SIAN CEINWEN

This book is sold subject to the condition that the reader gives the author tips on how best to control frizzy hair. It must also be accepted that the author reserves the right to have each member of the harem as her personal book boyfriends. This will remain so either for life or for perpetuity should she find a way to come back from the grave to claim them after her untimely demise due to too many orgasms.

ISBN: 978-1-922559-27-2 (eBook)
ISBN: 978-1-922559-28-9 (Paperback)

Front cover image by Mark Reid at **authorpackages.com** .
Book design by Lorna Reid at **authorpackages.com** .

Acknowledgement of Country

I would like to acknowledge the Traditional Owners of Country throughout Australia and recognise their continuing connection to land, waters, and community.

The Whadjuk people of the Noongar Nation are the traditional custodians of the land this book was written on.

I acknowledge that sovereignty throughout these lands was never ceded. I pay my respect to them and their cultures, and to the strength and resilience of Elders both past and present.

Dedication

This book is for you, dear reader, because you deserve *cocks* in the first chapter.

The lovely Vera Valentine coined the unit of measurement Smut by Volume (SBV) when I wrote Wicked Opportunity. The SBV of that book was 64.58%. This book has an SBV of 69.69%. Take from that what you will.

Make no mistake, though, major character developments are made through the smut. It's precisely what I love about this book and reverse harem in general.

In what other genre can the heroine make major shifts in the plot by being a cum dumpster for multiple men? Very few, I daresay.

Raise a glass with me to Lexi as she once again has at least one of her holes absolutely wrecked in (nearly) every chapter.

Chapter One

As Ash is My Witness

We need to talk.

I stare at the text Cassandra Foster sent me. I'm pretty sure those are the worst four words in the English language. I'm meant to be getting into a bikini so I can go swimming, but I stare at Cassie's text instead.

The guys suggested that I should reply later, so it doesn't ruin our day. I haven't even opened my phone, so the message won't show up as having been read. Instead, it just sits on my phone's lock screen…driving me nuts.

I throw my phone onto the bed and stride into the closet because I need to forget Cassie and her 'need to talk.' I pull out a metallic silver bikini and put it on. It has steel rings in between the cups and shows plenty of cleavage. The same hardware is used to hold the front and the back of the bottoms together.

I run a brush through my auburn hair before I pull it into a bun on the top of my head, then turn side to side and check out my rear in the mirror. The fabric of the bikini is really just a nod to modesty, and my ass is basically exposed. Even so, this is one of the few bikinis I have with me, and considering the others are either mesh or become see-through when wet, this is really my only option.

I head downstairs to the pool where the four members of the band Wicked Stallion are currently swimming. They all look up as I arrive, three of them obviously ogling me, and the fourth with a cheerful smile on his face.

"Hey, Angel. What took so long?" My husband, Dante Sullivan, asks from the other side of the pool as I sit on the edge and slide into the warm water.

All four men are topless and wearing boardshorts as they tread water in front of me. With their fit, muscular bodies on display for me, I can't help but enjoy the view myself.

"I was deciding what to wear," I say casually and pretend as though I didn't spend a solid five minutes just staring at Cassie's text.

"I like this bikini, Sexy Lexi." Nathaniel Walker turns his bright blue eyes to me and pushes his wet, black hair out of his face with a grin. "I think I'd prefer it on the bottom of the pool, though."

"I'm not sure Ash would appreciate that," I say with a laugh as I swim to where he is with our friend.

I kiss Nate, and he pulls me to him as the bulge in his shorts presses against me. My pussy aches as I think about what we would be doing if Ashton Woodford weren't here with us. He's the only member of the band that I'm not sleeping with, and I look over at him where he's swimming nearby. He's got blonde hair with blue eyes and is just as muscular and attractive as his friends. I can certainly appreciate his good looks even if I'm not sleeping with him.

Ash grins at me. "Sorry, I'm such a party pooper for you guys."

"Could've been worse. You could've knocked on the door last night and told us to keep it down," Nate tells him with a laugh.

"And stop the live sex show? Of course not."

Ash winks at him, and heat rushes to my cheeks at the thought of him listening to us having sex.

"Is voyeurism your thing, Ashton Woodford?" Nate teases him.

"Not until last night, apparently." He wiggles his eyebrows suggestively, and we laugh.

I swim over to where Dante and Logan Ballantine are talking as they hold on to the edge of the pool. Both men have brown hair and chocolate brown eyes, but Dante is a few inches taller than Logan. They look up as I approach, and both of their gazes darken as they look me over.

"Hi, guys," I say with a smile as I wrap my arms around Dante's neck and kiss him.

I wrap my legs around his waist as our tongues intertwine, and he gently strokes my back. When our kiss ends, I turn to Logan and give him the same treatment. He maneuvers me around, though, so my back is against the edge of the pool.

We're both breathing heavily when our kiss ends, and Logan murmurs, "Do you know what I would do to you if Ash weren't here, Alexandra?"

My full name. It's the codeword that tells me he's Domming me, and I need to reply in kind.

"I don't know, Sir."

He gives me a slow, sexy smile and says, "I would sit you on the side of this pool, spread your legs, and eat your pussy."

As he says it, he slips his hand between us and underneath the waistband of my bikini. Despite the fact I'm in water, my pussy is wet with my own juices, especially when Logan begins rubbing my clit.

"No reactions, Angel," Dante says, and the way he says my nickname is his codeword that he's Domming me.

"You don't want Ash to realize what we're doing," Logan agrees.

He lowers his head to nip my bottom lip with his teeth, and the pain is swiftly overtaken by arousal. It takes everything within me not to gasp or moan aloud as he continues his movements.

He raises his other hand to my breast, reaches into my bikini top, and twists my nipple before he kisses me. I'm lost in the pleasure he's giving me, and when our kiss ends, Logan stares into my eyes as he watches me.

"Come for me, Alexandra. Not a single sound or I'll spank you the second Ash is out of sight."

I bite my lip and stare at him with my eyes wide as I pant for breath when my orgasm crashes over me. My body shakes, and he continues to stroke my clit as I ride out the waves of pleasure.

He gives me a sexy smile and kisses me softly. He puts his arms around me, and I wrap my legs around his waist. Logan's cock is hard against me, and I can't resist rubbing my pussy against it as he hugs me.

"I'm definitely going to need some relief later," he says with a laugh, then looks at Dante. "What about you?"

Dante takes one of my hands from around Logan's neck and pulls it down into the water to place it on his erection. He rubs my hand up and down a few times before he lets go, and I stroke him a few times more before I take my hand away.

"Definitely," Dante says in a husky voice.

"Is it bad that I wish Ash weren't here?" I ask quietly.

Logan kisses my lips and chuckles, "You just had an orgasm. Why do you wish that?"

I look into his beautiful chocolate brown eyes and grin at him. "Because one is never enough, plus I can feel your cock is hard, and I want to fix that."

"There's nothing stopping you from fixing it," Logan says and shrugs.

My mouth drops open, and I whip my head around to look at Ash and Nate, where they're talking nearby.

"Not in front of Ash," I say with a gasp.

Logan chuckles. "No. Not in front of Ash, but he's having fun talking to Nate. There's nothing to stop Dante and me from taking you upstairs so you can fix our problem."

My pussy aches at the thought, and I nod my consent. Not that he really needs it. He can just use my full name, and I'll do anything he wants.

"We're going upstairs for a bit. We'll see you guys later," Dante calls out to Nate and Ash.

Nate gives me a wicked grin and says, "Have fun with her."

Heat rushes to my cheeks as he says it, and Ash asks, "So, is this what it's like for you guys now? People just taking off and having sex all the time?"

"Pretty much," Logan laughs. "It's just like Nate has been doing for years, except the woman is always Lexi, and sometimes none of us leave the room."

"Well, have fun then, I guess," he says with a grin.

We get towels and wrap them around ourselves, but as soon as we're in the hallway leading out of the pool area, Dante says, "Stop, Angel." I stop where I'm standing and look up at him. "Take off your bikini."

I hand my towel to Logan for him to hold it for me and reach behind myself to untie the top. I lift it over my head and hand it to Dante before I pull off my bikini bottoms and hand them to him as well.

Logan takes the towel and rubs the soft fabric over my skin. While he's on his knees rubbing my legs down, he leans forward and swipes his tongue through my wet slit. I bite my lip and moan in satisfaction before he stands up again.

"Okay, you're dry enough to go upstairs," he says in a husky voice.

My pussy aches to be filled, and the fear that Nate and Ash might decide to leave the pool hits me as I take my bikini back off Dante. We go upstairs to the room Dante slept in last night, and relief floods through me as we make it there safely. We drop our towels and swimming clothes in the bathroom before we head back to the bedroom completely naked.

"On your knees, Angel," Dante says, and I drop to my knees where I'm standing a few feet away from them.

Both men look at me while slowly stroking their hard cocks, and I bite my lip as I wait to see what they will do.

"My toy has a pretty mouth. Don't you think, Dante?" Logan says casually to him.

"She definitely does. You should probably put it to good use," he agrees.

Desire courses through my body I watch Logan take a few steps toward me. I love sucking cock, and both of these men know it. He pushes his cock into my mouth and holds my head in his hands as he fucks me.

I'm dripping wet, and I lower my hand to my clit even though I know Dante will probably stop me from giving myself an orgasm.

Sure enough, he says in a low voice, "No, Angel."

I remove my hand from my clit, and Dante moves next to me. Logan releases his hold on my head and pulls his cock from my mouth. I take it in my hand and stroke him as Dante pushes his cock into my mouth instead.

I alternate back and forth between the two men for a while. Sucking one and stroking the other until Dante pulls me up to standing.

He looks at Logan and grins at him. "You took the lube out of this room last night."

"Shit. Yeah, we did. Do you want her ass today?"

"I thought it might be nice," Dante says as he gives me a wicked grin. "Go get the lube, Angel."

My eyes widen, and I gasp. "You want me to go get the lube from Nate's room, Honey?"

I have just enough sense to use his name, so it sounds less like I'm questioning him.

"Yes. Do you have a problem with that?"

I shake my head, but my heart pounds in my chest.

"Well, you should go quickly. I don't want poor Ash to see you naked when he least expects it."

I have no idea where Nate and Ash are now. I walk quickly to the door. There's no question that I'll follow the instruction, and the longer I wait to do it, the more likely it is that I might stumble across Nate and Ash. Fingers crossed they're still in the pool, but we've been up here for a while now.

I close the door behind me as quietly as I can. Unlike last night when I snuck to this room for the lube in the dark, the hallway is bright, and I feel utterly exposed. I pad along the thick, plush carpet toward Nate's room.

The opening with the sweeping staircase which leads downstairs feels dangerous, and my already racing heartbeat doubles as I approach it. There's no sign of Nate or Ash, so I rush across the opening and make it to Nate's room, safe and sound.

The lube is on the bedside table from when we used it this morning, and I snatch it up before I head out of the room again. Just as I reach the top of the staircase and move into sight of the foyer below, Nate and Ash's laughter rings out.

I turn my head and am horrified when I see Ash walking toward the staircase with Nate. My pussy aches, and my nipples stiffen at the thought of being caught. It's erotic and exciting, but it doesn't mean I actually want it to happen, so I continue across the opening as quickly as I can.

It feels as though the safety of the hallway on the other side of the staircase is a mile away. My blood rushes around my body, and I'm heated as I rush across the opening.

Just as I enter the hallway, Ash's voice reaches my ears. "Um, was that Lexi?"

"Probably," Nate tells him with a laugh.

I reach the safety of Dante's room and slam the door shut behind me as soon as I can. Dante and Logan look over in surprise as I appear in front of them.

"Everything okay, Angel?" Dante asks.

I shake my head. "No. Ash and Nate were heading upstairs when I was coming back."

"Did they see you?" Logan asks as he tilts his head to the side.

"I think so," I tell him, heat rushing to my cheeks.

Dante shakes his head. "Naughty, Angel. You took too long if Ash saw you. Bend over the bed."

My pussy aches as I hand Logan the lube and bend over the bed to wait for my punishment. The room is filled with heavy breathing from the three of us, and my juices drip down my thigh. I don't know what has me turned on the most; the fact that I'm about to be fucked by Dante and Logan or the fact that I was exposed to Ash and Nate when I ran past the staircase.

Dante smacks my ass hard, and I bite my lip to stop myself from calling out, but he says, "You can react, Angel."

He smacks my ass again, and I gasp loudly. He does it a total of five times, and by the last one, I grunt as he hits my stinging ass.

"Do you want to do the other cheek, Logan?"

I bite my lip as I wait for Logan to reply because he hits harder than Dante, and I squirm in place as I think about him spanking me.

"Why not? Sounds like fun."

There are some shuffling noises before Logan trails his hand gently over my hot, stinging ass cheek. His hand disappears from my skin before he spanks my other ass cheek hard, and I shriek loudly. He gently strokes the place he's spanked me before he does it again, even harder.

I shriek again but then moan loudly again. I'm suddenly very aware of the fact that we're in the room across from Ash's, and they were coming upstairs.

Can he hear me?

Considering he heard us last night when we were in Nate's room, he probably can. My pussy aches just from knowing that, and I moan again as Logan spanks me a third time.

He gently rubs my ass, then lowers his fingers and pushes two inside me. "She's very wet, Dante. I think she's enjoying this punishment a little too much." He begins rubbing my clit with his other hand and asks, "Do you like being punished, Alexandra?"

"Yes, Sir," I groan.

"I see."

He pulls his fingers out of me and stops rubbing my clit as well before he spanks my ass hard again, which causes me to jump. It definitely hurts more now, and I'm filled with the need to be fucked.

Logan spanks me a final time, then lowers his head to kiss my burning ass cheek. He places a hand on each cheek and spreads them apart before he tongues my hole.

I bite my lip and moan loudly, "Oh fuck, that feels good, Sir."

Dante moves next to me so he can reach between my legs to

rub my clit, and I lose myself in the pleasure these two men are giving me. My ass is still stinging under Logan's hands, but it swirls together with the pleasure of him eating my ass while Dante strokes my clit.

I moan wildly, and at the back of my head, I'm aware that I'm being louder than usual. I'm playing this up because the idea of Ash listening to this is hot as fuck. I imagine him in his bedroom, lying on his bed, and stroking his cock while he listens to us fuck in the room across from him. The thought of it topples me over into orgasm.

I scream as my body shakes, and both Dante and Logan continue with what they're doing to me. My clit is painfully sensitive when they keep going, and it isn't long until I have another orgasm. Finally, they stop, and Logan climbs onto the bed.

He lies on his back and says, "Ride me, Alexandra."

I straddle him, then lower myself onto his thick cock, and I bite my lip again as my pussy stretches around him. He reaches his hands up and places them on my breasts to play with them while I bounce myself up and down on his hard shaft.

"You feel so fucking good," Logan growls, and I notice that he's not bothering to keep his voice down, either.

The thought of Ash eavesdropping on our scene makes me wild, and I moan loudly again.

"Kiss him, Angel," Dante says, and I notice that, unlike us, he's talking in a normal voice.

I lean down and kiss Logan, which is always incredibly pleasurable because he's so skilled at using his tongue. Dante drips cold lube onto my ass, and I continue fucking Logan as Dante pushes two fingers inside me.

When we first brought Nate into our relationship, I'd never had two cocks inside me at the same time before. I'm used to this now, though, and I don't think I'll ever tire of the feeling.

Dante pushes his cock into my ass, and I break my kiss with Logan to scream, "Yes. Yes. Fuck yes, that feels so good."

Again, the thought of Ash listening to us crosses my mind, and my pussy clenches tightly around Logan's cock. I'd be lying if I said I hadn't masturbated while thinking about Ash before. In fact, the concept of being fucked by all of these men at once has crossed my mind, but it's been a rare fantasy.

Now I get fucked by three men regularly, and even though I'm sexually attracted to Ash, I'm very aware that he's only just broken up with his girlfriend. So I think it's the exhibitionist in me that is loving this. I feel so exposed, and I love the idea of him using our show as inspiration while he pleasures himself.

Dante grabs my hips and fucks me as I lean down to kiss Logan again. I grind my pussy on his cock and squeeze him tight with my internal muscles. He places a hand on my breast and twists my nipple painfully, causing me to gasp loudly as he does.

"Sir," I scream out in ecstasy.

"Do you like that, Alexandra?" he growls at me.

"Yes, Sir."

"Is there something you want right now?"

"To come, Sir," I manage to say as I pant for breath.

"I can't hear you. What did you say?"

"I want to come, Sir," I moan loudly again, and Logan gives me a wicked grin.

"Beg for it, Alexandra."

This is new, and I'm certain the idea of having an audience is turning him on as well. If he wants me to give a show, then I'll give one.

"Please, Sir. I need to come." I give a loud moan that turns into a grunt as Dante slams into my ass, and I'm thrust down on Logan. "I need it so badly. Please let me come, Sir."

"Okay. Go wild," Logan says.

I change my angle and fuck him desperately while Dante fucks my ass. I'm so full with them both and so close to orgasm, especially when Logan continues to torment my breasts. When I reach my release, I take Logan's words to heart and literally go wild. I scream and moan and continue to fuck him desperately until he comes inside me.

I collapse on him as Dante gives his last few final thrusts into my ass and shoots his load in there. Dante leans down and kisses my neck before he pulls out of me. Logan pulls my face to his to kiss me, and his tongue intertwines with mine as the world glows around us. I'm in post-orgasmic bliss as we head to the bathroom to clean up. Dante uses a loofah to wash my body from head to toe and takes the showerhead out of the holder to aim the spray at me.

He uses it to rinse my body clean of the suds but also aims the spray at my clit for long enough that I moan in pleasure. Logan places his hand on my breasts from behind and thumbs my nipples as I turn my face to the side to kiss him. It doesn't take long for me to have an orgasm, and I moan my satisfaction into Logan's mouth as Dante finally moves the showerhead away from my pussy.

He hands the showerhead to Logan, who uses it to rinse the pool water out of my hair before handing it back to Dante again. Dante hangs it up as Logan gets shampoo to wash my hair. He massages my scalp, and I smile at the enjoyable feeling before Dante kisses me. He pulls me to him while Logan continues to wash my hair, and I'm lost in a combination of love and lust and sheer happiness.

Logan rinses my hair, then conditions it, and eventually rinses that out as well before we get out of the shower.

As Dante towels me dry, Logan kisses me, then says, "I love you, Lexi. Did you enjoy that?"

"Very much so," I tell him with a contented sigh.

"I wonder if Ash overheard us again," Logan asks with that same wicked grin at me.

Now that I'm coming down from my sex high, I'm mortified that I was as loud as I was. It seemed fine at the time, but now I'm horrified that our friend probably heard us. Let alone that he saw me naked.

"Oh my god, he saw me buck naked when I was getting the lube," I groan.

"You didn't seem to mind at the time," Dante says with a laugh as he hangs up the towel.

"Yes, but at the time, I was horny as hell and desperate to be fucked. Now that I've come all over Logan's cock, I'm faced with having to see Ash and travel back to Los Angeles with him."

Dante trails his fingers around the areola of my breast before he tweaks the nipple between his thumb and forefinger. "Ash probably considers himself lucky he got to see you naked. He's the only one of us that doesn't get to do that."

"Ash broke up with his girlfriend last night. I highly doubt that seeing me naked is high on his priority list," I laugh, but it turns into a moan with what Dante is doing to me.

"I don't know," Logan says with a grin. "What I'm hearing is that he now has to make do with his hand for company and needs the inspiration that you so kindly provided for him."

I shake my head. "You guys are terrible."

"And yet"—Dante reaches down and swipes a finger through my admittedly wet pussy—"you do seem aroused by this, Angel."

Heat rushes to my cheeks, and I shake my head again. "If you two don't mind, I'm going to go get dressed so we can travel back to Los Angeles with our *friend*."

I walk away from them toward the closet as they chuckle behind me. Yes, the thought of Ash overhearing us as we fucked was hot. Yes, I might have imagined him masturbating as he listened to us. That doesn't mean that I want him as anything other than a friend. Fuck knows our situation is complicated enough as it is.

This thought reminds me of Cassie's text, and any arousal I'm feeling vanishes instantly.

Chapter Two

Not Again

I lie on the bed with Dante for a while and enjoy his embrace before we head to the closet to get dressed.

I pull on a light blue dress that comes almost to my knees, and Dante looks over at me. "No underwear, Angel."

"Yes, Honey," I say, even though I wasn't expecting to get to wear any.

"Just making sure," he says with a smile as he walks over to me.

He reaches underneath my dress and pushes two fingers inside me.

"You need to be accessible at all times," he murmurs.

He raises a hand to my breast and strokes my hard nipple with his thumb as he continues to push his fingers in and out of me. He kisses me passionately, and I wind my arms around his neck as we kiss.

Dante pulls his lips from mine and removes his fingers from my pussy before he pushes them into my mouth and says, "Clean my fingers, Angel."

I suck my juices off his fingers as he watches me with a satisfied smile before he pulls his fingers out of my mouth. I'm sometimes amazed at how my men manage to keep me in a near-constant state of arousal when they fuck me so often. It's almost like the more sex I get, the more I want it.

"I'll pack our suitcases. Go see Nate, Angel."

I'm dismissed, and I'm aroused at the thought of seeing Nate as I turn to follow the instruction. I enter the hallway, and as I close the door behind me, I'm faced with the one into Ash's bedroom. Shame and embarrassment flood through me as I look at it. God, I fucking hope Ash went downstairs with Nate after I saw them. Preferably for a *long* walk outside and well out of earshot of our bedroom.

I'm tempted to peer in and see if Ash is in there, but Dante told me to go see Nate, and I couldn't handle the embarrassment if he is. I pad down the hallway and open the door to Nate's room.

My heart flutters in my chest as I take in the scene in front of me. Logan is on his knees in front of Nate with his mouth around Nate's cock.

Nate has his eyes closed, and he bites his lip as he groans in satisfaction. My pussy aches, but I'm not sure if they want me to be a part of this or not. I hover at the door in a quandary. Dante told me to come here, but they're in the middle of something. That being said, his instruction was to see Nate, which I've done.

I decide to leave them to it, and as I turn away to leave the room, Logan says, "Come here, Alexandra."

I give a small gasp and turn back to face them. Logan is stroking Nate's cock, and both men are smiling at me, though Nate is panting for breath and looks like he's lost in ecstasy.

"Nate overheard us, and he seemed to have a very similar problem to Dante and me in the pool earlier," Logan says as he continues stroking Nate's cock.

He's still only wearing a towel around his waist, and I assume that he came into Nate's room on the way back to his bedroom.

Nate moans softly, then looks at me with a grin on his face. "Yes, well, who can blame me when Lexi was begging so loudly for an orgasm that they could probably hear her back in LA?"

"Oh god, if you could hear me, then Ash probably could as well," I groan.

"I *know* he could hear you," Nate laughs, "because I was in his room with him when it started. I left when it got a little too awkward."

Heat rushes to my cheeks at the knowledge that Ash listened to us fucking, but the humilation quickly turns to arousal because it's hot as fuck to think about.

Nate e looks down at his cock, where Logan is still slowly stroking him, and Logan says, "Well, that should make for a fun trip home." He turns to look at me and raises an eyebrow. "I told you to come here, Alexandra, and you haven't. You'll be punished for that. Come here now."

I'm wildly aroused, and I wonder what my punishment will be as I walk over to the two beautiful men in front of me. I stop next to Nate, and Logan grabs the hem of my dress, then lifts it up to reveal my pussy.

"That's what I like to see," he says before he moves his mouth to me and licks my wet slit.

Nate leans across and kisses me. He moans into my mouth and reaches a hand into my dress to play with my breast. Logan has allowed my dress to fall back down, and he's covered by it as he pushes his fingers in and out of me.

Nate breaks our kiss and moves his mouth to my breast. He clamps his lips over it through the dress as he continues to pleasure my other breast with his hand. His tongue wets the fabric of my dress, which is slightly rough against my nipple, and I moan loudly.

Logan removes his mouth from my pussy, gets out from under my dress, and looks up at me. "I think that's enough pleasure for now, Alexandra. Nate can do whatever he wants to you, but you're not allowed to orgasm again until after we land back in LA."

I groan internally because that's going to be fucking *hours*, and when Logan takes Nate's cock back in his mouth, I squirm against the ache in my pussy. Nate is still playing with my breasts while Logan sucks him, and he takes my breast out of his mouth to give me the shit-eating grin he gets when he benefits from my sexual punishments.

"Sounds like a challenge. See if I can get Lexi to break the rules." He reaches underneath my dress and finds my wet pussy. "I don't think it'll be too hard."

I bite my lip as he rubs my clit for a few seconds before he takes his hand away and looks down at Logan.

"God, you're so good at that," he groans.

Logan looks up at him and pulls Nate's cock out of his mouth before swirling his tongue around the head and grinning at him.

"Good to hear. Do you want to come down my throat, or do you want to fuck me again?"

Nate's eyes darken, and he says, "I want to fuck you."

"I thought you might." Logan looks at me and gives me a wicked grin. "What a shame we took the lube to Dante's room. You'll need to go fetch it again, Alexandra."

"Yes, Sir," I say dutifully.

"Don't take too long, or Nate might come down my throat, and you'll have gone to get it for nothing," Logan warns me.

There's a tone in his voice that tells me there will be some kind of punishment involved if that happens, and he takes Nate's cock back in his mouth again. I know how skilled he is, so I turn to quickly leave the room.

At least I'm wearing a dress now, and he didn't say to take it off. We really need to get a second fucking bottle of lube. Until this weekend, it wasn't needed unless one of the guys wanted to fuck my ass. Now, with Nate fucking Logan as well, it seems to always be in the wrong room. My pussy aches as I consider the future possibility of Nate being fucked by Logan.

When I walk into the room, Dante looks up from where he's meticulously folding clothes to put into our suitcases. He raises his eyebrows as he looks at me.

"That was quick."

"We need the lube," I say as I roll my eyes.

"We'll have to get another bottle, it seems," Dante says with a grin.

I pick it up off the bedside table and nod. "We really will."

As I turn to leave the room, he chuckles and says, "Your dress seems to be wet."

I look down at my left breast, where I could feel the material wet against my skin, but I hadn't realized just how bad it was. The light blue material now has a big dark blue patch around my nipple, which is stiff and peaking against the fabric.

"Oh god," I laugh. "Nate did it. I'd better get back. I'm pretty sure Logan is going to punish me if Nate comes while I'm gone."

Dante strides over to me, pulls me into his arms, and kisses me. He uses his hand to pull and tweak my nipple under the wet fabric as he does, and I moan as we part.

"Go, Angel."

"Yes, Honey," I manage to say as I make my way to the door again, clutching the lube and lost in my arousal.

I'm smiling as I close the door behind me, but when I turn to face the hallway, Ash is standing across from me in the open doorway to his room. Heat rushes to my cheeks, and I burn with embarrassment as he looks at me.

"Uh. Hi, Lexi," he says. "I was just, uh, taking my suitcase downstairs. Are you packed yet?"

Ash has never in his life acted this way around me, and I feel as awkward as he's behaving.

"Yeah. I mean, no. I mean, Dante is packing for me because I'm, um, I'm busy." I can't stop myself from glancing down at the lube in my hand.

Ash's gaze follows mine, and there's an awkward silence as he looks at it. He moves his gaze up my body and, to my horror, stops at my chest. My nipples tingle as he looks at my breasts, and I have no idea what the fuck I should say to explain it.

"I, um, spilled some water on my top," I lie, and it sounds false in the air around us.

"I see. I mean, I'm not looking. I just noticed, of course."

My eyes dart to his crotch, and there's a very obvious bulge in his jeans. I swallow and shake my head to try and clear it. I'm not the woman Cassie accused me of being, and I'm not going to fuck

Ash just because he's single now.

I meet his gaze and say, "Well, I'd better hurry. We need to leave soon, and I'm—"

"Busy. Yup. Got that. Have fun," he says, and it's almost like we're back to normal because he says it in a casual tone.

I stride away from him, and I have to pant slightly for breath as I do. As I turn the door handle to Nate's room, I can hear his moans of ecstasy, and I'm not sure if I'm too late when I see him. He's staring down at Logan as he fucks his mouth roughly, and he has a look about him that tells me he's close.

Logan notices me about ten seconds after I enter the room, and he pulls his head back from Nate, who groans, "What? Why?"

"Lexi's back," Logan says with a grin. "She brought lube."

"I've changed my mind. I want to come down your throat after all."

Logan laughs and says, "You're just saying that because you're horny. Come here, Alexandra." I walk over to him and hold the lube out for him, but he shakes his head. "I don't need it. You do. I want you to get my asshole ready to take Nate, Alexandra."

My eyes widen because I didn't expect it, but a dart of arousal floods through my body at the thought of preparing him to be fucked.

"I don't know what I'm doing, Sir," I say.

"Yes, you do. You've had it done to you plenty of times. Do it to me now, Alexandra."

"Yes, Sir," I say as he bends over the bed.

I look at Nate, but he offers me no help and just strokes his cock slowly as he watches us. I open the bottle of lube and squirt some on Logan's ass. I use my finger to rub it around his hole, then carefully push one finger inside him. He groans softly, and my pussy aches at the sound.

I push my finger in and out of him a few times before I try to push a second one in, and Logan says, "More lube, Alexandra."

"Oh. Sorry."

I squirt a lot more lube on and have no trouble pushing a

second finger into his ass this time. I find it wildly erotic to be the one fucking someone for once, and when Logan moans, I push a third finger into his ass. I can't stop myself, and I reach under my dress to rub my clit without thinking. Logan's pleasure is doing things to me, turning me inside out, and I love it, but I'm aware that I'm not allowed to orgasm.

After about a minute, Logan says, "Enough, Alexandra."

I pull my fingers out of him, and he stands, then turns to look at us. Nate is rock-hard, and so is Logan underneath the towel. When he drops it, and his cock is displayed for us both, I desperately wish that I could come, and my juices run down my thigh.

"Lay on your back on the bed, Nate," Logan says in a husky voice before he looks at me. "Take off your dress, Alexandra."

I gasp because I'm not sure what he's planning, but I manage to say, "Yes, Sir."

I set the lube aside, then pull my dress off over my head and drop it on the floor. Logan straddles Nate and lowers himself onto Nate's cock as they stare into each other's eyes.

"Damn, you feel good," Nate says.

"I fucking love your cock, Nate."

Logan begins to slowly fuck him before he looks at me. His gaze roams my body from head to toe, and he strokes his cock as he moves up and down on Nate.

"Such a pretty toy. What should I do with you, I wonder," he says through panting breaths.

Nate reaches forward and wraps his fingers around Logan's cock to pump him as they fuck. They're both so beautiful, and I love them so much. I can still hardly believe that I get to be a part of this amazing thing.

Logan looks over at me and moans before he manages to say, "What's the point in having a toy if you don't share it with your friends? Sit on his face, Alexandra, and pray he doesn't make you come."

"Yes, Sir," I say as my pussy aches painfully.

Nate will make me come in a heartbeat. I have no doubt about that. I'm going to be punished, and I have no idea what the punishment will be. I dutifully kneel over Nate's face before I lower myself down to hover above him, and he starts licking my pussy.

"I said sit, Alexandra, and I mean it. *Sit.*"

I inhale sharply but do as instructed and lower myself the final inch, so I'm actually sitting on Nate's face. At once, he groans into my pussy, and the sound vibrates pleasurably against my clit. He takes his hand off Logan's cock and wraps both arms around my thighs as I ride his face.

Logan begins to fuck Nate faster. In turn, Nate translates this to his movements with his tongue on my pussy. Like true bandmates, they move in rhythm together, the three of us wrapped up in ecstasy as we moan and writhe in sync.

My orgasm is building, and I lock eyes with Logan, who grins at me. "You won't want the punishment. Trust me."

"What is it?" I breathe out around a moan.

"Try me, Alexandra. Allow yourself to come and find out."

He has a wicked gleam in his eye, and a part of me wants to do it. An unknown punishment in exchange for allowing the orgasm that I'm keeping at bay to wash over me.

Logan reaches up and twists one of my nipples, which causes a shock of arousal to my pussy as Nate laves my clit with his tongue.

"Sir," I moan loudly.

"Are you going to come, Alexandra?" he growls.

"No, Sir." I shake my head.

It's a blatant fucking lie. I am barely able to keep control of myself, and I only manage to avoid coming by angling my pussy a tiny bit to change the contact with Nate. It's still there, though, and Nate pulls me back into position again as he continues to eat me out.

We're all panting loudly for breath, and I look down at the place where Nate and Logan are joined. It's a mistake. The sight of Nate's cock plunging into Logan's ass is as hot as ever. Logan is stroking his cock again, and I wish I had it in my mouth. I've lost the ability to control myself, though, and my orgasm hits me in unrelenting waves.

"Nate," I scream out as my ecstasy overcomes me.

I grind my pussy on his face and accept that the unknown punishment will happen. I hope that this orgasm is worth it. Right now, it definitely feels like it is.

"Oh fuck, Nate. Oh god. Oh god. Oh god. I'm fucking coming, Nate. Fuck."

I scream and curse as he continues to pleasure me while I come. Logan reaches across and pulls my nipples. He twists them, rubs them, and pinches them, all while he fucks Nate. My clit is so sensitive now that I have tears in my eyes when I come again. I can barely breathe as my body shakes, and my orgasm rocks me to my core.

Nate is still going to town on my pussy, but Logan frowns at me and says, "Let her go, Nate." It takes him a second, but he releases his hold on my legs, and Logan says, "Get off him, Alexandra."

Relief floods through me as I get off Nate. My clit throbs painfully, and my body spasms sporadically as I collapse on the bed next to Nate. Immediately, Nate grabs Logan's hips and begins thrusting harder into him.

Logan grunts and places his hands over Nate's as they fuck. I watch as Nate buries himself deep inside Logan, and he screws his eyes shut tight as his body shakes.

"Fuck, Logan. Yes," he gasps through his ecstasy.

Logan leans down and kisses Nate passionately as they ride out the end of Nate's orgasm together. Nate wraps his arms around Logan and kisses him back. I smile as I watch them, and I love that we've come to this place together. My heart feels like it might explode with how much I love both of these men.

When their kiss ends, Logan leans over to kiss me as well. His tongue intertwines with mine, and he explores my mouth with it, teasing and taunting me with his skill. I'm sad when he breaks our kiss, but it's only another moment before Nate kisses me as well, and I'm lost in the pleasure of my connection with him.

Finally, Logan says, "Come to the bathroom with me, Alexandra. I need you to suck me dry, and I have an ass full of cum."

I bite my lip and say, "Yes, Sir."

Logan climbs off Nate, who lies in place, and he has a satisfied look on his face as we walk away. We get into the shower, and Logan doesn't even turn the shower on. He just turns to look at me with his cock jutting impressively toward his stomach.

"Fix my problem, Alexandra."

I drop to my knees on the hard tiles and wrap my lips around his cock. He holds my head in place and fucks my mouth roughly as I look up at him. He holds his cock down my throat until I gag, unable to get any oxygen, and he pulls himself out again. He does this a few times, and the lust I feel overwhelms me. I'm in subspace, and I feel like I'm floating on air as he fucks my mouth.

When he comes, he holds his cock in my mouth, and I suck him dry as he instructed. I swirl my tongue around the head of his cock as I increase the suction I have on him because I want to taste every last drop of him.

His eyes are hooded as he watches me swallow his load, and he murmurs, "Good girl, Alexandra."

My pussy clenches at his praise, and I slowly remove him from my mouth. "Thank you, Sir."

I get to my feet, and he pulls me into his embrace and kisses me before he washes me gently.

Nate joins us as Logan finishes cleaning himself, and he asks, "Are you two done? I need to shower before we leave, and pretty soon, Dante will be hassling us to go."

"Yeah, we're finished. Though I wouldn't complain about having another shower with you." Logan pulls Nate against him and kisses him.

I bite my lip as I watch them kiss, then they break apart, and Nate kisses me as well before he says, "Okay, fuck off, you two. You know you make me horny, and we really will need to leave soon."

Logan and I are both laughing as we get out of the shower. He pulls a towel off the rack and dries both himself and me.

"I love you, Lexi," he murmurs as he pulls me into his arms again after he hangs the towel back up.

"I love you, too, Logan," I say before he kisses me, and we head back into the bedroom. "I'm going to have to change my dress before we leave," I groan as I pull it on and the wet patch touches my breast.

Logan looks over at me as he wraps the towel he was wearing before around his waist, and he gives me a wicked grin. "It'll dry by the time we get to the airport."

"What if it doesn't?" I ask, even as my breathing rate increases.

"We can cross that bridge when we come to it." He shrugs his shoulders.

"Is this my punishment?" I wonder aloud.

Logan laughs and shakes his head. "As if that would be punishment enough for having not one, but two orgasms so good you screamed the house down."

A shot of arousal heads straight to my pussy at his words. Logan turns toward the door, and as he walks away, I realize that he still hasn't told me what my punishment is.

"What is it, then, Sir?"

I think it's me calling him 'Sir' that catches his attention enough to make him stop in his tracks. He has his hand on the door handle as he turns to look at me.

"You're sitting next to Ash on the way home."

Chapter Three

No Holes Were Wrecked in the Writing of This Chapter

My cheeks burn with embarrassment, and my pussy is drenched as we make our way into the garage to get in the SUV and drive to the airport.

As we approach it, Logan says, "We'll have to use the third row of seats. Do you mind sitting in the back with Lexi, Ash?"

"No, that's fine. Thanks for giving me a lift. I wasn't expecting this."

"As if we'd leave you stranded in Napa," Nate laughs.

He unlocks the SUV, and Logan opens the door before he pulls the seat forward and turns to look at me. "In you go, Lexi."

I climb into the car, and a rush of air hits my bare pussy as I lean over to get into the back seat. I yank the skirt of my dress down behind my ass as I maneuver my way into the back seat and drop down onto it.

Logan has a wicked grin on his face when I turn to look at him, and he steps aside to look at Ash. "Your turn."

It's only a moment before Ash is on the seat next to me, and my heart races in my chest. This seat seems too small, and he feels too close.

He smiles at me, then his gaze moves to my breast, and a dart of arousal shoots to my pussy. My nipples are both stiff and give away how turned on I am.

Ash raises an eyebrow at me. “You didn’t change your dress.”

“No. It’ll dry by the time we reach the airport.”

Logan turns in the middle row of seats to look at me. “If it doesn’t, you can get changed in the car before we go inside.”

“How kind of you to allow it,” I say in a dry tone, and he grins at me.

Ash looks back and forth between us a few times, and I realize that he doesn’t know about the BDSM aspect of my relationship with Logan.

“I have to say that it is strange seeing all you guys together now after years of Dante and Lexi being together,” Ash says.

Nate is sitting in the driver's seat with Dante next to him. He backs the car out of the garage, and we start down the long driveway toward the entrance to his estate.

“It definitely took me a minute to get used to the idea when Nate and Lexi first got together,” Logan agrees. “We’re all really happy, though.”

“Yes, I can tell by the multiple sex shows I’ve listened to in the last twenty-four hours,” Ash smirks at us both.

This reminder of what he’s overheard us doing is embarrassing as hell, and heat rushes to my cheeks.

“Kill me now,” I groan.

“I might as well ask, but was Lexi calling you ‘Sir’ earlier?” Ash asks.

I’m so turned on by this conversation as I look at Logan, and I’m unsure of whether he’ll confirm it or not. A part of me really wants him to because it’s so hot, but another part of me is screaming that Ash just broke up with his girlfriend and this is wildly inappropriate.

Logan smiles back at Ash. “Yeah. I Dom Lexi, so does Dante.”

Ash’s eyebrows fly up, and he whips his head around to look at Dante. “Since when?”

"Since forever," Nate laughs, and Dante nods.

Ash turns his face to mine. "Really?"

My BDSM relationship with Dante was hidden in plain sight for ten years, and the guys didn't have a clue. I guess since the other two have told Ash now, I might as well give him the rest of the information.

I sigh and shrug my shoulders as casually as I can manage despite my arousal. "Yeah. I don't call him 'Sir,' though. Instead, I call him 'Honey.' He calls me 'Angel' and, yes, you've been there when he's done it."

"What about you, Nate?" Ash asks.

"Nah. I just fuck her whenever I want to and reap the rewards of these two teasing the shit out of her."

I shift in my seat because my pussy is wet, and I feel so exposed with our sexual secrets being revealed to Ash.

He swallows as our eyes meet, and I catch him surreptitiously adjusting his jeans before he asks, "Would you guys have told me all this if I hadn't broken up with Cassie last night?"

I hate how much the knowledge that he's aroused by the conversation is turning me on. A huge part of me wants to unzip his jeans and either suck or fuck him, but I know that I shouldn't, and his reminder of last night is a testament to that fact.

Nate snorts. "Probably not. We've been hiding a lot of things because we were worried about how she'd react."

"I'm pretty sure this would've been too much for her." He grimaces. "She was pretty bad after she found out about Logan and Lexi."

His comment cuts through my arousal and reminds me that she sent me a text, so I pull out my phone to open her message. "What should I say to her?"

Ash leans over to look at my screen. He cringes as he reads the message and looks at me.

"I guess you should ask her what about. If she's figured out I really did block her, she's probably going to try and apologize."

I nod and write the text to her.

What do we need to talk about?

My heart races as the message shows up as delivered. I look at the screen for another thirty seconds or so, but it doesn't show as read, so I lock my phone again.

"I guess now we wait."

Ash nods and then sighs. "I really am sorry about last night, Lexi."

"No, I should apologize. I'm sorry that I'm the reason you and Cassie broke up."

"Don't apologize for that. You guys are happy, and she couldn't handle that. As soon as she insulted you, I realized that I should've ended it sooner. She'd been talking shit about you guys since we found out, so bringing her to Napa was a mistake."

I'm so grateful that he defended me last night, and I lean over to hug him. "Thanks for doing that. It means a lot to me that you stood up for me when she called me a slut."

"I would never allow someone to call you something like that." He wraps his arms around me and hugs me back.

I relax into his warm embrace, and the scent of his cologne fills the air around us. I'm hyper-aware of him in a way that I never have been before. Suddenly, my phone buzzes in my lap, and I look down at it as Ash and I break apart.

I'm sorry for last night. I think Ashton has blocked me. Can you get him to call me?

Fuck.

Cassie called me a slut last night and here I am, lusting over her ex-boyfriend as if that's even marginally appropriate.

My jaw tightens, and I dare to look over at Ash, who has read the message, and he scoffs, "Hard pass."

"You will have to talk to her. Won't she have stuff at your place or something?"

"Ugh," he groans. "You're right. She does."

"She'll probably try to talk you into getting back together with her," I warn him.

My blood runs cold at the thought. Yet another reason I

shouldn't be lusting after Ashton Woodford. It's entirely possible that Cassie will convince him to get back with her and it would be a shitshow if Ash and I had done something in the two seconds they were split up.

"She has no chance." He shakes his head at me. "Any feelings I had for her were diminished over the last month, and last night they disappeared entirely."

It should be reassuring, but I'm still concerned that she will, and I don't say anything for a few seconds as I think about it. Even if he doesn't get back with her, she knows about us, and I wish we'd never given her that information. I truly thought that she and Ash would be together forever, and we'd all be happy in our friendships.

"She knows our secret," I say around a lump in my throat as the fear that she might tell people takes me over.

Ash stares at me, and his jaw tightens. "I'll make sure she doesn't tell anyone."

The look of disgust on Cassie's face when I kissed Logan in front of her comes to my mind. I can imagine how the world would react if she told people.

"People can't find out. They wouldn't understand." I know that's the truth, and I blow out a breath of air as I think about what would happen if the world knew about me, Dante, Nate, and Logan.

"It'll be okay. Your secret will be safe, I promise." Ash gives me a reassuring smile.

I hope he's right, but I'm not sure he is. "What do I say to her?"

"Tell her I'll call her when I'm back in LA."

I nod and write the message to Cassie.

He said that he'll call you when he's back in LA.

It's only a few seconds before her response shows up.

He needn't bother. I'll talk to him on the plane, I guess, since we'll be sitting next to each other.

Ash groans. "Fuck. I forgot about that. I guess she chose not to go back to LA early after all."

"Probably because she knew you couldn't avoid her this way." I wrinkle my nose at him.

She'll have over an hour on the flight to convince him to get back with her. I can't stand the thought of having to be around her, knowing that she thinks I'm a slut.

He nods. "More than likely." He's silent for a few seconds, then he chuckles. "Do you think I should tell her that I heard you guys fucking this morning?"

Embarrassment floods through my body, and I shake my head as I say as casually as I can, "I doubt that would be a good idea."

"I guess not. What if I told her that I saw your naked ass run across the hall in front of me before that?"

He has a wicked grin on his face as he teases me, and my cheeks get hotter, even as my pussy aches at the confirmation that I was exposed. I know that I shouldn't enjoy his teasing, and I know that there is a very real chance that Ash might get back together with Cassie today, but that doesn't stop how much it turns me on.

"I was hoping you hadn't seen anything." I cringe.

"I didn't see much. Just as we were coming up the stairs, I saw you disappear into the hallway."

"Sorry about that. You weren't meant to see anything." I look over at Logan, who's looking out the window. "I got in trouble when I told the guys. Right, Logan?"

I bring Logan into our conversation to desperately try to stop myself from the completely inappropriate thoughts I'm having about Ash.

He turns to look at us. "Huh?"

"When I told you guys that Ash saw me getting the lube."

"Oh, yeah." Logan looks at Ash. "It's a consent thing. You weren't meant to see because you didn't consent to play with us. Even if Lexi likes being exposed." He looks me over, and my nipples are stiff under my dress, a clear indication of how much talking about this is turning me on. "It doesn't mean you necessarily want to see."

"What if I didn't want to overhear?" Ash raises an eyebrow at him.

"I figured you would knock on the door if you had a problem. You also didn't seem offended at breakfast when you said you overheard us last night." Logan grins at him.

"True. Well, this *has* been an enlightening weekend. Now I know what my bandmates get up to when I'm not around. You dirty, dirty fuckers."

Logan laughs, "Yeah, you don't know the half of it."

"That was less than half of it?" Ash raises an eyebrow. "I mean, even just listening to it was a pretty good porn."

"I like your thinking, Ash." Logan grins wickedly at me. "We should make a sex tape with the four of us sometime."

"I can be your cameraman," Ash suggests, and as they burst into laughter, my pussy aches, along with my painfully hard nipples.

Logan turns to the front of the car, where Dante and Nate are talking, and says, "Hey, guys, what do you think about us filming a porn movie with Lexi sometime? Ash has offered to be the cameraman."

Nate just laughs but doesn't say anything while Dante turns in his seat to look at me. My cheeks burn with heat, and I clench my legs tightly together against my arousal.

"Well, the whole world's seen Nate give her an orgasm. What's the difference if they see us give her one, too?" Dante says in a level voice, but there's clear amusement in his gaze.

"Wait? When did the whole world see Nate give her an orgasm?" Logan asks, and I realize that we haven't told him about that.

Dante looks over at Nate, who darts a grin at us before he turns back to the road again and says, "I'll give you a hint. You were both there the first time I made Lexi come."

I can barely breathe as Logan and Ash take this information in. Ash's mouth drops open, and he stares at me for a second before his gaze slowly traverses my body.

"I congratulated you on your acting skills," he says and gives me a meaningful look.

My body is aflame with lust as I meet his gaze. Memories of coming for Nate while our friends and the crew members on the set of their music video watched flood my mind. It's hot knowing that they were there when it happened.

"I wasn't exactly about to say, 'thanks, but I wasn't acting. Nate just made me come while you were watching.'" I give him a wry grin.

"I don't think I'll ever look at that music video the same way." Ash shakes his head.

He pulls out his phone and, to my horror, immediately opens the video on it.

"Oh my god, don't *watch it*!" I gasp.

"It's not like I haven't seen it before," he points out.

On his screen, I walk across a nightclub, and Nate follows me.

"Yes, but now you know I was coming in the video. It's different. Please turn it off," I beg him because the part where I'm actually having an orgasm ended up about a minute before the song ends.

Ash looks at me and says, "If you really want me to turn it off, I will."

"Let him watch the video, Alexandra," Logan says with a look at me.

My goddamn full name. He knows I can't stop Ash from watching it unless I safeword.

I scowl at Logan and say, "That's not fair."

Ash pauses the video, and he looks between us a few times. "Am I watching this or not?"

Logan looks at me, and I purse my lips. I don't want to safeword. I want Ash to watch the video, but this feels dangerous. Whatever we do now could cause so many problems in the future. Cassie already thinks I'm a slut and, obviously, she's right since so much of me wants to continue down this path.

I can barely breathe as I say, "Fine. Go ahead and watch it."

Ash hits play, and the song rings out through the car again. I look over, and scenes from the three different sets are interspersed throughout the video. The nightclub where I 'meet' Nate, a restaurant where we go on a 'date,' and the bedroom where he made me come.

My heart races as the second chorus ends and it moves to the bridge. This is the point where the video focuses more on the bedroom scenes. My eyes go to Ash's face as he stares intently at the phone. When the line plays that I know is timed with my orgasm, his mouth drops open slightly.

He keeps watching until the video ends, then locks it and stares at me before he asks in a husky tone, "It happened during the bridge, didn't it?"

I nod my head because I can't form any words right now. I'm so turned on at him watching me orgasm. My pussy is drenched, and I think I'm going to leave a mess on the seat. I also have a desperate need to be fucked.

"Wait a minute, though." Ash's look of shock turns into a frown, and he looks back and forth between Nate and me. "We weren't there when you two shot topless."

I still can't form words because I'm worried that if I say anything, my blatant arousal will be highlighted to him if it isn't already.

Luckily, Nate answers his unasked question for me in an amused tone, "I said you were there the first time I made her come. I didn't say that was the only time I made her come that day."

"Wait, this was before you two actually got together, right?" Ash asks.

"Yeah, they got together the day after when I invited Nate around to our place," Dante tells him.

"Did you know when they were shooting this?" Ash lifts his phone up for Dante to see.

He chuckles and nods. "Yes. I could tell Lexi was having an actual orgasm. It was hot as fuck, so I was glad I got to see it happen again when she shot topless."

There's silence in the car for a few moments before Logan turns to me. "Lexi likes being looked at." His gaze travels slowly over my body, down to my feet, and back up again. "Do you like knowing that Ash can watch you come any time he wants to now, Alexandra?"

Ash shifts in his seat, and I notice he's semi-hard in his jeans. I still don't want him as anything other than a friend, but this whole situation is arousing to me. I like that he watched me come. I like them talking about fucking me. I like that my nipples are so hard they're clearly visible in my dress.

The word 'pineapple' is on the tip of my tongue, though. I'm tempted to say it just to get out of this conversation, but I also like the arousal flowing through me despite my embarrassment.

"Yes. It's hot," I murmur.

Logan reaches over the back of the seat, places a hand on one of my breasts, and strokes my hard nipple with his thumb. "Yes, I can tell you think it's hot."

I gasp and can't resist looking over at Ash, who watches us with a mixture of what seems to be both amusement and arousal in his eyes. Logan places his forefinger and thumb around my nipple and tweaks it through the fabric, which causes me to moan softly.

"Are you okay with watching me do this, Ash? I can stop if you're uncomfortable," Logan says.

"Fine by me. I'm just amused by this. Honestly, I'm learning *so* much." His voice is thick with lust, and his cock seems to be stiffer each time I look his way.

"You know, maybe you should change your dress, Alexandra. We can all still see where Nate had his mouth around your breast earlier," Logan says.

I blink at him. It's a step too far. All of this flirting and showing me off in front of Ash has been fun, but actually getting naked is too much.

"I thought you spilled something on yourself, Lexi?" Ash asks dryly.

Logan trails his hand over to the breast with the wet patch and traces around the outside of it, and he laughs, "Nate's something, all right, but I wouldn't say she 'spilled' him on her. More that her breasts are so glorious that he couldn't wait for them to be exposed to suck on them." He turns his face to mine. "So, do you think you need to change your dress, Alexandra?"

"No, I really don't think I should." I sigh and cringe. "I don't want to be the slut that Cassie said I am."

It's like I've thrown a bucket of cold water into the car, and the sexual tension in the air dissipates immediately. Logan pulls his hand away from my breast, and Ash takes a sharp intake of air.

"You're not a slut, Lexi," Ash says to me.

"Am I not? I mean, Cassie certainly thinks I am for sleeping with three guys. Now I'm here being felt up by Logan in front of you after you've watched me have an orgasm. Not to mention seen me naked and listened to me have sex. Would any of this have been okay if Cassie was here with us?"

Ash frowns at me. "No, it wouldn't have, but she's not here for a reason. Anyway, it's not like we're about to have sex or anything. I thought we've just been having some fun, and it's been a nice distraction from everything."

It's definitely been hot being shown off for Ash, but I have to try and be reasonable. We can't do this, no matter how much I want to. I have to think about what might happen in the future, not what will just happen on this car ride.

"You only just broke up with Cassie last night, basically because of me and what we're doing now. This is exactly what Cassie thought would happen. Even if we don't fuck, you have to admit that this is *very* different from our friendship in the past."

"In the past, you were very much off-limits. Dante's wife and one of my oldest friends. When this whole thing with Nate and Logan started, I was with Cassie, so you were still off-limits. If you like being looked at, let me look because I certainly don't mind looking. It's just a bit of fun, nothing serious. It's not like I'm going to fuck you or anything."

I swallow and shake my head. "It's a bad idea."

"I already saw you naked once today. How is this different?"

He raises an eyebrow at me.

"You know very well how it's different," I scoff.

He looks at Logan and asks, "Can you make her do it?"

"I can." He looks at me and tilts his head to the side. "Should I make you do it, Lexi? I could have you take that dress off and not put another one on until we reach the airport. I could tell you to spread your legs wide to give Ash a *really* good view or even make you give yourself an orgasm so he can see it in person. Want me to do those things?"

I struggle to breathe as he makes these suggestions because I can see them happening in my head. I'm wildly aroused by the idea of being fully on display like that, and I kind of want Logan to do it. I also love that he can force me to do it unless I use my safeword.

"Whoa. That's fucking hot, Logan," Ash murmurs. "Also, it's totally fascinating to see how turned on Lexi is by this. Is this what you guys do now? Just play with her like this all the time?"

Logan chuckles. "Pretty much. It's a lot of fun. If you're down, as I said, we can do stuff in front of you, but only if you're okay with everything."

"More than fine with it. As I said, this has been a nice distraction." He turns to run his gaze over my body. "A *very* nice distraction."

"Is Ash going to fuck Lexi?" Nate calls from the front of the car with a laugh. "Do I need to adjust the rear-view mirror so I can watch?"

"Only if he wants to, and I tell her to do it," Logan says.

Ash gives me a wicked grin. "Well, I *did* say that we weren't going to fuck, but maybe we should. What do you think, Lexi?"

I'm hot as hell at the idea of Logan instructing me to fuck our friend. Of being the slut that Cassie accused me of being. I don't want it logically, but my body aches for that to happen.

"No. It's a bad idea," I breathe out, even as I shift in my seat because my pussy aches so badly.

"So even though she's said no, you can still make her do it?" Ash asks as he looks at Logan.

"Correct. Her consent is in not using her safeword. The second she says that word, everything stops. If she doesn't use it, then she has to do anything I tell her to do, even if she doesn't want to do it or says no."

"Think we could make her use it?" He raises an eyebrow at Logan.

Logan nods. "We definitely could, but it's not a good thing if we do. It means we've done something so far beyond her comfort zone that she couldn't stand it. Trust me. It's not an achievement to make your sub use their safeword."

I love Logan so much, and I appreciate that he would never attempt to force me into safewording.

"Well, now I feel like an asshole. I was only joking." Ash cringes.

"It's all good. I knew you were joking, but I wanted to explain how it works anyway, so that you know. I'm guessing you've never done BDSM."

Ash shakes his head. "Nope."

"It's a bit of a learning curve, and knowing Lexi as well as I do helps. So I generally won't do anything that will make her use it." He looks me over again and takes me in. "Lexi, do you want to pull your dress down and show Ash your breasts?"

I inhale sharply, and a dart of arousal heads to my pussy as I shake my head. "No, I don't."

A slow, seductive smile comes across Logan's face as he says in a husky voice, "Pull your dress down and show Ash your breasts, Alexandra."

I can barely breathe as I follow the instructions. I reach up and slide the straps of the dress down my shoulders as I turn to look at Ash. His jaw is slack, and he stares at me with wide eyes. I pull the dress down under my breasts and expose them to his view.

My nipples are so hard and stiff that they hurt, and as Ash stares at my chest, Logan reaches across and tweaks one with his fingers. I moan softly and close my eyes, unable to look at Ash any longer because I'm so embarrassed that I'm doing this in front of him. That I'm doing the exact thing I swore I wouldn't do.

Logan twists my nipple painfully, and I gasp as my eyes fly open to look at him. He smiles at me, as obviously turned on as I am, and I'm sure Ash is as well. I don't know how much Dante and Nate are paying attention, though, because I'm lost in lust right now.

"Are you enjoying the show, Ash?" Logan murmurs.

"It's a very good show," he agrees.

I dare a glance at him, and his cock is fully erect in his jeans. He meets my gaze, and I bite my lip as Logan continues to play with my breasts.

"Now you can see why Nate wanted his mouth around her breast."

"Definitely. I mean, I knew she had great tits, but it's still nice to see them like this." Ash winks at me.

"Lexi can come just from someone playing with her breasts. I've done it to her before," Logan tells him.

Ash's eyebrows fly up. "Really?!"

"Yup. Want to see if you can make her come without touching her pussy?"

It's too much. We can't do this. We've already crossed a massive line.

Ash doesn't seem to care about lines, though, because he smirks at me. "I bet she'll say no, though."

"Lexi, do you want Ash to try and make you come?"

It's a terrible idea, and I feel like I'm proving Cassie right because I'm wet as hell, and I know I'm not going to use my safeword when Logan inevitably forces me into this.

"No, Sir. I don't want him to touch me because it's crossing a line."

"Ooh, ouch. She doesn't even want me to touch her. I'm wounded," Ash says.

It's clear that he doesn't believe me, and I don't blame him. I do want him to touch me, and it's blatantly obvious because I haven't used my safeword.

"You can touch her," Logan laughs as he twists my nipple roughly one last time. "Ash is going to try and make you come now, Alexandra."

My pussy clenches, and I'm pretty sure I'll be coming soon because I'm so turned on. Logan pulls his hand away from my breast and gestures to Ash that he can go ahead. He moves next to me, and his body touches mine before he does anything with my breasts. I can smell his scent, and it's intoxicating, adding to my arousal.

"What are the rules here?" he asks, and I don't bother answering because I know he's not asking me.

"You can't touch her pussy. You can't kiss her. You have to make her come only with what you do to her breasts."

"Can I say dirty shit to her as well?" he asks.

"Sure. That's fine. I'd tell you some of the stuff she likes, but I don't want to make it too easy for you," Logan laughs.

Ash finally lifts a hand to my breast and softly strokes my nipple with his thumb. I have to resist the urge to pleasure myself, and I remember that I'm not meant to have an orgasm until we get back to LA.

I guess all bets are off now.

He lowers his head to my ear and murmurs, "Still don't want me to touch you, Lexi?"

"It doesn't matter what I want. Logan told me to do it."

"So use your safeword. I think you want this. You want me to make you come, don't you?" Ash asks as he pulls back his head to look at me, a smug amusement in his expression.

"No, I don't," I tell him, even as my nerves are set aflame by everything that's happening.

"Liar." Ash twists my nipple roughly. "For years, you've paraded these tits around in tiny little bikinis and tight shirts. Now I finally get to see them uncovered." I moan softly, and he laughs. "Tell me again how you don't want this, Lexi."

"I don't want this," I manage to say before moaning again.

"If you say so. I'll believe it when you use your safeword, whatever that is. I don't expect I'll find out today."

Heat floods to my cheeks because he's right. I'm nowhere near using my safeword. I'm enjoying this and the humiliation of becoming what Cassie said I was. Of letting Ash do this to me. Because as much as I can say that Logan told me to do it, I know that I have the power to stop it. Everyone in this car knows that this is a choice I'm making.

Ash lowers his mouth to my breast as he continues to play with my other one. He sucks and bites and licks both my breasts as he alternates between the two.

When he twists one nipple roughly, a shock of arousal goes straight to my clit, and I moan, "Ash."

"Mmm, you fucking like that, don't you?"

"Yes. It's good," I groan.

He lowers his lips to my ear again as he continues to roughly play with my breasts. "Imagine me pulling you onto my lap. My cock buried deep inside your cunt. You bouncing up and down on me as I fuck you so hard that you scream like you did this morning."

I gasp as the images play in my mind and I moan his name again with my orgasm rapidly approaching.

"I know you want that. I bet your pussy is wet just thinking about it. Maybe I should tell Logan to make you fuck me. God knows my cock is hard enough right now, and I don't have anywhere to put it except in you."

The thought of being forced to fuck him breaks me. My orgasm hits along with the realization of what we're doing and how wrong it is that twenty-four hours ago, he had a girlfriend who accused me of wanting to do exactly this.

"Oh, Ashton," I moan as my orgasm hits.

He twists my nipple roughly as he lowers his head back to my breast while I come. My body shudders, and my pussy aches to be filled. Ash nips my breast with his teeth one last time before he sits back up and slides back to his seat.

"That was pretty fucking hot," he says in a low tone.

"No kidding. I might need her to fuck me in a minute," Logan laughs.

"That's what I told her that sent her over the edge," Ash smirks. "I said I had nowhere to put my cock right now except in her."

For a few seconds, I'm on edge. I'm unsure if Logan will make me fuck Ash or not, while Logan looks me over from head to toe. "No. We shouldn't do that. I do think she should change her dress, though."

Because we needed to use the third row of seats, our luggage is sitting next to Logan. He turns around and rummages in my bag before he pulls out a white floral dress made of soft, floaty material that he hands to me.

"Put this on, Alexandra."

Ash's eyes are on me as I take the dress from Logan. I set it on the seat between us, then unbuckle my seatbelt before I lift my dress up and off over my head. I hand it to Logan, whose eyes are dark with arousal, before I turn back to pick up the floral dress.

Ash's gaze catches mine, and as I look at him, he lowers his hand to his crotch and strokes his cock through his jeans. "Looking good, Lexi."

"Look how wet her pussy is," Logan murmurs. "Spread your legs for us, Alexandra."

I pant for breath as I follow his instruction, spreading my legs wide and putting my pussy on display for them.

"Very nice. You can put your dress on now."

I pull the dress over my head, but the damage is done. Ashton Woodford has already seen me naked, and putting this dress on won't change that.

Chapter Four

Ashton Woodford, Pudding and Pie

The rest of the car ride to the airport passes with flirty innuendos being thrown my way, but Logan doesn't make me do anything else dirty with Ash. A part of me is sad, but I'm mostly relieved.

I think the image of him looking at my naked body while he stroked his cock is one that will be hard to forget. He was right that what we did was fucking hot, but he's also about to spend an hour and a half sitting next to Cassie on the plane ride home.

Who the fuck knows what will happen or if she'll put thoughts in his head about me. He said he was done with her, but she might persuade him not to be. I can't imagine what will happen to the band if Ash gets back with Cassie, not after what just happened. I knew it was a bad idea. I should've used my safeword back at the beginning of the conversation.

These thoughts weigh heavily on my mind until we reach the airport to drop off the rental car.

As Logan opens the door to get out, Ash says, "Lexi, you can go first."

"Huh? You're nearer, though." I blink at him.

"Get out first, Alexandra. That way, Ash can enjoy the view if he wants to."

I swallow and nod before I shuffle across the seat toward Ash. I pull myself up to stand in front of him, bracing myself on the middle row of seats, and as I'm about to move out of the car, Ash's hands grip my hips.

I halt as he touches me, and I look at Logan. Arousal is written across his face as he watches on.

"Let me just see it one more time," Ash murmurs in a husky voice.

Cold air hits my pussy as he pushes the hem of my dress up to my hips. I'm exposed to him again, and he's so close that I know he could lean forward mere inches and eat me out.

"Is she always this wet, Logan?"

"Pretty much. Especially if you're going to do something like that. Right, guys?"

Dante and Nate have joined Logan to watch what's happening, and they both nod before Dante moves in front of Logan to kiss me. He slips his hand into the top of my dress and tweaks my nipple as his tongue explores my mouth.

Ash places his hand on my ass and rubs it softly as my pussy clenches in arousal. "Such a nice ass. I can't resist touching it. I was admiring it just this morning in your bikini, Lexi. Did you know that?"

"No, I didn't," I tell him as Dante breaks our kiss and grins.

"Not everyone is as obvious as Nate when they're checking someone out," Dante teases him.

"I like what I like." Nate shrugs. "I like checking out Lexi the most, though."

Ash puts his other palm on my ass and holds both cheeks in his hands for a moment before squeezing them. My pussy is drenched, and the juice runs down my thigh. I gasp when Ash's wet tongue trails up my inner thigh and stops just before he hits my pussy.

"She's literally dripping wet," he murmurs in a husky voice. "I had to lick her clean. I hope that's okay."

"I did tell her to let you enjoy the view. If that's how you want to enjoy it, that's your choice," Logan chuckles.

This is too much. I know he's going to see Cassie soon, but, fuck, I'm enjoying this so much. I want Ash to eat me out so I can come on his face, and my pussy aches at the thought of it.

Ash squeezes my cheeks one more time, then pulls my dress back down. "Get out, Lexi. Or I might actually pull you onto my cock and fuck you. I'm not sure you really want that, so you should move now."

For a second, I'm bombarded with images of Ash doing just that, and I can't move. I want it so badly that I can barely breathe through my lust. Then I remember that it's a terrible idea, and nobody is making me fuck Ash, so I should get the fuck out of this car and to relative safety immediately.

I climb through the gap from the pulled forward middle seat and step out of the car in front of the three waiting men. I'm so aroused that even the smell of the different colognes they're wearing is hot. Their beautiful faces look at me, and I want them to bend me over and fuck me right here.

Dante looks into my eyes for a few seconds, then says, "I'm a lot more sure than you, Ash. Whether she thinks it's a good idea or not, Lexi definitely wants that."

He knows me so well that he even knew I was in love with Nate before I did. He gently strokes the side of my face and smiles at me.

Ash gets out of the car and presses his body up against mine from behind as he leans down to murmur in my ear, "Good to know. Maybe I'll get Logan to make you fuck me after all."

I shiver and swallow heavily as I think about how good his hard cock would feel inside me, but I counter, "Maybe you should tell Cassie your plan on the plane and see what she thinks of it."

"Maybe I'll get you to fuck me in the seat next to her."

I turn to look at him, as well as to put some space between us because we're out in the open where we can be seen, and I'm also struggling to focus.

"Yes. Prove her right that I'm a slut. Good idea, Ash." I glare at him.

Ash's gaze roams over me from head to toe, and my breathing is shallow as he does.

"The only one who's called you a slut today is you, Lexi. I don't think you're a slut, just a lot of fun to play with."

His gaze hovers at my chest, where my nipples are stiff against the fabric, but I know it won't be as obvious in this patterned dress as it was in the solid blue-colored one.

"Yes, well. On that car ride, I proved Cassie right. Maybe you should get back together with her since she's been vindicated by what we just did. The whole reason she was uncomfortable was because she thought I'd do exactly that." I'm talking out of anger and frustration and fear, but there's more than a nugget of truth in my words.

I push past the guys and start toward the airport as Dante calls, "Angel!"

There's no instruction with it, so I ignore him, and I've only taken two more steps when Logan's voice rings out, "Come back here, Alexandra."

I whirl to glare at the four people I love the most in the world. "*Fucking pineapple!*"

I spin on my heels and continue to the terminal, secure in the knowledge that right now, they can't make me do anything. Throwing out my safeword like that feels strange. I needed it, though. I couldn't do this plane ride following instructions from Dante and Logan. Not with Ash threatening to make them force me to do sexual things with him.

I don't look back as I keep walking quickly to the building ahead. Despite my mood, my body is suffering from the remnants of my former arousal. My pussy is still wet, and I have no underwear on. Considering I used my safeword, I'm tempted to buy a pair at the airport and wear them.

I didn't bring my phone or purse with me, though, so I can't. I'm feeling shaky, and I head to the bathroom, where I make do with wiping myself dry with toilet paper.

Everything that just happened hits me at once, and I start to cry. What happened in the car was so intense because, even though I enjoyed it, I shouldn't have done it. I should have used my safeword and put a stop to everything before Ash ever touched me.

He was right that what we did on the way here was a sufficient distraction, but as soon as we got here, reality hit me.

My concern about this fucking everything up is overwhelming. Cassie knows about us, and that is bad enough. If she had any idea about what happened on that car ride, who knows what she would do.

Two women walk in as one says, "Oh my god, did you see Nate Walker? He's *so* hot!"

"Yes. Holy *shit*," her friend gasps.

They continue their conversation about Nate as they enter stalls. I obviously can't hide out in this bathroom forever, so I quickly flush the toilet and wash my hands. I splash my face with water, but it's obvious that I've been crying.

When I leave the bathroom, I find Nate leaning casually against the wall waiting for me.

"Hey, Sexy Lexi. Are you okay?"

I shrug and bite out, "Just fine."

He stands up and takes a step toward me, forcing me to look up into his beautiful blue eyes. "You don't seem fine. What's up?"

My jaw is tight, and I'm still full of emotions, but Nate looks concerned, and he wasn't really a part of what tipped me over the edge.

"I'm just stressed. I shouldn't have done all that. I used my safeword about an hour too late."

The two women from the bathroom come back out and gape at Nate as I finish speaking. He smiles at them, but thankfully they don't attempt to strike up a conversation.

"Let's get through check-in and go to the first-class lounge. We can talk there."

I nod, and we head toward the desk. My heart pounds in my chest as we approach Dante, Logan, and Ash, who are standing near the first-class check-in and garnering a lot of attention from the people around them. All three of them look guilty as we join them.

"Lexi, I'm so sorry," Logan says quietly.

Dante wraps his arms around me, and it's calming as he whispers, "Logan knows he can't hold you right now, so he asked me to do it."

I wrap my arms around Dante's waist, and he kisses my head softly. I still feel shaky, and I'm aware of all the people around us who are bearing witness to this. I need it too much to care, though.

"I'm sorry, too, Lexi. I really am," Ash says.

I don't acknowledge either of them because I still feel raw about what happened. We can't really talk here, anyway.

Dante holds me for a long time before he says, "We should check in, Angel."

"Okay," I agree.

He holds me close all through the process of checking in and heading to the first-class lounge. The only time he lets go of me is when we go through security.

We end up sitting in a booth in the lounge. I'm in between Dante and Nate, sitting across from Logan and Ash, who look at me.

"Can we talk, Lexi?" Logan asks.

I nod, and Dante squeezes my hand.

"I fucked up. I should've realized I was pushing you too far."

There's silence in the wake of his words, and I sigh.

"I should've used my safeword sooner. I was caught up in what we were doing, but I knew we shouldn't be doing it, which is why I said no."

Logan grimaces and looks forlorn. "Perhaps, but it's also on me to recognize your boundaries. I knew what you absolutely wouldn't do, but I had you do things I shouldn't have because I knew you would, and that's my fault. If you felt you had to use your safeword, then that means I pushed you too far. I'm sorry."

"And I was just an asshole in general," Ash adds. "I got carried away with what I was able to do, and it took my mind off the flight today. Basically, I took advantage of you, and it wasn't okay. I'm sorry."

I nod my acknowledgment of their words but don't say anything.

"Where do you want to go from here, Lexi?" Logan asks, a note of fear creeping into his voice.

I look at him and realize that he thinks I'm going to break up with him because of today.

"I still love you, Logan. I'm stressed to the gills about this flight with Cassie, though, and I didn't want to have Ash's threat hanging over my head for it," I admit.

Dante pulls me close to him and hugs me tightly in his warm embrace as he says, "You could've just said that, Angel. Neither Logan nor I would ever have made you do anything with Ash in public or in front of Cassie."

"I know that logically. I was just on edge because of the car ride."

"Again, that's my fault," Logan says. "If you still want to be in that type of relationship with me, what if we leave your safeword in place for the trip home, and we can see how you're feeling when you come to my place tomorrow night after work?"

I nod in agreement. "Okay." I meet his eyes and say again, "I do love you, Logan."

"I love you, too," he says back.

I hate that I can't hug him right now. I appreciate the comfort from Dante, but Logan is the one who I need aftercare from after such a heavy scene.

"Nate, can you switch places with Logan?" I ask him.

"Of course. I'll go get a drink, and Logan can move while I'm gone. Do you want anything?"

I smile at him. "Can you get me a Coke?"

Nate agrees and walks away from the table, which allows Logan to move next to me. He links his hand with mine underneath the table and squeezes it.

"I'm so sorry," he says again.

"I know, Logan."

I look into his beautiful brown eyes and sigh. At least having him here next to me is helping. I'm still feeling shaky, though, and Ash sitting across from me isn't helping. I have vivid memories of coming for him in the car, and it was hot as shit, but the shame of doing exactly what Cassie said I would do is overwhelming.

My body stiffens, and Logan frowns at me as he lets go of my hand and softly strokes my leg instead. "Are you okay?"

"No. She said it's what I would do," I murmur while looking at the table.

"Fuck it," Logan says.

He wraps his arms around me and holds me close. It's enough to send me into tears again, and Dante rubs my back, which helps soothe me. I know that I'm in sub drop and that a huge part of why I've been affected so much is because I enjoyed what we did.

"What can we do to help you feel better, Lexi?" Logan asks quietly.

Ash being here reminds me of what we did, and it's too hard to ignore him. Mostly because a part of me wants to do it again, and I feel like the slut Cassie accused me of being.

"I need Ash to leave."

I can't see anyone's face because mine is buried in Logan's chest, but there's silence in the wake of my words. I'm not sure if they're going to make him leave or not, and a part of me feels guilty for asking. They're all best friends, and I don't want this to fuck everything up, but I can't be around him right now.

"Can you go, please, Ash?" Logan says quietly.

"Of course. I'll see you guys later."

After about ten seconds, Nate says, "Is it okay if I go with him, Lexi? I don't want him to be left alone, and Dante's better to stay with you than me in public."

I wasn't even aware that Nate had returned. I don't really want Ash to be on his own, if only for the optics of it, so I sit up from Logan and wipe at the tears on my face as I nod.

"Sure. Go ahead."

Nate gives me a reassuring smile and walks away to where Ash is now sitting in a booth on the other side of the lounge. He catches my eye, and I look away quickly.

"Is our flight boarding soon?" I ask Dante because I know he'll know.

"Another twenty-five minutes."

I nod and take a sip of the Coke Nate has left for me. The sugary drink is good, and I try to focus on my breathing as well as Logan's comforting touch. He's gone back to softly stroking my leg where no one can see.

"What a birthday weekend. I wish we'd never gone out to Napa." I cringe. "Ash would still happily be with Cassie, and none of that shit would've happened."

"It would've happened eventually," Dante says. "She was unhappy with us, and if it wasn't your birthday weekend, something else would've tipped her over the edge."

"Which wouldn't have happened in Napa, and we wouldn't have driven back to the airport with Ash." I give him a pointed look.

"Ah. I see your point," he says with a frown.

We fall into silence, and I drink my Coke while watching the other people in the lounge but keep my gaze firmly away from where Nate and Ash are sitting. It's about five minutes later that Cassie appears near the entrance. I gasp, and my entire body stiffens.

Logan follows my gaze and says, "Oh, shit."

We watch as Cassie looks around and her eyes land on us. She immediately glares at me, then her look turns to one of confusion, and she continues to look around the area. When she sees Ash and Nate, she strides toward them. I grip both Dante and Logan's hands tightly as she approaches their booth.

"What if he tells her what happened in the car?" I whisper in horror as they start a conversation.

"Ash won't do that," Dante assures me.

Ash has a frown on his face and says something vehemently to Cassie, who glares back at him. Nate is relaxed in the booth with a grin, and he adds something to the conversation that causes Ash to laugh as Cassie turns to glare at him as well.

"I wish I knew what they were saying," I murmur.

I kind of wish I hadn't asked Ash to leave, but the way I feel toward him at the moment, I would probably have been the one to give shit away.

"Me, too," Logan agrees.

Ash shakes his head at Cassie, and she says something to him before she turns to shoot daggers at us. She says something else before Ash shakes his head again, and he looks angry now.

Whatever he says makes Cassie put her hands on her hips as she listens to him. The conversation continues for another couple of minutes before Ash says something that makes Cassie cry, and my mouth drops open as I watch them.

I know Ash so well, and I can see how tense he is. He doesn't look at Cassie, but even though he looks at Nate instead, I know he's fully aware of her. How could he not be? We can hear her crying from here.

People are turning to look at her, and I ask, "What the fuck did he say to her?"

"Probably that he doesn't want to be with her, I guess," Dante says quietly.

After about thirty seconds, Cassie turns and heads toward the bathroom. As soon as she's walking away, Ash turns to watch her go. He looks relieved, but he has that same guilty look on his face he had when he apologized to me for what he did in the car.

Nate says something to him, and Ash shrugs, then says something back before he looks over at us. His gaze finds mine, and I don't look away. I still feel weird about earlier, but my curiosity is burning, and I need to know what happened in their conversation, so I jerk my head back to indicate that he should come to join us again.

Nate laughs and says something before they slide out of the booth and walk over to us.

"What did Cassie say?" I ask as they stand in front of us.

"She couldn't believe I would choose you over her, and I told her that I would choose any of you guys over her." He shrugs.

My heart thuds in my chest as I remember that, despite everything, I do love Ash, and he's loyal to all of us like that.

"Of course you would. Thank you."

He smiles at me and then rolls his eyes. "She had a big problem with the fact that I spent more money on your birthday gift than hers."

This information takes me by surprise, and my mouth drops open as I stare at him.

"Really?" Dante asks.

"Yup," Nate confirms and then laughs. "She said Ash shouldn't be buying jewelry for any woman who isn't his girlfriend."

"That's ridiculous," Logan scoffs.

"Pretty much what I told her, but you were nicer," Nate smirks at him.

"Then I told her I would courier her things to her when I get home, and she took off crying. I'm dreading the plane ride." Ash cringes.

I frown at him for a few seconds, then look around the lounge. Other passengers are watching us, and I realize that anyone who's been watching us since we arrived will be coming up with a narrative in their mind.

"We're still not okay, Ash," I say truthfully, and his expression tightens. "Sit down, though. People are looking."

Nate and Ash take seats, and Ash says, "I really am sorry, Lexi."

"I know. Saying it repeatedly isn't going to change what happened, so please stop. I'll be fine, but the last twenty-four hours have been a lot, and I need a minute to process it. I don't want to talk about it anymore right now." He gives me a solemn nod, and I sigh. "I still love you, too, Ash. You're one of my oldest friends. We're not okay right now, but the same way I'll be fine, we'll be okay, too."

"Okay."

The conversation is stilted after that, and I'm grateful when our boarding call comes over the speakers. We head to our gate and see Cassie in the line to board the plane. She glares at us, and her eyes are red-rimmed.

"God, this sucks. I'm going to put on my noise-canceling headphones, but it's still going to be awkward as shit," Ash murmurs.

"If it gets too bad, I'll switch seats with you if you want," Logan offers.

Ash smiles at him and nods. "I might take you up on that offer."

Dante has his arm wrapped around me, and I snuggle into his warm embrace as we wait a minute or two for them to actually let us onto the plane. When we get to our seats, I'm at the window, and Dante is next to me. Across the aisle are Nate and Logan, and one row in front of them, Cassie is by the window. I can't resist watching Ash as he takes his seat next to her.

She immediately says, "Ashton, can we talk?"

"No," he says firmly as he pulls out a pair of noise-canceling headphones.

"You're really never going to see me again after this flight?"

Ash settles the headphones on his head and says, "Yes."

He reaches up to press the button to turn them on, but before he can, Cassie snarls, "You really think that slut is better than me?"

Shame floods through me at the knowledge that a short while ago, Ash had his hands on my breasts and was making me moan his name.

"Calling her that isn't helping you out, but yes. We're done here." His voice is full of cold anger as he defends me to her.

"You can't do this, Ashton. *I know things.*"

She looks past him, and her eyes meet mine. My blood turns to ice in my veins, and I think I might be sick. This is exactly what I was afraid of. She looks at me with pure hatred and disgust before she turns her gaze back to Ash.

His voice is still cold but also measured when he replies. "It's already done. Whatever you know doesn't matter, and you're not going to force me to be with you because of it."

Ash presses the button on his headphones, effectively ending their conversation as Dante takes my hand in his, and I grip it for dear life. The fear that she'll tell the world what she knows is overwhelming, but Ash is right that she can't use it to keep him in a relationship. If only because none of us wants her in our lives anymore.

Dante leans over and kisses me softly before he whispers in my ear, "It'll be okay, Angel."

I'm not sure that it will be, though.

Chapter Five

Secret Fantasies

Ash keeps his headphones on all through the flight and until he's off the plane and on the air bridge. He steps aside to let Cassie pass, and she stops, blocking the path of everyone behind her.

"Ashton," she says as he takes his headphones off.

"No, Cassie. You're holding everyone up." He indicates to the people behind her as someone pushes past her to continue up the bridge.

There's only one person between them and us now, and I have no desire to talk to Cassie, so I'm grateful when she turns and strides away.

I release a breath of air in a whoosh and say, "Thank fuck."

"No kidding," Nate murmurs from behind me.

The person in front walks past Ash, and we join him as we start walking toward the airport.

"Are you okay, Ash?" Nate asks.

"Yeah. That sucked. I kind of can't believe how this weekend has turned out." He looks at me, and for a second, desire flares in his eyes before his jaw tightens, and he looks away. "I'm glad I saw the truth about Cassie, though. To think I was considering a long-term future with her. I feel like I barely even know her."

We stand as far away from Cassie as we can at the baggage claim. I'm on edge the whole time we're waiting for our luggage, and it's a relief when she doesn't attempt to confront us at all.

When we get outside safely, I feel like I can breathe again. We head toward the car service we have booked, and I grip Dante's hand tightly.

"Does Ash still have his own car service booked to go home?" I ask quietly.

"I'm pretty sure he does. Why?"

I chew my bottom lip for a few seconds, unsure if I want to do this, but then I say, "Can Logan go in a car with him?"

Dante looks surprised and says, "We can ask him."

I nod, even though a part of me hates this. I'm just not ready to be back in a car with Logan or Ash right now.

"Hey, Logan," Dante says.

Logan turns from where he's been talking to Nate and Ash. "Yeah?"

"Could you possibly go with Ash? His car could take you home."

Logan's eyes dart to mine, and it's obvious that he knows the request came from me, and he's hurt by it.

"I can if that's what you want. My car's at your place, though."

"I can drive it to work and take it back to your place tomorrow night," I tell him. "I just need some space tonight."

Logan's jaw tightens, and he looks as sad and forlorn as he did earlier. "Sure. That works. I'll see you tomorrow, I guess."

He and Ash say goodbye to us solemnly, but neither comes near me before they walk away to the car that will be taking them home.

I hate watching them go, and despite everything, I feel guilty. It feels wrong sending them away, especially Logan. He was meant to come back to our place when we got home, and we would have some time together at home before he went back to his apartment.

We get into our car in silence, and once I'm seated in between

Dante and Nate, I'm grateful to be going home. I just want to be out of public, so I can hug Nate. Even in this car, though, we need to be mindful of the driver.

As soon as we're safely behind our apartment door, I throw my arms around him. He hugs me back tightly, and I kiss him. Our tongues intertwine, and I feel the freedom to do whatever I want with him.

"Hi, Sexy Lexi," he says with a smile.

"I've missed you," I tell him.

"I've been right with you the whole day," he laughs.

I shake my head. "No. You were driving and then I couldn't be near you. It doesn't count."

"Well, do you want me in bed with you tonight?" he asks.

I look over at Dante and smile at him. I spent last night with Logan and Nate in Napa. Tomorrow I'll be at Logan's, so there's only one solution.

"Both of you."

"Whatever you want, Angel," Dante says gently.

He holds his hand out to me, and I link mine with his before he leads me over to the sofa in the living room. He sits me on his lap and wraps his arms around me.

"How are you feeling after today?"

I look down into his beautiful brown eyes and sigh. "Still strange. It was really intense. It wasn't bad, but it was too much."

"Is your safeword still in place for me?"

I shake my head. "No. But nothing too heavy today."

"I know." He kisses me softly. "I wasn't even planning on having sex with you tonight if you don't want it."

I can barely speak around the lump in my throat because I love him, and he knows me so well. "Thank you."

He holds me on the sofa for most of the evening while we have dinner and watch movies with Nate. I spend a decent amount of time in Nate's lap as well.

When we go to bed, we all get naked, and I lie in between the two men. I know they're waiting for me to initiate something, and

I'm not sure if I want to.

I remember the car ride to the airport, along with the look on Ash's face as he looked at my breasts, and my pussy aches. He knows about the music video now, too. I can't help but wonder if he's at home watching it right now.

I envisage him lying in bed watching me orgasm while he strokes his cock, and my pussy gets wet. I think about what could've happened if I hadn't moved out of the car, of Ash burying his face in my pussy and eating me out.

I can't resist sliding my hand down to Nate's cock where he's lying in front of me. It's semi-hard, and I stroke it slowly.

"Mmm, Lexi," he says in the darkness.

Dante's arm is around my waist, so I place my hand on his and guide it down to my wet pussy. He takes the cue and starts rubbing my clit while he kisses my neck.

My lips find Nate's in the darkness, and I kiss him as I continue to stroke his cock. I keep this up until Dante brings me to orgasm, and then I push Nate onto his back as I climb onto him to ride him.

Dante's lips find my breast, and I'm forcibly reminded of Ash's mouth being on it earlier today. I wonder again if he's getting himself off tonight with thoughts of me.

Dante plays with my breasts, and I moan his name loudly, almost as if to scold myself for even thinking of Ash like that.

Nate's cock is thick and hard inside me, filling me completely, and I focus on how good he feels in this moment rather than anything else from today.

I lean down to kiss him, then sit up and ride him while Dante goes back to playing with my breasts, and I reach down to stroke his cock as he does.

It isn't long before I come loudly as I moan, "Nate."

"God, I love when you come on my cock," he groans as he continues to thrust in and out of me.

Eventually, he pulls me down on him and buries himself deep inside me as he comes. I lean down to kiss him, and Dante's voice, husky with lust, sounds out from next to us.

"Ride me, too, Angel."

My pussy clenches around Nate's cock at the instruction. I climb off him and onto Dante, who is lying on his back, waiting his turn.

He feels good inside me, and this is definitely a nice, easy scene. I do as he told me to do and begin to ride him. He raises his hands to my breasts to play with them, and I moan in satisfaction.

"Stop, Angel."

I stop moving, but Dante continues to play with my breasts. He strokes and tweaks my nipples as I grind on him.

"Come on my cock, Angel."

I jump as Nate's hands find me in the dark because I was so focused on Dante that I didn't realize he'd moved. His hand reaches around me from behind, and he rubs my clit as Dante continues to torment my breasts. Nate kisses my neck and strokes me faster, not stopping until I've had an orgasm.

Dante rolls me onto my back and braces himself over me as he begins to fuck me faster. I wrap my legs around his waist as he thrusts into me.

"Lexi," he moans as he comes. When he's finished coming, he kisses me and says, "I love you, Angel."

"I love you, too, Honey." I kiss him again, then kiss Nate as well. "I love you, too, Nate."

We head to the bathroom to clean up, and Nate leaves Dante and me in there while Dante washes me, then dries me. Finally, we end up tangled in one another in the bed as we drift off to sleep.

Guilt at thinking about Ash during sex and about what we did during the car ride home floods my mind. It leads to thoughts about Cassie, and I fall asleep thinking about her words on the plane.

I know things.

*****

I drive Logan's car to Black Lilac's Rodeo Drive store on Monday morning, and I greet Jasmine, the store manager, on the way in.

"Did you have a good birthday weekend?" she asks with a smile on her face.

I don't even know where to begin with everything that happened. The news of Ash and Cassie's breakup isn't public yet, to my knowledge, so I decide to give an abridged version of the truth.

"Yeah. We went out to Nate's estate in Napa and hung out. We had a lot of fun out there."

Ash and Cassie's breakup aside, this is the truth. It was really the trip home that was the shitshow.

"That sounds awesome," she says.

"Yeah, it was. So, anything new with the store?"

I own three stores around Los Angeles, and I rotate the days I spend at them. Because we went to Napa on Friday, I haven't been at this location since Tuesday last week.

"Nothing big. Brittany's last day was Friday. She's off to college."

"Oh, I'm sad I didn't get to say goodbye." She was a good worker, and I value all of my employees for the effort they put into keeping my stores running.

Jasmine and I talk for a few more minutes before I head to my office at the back of the store. I dock my laptop, and as it's starting up, I pull out my phone to send a text to Logan.

Hey. I hope you had a good night. I can't wait to see you after work.

I hate the way we left things yesterday. I'm nervous about the conversation we're going to have tonight, and a part of me is worried that what happened yesterday will have broken something between us. I don't know how I'll feel the next time he's going to Dom me, and we've never really had a vanilla relationship.

I log into my laptop, and as I'm opening my email, Logan's reply comes through.

It was okay. I missed you guys. I look forward to you coming here.

Now that we're back in LA, we're meant to start looking for apartments to buy together. A stab of fear hits me that maybe that won't work now.

No.

Logan and I still love each other. We're going to talk things through tonight, and it'll be okay. I think that being apart is just messing with my head. I focus on going through my emails to catch up on the ones I missed over the weekend. My heart races when I see the name 'Heather Fletcher' in the list, and I click on it immediately.

To: Lexi Sullivan
From: Heather Fletcher
Subject: Stocking Serenity
Hey Lexi,
I hope you're doing well. Could we schedule a time to meet regarding you becoming a stockist for Serenity? Call me to discuss.
Heather

I blink a few times and then grin at the screen. It was actually Cassie who suggested I try to get the designer to allow us to stock her clothes. I should probably send her a thank-you card if this goes through.

I give a bitter laugh at the idea as I pick up my phone and dial Heather's number.

"Hi, darling. You got my email?" Heather answers the phone in a cheerful voice.

"Yes, I did. I'm so happy you're on board with us stocking your clothes."

I can't help but grin as I say it because she's become one of my favorite designers in the last three years. Her first fashion show was right around when we opened our first store, and I was stunned by her designs. That infatuation with her clothes grew when I started actually buying them. I never imagined I'd get to stock them in my stores.

"Of course I am. So, I have some pretty standard contracts in place with our stockists. If you can send through the name of your lawyer, we'll get it sorted out. However, April has invited me to LA in a few weeks to visit the set of her movie. Would you like to catch up? I'd really love to see your other stores as well. We can discuss merchandising my clothes."

I'm stunned by her request, but I manage to say, "Sure. Not a problem. Just give me dates, and we can make a day of it. I can't wait to show you the other stores."

"Excellent. I'll send through the details when I've got them."

We end our call, and I stare at the phone for almost a minute, completely astounded by what just happened. In the past, I would've called Cassie to tell her about this new development. The guys are all supportive, but none of them would get how huge this is.

I sigh and head out of my office as I call, "Hey, Jasmine. Guess what just happened!"

"What?" she asks from the break room where she's making herself a coffee.

"You have to keep it on the down-low, but Heather Fletcher is coming to LA to look at the stores. We're going to stock Serenity."

Jasmine gasps. "For real?"

"Yes. No contracts have been signed yet, so please keep it quiet."

"Oh my god, that's fricking amazing!" Jasmine whispers, and we do a little excited dance together while we try to keep quiet so no one hears us. "My lips are sealed."

I trust Jasmine because she was one of my first employees. She has exactly the reaction I expected, and we spend the rest of the day whispering excitedly about it out of earshot of the other employees or any customers.

I'm still flying high when we close the store for the day, and Jasmine walks out to the parking lot behind the store with me.

"Whose car is that?" she asks as I approach Logan's AMG CLS.

"Oh, it's Logan's. We traveled to the airport together, but he traveled home with Ash, so I agreed to drive it over to his place today." Heat rushes to my cheeks even though Jasmine can't possibly know any of the true circumstances surrounding this.

She shakes her head. "Will I ever get used to you and your famous friends?"

"It's been three years, Jazz," I laugh. "You probably should have by now."

We say goodbye as I get into the car and send Logan a text to let him know that I'm on my way. When I arrive at his apartment building, I park the car in his spot, then head upstairs and let myself into the apartment.

Logan is waiting for me when I arrive, and I smile at him before I head over to the wicker basket where I normally leave my clothes when I get here.

Logan has a rule that I can only spend one minute wearing clothes in his apartment, so I'm surprised when he says, "No, Lexi. Keep your clothes on."

"Huh? Why?" I whirl to stare at him.

Maybe he's the one who doesn't want to do BDSM with me now.

He smiles and walks over to wrap his arms around me. "We need to talk, and I want to do it as equals."

"Okay," I breathe into his chest as his intoxicating scent invades my senses.

I hug him back, and everything from yesterday feels like so long ago. Still, we can't move forward without discussing it properly. Logan leads me to his living room, where we take seats on the sofa.

"Would you like a drink or anything?" he asks, and I shake my head.

"No. I'm kind of freaking out about what we have to talk about," I admit.

"Is there anything I can do to make you more comfortable?"

I shake my head again, and he sighs before he falls silent. I don't say anything because I want to see where he takes this conversation.

"I want to apologize again, but I heard what you said to Ash yesterday, so it seems redundant. An apology is meaningless without action, anyway. We never really had a proper discussion about consensual nonconsent, which we should do now. What would you like to do in that regard?" He has a solemn look on his beautiful face as he asks the question.

"It's strange because Dante and I had a CNC agreement in place since we first started kink, but he never used it until Nate. With Nate, my opposition to it was mild at best, and only because I was worried that I would fuck up our friendship. What happened yesterday…"

I trail off as I blow out a breath of air slowly as memories of the car ride bombard me. "I promised you that I would use my safeword if I needed to, and I didn't. For that, I'm sorry. I was so into it, but I didn't want to be, and I still don't want to be."

Logan is silent for a few seconds, and I can see him processing what I've told him. "You are still into it despite not wanting it, though. Am I correct?"

"Yes," I admit, because there's no point in lying about it.

He's quiet for an even longer time this time, and the space between us feels too big. I want to touch him, so I slide closer to him on the sofa and place my hand on his thigh. He smiles at me and links his hand with mine.

"Okay, I want you to imagine something for me." My eyebrows raise in surprise, but I nod at him. "Imagine Ash is here now, and I ask you if you want to kiss him. What do you say?"

It's a no-brainer for me. "No."

"What if I then tell you to kiss him anyway? What would you do?"

Arousal floods through me at the thought of it. I love the idea of being forced to kiss Ash. I want to feel him hard underneath me as we kiss before he fucks me.

"I would kiss him," I confess quietly.

Logan looks into my eyes. "Lexi, I can't do this if you won't use your safeword when you need to. I mean, obviously, I know your limits in regards to that now. So CNC is the only thing I can't do with you, and Ash is out of bounds."

A wave of disappointment crashes over me because I want Logan to have full control over me. "I don't want that, Logan. I give you my consent to do anything you want to me."

His jaw tightens, and he says, "Lexi, do you want to fuck Ash?"

"No." I shake my head even though it's something I've imagined doing multiple times.

"Take my car to Ash's apartment and fuck him, Alexandra. I'll call him and tell him you're coming."

I inhale sharply as I look at Logan. This is a test. I know it is. He said in the car that he wouldn't force me to safeword, though. Except, I failed the practice test, and now I'm about to fail the real thing. I know that the second I move to leave this apartment, Logan will stop me and tell me that CNC is off the table. I ache to do it because I want it so badly.

So I say the only thing I can say right now. "Pineapple."

"I'm still not sure you would do it if he were actually here."

"I will. I promise. I'll safeword if it gets too much."

I'm on edge as I wait for his response, unsure if he'll agree to it or not.

"I want to give you what you want, Lexi, but I don't know how. I felt like shit yesterday when I realized how much further I'd pushed you than I knew at the time. I certainly don't want to do it again."

"Yesterday was also different," I point out. "I was stressed about Cassie." I sigh and tell him honestly, "She was at the back of my mind the whole time. I was worried that she would convince Ash to get back together with her during the flight. I should've had more faith in Ash, I guess." I shrug my shoulders.

Logan considers it for a moment, then asks, "Would you still have said no if Cassie wasn't going to be on the flight?"

I chew my bottom lip, unsure of whether I would have or not. "I don't know because she was." I take a deep breath and blow it out slowly. "A part of what was so hot about it was you forcing me to do it after I said no."

I'm worried that this is going to take CNC off the table again, and when Logan frowns, I become certain it is.

"I'll safeword," I promise again.

"Let me think about it while we have dinner. Is your safeword still in play?"

"No, Sir," I answer, and Logan's eyes darken.

I'm determined to be the best sub ever tonight, so I can be fully Logan's in the future.

"Go take your clothes off, Alexandra. Then make us dinner."

Despite his instruction, Logan helps me make our dinner of grilled chicken and salad. As we wait the last few minutes for the chicken, Logan's gaze roves over my body from head to toe.

"Link your hands together behind your head, Alexandra."

"Yes, Sir."

I do as instructed, and it pushes my breasts forward. My nipples are stiff and painful, while my pussy aches.

"Very nice. Spread your legs wider."

After I do, Logan walks around me in a circle. He pulls his phone out of his pocket and takes a picture of me.

"Are you my toy?"

"Yes, Sir."

He gives me a seductive smile and asks, "Do you want me to send this picture to Ash?"

My pussy clenches, and I gasp. "You wouldn't."

"Why wouldn't I if you're my toy? Should I do it?"

"No, Sir."

He steps forward to kiss me, his tongue expertly exploring my mouth as he strokes one of my nipples with his thumb.

"I won't do it, but I could. How does that make you feel?"

I think about him sending Ash a picture of me naked, legs spread, and ready to play with. It reminds me of the way Ash stroked his cock while admiring my body, and my nerves are set alight at the thought.

"Aroused," I admit.

Logan easily pushes two fingers in and out of my wet pussy. "I can tell." He pulls his fingers out of me and places them in front of my lips. "Taste yourself, Alexandra."

I suck his fingers, and I'm desperate to be fucked, but the timer goes off for the chicken, and I groan while Logan laughs. He keeps me on edge as we eat our dinner and clean up afterward.

As I'm bent over to put the dishes in the dishwasher, Logan places his hands on my hips and says, "Don't move." I pause, and he moves his hands onto my ass as he crouches down and moves nearer to my pussy. "So this is the view Ash had," he murmurs.

I gasp at the memory of Ash's face being inches away from my pussy like Logan's is now.

"It's a very nice view. God knows how he managed to stop himself from eating you out or fucking you. I sure as shit won't be."

He buries his face in my pussy, and I have to hold on to the dishwasher as he brings me to orgasm. He pulls me up to standing and spins me to face him.

"Do you wish Ash had fucked you?"

"I know it would've been a nightmare if he had, but I definitely wanted him to do it."

Logan looks me over from head to toe but doesn't say anything. My pussy is drenched, and my nipples are stiff as I wait eagerly to see what he'll do next.

He keeps my gaze as he unbuckles his belt and drops his jeans to his ankles to release his cock. Logan spins me back around and bends me over the kitchen bench as he enters me from behind. I moan in ecstasy as he fills me completely.

He moves in and out of me slowly, nowhere near the rough sex we usually have.

He leans forward as we fuck and growls, "Pretend I'm Ash, Alexandra. Say my name."

I can barely breathe as I take it in, and as he slowly fucks me, I imagine it's Ash instead. I imagine I'm bent over in the car as Ash pulls his stiff cock out of his jeans to fuck me.

"Ash," I moan.

"I've never been allowed to fuck you, Lexi, but now I can. You're so sexy, and I should've done it sooner."

I don't know if this is something Ash told him on the car ride home yesterday, but it's fucking hot.

"Fuck me, Ash," I moan. "Your cock feels so good, and I want you to come inside me."

As I say the words, I really do wish I was fucking Ash, and shame floods through me as I remember that Cassie thought I would do exactly that.

I have no idea what it would be like to fuck him, but Logan does a good enough job of fucking me differently from his usual technique that it's easy to pretend it is.

I'm so wildly aroused by this experience that it isn't long at all before I come, and I moan, "Ash."

My pussy clenches tightly around Logan's cock, and he changes his rhythm to something I'm more used to from him until he comes buried deep inside me. As he comes, he leans down and kisses my back softly.

He pulls out of me, then swiftly picks me up in his arms and carries me towards his bedroom. "Are you okay?"

He looks down at me with concern in his expression, and I smile at him as I nod. "Yes."

"How do you feel?"

"Like a slut," I admit. "But it was hot as hell."

He turns the shower on and kisses me softly as he waits for the water to warm up. "You're not a slut, Lexi. That word really seems to have gotten in your head, and I hate Cassie for doing that to you."

I don't know what to say to that, so we fall silent as he stands me in the shower. He washes me carefully, and I enjoy his loving touch. After we're done, he dries himself and me, then takes me to bed with him.

As we lie together in the dark, he asks, "Do you want to play with Ash, Lexi?"

It's easier to answer honestly because I'm tired, he can't see my face, and I feel so loved by this experience tonight. I know that I trust Logan to keep me safe, too.

"Yes."

Chapter Six

So Much Love

I leave the Beverly Center store early on Wednesday to head to our apartment. The four of us are meeting with a real estate agent to look at apartments tonight, and I'm excited.

I walk into the living room to the sound of Nate's voice ringing through the apartment, and I smile when I find the three men together. Dante has an acoustic guitar that he's playing even though he doesn't play guitar often. They harmonize on the chorus of a song I haven't heard before, and I figure that's probably because Logan has staff paper in front of him with music notes and lyrics on it. I drop onto the sofa next to Nate, and he puts his arm around me.

They sing a verse after the chorus before Dante stops playing and smiles at me. "Hey, Angel."

"Hi, Honey."

Nate kisses me, and I kiss him back before I move over to kiss Dante, who has set the guitar aside, then I walk over to where Logan is sitting on an armchair. I straddle him and wrap my arms around his neck before I kiss him as well.

A sense of overwhelming rightness comes over me because Logan is here with us, and I smile into his beautiful face. "Hi. I missed you last night."

"I missed you, too. The sooner we have an apartment together, the better."

He starts to get hard underneath me, and I turn to look at Dante over my shoulder, hopeful that we have some time to play before our appointment. "How long until the agent gets here?"

"He won't be here for another hour. We should discuss what things we're prioritizing in apartment choices," he tells me.

I turn back to Logan and kiss him as I grind myself on his growing erection. I don't really want to waste time talking about the apartment right now.

"Should we?" I ask cheekily. "We know what we want. A place for us all to be together. I don't care about anything else."

Logan reaches a hand up and places it on my breast before he pulls my head down to his and kisses me. Arousal flows through me as our tongues dance together, and I moan when he reaches into my bra and tweaks my nipple.

"I see." Dante chuckles from behind me. "Take your clothes off, Angel."

I bite my lip as Logan ends our kiss and takes his hand out of my top. I stand and face Dante before I pull my top off over my head. I fold it neatly and place it on the coffee table before I remove my bra and place it on top.

"I love her breasts," Nate murmurs.

"Turn to show Logan, Angel," Dante says.

I turn to face him as my pussy aches with desire. My nipples are taut and painful, and I'm already drenched, probably making a mess of my underwear.

"I want to watch you play with them, Alexandra."

I raise my hands to my breasts and squeeze them before I tweak and pull my nipples as I moan.

"Very nice. Let Dante and Nate watch, too."

My heart races as I turn to face the other two while I put on a show for them. Arousal floods through as they watch me with hungry eyes, and I love being put on display like this.

Dante says in a husky voice, "Remove your pants, Angel."

Nate and Dante's cocks are already rock hard, and I know Logan's will be, too. I can't wait to be fucked by these three men. I unbutton each button on my pants deliberately slowly, though, to draw out the tease.

The sound of our breathing is loud in the room as I bend at the waist and push them down to my ankles. I gasp as Logan softly strokes a vertical line on my pussy over my thong.

"Wait until you see the mess she's made of her thong."

The comment causes heat to flood to my cheeks, even as it sends a dart of arousal to my pussy. I swallow heavily as I step out of my pants and straighten up with them in my hands. I fold them and put them on the growing pile of clothes on the coffee table.

"Come here, Angel," Dante says.

I walk over to him, and he strokes the same line Logan did.

"Quite the mess she's made of it, Logan. I'll have to take them off her, I think." He pulls my thong down, and I step out of it before he tosses it to Nate. "Here. Look."

I'm dripping wet, and I ache to be filled as Nate lifts my thong to his face and smells it. "Mmm, she's going to be tasty, Dante."

Dante places a hand on either of my hips as he leans forward and begins to eat me out. I thrust a hand into his hair as I gasp.

"Honey," I moan.

Pleasure rocks my body, and I throw my head back and close my eyes while I focus on the sensations of what Dante is doing. He licks and sucks my clit as he pushes two fingers in and out of my pussy. It's nowhere near as satisfying as having a cock in me, but it doesn't take long for him to bring me to orgasm.

I moan Dante's name when I do, and I open my eyes to look down at his smiling face before I look over at Nate. I gasp, and my pussy aches when I do. Logan has moved over to the sofa, and they're currently kissing passionately. Nate's jeans are unzipped, and Logan has pulled his cock out to stroke it. Nate moans into Logan's mouth, and I love the sound of his ecstasy.

"Logan's cock looks like it needs sucking, Angel," Dante murmurs.

I nod as desire floods through me, and I move over to them before I drop to my knees in front of Logan. I rub his cock through his jeans, and Logan's eyebrows raise as he breaks their kiss, then turns to look at me.

"Hello, Alexandra."

"She's going to worship your cock," Dante tells him.

Logan continues stroking Nate as he looks down at me. "Lucky me. I know plenty of men who wish they had a woman like Lexi doing that."

I swallow as our eyes meet, and I wonder if I'm friends with at least one of them as I unzip Logan's jeans. The thought of Ash thinking about me sucking his cock makes me hot all over, and I pant for breath. Logan lifts his ass so I can pull his jeans and briefs to his ankles, freeing his stiff erection.

He leans over to kiss Nate again as I take Logan's cock in my mouth. I enjoy the sound of Logan's moans and pants for breath while I suck him.

"Bend over so I can fuck you, Angel," Dante says.

I shuffle my knees back so Dante can get into position behind me, and I groan onto Logan's cock as Dante enters me. I'm lost in a daze of lust as he fucks me while I blow Logan. I love this, and I reach over to gently squeeze and play with Nate's balls because I want to be connected to him as well.

"Oh god, that's good," Dante says when he grips my hips tightly and holds himself deep inside me as his cock jerks when he comes.

I moan around Logan's cock and take him as far in my mouth as I can just to tether myself to something as Dante's orgasm tips me into my own. My body shakes, and I have to pull Logan out of my mouth so I can pant for breath.

"Fuck, I love you, Honey," I moan.

Dante holds himself inside me while I come, and then he pulls out, leaving me empty.

"Do you have lube we can use?" Logan asks Dante.

"Sure. I'll go get it," he says.

He walks away, leaving me with Nate and Logan. I don't know who the lube is for, and I don't ask because I don't care.

"Suck Nate, Alexandra. If you spill any cum on the carpet, you'll be spanked."

My pussy clenches tight, and I carefully crawl over to Nate. I arch my back and keep my ass high to try and keep Dante's cum inside me as I take Nate in my mouth. He places one hand on the back of my head and reaches over to stroke Logan's cock as well.

"Want me to prepare her ass?" Dante asks from behind me.

"It looks pretty fuckable, doesn't it?" Logan asks, sounding amused.

"It really does."

"If only there were a fourth person here to fuck her, but no." He pauses just long enough for me to envisage Ash giving me anal before he continues, "Lexi's ass will remain sadly unfucked today. The lube is for me, and if you want to prepare my ass, you can. Otherwise, Nate or Lexi will do it."

Dante sounds mildly surprised when he responds. "I see. Who am I giving the lube to, then?"

Logan laughs, "Tactful. Give it to Lexi. She has to make sure she doesn't get any cum on the carpet, or she'll be spanked. Let's see if she can prepare my ass and keep your cum safe in her pussy. Stop sucking Nate, Alexandra."

I moan softly as I remove him from my mouth because I want to keep blowing him and I can't. Logan gets onto his knees next to me. He leans up to kiss Nate, and I clench my pussy tight as I straighten up to take the lube from Dante.

I'm fucked.

There's no way this cum won't drip out of me, but I keep trying anyway.

"I'm fucking your ass today, huh?" Nate asks Logan in a husky voice.

"Yes. I want your amazing cock in my ass while I fuck Lexi's tight pussy, and I consider myself lucky to have two partners who are so damn perfect."

I enjoy the sight of them kissing again as I squirt lube on Logan's ass. I push a finger into him, and when I'm able to push it in and out easily, I add more lube before I push in a second finger.

I gasp as I feel Dante's cum seep out of me and run down my thigh, and he chuckles from behind me. "What are you going to do, Angel?"

I continue fucking Logan with my fingers as I use my other hand to swipe at the cum on my leg. I suck my fingers clean and taste Dante's salty cum as I do. I pant for breath as I squirt more lube on Logan's ass and push a third finger in. He moans, and I'm so turned on by doing this and knowing that Nate's cock will be taking the place of my fingers soon.

I straighten up more to get a better angle, and I feel some cum drip out of me just before Dante says, "Oh dear, Angel. You weren't meant to make a mess on the carpet."

"Stop, Alexandra, and bend over the sofa," Logan says.

I can barely breathe as I follow the instructions. Dante has me move, so my head is resting on his lap as I present my ass to Logan. He doesn't give me a number or tell me to count before I feel the stinging sensation of his hand hitting my ass cheek.

I gasp as it happens, and I barely have a second to breathe before it happens again. My pussy is so wet, and I'm sure more cum is going to leak out of me as Logan spanks me again. He repeats this process over and over, and it drives me wild. My ass is hot and stings to hell by the time he's finished.

"Lie on your back on the sofa, Alexandra. Dante can be your pillow."

I do as instructed and rest my head on Dante's legs before Logan climbs onto me. Dante uses a hand to tweak and play with my breasts as Logan finally pushes his cock into me, and I moan in ecstasy.

"Get in my ass, Nate. I need you to fuck me," Logan growls.

I have the pleasure of watching as Nate positions himself behind Logan. Logan's weight on me gets heavier as Nate thrusts into him. I have to take shallow breaths because of Logan's and

Nate's combined weight, and Dante's hand stills as it's trapped between Logan's body and mine. He manages to pinch my nipple, though, twisting it roughly as Logan lifts himself slightly and starts to fuck me.

Nate kisses Logan's neck before he pulls himself up to fuck Logan. With each thrust forward from Nate, Logan is forced deeper into me, and it's amazing. The room is filled with our moans and the sound of fucking, along with our loud breathing.

Dante plays with my breasts and says, "I love watching you get fucked, Angel. I don't think I'll ever get tired of watching someone shove their cock deep inside your pussy."

My pussy clenches around Logan's cock, and I can't help but think of Cassie calling me a slut. Right now, I don't care if I'm a slut. Nothing about this is dirty or shameful. I love the men I'm fucking, and they love me.

"I'll never get tired of being balls deep in Alexandra," Logan grunts. He pushes himself roughly into me. "She's so tight." He pulls out and thrusts in again. "And wet." I gasp as he does it another time. "And hot." Another thrust. "And I"—he pounds into me—"fucking"—another thrust—"love her."

Logan's rough fucking tips me over the edge into another orgasm, and I moan, "Logan."

I grip his cock tightly with my internal muscles as I come apart around him. Dante is still tweaking and thumbing my nipples as I lose myself to everything. Logan thrusts one last time, followed by him being pushed further in by Nate as Logan groans loudly.

"Alexandra." Logan's guttural groan is followed by his release.

He collapses on me as his lips find mine. His tongue explores my mouth, and we're both jolted every time Nate pounds into Logan's ass. I can barely breathe with the weight of Logan and Nate on top of me, but I love this, and I kiss him back.

It's a relief when Nate empties himself in Logan's ass and pulls out of him, though. Nate moves around and kneels next to us. He kisses Logan first, then me, and then I can't resist kissing Logan again.

"I love you guys so much," Nate says.

"I love you, too, Nate," Logan says, and they kiss again.

"I love you as well," I say with a smile.

Logan pulls out of me and stands up before rushing off toward the bathroom. I move upright and kiss Dante quickly.

"I love you, too, Honey," I say as I rush off to follow Logan.

He laughs and calls out, "Love you, Angel."

I follow the sound of running water to the room that I share with Nate and find Logan in the shower. He usually spends nights in this bedroom when he stays in our apartment. He's even got some clothes stashed in the wardrobe and dresser.

"Hey, Alexandra." Logan's lips claim mine as I join him under the warm spray.

He pulls me against him, my back to his front, and I moan as he rubs his hands over my skin. He slips his hand down to find my clit.

"So beautiful," he murmurs in my ear before he kisses my neck. "Come for me, Alexandra."

He uses one hand to play with my breasts while he continues to stroke my clit.

"Imagine if we'd had someone else here today. They could've fucked your ass." He keeps rubbing my clit but trails his hand from my breast down to my ass and squeezes it. "Would you have enjoyed that?"

"Yes, Sir," I moan.

"Any idea who you'd like to join us and fuck your ass, Alexandra?"

"Ash," I whisper, barely audible above the running water.

I'm not sure if Logan heard me or if he just knows, but he puts a little pressure against my asshole with his finger, not pushing it in but pressing just hard enough to make me gasp.

"I'm sure you'd love Ash to be here right now. He could bend you over and fuck that pretty little ass of yours. Now it doesn't get fucked today, and that's a damn shame."

I moan as I think about it, and I'm close to coming when

Logan strokes me much slower and keeps my orgasm at bay instead of tipping me over the edge.

"Oh no, you don't get to come yet, Alexandra. I want you to spend some real time thinking about it first. Tell me what you would've done if Ash were here today."

My pussy clenches tightly, and I pant for breath as Logan moves his hand back to my breast.

"Fucked him," I admit. "I'd have given him any hole he wanted."

"How does the thought of fucking Ash make you feel?"

I think about the way I felt when I thought of Cassie during that scene, and I think I've finally made peace with what she called me.

"Like a slut, but in a good way," I admit. "Because if fucking the men I love makes me a slut, then fine, I'm a slut. Just keep filling my holes, and I'll be the happiest little slut ever. I just can't believe that us all loving each other is wrong in any way."

Logan stops doing what he's doing and moves his hands to my shoulders to spin me to face him. He looks down into my eyes with a solemn look on his face.

"Seriously?"

"Yes, Sir." I nod my head.

He gives me a loving smile and kisses me gently. "Good. Because there *is* nothing wrong with what we're doing. We're all happy, and that's what matters." He gives me a seductive smile. "Are you my happy little slut toy, then?"

My pussy aches, and I nod. "Yes, Sir."

"I'm going to talk to Dante and Nate about us hanging out with Ash on Saturday if he wants to."

I bite my lip as I think about what this means. Ash fucking me. A fourth cock in a scene like today's, and, honestly, I can't fucking wait.

Logan pushes me back, so I'm pressed up against the cold tile wall facing him. "I'm going to watch my beautiful slut come for me."

He reaches between my legs again to rub my clit, and I moan.

"Such a good little toy. Ready to be used whenever I want to use it. Say my name," he murmurs.

"Logan," I gasp as my orgasm nears.

"Pretty soon, you'll be moaning Ash's name. I'm going to enjoy watching him satisfy himself with your body."

I pant for breath as I envisage myself fucking Ash.

"Mmm, are you thinking about it, Alexandra?" I nod my head. "Me, too. I can imagine how good you'll look with Ash balls deep inside you as he licks and sucks your gorgeous breasts. I want you to come while thinking about all the things Ash is going to do to you."

Logan tweaks one of my nipples as he says this, and it reminds me of Ash doing it to me, which finally tips me into orgasm.

"Fuck, Logan," I groan.

I look into his beautiful brown eyes as my body shakes, and my orgasm rocks me to my core. Once my body has stopped shaking, Logan moves forward and kisses me lovingly.

"I love you so much, Lexi."

He pulls me into his arms as he kisses me. I wrap my arms around his neck and press my body against him as I kiss him back.

Logan gets the soap and washes me from head to toe. I love his gentle touch, and when we're done in the shower, he wraps me in a towel, and I sigh in satisfaction.

"I've never been happier," I tell him.

He kisses the top of my head as he pulls me against him. "I'm glad. Go get dressed, Lexi. I'm pretty sure Dante's going to kill us for taking too long in the shower."

I laugh as I head to my bedroom with Dante and get dressed as quickly as I can. I don't put any underwear on underneath the floaty Serenity purple skirt and cream blouse that I put on. I slip on some cream heels and meet up with Logan as he's heading back to the living room.

"The agent's going to be here in fifteen minutes," Dante grumbles as soon as we appear.

Both men have their clothes back on, and I walk straight over to Dante and kiss him. "Sorry, Honey."

"Hmph. Well, I'll be back in a couple of minutes."

As Dante leaves for his shower, I climb into Nate's lap and kiss him.

"You guys are in trouble," he says with a laugh. "Dante was threatening to go interrupt you just before we heard the water turn off."

"What can I say? Lexi takes ages to get clean." Logan winks at me, and both Nate and I laugh in response.

After a couple of minutes, Dante yells to Nate that he can have a shower while Dante gets dressed. Nate kisses both Logan and me quickly before I climb into Logan's lap, and Nate walks away.

Logan places his hand on my breast and thumbs my nipple. "I can just see the dark outline of your nipple, so I know you're not wearing a bra, and I like that."

My nipples have hardened from what he's doing. "Well, it's even more obvious now."

"Yes, it is. I can't wait to show you off on Saturday. Are you looking forward to that?"

"Yes." I nod my head and smile at him. "Only if Dante and Nate are okay with it, of course."

"I'm pretty sure they will be." Logan laughs and then cringes. "I'm actually more nervous about telling Ash that Nate and I are together as well."

My heart swells as he says it, and I'm so happy for them. "Are you officially a thing now?"

"Yeah, we are. We talked about it today. Are you okay with that?" He looks as though he thinks I might ever have some kind of objection to them having a relationship.

"Of course I am. I'm so happy for you both. Does this mean we don't have to move? Couldn't you just share a room with Nate? You've been sleeping in his room anyway."

Logan shakes his head as Dante walks back into the room and says, "No. We want our own rooms because we each have a separate relationship with you. If we shared a room, we wouldn't be able to be alone with you when we want to be."

I nod as he says it because I see what he means. They can always visit each other's rooms to spend time together, like on nights I'm with Dante, but when I want to be with just one of them, we can do that.

I frown as I come to a realization and say, "Hey! Does this mean that I'm the only one of us that doesn't get their own room?"

Dante and Logan both look at each other, then burst into laughter, and I can't help but laugh with them.

"I suppose it does, Angel," Dante says.

"That's not fair," I pout.

"Maybe we can find a place with another room so you can have your own room as well," Dante suggests.

"We were planning that, anyway," Logan smirks at me. "It's going to be filled with sex toys. That's your room, Lexi."

"My room is the sex room?" I raise an eyebrow at him.

Logan pushes my skirt up and slides his hand up my thigh to my pussy. He softly traces my wet slit and nods.

"Indeed. You're a good little slut toy who likes to be used for sex, aren't you?"

Dante whips his head around to look at us when Logan says this, but when I moan and nod my head, he relaxes.

"Yes. That's why my room is the sex room."

"Precisely."

There's a knock on the apartment door, and as Dante stands to answer it, he says, "You should probably get off Logan's lap, Angel."

I wrinkle my nose and nod. I slip off his lap and move a reasonable distance away from him as Nate comes back from the bathroom, dressed in jeans and a t-shirt. He smiles at us and takes a seat in an armchair as Dante brings the agent over to us.

"Did you want a coffee, Anthony?" Dante asks.

"No, I'm fine." He takes a seat in the other armchair as Dante sits next to me.

"I've found a few apartments that seem to meet your needs. You said a minimum of four bedrooms, ideally with a separate theater as well as a games room and a study. Is that correct?"

Dante nods. "Yes, that's right."

"There are very few apartments that meet those criteria, but I've found three penthouses that I think you might like. You're all coming to look at them?"

"Yup, we are. We couldn't possibly make a decision like this without feedback from the guys," I say with a casual laugh.

He looks through our group with a quizzical look but doesn't comment. We head downstairs to his BMW sedan, and Dante sits in the front seat while I squish into the back, in between Logan and Nate. I have to resist the urge to cuddle into them and work hard to look like the dutiful wife who's sitting with her platonic friends.

Anthony shows us the three penthouses, and they're all gorgeous. As promised, they have all the things we asked for, and they ooze luxury. I like the second apartment the best, though. It has remote-controlled blinds and is fully smart-wired. It's also in a building that's a lot more modern, and I love it.

Anthony gives us some time to talk in private after we've looked through the third apartment.

"Thoughts?" Dante asks.

"I still like the second one best," Nate says.

"Me, too," I agree with a grin.

"The theater was a bit bigger in the first one, though," Logan says.

"But the bedrooms were bigger in the second. You know you want a big bedroom to watch The Lexi Show," Nate teases him.

Logan laughs and says, "Maybe. I'm happy with either the first or the second. Not a fan of this one."

"We'll put an offer in on the second one, then," Dante suggests, and I squeal.

Anthony is thrilled when he writes up the offer, and he tells us that he'll let us know before he drives us back to our apartment.

We order Chinese for dinner, and after we've cleaned up, we

have coffee in the living room. I'm sitting on Dante's lap as we talk, and everyone is in a good mood.

"So," Logan says. "I wanted to ask you guys something."

Both Dante and Nate look at him, and butterflies fly around my stomach, knowing what Logan is about to suggest.

"I want to ask Ash if he'd like to come and play with us on Saturday."

"No," Dante says in a stern voice as he glares at him.

"Lexi wants it," Logan tells him.

Dante turns his face to mine, and his eyebrows raise. "Really?"

"Yeah. Logan and I have talked about it this week. I think it will be fun."

There's silence in the room for a few seconds, and Dante's face is inscrutable. I hate that I can't tell what he's thinking.

He sighs and frowns. "It's not a good idea."

"We've roleplayed it, Dante. You'll be properly involved this time. I was going to ask you to keep an eye on her, and you can stop everything if you think she's getting too overwhelmed."

"You've roleplayed it?" Nate raises an eyebrow at Logan.

"Yeah, she called me Ash while I fucked her on Monday." Logan shrugs.

Nate blinks at him. "I'm sorry, she *what*?!"

"I wanted to see how she would react. We practiced her using her safeword and then roleplayed her fucking Ash. It was the stupid shit Cassie said getting in her head. I'll give you the call on making her fuck him, Dante. If you don't think it's a good idea on the day, it won't happen."

There's silence in the room for a long time, and I can barely breathe as I wait for Dante's answer. I don't know if he'll agree or not, and I really want this. Dante looks into my eyes, and I can't look away from him. He searches my face for about ten seconds before he sighs.

"If Ash wants to play with her, he can."

Chapter Seven

Play Time

By Saturday afternoon, I'm wound as tight as a spring. Ash is coming over soon, supposedly to 'hang out,' but I know that Logan specifically asked him about playing with me.

About half an hour before Ash is due to arrive, Logan says, "I'm going to take her to get dressed."

"Okay," Dante agrees.

I follow Logan to Dante's and my bedroom and into the closet. He looks through my lingerie first, and I'm surprised.

"I'm going to wear underwear?"

He smiles at me. "You'd be surprised by how hot not seeing something can be."

He chooses a tiny black thong and bra that are made of black mesh.

"Put these on while I choose the rest of your outfit, Alexandra."

I nod and strip off the dress I've been wearing, then pull on the lingerie. Logan flicks through my clothes and pulls out a blue silk mini-skirt, followed by a tight pastel pink shirt.

He turns to face me, and his eyes darken in arousal. He lowers his head to my breast and clamps his lips around one nipple. He swirls his tongue around the hard pebble before he bites it roughly, and I moan.

"Ash is going to enjoy you a lot," he says in a husky voice.

"I hope so."

Logan hands me the skirt, and I pull it on. It's so short that it ends barely an inch below my ass cheeks.

"Turn around," Logan says, and I do as I'm told.

When I'm facing him again, he steps forward and places his hands on the waistband of the skirt. He rolls it over, raising the skirt approximately the single inch that was giving me any modesty.

"Turn around." When I turn this time, he says, "Perfect."

He hands me the shirt, and I pull it on. It's from the 'sex clothes' section of my wardrobe with Dante. It's about two sizes too small, and I struggle to get it over my breasts. The fabric strains and the neckline pulls so low that my cleavage and the top of the bra cups spill out from it.

"Beautiful," Logan murmurs. "Have a look at yourself."

I turn to the mirror, and the black bra is clearly visible beneath the tight fabric. My nipples are an obvious outline as well because the mesh is doing nothing to hide them. I turn to check out my rear, and the bottoms of my ass cheeks are visible underneath the hem of the skirt.

"Do you think Ash will like this outfit?" Logan asks.

"I think he will." I bite my lip as I think about Ash seeing me in this.

"One last thing." Logan pulls out a pair of thigh-high boots, and my pussy clenches as he says, "Perfect boots for a slut to wear."

Logan unzips one, and I put my right foot into it. He slowly pulls the zip up, past my knee, and to my upper thigh. When he reaches the top of it, he continues the movement of his hand until he gently brushes my pussy.

"Whoops. Too much momentum," he says with a grin.

He does the same thing as he zips up the left boot. This time, he rubs my pussy for about ten seconds.

"I'm so clumsy," he says. "You're ready, though. Let's go."

I'm absolutely soaking this thong. Ash isn't even here yet, and my senses are on fire as I take Logan's hand, and he leads me back to the living room.

"Fucking hell, you look good, Lexi," Nate groans.

"I'd tell you to sit on the coffee table, Angel, but I think Nate's going to struggle to focus as it is," Dante chuckles.

I sit between them, and Dante takes my hand in his as I lean over to kiss him, then I lean over to kiss Nate as well.

Logan sits in an armchair opposite us, and his cock is stiff in his jeans. "Ash should be here soon."

"You'll use your safeword if you need to?" Dante asks me, and I nod. "I get to decide if you fuck Ash," he reiterates, and I nod again.

"Do you want to say no and have me force you to do things? Logan asks.

"Maybe? I liked you exercising your control over me."

Dante looks at Logan. "Did Ash have any rules for her?"

Logan chuckles, "No. I asked if he wanted to play with Lexi, and he asked if I was shitting him. When I said no, he said to name the time and place and that nothing short of bodily harm would stop him from being here. He also got his STD test results back, and he's negative."

A dart of arousal shoots to my pussy when I hear that Ash was so into doing this. Nate reaches over and circles around my nipple with his pointer finger.

"I'm jealous of Ash. I wish I could go back and fuck you for the first time again. It was glorious," he murmurs.

"They might not fuck today," Dante says sternly.

"Of course," Nate concedes. "Maybe he'll just eat her out. Or she'll swallow his cum. Or jack him off. Whatever she does, no doubt Ash will consider himself a lucky asshole. He was jealous of me when I pointed out that I get to touch her in private."

"He was?" I whip my head around to look at Nate.

"Yes," he says. "He said you were always off the table, so he'd never considered you before."

"Oh, he'd considered her," Logan laughs. "He was just not touching her because she was off-limits."

When the doorbell rings, Nate goes to answer it, and when he comes back, he sits in the other armchair. It leaves a space on the sofa next to me, where Ash takes a seat.

I give him a small smile as butterflies fly around my stomach. The sexual tension in the room is so thick it could be cut with a knife as Ash greets us.

He starts with the guys before he says, "Hey, Lexi."

I look into his beautiful blue eyes, dark with arousal, and say, "Hi, Ash."

His eyes travel over me from head to toe. My pussy is barely covered by the skirt, and my breasts are straining against the shirt.

"I like those boots," Ash says.

"Thanks," I breathe.

"I think we could all use a drink. Get one for everyone, Angel," Dante says.

"Yes, Honey," I reply dutifully.

As I stand from my seat and walk over to the bar, the cold air hits my ass and pussy, and I remember what Ash is seeing.

I can barely focus enough to pour the drinks and take them one by one to the guys. I start with Dante, who kisses me and rubs my breast as I hand it to him.

Next, I serve Nate, who reaches under the skirt and rubs my pussy through my thong.

Then comes Logan, who reaches behind me and pushes my skirt up a little as he squeezes my ass cheek. "Do you like her skirt, Ash?"

"I certainly do. I'm also waiting very patiently for my drink," he murmurs.

Logan doesn't pull my skirt back down, and I know without being told that I'm not allowed to adjust it. Finally, I carry Ash's drink over to him. His cock is already stiff in his jeans as I hand it to him.

"Thanks, Lexi." He takes a sip, then says, "Nowhere near as

tasty as your pussy juice was on Sunday."

I gasp as he says it, and my pussy aches for him to fill it.

"We were having a discussion before you arrived about whether or not you've masturbated while thinking about Lexi," Logan says casually as I take a seat with my own drink in hand.

"Of course," Ash laughs, and his gaze travels over my body. "More this week than ever, but yes." He gives Dante a chagrined smile. "I did feel like a piece of shit, though."

"I forgive you," Dante says with a smirk. "If I didn't, you wouldn't be here."

Ash relaxes, and I think they're talking more about Sunday than some past masturbatory fantasies Ash had about me.

The guys talk for a few minutes, not even looking at me, while I drink my drink quietly and wait for whatever will happen next.

"Do you want to touch her, Ash?" Logan asks.

"Of course I do." He finally looks at me, and I gasp.

His gaze is full of intense desire, and I'm desperate to be fucked by him. He takes my drink out of my hands and sets it aside with his own, then turns to look at me again.

"All week, I've been imagining my hands all over her body."

He seems to be watching for a reaction, and I give one. I bite my lip and moan softly as my pussy aches with desire.

"I've been thinking about your 'O' face while I jerked myself off. Have you thought about me?" Ash raises an eyebrow at me.

Heat rushes to my cheeks as I think about using his name while I fucked Logan on Monday.

"Answer the question, Alexandra, *and* tell him when," Logan says.

I can barely get the words out because I'm so embarrassed and aroused. I don't want to tell Ash when it happened. It's too embarrassing, so I cop out.

"Yes, I have. When I've been horny."

Before Ash can reply, Logan grinds out, "Come here, Alexandra."

I knew this would happen, and I'm horny as shit to get a

punishment from Logan in front of Ash.

"Get over my knee," Logan growls.

I bend over his knee, and Logan flips my skirt up and over my hips.

"Look at Ash while I spank you. If you stop looking at him, you won't get an orgasm until after dinner."

I gasp and stare at Ash. He meets my gaze and strokes his cock through his jeans as Logan brings his hand down roughly on my ass.

The sound of his stinging hit rings out around the room, and I jump. Logan's cock is hard under my stomach, and I desperately want it in my mouth.

The embarrassment of being spanked in front of Ash is hot as shit, though. Part of it is knowing that when he's done, Logan is going to make me tell Ash the truth.

"I'm assuming she didn't tell me everything," Ash says.

Logan smacks my ass again. "Not even close."

I squirm against my arousal and embarrassment as Nate chuckles, "Lexi's naughty all the time."

I resist the urge to look at him when he says it and keep my gaze firmly locked with Ash's as Logan spanks me again. By the time he's done, my body is on fire with arousal.

Both the cheeks of my face and the cheeks of my ass are equally hot, and my embarrassment is heightened when Logan says, "Walk over and show your ass to Ash so he can see what happens when you don't tell the whole truth."

I walk over to him and turn to face Logan again as I lift my skirt up over my ass cheeks to show it to him.

I gasp when Ash's cool hand touches me, and my pussy clenches. "Damn, you did a good job. Her ass is bright red and even hot to touch." He chuckles. "I mean, it's hot to touch either way."

The guys all laugh, and Ash rubs my ass cheeks for a few seconds before he allows my skirt to drop down again.

"Turn around and tell Ash when you thought about him this week," Logan says sternly.

I turn to face Ash, and I think I might die from embarrassment when I say, "I fucked Logan while I called him 'Ash.'"

Ash's mouth drops open in shock as he blinks at me a few times, then a dangerous look of arousal takes over, and he looks past me to Logan.

"That's some kinky shit, dude."

When Logan replies, I can hear the smile on his face. "Maybe. I wanted to see if she would fuck you or not. You missed out. I told her to go to your place and fuck you, but she used her safeword."

"You didn't want to do it?" Ash asks me.

"Oh, no. She wanted to do it," Logan answers for me. "She only used it so I would let her do this."

"I'm confused," Ash says.

"Dude, just go with it. I don't even try to understand it anymore. I just let them torture her, and look at how fucking hot she is from it," Nate laughs.

Ash looks up at me again, then trails his gaze over my body from head to toe.

"Are we going to fuck today, Lexi?"

"That's up to Dante," I admit.

Ash looks over at him, and Dante says, "I hold her consent today. We'll see how it goes."

"Hey, I could go home now and have enough masturbation material to last me a lifetime." Ash grins at him, then lifts my skirt and looks at my pussy. "I mean, just getting to see this again is better than my wildest dreams."

He stares at me for a solid thirty seconds before he lets my skirt drop again.

"Remove your skirt and take a seat on Ash's lap, Angel," Dante murmurs.

I do as instructed, and I sit on Ash's lap after I place my folded skirt on the coffee table. His cock is hard underneath my ass, and I gasp as the pain of sitting down on my stinging ass cheeks hits me.

I allow my legs to drop either side of Ash's, so I'm spread wide, and both Logan and Nate seem to appreciate the view.

Ash puts his arms around me, just under my breasts, and pulls me back against him. I tilt my head back to rest it on his shoulder, and in this position, my breasts are pushed higher in the air with my nipples prominently displayed under my tight shirt.

"God, you're so fucking hot," Ash murmurs.

I moan as he slides his right hand up to my breast and strokes my hard nipple with his thumb.

"Are you enjoying this, Angel?" Dante asks, his voice coated with thick lust, and I nod.

"Do you want Ash to touch your pussy?" Logan asks, and as I look at him, he gives me a meaningful look.

"No, Sir. This is enough," I tell him.

"Ash is going to touch your pussy, Alexandra."

I squirm as Ash takes this as his cue to lower his hand toward my pussy.

"No, Sir. I don't want him to touch me there."

Ash pauses and asks, "Um, should I do it?"

"Yes," Dante answers. "Our angel can't stop you unless she uses her safeword." I bite my lip and moan as he says it. "She doesn't want to do that. She wants you to touch her, so go ahead and do it."

"No, I don't," I gasp.

I turn my gaze to Ash's, and he leans down and crashes his lips against mine. I wasn't expecting this, and when I gasp in surprise, Ash thrusts his tongue into my open mouth.

He kisses me roughly, exploring my mouth with his tongue, and he tastes like whiskey and some arousing taste that I think I'll always attribute to sex from now on.

He doesn't touch my pussy and leaves his hand where it is on my pubic bone, but he uses his left hand to stroke and tweak my left nipple. I'm lost in ecstasy by the time he ends our kiss.

"I didn't expect that," Logan laughs. "That was quite a kiss, Ash."

"Mmm, it was. She's a good kisser."

He's still playing with my breast as he speaks, and I moan loudly, "Ash."

"You want me to make you come. Don't you, Lexi?" he growls

at me. I nod my head, and he says, "You want me to touch your pussy, don't you?"

"No," I moan. "Please don't do it."

Ash seems to understand now, and he gets a wicked grin on his face. "You can't stop me, Lexi. Logan and Dante have both told you to let me do it." His hand toys with the band of my thong, and he lifts it away from my body, then lets it snap back down as he growls in my ear, "Say 'pineapple,' Lexi."

I pant for breath as his fingers slide down over my thong to rest above my pussy. He doesn't move his hand, just holds it there. The three other men are watching us with interest, and all three have cocks that are stiff as a rock.

Ash grabs my thong and bunches it together before pulling it tight and hard up my slit. I gasp in shock at the slight pain as my pussy lips surround the fabric of my thong.

"This is how you should wear it." Ash yanks on it again, and I moan at the pain. "Get this fucking thong off and sit back down on my lap so I can play with your cunt like you want me to, Lexi."

I can barely breathe as I stand and remove my underwear before I drop it on my skirt on the coffee table.

Before I can walk back to Ash, Dante says, "Take off your shirt and bra, Angel. Face Ash while you do it."

I turn to face Ash, and he's grinning from ear to ear as I pull my top off over my head, fold it, and place it on the coffee table. I unclip my bra and drop it there as well before I walk slowly back to Ash wearing nothing but the black thigh-high boots. I enjoy the greedy look in his eyes as they rove over my naked body.

"God, this fucking view," he murmurs. "You assholes have been looking at it for months. Years for you, Dante."

The others all laugh, and Dante says, "Well, we're sharing her with you now."

I take my place on Ash's lap again and lean back again as I spread my legs.

"She's so wet that she's literally dripping juice on your jeans," Nate murmurs.

"Do you want me to touch your pussy, Lexi?" Ash asks as he begins to pull and tweak one of my nipples.

"No, I don't," I say, even though it's nowhere near the truth.

Ash chuckles in my ear, "You're a fucking liar who gets no say in this. I'm going to touch you, and you can't stop me." I squirm on his lap, eager for him to follow through on this threat.

He kisses me again, and it's just as good the second time. His hand hovers over my pussy, so close that I can feel it's there, but he doesn't touch me at all.

When our kiss ends, Ash gives me a wicked grin. "Actually, I won't touch your pussy after all. I'm going to let you writhe and squirm and ache for me to do it."

He trails his pointer finger around the outside of my pussy, up the outside of my labia, across my pubic bone, and down the other side.

I moan, "Ash, please."

"Ash, please what?" He raises an eyebrow at me.

"Please touch my pussy. Make me come for you," I beg.

"Is that what you want?"

He tweaks a nipple roughly, which sends a dart of arousal straight to my aching pussy, and I nod.

"Use your words, Alexandra," Logan says, as though I'm a precocious toddler.

"I want you to make me come, Ash."

"Maybe I will. I've had the image of your face when you orgasm burned into my brain, but that hasn't stopped me from watching our music video about five hundred times this week."

My pussy clenches, and I murmur, "I imagined you stroking your cock while you watched it."

"Did you like that idea?"

"Fuck, yes. Did you do it?" I turn to look at him and bite my lip as he grins at me.

"Of course." He finally reaches between my legs, finds my wet clit, and slowly rubs it. "I was so jealous of Nate all week. I imagined what it would be like to have you get yourself off on me."

"Why don't you do it?" Dante suggests.

Ash pauses and says, "Huh?"

"Take her to one of the bedrooms and give her an orgasm the same way Nate did."

Ash gives him a slow smile. "Okay."

We make our way to Dante's and my bedroom because it's the biggest. Ash removes his jeans and shirt, so he's only wearing briefs, the same way Nate was in the music video, while I remove my boots.

I lie in bed with him, and he wraps his arms around me as he smiles down at me and murmurs, "God, you're amazing."

"Action," Logan yells with a laugh, and I smile as their song starts playing from someone's phone behind me.

Ash rolls onto his back as he pulls me on top of him, and I'm surprised by how accurately he's timed it to the song and the exact moment Nate did it when filming. I kiss Ash and then grind my pussy against his hard shaft.

There's so much that's different about this, but there's so much that similar as well, and it's all so wildly erotic that it isn't long before I'm coming with my clit pressed against Ash's cock.

Unlike Nate the day that we filmed, Ash doesn't kiss me to cover up my orgasm, and I throw my head back in ecstasy as waves of pleasure crash over me.

"Ash," I moan, and I continue grinding against him.

He rolls me onto my back and thrusts against me the way Nate did that day. I want Ash inside me, though, and I wrap my legs around his waist.

"Fuck me," I groan.

He blinks at me. "For real?"

The music stops playing, and I stare into Ash's eyes as I beg, "Yes. Fuck me. Please fuck me." I bite my lip and squeeze his waist with my legs. "I need you inside me so bad."

Ash stares at me, then says in a strange voice, "Okay."

He pulls his briefs off and then moves his head toward my pussy but stops before he goes any further.

He turns to look at the three men at the side of the room. "Dante, can I do this?"

"She can do whatever she wants, Ash. I was only going to put a stop to it if I thought she didn't really want it. I have zero doubt in my mind that she wants to fuck you right now."

I have time to smile over at him before Ash dives face-first into my pussy, and I close my eyes as I moan in ecstasy. I thrust my hands into his hair and hold his face hard against me as he tongues my clit.

It takes less than a minute for him to bring me to orgasm again, and I moan, "Fuck me, Ash. I need you to fuck me."

He ignores me and continues to eat me out instead. My clit is so sensitive that I can barely stand it.

As another orgasm crashes over me, I beg again, "Please, Ash. Please, please fuck me."

In answer, he lifts a hand to tweak one of my nipples roughly as he continues his onslaught on my clit. With his other hand, he begins to fuck my pussy with three fingers.

My body shakes as the fourth orgasm hits, and it's so pleasurably painful that tears come to my eyes.

"I can't, Ash. Please fucking fuck me because I can't take it any longer. I need you to stop that and fuck me." My voice is shaky, and Ash finally stops and moves over me.

He kisses me, thrusting his tongue into my mouth and forcing me to taste my own juices before he pulls his head back and growls, "Okay. Let me fill that juicy cunt of yours."

He thrusts roughly into me, and I moan in satisfaction. His cock is thick, really thick, and it stretches me wide as he fills me the way he promised.

"Do you like that, Lexi?"

"Yes, Ash."

He continues to just hold himself there, his cock deep inside me, as he asks, "Is it as good as you imagined?"

"Better. You're so thick, and I could never have imagined what it would be like to have you inside me."

Ash grins and leans down to kiss me before he begins to move. He pulls his cock out of me before he thrusts forward roughly, and it makes me gasp. He does this about five times before he starts doing shorter thrusts, only pulling himself out about halfway before thrusting back in.

He reaches between us to rub my sensitive clit, and I can barely stand it. "Oh my god, it's too much."

"It's not too fucking much," Ash growls. "I want you to come on my cock."

I half expect Dante to stop him, but he doesn't, and the pleasurably painful contact between Ash's fingers and my clit continues until I come again.

My pussy contracts around Ash's cock as he continues to thrust in and out of me. "Yes, baby. Come on my cock. God, that's fucking hot."

He lowers his mouth to my breast and takes it in his mouth as he continues to pound me. I'm enthralled by watching him when he comes. He clenches his eyes shut tight and grits his teeth as he groans, and his body shudders. His cock spasms inside me before his load is deposited in my pussy.

Ash collapses on me, panting for breath, and he rolls onto his side while pulling me with him. "Fuck, that was good."

"Yeah, it was."

I kiss him, and this time there's no urgency to it. Ash's tongue dances with mine as he softly thumbs one of my breasts.

When our kiss ends, he smiles at me. "Tell me you wanted me. Cause I was freaked out for a second there."

"Yeah, I wanted you." I nod my head. "Being forced to do stuff on Sunday was hot, so I wanted to play with that."

"I see."

"Sorry, I should've warned you about that," Logan says from behind us, and Ash jumps.

"Shit. I'd kind of forgotten you guys were here," he laughs.

"Lexi will do that to you," Nate says with a grin.

"We'll leave you guys alone now," Dante says.

"You're not going to fuck me, too?" I ask in surprise because I'd honestly expected it.

"We've got all evening for that, Angel. I think you and Ash probably need a moment."

My men leave the room, and I'm left alone with Ashton Woodford still inside me.

He kisses me again and says, "Fuck, that was so much fun."

"We should go clean up, though," I say, and he nods.

We head into the bathroom, and I wash myself before Ash does as well.

I hand him Dante's towel to dry himself when we get out, and as I do, I say, "I'm going to need cuddles in bed with you if you're okay with that?"

"Huh? How come?" He gives me a quizzical look.

"Sub drop. When I do a BDSM scene, it feels absolutely amazing, but the comedown is rough, and I need aftercare. We did intense shit, and normally one of my Doms does it for me, but they left me with you. I'm guessing they thought we'd cuddle." I can feel the endorphins seeping away as I speak.

Ash nods. "Of course. Whatever you need, Lexi."

He hangs up the towel and takes my hand as he leads me back to the bed and pulls me into his arms.

"Is this okay?"

"Perfect," I murmur.

"How long do we do this for?"

"However long I need. If you're uncomfortable, I can get Dante or Logan back here."

Ash tilts my face up to look at him. "I'm not uncomfortable at all. I just want to make sure I do it right."

"Oh, you did it right, don't worry," I smirk at him, and he laughs.

"Good to know." He kisses me softly, and we fall into silence as I snuggle into his warm embrace.

Everything finally hits me. My entire body aches with fatigue, and I yawn loudly.

Ash squeezes me tightly and says, "If you need a nap. I'll be right here."

"No, I'll be fine," I say, even as my eyes drift closed.

"Sure, you will," Ash chuckles as he kisses the top of my head.

Chapter Eight

Too Much of a Good Thing

I wake in Ash's arms and blink as I look around. "How long have I been sleeping?"

"About an hour."

I smile up at him as I squeeze him tightly. "Thanks."

"For letting you sleep?"

"Amongst other things," I laugh.

I run my hand down his taut stomach and then kiss his chest. Ash pulls me up to him and kisses me. He gently strokes my back with his hand as we kiss, and I feel happily at peace with everything that's happened since my birthday.

"Do you think you'd like to play with us again?" I ask.

"Look, it'll be a hardship, but I could probably do you a favor and make some room in my schedule," he teases me.

I tap his stomach playfully with my hand. "Shut up, douchebag."

"Hey, just because you like to be spanked doesn't mean I do," Ash laughs.

On cue, my ass smarts as I remember the spanking I got. I reach down and rub it as I cringe.

"Don't remind me. My ass still hurts," I groan.

"I probably need to have a look at it to see if it's okay." Ash gives me a wicked grin.

I throw the covers off us and roll onto my stomach. Ash moves down to look at my ass.

"Yes, it's very red." He leans down and kisses my left ass cheek, then asks in a husky voice, "Does that feel better?"

"A little bit. What about the other one?"

Ash kisses that one, too, and my pussy aches as he does. "Better?"

"Getting there." I grin into the pillow.

Ash softly strokes my ass cheeks, then holds them in his hands and squeezes them as well. He does this for about thirty seconds, but when I moan softly, he stops.

"I think you'll survive," he laughs.

"Are you sure? It could be fatal. You should probably continue treatment just in case."

Ash moves his hand down and pushes a finger inside my pussy. "What about this? Does this help?"

"Yes," I moan.

Ash pulls his finger out of me and moves back to lie on his back in the bed again.

"You're all better," he announces.

"No, I'm not," I groan.

As I sit up and look at him, he looks me in the eye and sucks the finger he had in me a moment ago. "You taste so good."

"Thanks." I move closer to him and smile. "We should probably go talk to the others. I'm glad you're on board with playing again because that was fun."

He nods. "Definitely. I can't believe I can touch you now. It seems like a cruel trick that my brain is playing on me, and I'll wake up soon."

"You wanted me that bad?" I raise an eyebrow at him.

"In the past, it was just a general desire because you were hot. This week, though"—he blows out a breath of air—"I haven't had wet dreams since I was a teen…until this week."

I'm suddenly very aware that we're both still naked when my nipples stiffen, and Ash's gaze moves to my chest.

"Yeah. I'm fucked now," he laughs.

"Sorry." I grin at him. "If you wake in the middle of the night from a wet dream, I promise you can call me and wake me up as payback."

Ash gives me an evil grin. "Watch out. I might actually do that."

"Good. Do it. I look forward to it."

"Well, great. I will do it."

"Fine. That'll be excellent."

"Yes, it will."

We burst into laughter, and I shake my head. "We're idiots."

"Mostly you," he teases me. "Should we go out and see the others now? Are you okay, or do you need more cuddles?"

"One thing you should know about me, Ashton Woodford, I never say no to more cuddles."

He pulls me into his arms again, and I sigh at how good it feels. After everything that happened last week, I actually feel good about Ash playing with us. It doesn't matter what Cassie said because Ash dumped her for it. He's now single and can do what he wants until he gets another girlfriend.

"I'm so glad you came to play with us today," I say with a smile.

"Me, too. I couldn't believe it when Logan called me. I honestly thought after Sunday that I'd fucked everything up, and I might even be kicked out of the band for what I did." His jaw is tight, and he has a frown on his beautiful face.

"Oh my god, Ash. I'm so sorry." I reach up and put my palm on his face before I move my face up to kiss him. "I just needed space. You saw me before. What happened in the car was really intense, and I hadn't had any aftercare. It was just too much for me. If I'd known you thought you'd be kicked out of the band, I'd have told you not to be a dumbass."

He wraps his arms around me and kisses me again. "Well, you did say that we would be okay at the airport, but then we went our separate ways in LA. I know you're with all the other guys, and they'd choose you over me."

I frown and swallow heavily as I take it in. He's right, though. I know they would choose me if it ever came to it. That was part of what I was concerned about with him flying back next to Cassie because I didn't know what we would do if they got back together. That means I'm the only one who can reassure him on this.

"I love you, Ash. Let's make a deal. Us playing together will never come between the band. We're just going to have fun with you joining us, and you won't be shut out. If you find another girlfriend, who I'd hope like hell wouldn't be anything like Cassie, then we'll stop with no hard feelings. Deal?"

He smiles at me and nods. "Deal. Last Sunday was the first time I've ever felt like an outsider, so it's nice to be included in this." He lifts a hand to my breast and softly strokes my nipple. "It's *very* nice to be included."

"Mmm, I couldn't agree more. Man, how come you never told me your cock was so thick it would practically split me in half when you put it in me?" I ask.

Ash throws his head back and laughs. "Well, for a start, because I didn't think Dante would appreciate me waxing poetic about my cock to you."

I want to play with Ash some more, but I know we should go see the others. My pussy is wet again, and I know they'll probably want to fuck me. Ash is probably up for it again, too, and the thought of a scene with four men makes me hot as hell.

"Let's go see the others. Maybe you can split me in half again soon."

Ash agrees, and he pulls on his clothes before we walk out to the living room to find the guys playing *Call of Duty*. They have drinks and snacks on the coffee table in front of them.

"About time you two showed your faces," Logan laughs.

"Did you fuck again?" Dante raises an eyebrow at us.

Ash shakes his head. "No. Lexi had a nap, and then we just talked."

Dante looks at me, then over at Logan, and says, "We've got about ten minutes left in this game. Lexi can sit on your lap while we wait, Ash. If you want that, of course."

"Sure," he says.

He takes a seat on one of the armchairs. It's angled so we can see both the TV as well as the guys sitting on the sofa and playing the game. I get onto his lap, and Ash looks surprised.

"You're not going to put your clothes on? I assumed you were coming out here to get them."

My clothes are piled neatly at the side of the room, and I have no doubt that it's Dante's doing.

I shake my head. "No point. I'm naked most of the time." I snicker, "Logan has a rule that I can only spend a total of two minutes wearing clothes at his place."

"Have I mentioned how lucky these fuckers are?" Ash laughs.

"Once or twice," I say in a dry tone, even though my pussy is wet right now.

Ash places a hand on my leg and gently strokes my inner thigh. "How do they manage to not just bend you over and fuck you all the time if you're as readily available as this?"

He slides his hand all the way up to my pussy and rubs it, which causes me to moan. Nate glances over at the sound and promptly dies in the game.

"Dammit, Lexi. You're so distracting," he grumbles.

I laugh and say to Ash, "Exactly like that. They don't. Nate gets very distracted by me, and you've seen what the other two do. Basically, whatever they want whenever they want."

"I definitely have some things I want to do to you," Ash says in a husky voice.

I scoot my ass forward and reach behind myself to stroke the bulge in his jeans with my hand. "I figured as much."

Ash unbuttons his jeans and pulls his cock out of his briefs. It's stiff and points toward his stomach. I wrap my fingers around it, and he's so hard and thick in my hand. I stroke him up and down a few times before I let go because it's a really awkward position. I sit sideways on his lap and kiss him as I stroke him in this much more comfortable position. He moans into my mouth, and I reach between my legs to rub my clit as I jerk off Ash.

I break our kiss and look at him, "Did you imagine me doing this when you were thinking about me this week?"

"No," he breathes. "I was honestly more focused on watching you come, especially after I'd seen it in person and had a way to watch it on demand."

I moan at the thought of him watching me, and he kisses me as he puts his hand on mine to remove it from his cock.

"Logan said you like to be looked at. Is that true?"

My pussy clenches, and I nod. "Yes, it is."

He pulls me back, so my ass is resting on his warm, hard cock, and he reaches between my legs to go back to pleasuring me. "Let me tell you about all the times I've looked at you, Lexi."

I gasp and bite my lip while I play with my breasts as I say, "Okay."

"Any time we've been swimming. Without fail. You wore some tiny bikini with your tits and ass hanging out. I would go somewhere private and jack off while picturing doing it on your chest."

"Fuck," I moan.

"Yup. Oh, I remember one time you came to one of our soundchecks. You were wearing leggings that gave you a cameltoe." He squeezes my labia together, and I grind my ass on his cock. "I wanted to rip your leggings down and bury my tongue in your cunt before I followed it with my cock."

Ash goes back to stroking my clit, and I'm wildly aroused by his confessions.

"Why do you call it that?" I ask.

He grins at me. "I said it in the car just to shock you, but you're fucking hot when I call it your cunt. You do this little shocked gasp, and your eyes go wide every time. It's hot as shit."

Heat rushes to my cheeks, and I say, "I had no idea."

"Well, now you do. I don't want to use it too often, though, because I don't want it to lose its effect."

"Are you guys all right?" Dante asks in an amused tone, and I notice that their game is finished, and they're all looking at us.

"I didn't want Lexi to be bored while you were playing," Ash deadpans.

"She does like to be entertained," Logan agrees.

"So, I'm assuming that you two are together now," Dante says.

I blink at him and shake my head as I turn to look at Ash. "We're just friends, aren't we?"

"You don't want more than that, do you?" He raises his eyebrows at me.

I look back at my three other men. I love them as much as I love Ash, but it's different with them. Ash is a friend…with a satisfying cock. I want to play with him for sure, but I'm happy just being friends.

"No. Do you?"

"No offense, but this whole thing you guys have seems like a lot. Don't get me wrong, I definitely want to fuck the shit out of you as often as I can, but I don't think we need to be in a relationship for that to happen."

I smile at him and reach down to find his stiff cock with my hand again. "We definitely don't. As long as you promise to stick this cock in my pussy, ass, and mouth regularly, I can handle just being friends."

"That's quite a friendship," Ash laughs.

I kiss him, and our tongues intertwine as I turn on his lap to straddle him. I hold his thick cock in place as I slide it into me, reveling in his groan as I do.

"Yes, it is. Do you want my friendship or not, Ashton Woodford?" I look into his beautiful blue eyes.

"Of course I fucking do."

I squeeze his cock with my internal muscles. "That's what I thought."

I fuck him slowly, and I don't attempt to give either of us an orgasm. Instead, I just enjoy the feeling of having him fill me so completely. Ash leans back in the chair and watches me ride him.

"What's your plan here, Lexi?"

"I don't have one." I circle my hips on his cock. "I suppose my plan is to just enjoy your cock being in my pussy, and I'm doing that."

Ash looks past me and asks, "Is she allowed to do this?"

"Certainly not for Logan or me," Dante says. "She wouldn't be able to sit for a week if she did this to us."

"Oh, but I'm fair game?" Ash groans.

"Apparently," Logan laughs.

I keep doing what I'm doing, and it's ridiculously erotic. I love Ash's reaction, and after a few minutes, he moans when I grip his cock as I move painfully slowly on him.

"Lexi, you have to stop. It's doing my head in."

I laugh and kiss him as I move slightly faster. "Do you want me to make you come, Ash?"

"Yes. I need to fuck you properly."

I slow down again. "I don't want this to end, though."

"Guys, can you please help me out?" Ash begs.

"Lexi, do you want to make Ash come?" Logan immediately asks, and I'm wildly aroused because I know what's going to happen.

"No, Sir."

"Why not?" he asks.

"It's fun teasing him, and I want this to last."

I luxuriate in moving slowly on Ash as he groans loudly.

"I see," Logan says. "Are you sure you don't want to make him come?"

I kiss Ash and squeeze his cock tight with my pussy as I move on him. "No, Sir."

"Make him come, Alexandra."

I sigh and give one more slow thrust before I fuck Ash properly. He groans and pulls my face to his to kiss me as he fucks me back.

He thrusts into me roughly and groans, "God fucking damn, that was torture. I'm barely going to last five seconds now."

I bury him inside me and stop moving as I reach down to rub my clit. Ash keeps thrusting up into me, but I try to keep him as deep as possible while I rub myself to an orgasm.

I come around him and moan, "Fuck, Ash. Come inside me."

He grips my hips as he continues to pound me, and he growls, "I'm going to come inside you all right." He thrusts roughly into me and continues, "This is my cunt to come in whenever I want now. As long as the guys are okay with it. I hope you enjoyed that, Lexi, because you get no fucking say anymore. Got it?"

He raises an eyebrow at me, and I can barely breathe at how motherfucking hot this makes me. My entire body is on fire, and I nod as another orgasm crashes over me.

"Yes, Ash. It's your cunt to come in whenever you want." I can barely get the words out because it's so erotic to say.

Ash's lips crash against mine as he holds me down on him and does exactly that. His tongue dances with mine as he comes deep inside me.

I'm lost in the ecstasy of fucking him for a second time, and he's still coming when Nate appears next to us. He has his cock out and is stroking it.

"Open your mouth, Lexi," he says.

I take Nate's cock in my mouth, and when my pussy clenches around Ash's cock, he groans, "Damn. She's so hot, Nate."

"She really is." Nate softly strokes my head as he says it.

Ash places his hands on my breasts and plays with them while I suck Nate. Ash's cock is softening inside me, but I still enjoy the sensation of having him there, and I moan around Nate's cock at the pleasure Ash is giving me.

Logan appears on the other side of me, and I stroke his cock with my hand before I switch and suck him while I stroke Nate.

We've been at it for a few minutes when Dante says, "Come here, Angel."

I slip off Ash and feel every inch of him slide out of me. I clench my pussy tight to stop his cum from leaking out of me as I walk over to Dante.

"I'm going to fuck your ass while Nate and Logan take turns in your pussy, Angel," he tells me as he holds up the bottle of lube he must've gotten while I was busy with the others.

"Yes, Honey," I breathe.

Logan comes over to the sofa and lies down on it. "Sit on my face and suck my cock, Lexi. I can clean you out while Dante gets your ass ready for fucking."

I groan and nod as I climb over him. He begins eating my pussy, and I moan in ecstasy before I take his cock in my mouth.

"Logan's eating my cum out of her?" Ash asks in a strange voice from nearby.

"She'll get it everywhere if he doesn't," Nate points out.

"More power to him for saving the cleaning bill, I guess," Ash laughs. "God, you guys really are kinky as fuck. This is hot, though. By the time you're all finished, I'll probably want to fuck her again."

"Welcome to my world. The good news is that you can do her whenever you want," Nate tells him, and I moan at the thought of Ash doing me whenever he wants.

Dante drops cold lube onto my ass and pushes a finger inside me. Logan continues to tongue my clit, and all of these sensations combined with listening to Ash and Nate's conversation tips me into orgasm.

I gasp and whimper, "Logan."

Dante squirts more lube on my ass and pushes a second finger in me. He fucks me with his fingers while Logan continues eating me out until I come on his face again.

"Can I fuck her now, Logan?" Dante asks.

Logan removes his mouth from my pussy and rubs my clit with his fingers instead. "Sure."

I climb off Logan so he can stand up, and Dante takes his place on the sofa. I ease myself onto him, and his cock stretches my asshole in a pleasurably painful way.

Logan and Nate stand next to us as Dante begins to fuck me.

"Do you want her pussy first?" Logan asks.

Nate leans over and kisses Logan. A shot of arousal goes straight to my pussy as I watch him do it, and Nate reaches between them to stroke Logan's cock while they kiss.

"I want to fuck her with your cum inside her and while knowing that your beautiful cock has been there first," Nate murmurs.

Logan kisses Nate back and reaches down to stroke his cock as well. Watching them make out and play with each other gets me as hot as usual, and I want one of them to fuck me soon.

Logan ends their kiss and moves closer to me. Dante takes my left leg and lifts it over the back of the sofas, spreading me wide.

Logan braces himself over me and pushes his cock into me as he gasps, "Fuck, that's good."

He thrusts into my pussy in sync as Dante thrusts into my ass, though I can tell that Dante is holding off, so he doesn't come yet.

I'm in complete ecstasy, and I writhe and moan while they fuck me. When Nate shoves his cock in my mouth as well, I'm completely lost to the scene as every one of my available holes is filled. I suck him until Logan comes, and Nate pulls out of my mouth as Logan pulls out of my pussy, and Nate swiftly takes his place there.

"Clean my cock, Lexi," Logan murmurs as he places it near my lips.

I lick and suck his shaft gently to the soundtrack of his groans, as well as Dante and Nate's fucking. I clean the salty cum off Logan's cock, and he leans down to kiss me.

As we kiss, a mouth clamps around my breast, and I assume it's Nate until Logan ends our kiss, and I gasp when I see that it's Ash.

He grins up at me while he swirls his tongue around my nipple, and he reaches between Nate and me to rub my clit. Logan kisses me again, and I lose control. My senses are on fire from everything they're doing, and I come three more times before Nate dumps his load in me.

Dante gives a few final thrusts in my ass before his cock jerks, and he fills my back hole as well. The room is full of panting breaths as he comes.

"Well, that was *very* interesting," Ash drawls.

I assume he's talking about what just happened, so I grin at him. "Yeah. I just needed someone to come down my throat, but I do like getting fucked in the ass and the pussy at the same time."

"I'm sure you do, but I was talking more about Nate and Logan jacking each other off." He raises an eyebrow at them.

Both of them turn bright pink, and Logan says, "Yeah. We do that sometimes."

"No point trying to hide it," Nate says and kisses Logan before turning to Ash. "We're together as well."

"You're *bi*?!" Ash gasps. "Since when?"

"Probably since Logan gave me the world's hottest fucking blow job in Napa," Nate laughs.

Dante chuckles underneath me. "I'd like to point out that, while Logan's blow jobs are excellent, I don't consider myself bisexual after having had one."

"What the fuck have you all been doing?" Ash's mouth is hanging open.

"We can talk about it," Dante laughs. "But let's get cleaned up first. Lexi is full of cum right now."

"That's just how I like it, to be honest," I smirk at Ash, who is still looking stunned.

Dante takes me to our bathroom to clean up. He kisses me and holds me tightly in the shower. Afterward, he gives me a floaty green dress to wear.

"I think you'll be too distracting for some people if you're naked," he says as he hands it to me.

"They can't all have your level of self-control," I tease him.

Dante pulls me against him. He settles his hand on my ass and kisses me thoroughly before he lets me go again.

"I hope you don't think that I don't find you at all distracting. You take all of my available self-control some days."

I'm pleased to hear this because he's normally so calm and controlled that I think I don't affect him as much as the other two.

"Good to know. I'll make more of an effort to make you lose it in the future." I give him a wicked grin.

Dante chuckles, "And I will forbid you from coming for a month, then let Nate and Ash do whatever they want to you, and I'll punish you every single time they inevitably make you come.

Do you really want this?"

"I've given it some thought and decided that maybe it's not quite worth it after all," I joke.

"That's what I thought." Dante grins at me as he takes my hand and leads me back to the living room.

We find Ash sitting alone on the sofa, but the water was running in Nate's room as we passed, so I assume the other two are still cleaning up.

I drop next to Ash and smile up at him. "Having a good day?"

"You could say that. I have so many questions. Also, I never thought I'd say this, but I'm glad you're wearing clothes."

Dante laughs, "Is Lexi a tiny bit distracting, Ash?"

"Even now she's wearing a dress, I can still imagine her naked."

I lift my dress and flash him my pussy. "Does this help?"

"A little too much," he groans. "Do you guys get tired of fucking? Cause I could probably go again, except I'm tired at even the thought of it."

"We don't always do group scenes," Dante says with a grin at him. "Lexi alternates nights between us. So, really, she gets the most sex."

"The guys are pretty good about not making me do stuff if I'm too tired. I like being used, though. So sometimes, if I'm tired and don't want to have sex, that's when it ends up being the hottest for me."

Ash shakes his head in apparent amazement. "God. Why are you so fucking hot?"

"I don't know. You tell me." I lift my skirt to flash him my pussy again.

"Make her stop," Ash groans.

Dante chuckles. "I probably won't. I find it interesting to watch her tease you, and that's kind of the point of having a sub. I get to play with her however I like."

"Ugh. Can I Dom her, too?" he asks.

"No." I give him a wicked grin and climb onto his lap to straddle him. "You can't. Still want to play with me?"

Ash kisses me and raises a hand to my breast to stroke my nipple through the fabric. "Yes. Even though I think you're going to be the death of me."

I grind my pussy against his crotch, and he shakes his head before he kisses me again. We kiss for a little while before I laugh and climb off him. He's semi-hard again, and I really love teasing him like this.

"I thought I was meant to be playing with Lexi today. It feels a lot like she's playing with me," Ash grumbles.

"Is that a bad thing?" Nate asks as he and Logan appear from the hallway.

They sit next to each other down the side of the sofa, and I smile at them. They're so beautiful, with their hair wet from their shower and both wearing jeans and t-shirts.

Ash looks over at them and says with a grin, "I'm not complaining." He raises an eyebrow at them. "So, you two are together. Logan has given Dante at least one blow job. What else have you lot been hiding from me?"

"We wrote a song about Lexi the other day," Logan says.

"That was about me?"

I raise my eyebrows at them as I remember the song, because nothing about it seemed relevant to me.

"The moonlight that shines on us all was you."

Heat rushes to my cheeks. "I thought you were talking about literal moonlight."

"Well, I'm hardly going to sing, 'Lexi fucks us all, and we love her.'" Nate chuckles.

Dante gets his guitar while Logan grabs the sheet music and shows it to Ash, who plays the guitar this time. Nate sings as much of the song as they have written while looking at me. As he sings, I can clearly hear that it's about me now, and I smile at him. I don't think I've ever been happier.

Chapter Nine

An Unexpected Call

"Should I wear a Serenity dress, or is that stupid?" I chew my bottom lip as I ask Dante and Nate this question.

"I think Heather will be flattered by it," Nate says.

"Will it look like I'm trying too hard, though? I was wearing a Serenity dress at the concert. I'll look stupid."

"Then don't wear one." Nate shrugs.

I turn to frown at him before I spin back to face my clothes. "I don't know what to do."

Dante's arms wrap around me from behind, and he kisses my neck softly. "Don't wear a Serenity dress, Angel." He steps around me and pulls out a pair of high-waisted patterned Gucci pants and a black Gucci belt. Then, he gets a black woolen turtleneck and hands the clothes to me. "Wear these."

I'm relieved to have the choice taken out of my hands, and I kiss Dante as I take the clothes from him. "Thank you, Honey."

He looks into my eyes for a few seconds and asks, "What time are you meeting her at Rodeo Drive?"

"Not until nine. I'm nervous as shit, though. Even though the contracts are all set in stone. I'm worried she'll want to pull out."

"She won't," Nate says.

I wrinkle my nose at him. "Probably not. Doesn't mean I'm not worried about it."

"Put those clothes aside, Angel."

I resist the urge to gasp and set the clothes carefully on a shelf nearby before I turn to look at Dante.

"Take off your robe," he instructs.

I untie my robe and place it in the hamper. My breathing is shallow as both men look at me.

"I think our angel needs help getting dressed today, Nate."

"I mean, obviously." Nate laughs.

"But first, I think an orgasm would probably help ease her nerves." Dante takes a seat on the bench in the center of the room next to Nate. "We want to watch you come, Angel."

I reach between my legs to rub myself. I'm wet and turned on by them watching me do it. I bite my lip to stop myself from making any noise, but the sound of my fingers on myself fills the room.

"React, Angel."

I close my eyes and throw my head back as I moan loudly. I've been doing this for a little while when there's a ringing sound in the room. I gasp and open my eyes to see Nate's video calling Ash. He has his screen turned to me, and the ringing cuts off as Ash appears on the screen.

"Hey, Nate, what's—Lexi? Well, hi."

"Did I tell you to stop, Angel?"

Dante stands and strides over to me. He spins me toward my clothes and smacks my ass hard before he turns me back to Nate and his phone.

"Continue, Angel."

I return to what I was doing, and my eyes meet Ash's as I do. I moan loudly and play with my breasts until my orgasm crashes over me.

"Very nice. Thanks for calling, Nate," Ash murmurs.

"You're welcome."

"Can you take a picture of her and send it to me? I'm going to masturbate while I think about her as soon as you hang up," he says.

"Why wait?" Dante says. "She's here and watching."

I bite my lip as Ash switches the camera on his end and focuses on his cock. I watch him wrap his hand around it, and he groans.

"Turn around and bend over, Lexi," Ash says, and I do as instructed. "Mmm, that's such a nice sight. Now I can pretend I'm ramming into you from behind."

I hate that I can't watch him masturbate now, but I'm dripping wet because I know he's using me as inspiration. Listening to his grunts and groans is even more erotic because I don't get to see it.

Eventually, he moans, "Lexi."

"Turn around, Angel."

I turn in time to see the last of Ash's cum squirt onto his stomach, and I murmur. "I wish I was there to lick you clean, Ash."

"Me, too, baby. I'll see you on Saturday, and I promise you can taste my cum when we play."

"I can't wait." I grin at him.

Ash says goodbye, and Nate ends the call before he drops his phone next to him. He stands and looks me in the eye as he undoes his jeans and drops them with his briefs to his ankles before he sits back down.

"Put on a thong, then come suck my cock, Lexi."

"Huh? Why am I wearing underwear today?"

Nate gives me a sexy smile. "I want you to drench them as a gift to Logan from me tonight."

I shudder and bite my lip at the thought of delivering a pair of wet underwear to Logan for Nate. I pull a thong out of a drawer and step into it before getting onto my knees in front of Nate. I wrap my lips around his cock, and it's as glorious as ever. I worship every inch of it and revel in the noises he makes while I suck him. Dante moves behind me, but he doesn't fuck me. Instead, he rubs my clit through the thong.

"I'll make sure these panties are ready for Logan," Dante growls as he leans forward and twists my nipple sharply.

I gasp onto Nate's cock, and Dante does it again. He continues his onslaught of my breasts while he rubs my clit, and it isn't long before I'm coming again. When Nate comes, I swallow his load and clean his cock with my tongue while Dante moves in front of me.

I move upright as Dante places a hand on either side of my face and holds it in place. He pushes his cock into my mouth and fucks me roughly. I gag on his cock multiple times, and I love it so much. When he comes down my throat, I gag on his cock as well and have to work hard to swallow his cum. After I clean his cock, he pulls me up to standing and kisses me. I turn to kiss Nate before I put on my bra as Dante picks up the turtleneck.

"Arms up, Angel."

I end my kiss with Nate and follow his instruction. Dante pulls the top over my head and then pulls me against him to kiss him again before he turns to pick up the pants.

He crouches below me and says, "Step into the pants, Angel."

I do as instructed, and he pulls them up slowly before he zips them up. He grabs the belt to feed it through the loops while he stands in front of me. When he puts it through the back loops, his arms are wrapped around me, and he kisses me softly, then leans back to buckle it up between us.

He holds my chin between his forefinger and thumb while he kisses me tenderly. "I love you, Angel."

"I love you, too, Honey. Thank you."

He wraps his arms around me and holds me tight against him for a while before he says, "Okay. You'd better do your hair and makeup so you can go. Nate and I have a meeting with the guys and Isaac at eleven. We're meeting up at Logan's first."

"Tell him I love him, and I can't wait to see him tonight," I say with a smile.

"I will. Anthony sent through some more apartment options last night after you and Nate went to bed."

Unfortunately, the offer we put in on the apartment was beaten out by another buyer. Anthony has sent us through a few options, but nothing that we've wanted to put an offer on yet.

"Awesome. I'll have a look when I get to work."

I'd normally have been at the Orange County store today, but Heather wanted to meet at Rodeo Drive, so I head there instead. When I arrive, I greet Jasmine, and she gives me an update on the store.

I enter my office and dock my laptop before I look through my email. Of the apartments that Anthony has sent us, there's only one that I like and think we should go see. I send an email to the guys telling them so, and it's about fifteen minutes later when Jasmine rushes in.

"Heather's here. I just saw her bodyguard, and then she got out of an SUV."

"Ooh, thanks, Jazz." I smile at her and shut my laptop before I follow her into the store.

Heather has just walked in, followed by the suited man I met when she visited my store last time. She's tall and thin with blonde hair and blue eyes, and she's wearing a pale blue dress that matches her eyes. Her hair is neatly tied up, around her neck is the same heart lock necklace she was wearing the last time she was here in Los Angeles.

"Hi, darling." She smiles at me as she greets me with a hug. "It's so good to see you again."

"You, too. How was your flight to LA?"

"Really good. Harrison had a break in his schedule, so he came over with me. It's nice to get away sometimes." She gets a dreamy smile on her face when she talks about her husband.

"It must be hard with your busy schedules," I say.

She nods. "Yeah, it is. Especially now that I've got so much going on with Serenity. It just gets bigger and bigger, which is more work for me."

"You probably need to get yourself some help." I cringe.

"I know, I know," she laughs. "Anyway, what about you? How is Dante?"

"Yeah, the guys are good," I say without thinking, and heat rushes to my cheeks. "They've got a meeting with Isaac today."

"Oh, Isaac's great, isn't he? I'm *so* glad that Cruise Control changed its management. Their old manager was an asshole, so the bar was pretty low for Isaac to beat him," she laughs.

We talk for a few minutes about the bands and their manager, which turns into a conversation about April's movie and the set visit Heather did yesterday.

"It was pretty cool getting to visit an actual movie set. I got to watch April and Toby film a few scenes as well. I can't wait to see the movie. I think it's going to be really good." Heather nods her head.

"That sounds amazing. I've never been to a movie set. The closest I came was when I filmed the 'Heavenly Promises' music video with Nate." Heat rushes to my cheeks as I remember the day and the fact that everyone in the world has seen me orgasm, whether they know it or not.

Heather fans herself and says, "I've seen that video. It was hot as shit."

"Yeah. You do one favor for your friends, and next minute the whole world thinks you're having an affair."

Stop talking.

I chide myself internally because I'm not exactly making anything better for myself. She didn't even bring up the rumors, so I didn't need to defend myself.

"Oh god, don't I know it. The paparazzi love to think Sebastian and I are screwing. We're not, though." She rolls her eyes as she shakes her head.

Unlike Nate and me.

"Of course not. Everyone knows you love Harrison." I give her a too-bright grin. "Anyway, want to have another look around the store?"

"Sure," she says, seeming disconcerted by the quick change of topic.

"You mentioned that you wanted to discuss how we plan to merchandise your clothes?"

"Yes, I do. I'm not too specific with how my line is displayed, but I like to see the stores and make sure we're not tucked away in a back corner." She gives me a charming smile, and I laugh.

"I would never." I act offended, and she laughs in return. "I'm so excited to be stocking Serenity, so we'll be giving you pride of place in each of the stores."

I show her the section near the front of the store that I'm planning to show the Serenity stock, and Heather seems pleased.

She has a look around the store again and groans, "I promised Harrison I wouldn't buy your entire stores out today, but have you gotten even more awesome clothes in since I visited last?"

"Yeah, the stuff you're looking at came in from a local designer a few weeks ago," I tell her with a grin.

Heather pulls out a burgundy jumpsuit with spaghetti straps that cross at the back and a silver chain belt. "Okay, I'm buying this and *only* this…from this store. I can't speak for what I might find at the other two stores, of course."

I take the jumpsuit from her and take it to the desk where Jasmine rings up the sale. She carefully wraps the jumpsuit in paper and sticks a Black Lilac sticker on it before she places it in one of our bags and hands it to Heather.

As we leave the store, a group of paparazzi crowd around us, and I realize how much more famous Cruise Control is than Wicked Stallion. Heather has become a full-on celebrity in her own right due to her success with Serenity, but in general, they just get way more attention than the guys do.

"Heather, where's Harrison?"

She doesn't say anything in response and her bodyguard, Callum Archer, pushes the crowd back.

"Lexi, how do you know Heather?"

I take a cue from her and don't respond, grateful as hell that the black SUV isn't far away.

"Is it true that Hayden got married at Nate's estate in Napa? Is that how you two know each other?"

"Are you going to stock Heather's clothes in your store, Lexi?"

Callum opens the car door, and Heather slides into the SUV.

I follow her quickly and thank him as he closes the door behind me.

"Damn. They found me fast today." Heather cringes.

"It's a good thing we're doing Beverly Center next. I think we're the most exposed there. Once they figure out we're visiting all the stores, they'll know to go to the third one, but in Orange County, we can park in my spot at the back, and they won't be able to get to us."

Sure enough, we're harassed by the paparazzi on the way into the Beverly Center store. We're met by Sherry, the store manager, and I show Heather where I plan on displaying her line here. When we leave, the paparazzi follow us to The Henry, where Heather has made a lunch reservation for us.

As we drive there, my eyes are drawn to Heather's necklace again. I think about the times I've seen Heather with Harrison. I know about the cheating scandal, of course, but they're such a high-profile couple that I've seen them in public together many, many times.

Aside from that breakup, they've been rock solid for years, and if I had to put money on it, I would bet that she's collared. If only because a woman like her wouldn't wear the same necklace on multiple occasions for many other reasons.

I'm desperately curious about it now, so I say casually, "Your necklace is pretty."

"Thanks." Heather gives me a dreamy smile as she reaches up and toys with the diamond heart.

"I notice you wear it all the time. Is it special?"

Heather nods. "It is. Harrison gave it to me for our wedding. It's my favorite piece of jewelry after my wedding and engagement rings."

I smile at her and turn to look out the car window. I should let this drop right now and resist the urge the pry into her private life. At the same time…if I word my question well enough, nobody out of the scene would understand its true meaning.

"It looks like it would be very difficult to take off. Do you need help to do it?" I keep my eyes on the scenery flashing by as I ask the question.

Heather chuckles. "Yes. It's quite difficult for me to take off myself. I'd only ever attempt it in an emergency."

"I knew it." I turn to grin at her, then glance ahead to make sure her bodyguard isn't listening in as I ask quietly, "Is it a collar?"

"Indeed. You're in the scene?"

I nod and say, "Yup. Dante and—" I almost fuck up by saying Logan's name, so I quickly pivot, "—I have been into kink for a long time. I don't have a collar, though."

Dante and I discussed it a few years ago and decided that it would be too conspicuous. Heather is ballsy, but playing it off as a sentimental piece of jewelry works for her, I guess.

"I've never been happier. We'd been through a lot, so being collared after all that was amazing."

She has that same dreamy smile she gets on her face whenever she talks about Harrison, and it's obvious how in love with him she is.

"That's awesome."

"Will Dante collar you?" she asks.

I shake my head before I explain the reasoning, and our conversation continues until we arrive at the restaurant. As soon as we're out of the car, we're swarmed by people taking our pictures and yelling questions at us. Callum escorts us inside, and we're taken immediately to a table at the back of the restaurant.

As we're waiting for our food after we've ordered, I comment, "I'm exhausted. I can't imagine being followed around by paparazzi *all* the time like this."

"You get used to it after a while." Heather shrugs as she takes a sip of her wine. "Don't get me wrong, it *is* exhausting, but it's become my normal."

"That's depressing."

She wrinkles her nose. "Kind of. It's allowed me some pretty fantastic life experiences, though. I don't know if you heard, but I visited a *movie set* yesterday."

"You know, I did actually hear something about that," I laugh.

Our food arrives, and we're having an enjoyable time when my phone lights up with the name 'Cassie Foster' displayed on the screen and the same message she sent weeks ago displayed underneath it.

We need to talk.

My heart thumps in my chest, and, as I look at it, a notification that she's sent a picture as well comes through.

Nausea threatens to overwhelm me, and I force a smile at Heather. "If you'll excuse me, I just need to visit the ladies' room."

"Of course." She looks up and sees my face. "Are you okay?"

"Fine. Yes. I just need the bathroom."

I rush away, and as soon as I've locked the stall, I open Cassie's message. Immediately, I retch at the sight of it and spin to drop in front of the toilet before I vomit the contents of my stomach into it. I retch a few more times and use a piece of toilet paper to wipe my mouth.

Cassie has sent through two pictures that are from the same night. When we went to a charity concert with the guys. One picture is of Nate and me hugging backstage when he was comforting me after the show. It would, perhaps, be acceptable…except for the fact that we're just a little too close together, and his lips are on my head as he kisses me. Plus, we're already rumored to be having an affair.

The other picture, however, is even worse. I'm in Logan's arms in the VIP area of a club during the after-party. His jacket is on my lap, and you can't see it in the picture, but his fingers are in my pussy. What you *can* see is me staring up at him as I bite my lip in ecstasy while he looks down at me with a similar look of lust on his face.

She's sent another message as well.

Now.

I flush the toilet and wash my face at the sink before I call Cassie.

"What do you want, Cassie?" I ask as soon as she answers.

"I want to talk to Ash in person. He won't answer my calls, even though I've called him from other people's numbers. As soon as he knows it's me, he hangs up. I thought this might get your attention and help you persuade him to talk to me."

My jaw clenches, and I take a deep breath. "I can't make him get back together with you."

"Can't you? We'll see. I'm sure you can do a lot more than you think if you're sufficiently motivated."

"You're blackmailing me to get Ash to see you?" I growl.

"That's an ugly word, Lexi. I'm just giving you the motivation to make it happen."

She falls silent, and I think it over. I have no idea what the fuck to do, and I'm terrified of what she might do.

"I'll talk to Ash," I whisper.

"You should know that I didn't want it to come to this. As if I want a slut like you to have any contact with my boyfriend."

Shame washes over me as I think of the multiple times I've played with Ash since they broke up, and I say defensively, "He's not your boyfriend anymore."

"Not for now. Let's see how much he cares about keeping your disgusting secret, though. I wonder what your new bestie would think about being tied to a slut like you. Maybe I should send these pictures to Heather Fletcher."

My blood runs ice cold. "Cassie, please don't. I'll talk to Ash, and I'm sure he'll see you in person."

"You'd better. Let me know, and don't take too long."

She ends our call, and I want to be sick again. I don't have anything left to vomit up, so I retch a few times before I call Ash.

"Hey, baby. What's up?" His voice is cheerful when he answers my call.

"I'm stuck in a bathroom because your ex-girlfriend sent me a lovely message. Are you with the guys?"

His tone changes, and he sounds concerned when he responds. "Shit. Yes, we're all together. What did she say?"

"I called her, and she wants to see you. She's got pics she's threatening to send to the media. I'll send you a screenshot of our messages. I'm at lunch with Heather right now."

"Are you okay?" he asks, and he sounds worried for me.

"No," I manage to say around a lump in my throat.

"One sec, Lexi."

As Ash mumbles an explanation to the guys, the fear of the pictures being leaked is overwhelming, and nausea threatens to take hold again.

Dante's voice comes through the line, "Make your excuses to Heather and go home, Angel. We'll meet you there."

"Thank you, Honey," I whisper because it's an instruction, and that will help me to get through this easier.

"I love you, Angel."

I end the call and send Ash the screenshot of my messages with Cassie before I walk back out to where Heather is sitting at our table.

"I'm *so* sorry, Heather, but something has come up, and I need to go home."

Her eyebrows raise, but she nods. "Of course. Are you okay?"

"Not really," I manage to say.

I'm grateful that she doesn't press me on what has happened, but getting through the paparazzi to get to the SUV is even more stressful than it was earlier. All I can think about is how much worse it will get for us if Cassie leaks those photos.

As soon as the SUV door is closed, I retch a few times, and Heather looks concerned as she asks, "Are you going to be sick?"

"Probably not. I already vomited my entire lunch in the bathroom," I say in a grim tone and immediately wish I hadn't. "Please forget I said that."

There's an awkward silence for a few seconds before Heather says, "You don't have to tell me anything, but if you ever need to talk, you have my number."

I think about Cassie's threat to tell Heather about my relationships, and I don't want to risk the Serenity deal, so I just nod with my jaw tight. "Thanks."

I don't know if there's any kind of morality clause in place within our contract, but I'm pretty sure that my alternate relationships would void the shit out of it if there is.

Heather has her bodyguard drive us straight back to the Rodeo Drive store. He takes us to the back parking lot, and before I get out, Heather looks at me.

"Are you going to be okay to drive? Cal could take you home, and you could get your car some other time."

"I'll be fine." I force a laugh. "My car practically drives itself."

Heather smiles at me. "Yeah, I have the same car. I'm still worried about you, though."

"I really will be okay. It's only a twenty-minute drive."

"Okay." She sighs and nods. "If you need anything, let me know. We'll talk when you get the clothes anyway, no doubt."

"Of course." I smile at her. "Thanks. I appreciate your understanding about cutting our day short, too."

Heather hugs me before we say goodbye, and I get out of the SUV. I head into the store, say a quick hello and goodbye to Jasmine, then grab my laptop and car keys before I head out. I drive home in a daze and reach our apartment before the guys.

They arrive about twenty minutes after I do, and Dante rushes over to hug me first. I receive hugs from all of them before we settle on the sofa, and Dante gets us all coffees. I end up between Dante and Nate while Ash and Logan sit on the other side of the L-shaped sofa.

"So, what did Cassie say?" Ash asks in a voice like ice.

"She seems to think that you'll get back together with her because of those photos."

Nausea rolls over me, and I retch again at the thought of them being released for public viewing. For the entire world to see and judge me as a slut the same way Cassie has done, and I clutch Dante and Nate's hands for comfort.

"She's wrong. I'm never getting back together with her."

I look up into Ash's beautiful blue eyes and frown. "What if she releases those photos?"

He sighs. "I don't know, Lexi. I do know that I can't be with her. I'll do anything to stop her from going public, but I won't do that."

There's an awkward silence in the room before I nod at him. "Of course. I couldn't ask you to do that. What are you going to do long-term? Marry her to stop her telling the world about us?"

"Cassandra Woodford. It has a certain ring to it, don't you think?" Ash gives a hollow laugh.

I snort. "I bet she's imagined it."

"Fuck. I imagined it before she revealed herself to be a Grade-A bitch." Ash shrugs.

I let go of Dante and Nate's hands, walk over to Ash, and throw my arms around him when I reach him.

"I'm sorry everything has gone to shit," I murmur.

Ash pulls me to sit on his lap as he hugs me back. "It's not your fault, Lexi. I would one million percent prefer this, even with the threat of her going public, than being tied to that woman long term if I'd stupidly proposed to her before she revealed her true self."

Everything that's happened today hits me, and I burst into tears. Ash squeezes me tighter and kisses my head as I cry into his chest.

When I finally manage to get myself together, he rubs my arm gently and asks, "Are you okay?"

"I guess." I cringe at him.

"Can you call Cassie, or do you want me to do it?"

Relief floods through me that he's willing to call her, and I nod my head. "Can you do it, please?"

"Of course."

When he pulls his phone out of his pocket, I notice that he pulls up Cassie in his contacts rather than going to his favorites. I get a small amount of satisfaction from her demotion as he dials her.

"When do you want to meet?" he asks without preamble when she answers.

Her tinny voice comes through the phone. "Have you unblocked me?"

"No. You're still blocked. When do you want to meet?"

"Ashton, you don't have to be—"

He growls, "Cassandra. When do you want to meet?"

"Tomorrow."

"Fine. Lexi and I will see you at my place tomorrow night."

Cassie's shocked gasp comes through the line. "No. I don't want that slut involved."

Despite everything, shame floods through me because I'm literally sitting on his lap and have had sex with him exactly like she thought I would.

Ash's expression turns into a glower as his voice gets that ice-cold note to it again. "You involved Lexi, not me. Call her that again, and I won't see you tomorrow. I want this resolved once and for all."

I'm so grateful to Ash for defending me, and I love him so much for that. I still have my arms around him, so I squeeze him tightly to show my gratitude. He looks down at me and gives me a quick smile as he gently rubs my back.

"Well, I don't want her alone with you."

"And I don't want to see you ever again. We can't all get what we want."

"That's so hurtful, Ashton."

"I don't give a fuck. I'll see you tomorrow at my place at seven."

Chapter Ten
Morning Delight

Instead of Logan going home, he stays at our apartment, and I spend the night with both him and Nate after Ash leaves. Even though we don't have sex, I wake early on Friday in a tangle of limbs. I'm hot and sweaty, with fear oozing from every pore.

I have no idea how I'm going to get through this meeting with Cassie today. I slip out of bed and head to the kitchen. I've only had time to turn the coffee machine on in the dim morning light when Logan appears.

"Everything okay, Lexi?" he asks as he walks into the kitchen.

"No. I'm nervous as fuck."

He sighs and wraps his arms around me from behind. "I can imagine. I'm sorry for my part in it. I was drunk, but I should've known better than to do stuff with you in public."

I set the coffee machine to make us both coffee, then turn in his arms to wrap mine around his neck and kiss him. "The only person to blame is Cassie for taking the photo and using it against us."

"That's right," he murmurs and kisses me again.

I reach between us to stroke his cock through the gray

sweatpants he's wearing, and he smiles at me.

"Our coffee will go cold."

"I like iced coffee," I joke.

"Are you sure?" Logan traces around my nipple with one finger as his cock stiffens in my hand.

"I could use the distraction, and I think you can probably wake me up better than any coffee could."

Logan tweaks my nipple painfully, and a shot of arousal heads straight to my crotch.

"Is that what you think?"

I smirk at him. "Yes, it is."

Logan wraps his fingers around my wrist and pulls my hand away from his erection. "Well, then, what the fuck are you doing with your hand? I want your mouth on my cock, Alexandra."

I drop to my knees and pull his sweatpants to his ankles before I wrap my lips around his hard shaft. Logan groans as he hits the back of my throat, and I love the sound of his ecstasy. He lets me suck him for a while before he holds my face in his hands and fucks my mouth. He does it for so long that I think he might have decided to come down my throat this morning. Finally, he pulls himself out of my mouth and spins me to face the kitchen bench. He bends me over it, and I gasp as my breasts touch the cold marble before Logan grabs my hips and plunges deep inside me.

"Logan," I moan in pleasure as he fills me.

In answer, he grabs hold of my hair and wraps it around his fist as he pounds into me. I moan as he pulls my hair while we fuck, and it's slightly painful at times, but I also love it.

He thrusts into me roughly and growls, "I love fucking my toy."

I'm lost in ecstasy, and his words tip me into orgasm. I grip his cock with my pussy as I come apart around him.

"Fuck yes, Sir."

"Did I tell you that you could come, Alexandra?"

"No, Sir," I gasp.

He spanks my ass hard. "No." Spank. "I." Spank. "Didn't."

He hits me harder again, and my ass stings with fire, even as my pussy clenches and another orgasm threatens to hit me. Logan seems to know how close I am because he reaches around my legs to rub my clit, and I gasp.

"You're not going to come, are you?" His breath is hot in my ear.

"No, Sir," I moan.

"Are you sure?"

He rubs faster, and I pant for breath as I respond. "No, Sir."

"Good girl."

He gives me some relief by returning his hands to my hips as he continues to pound roughly into me.

"You're not allowed to come again until it's around Ash's cock when you're at his place."

I swallow and manage to ask, "You want me to fuck Ash at the meeting with Cassie?"

"I don't think that would be a good idea. After she's gone, though. I don't expect Ash will mind fucking you, but if he's not up for it tonight, then I guess you'll have to remain on edge until he's willing to fuck you at his place sometime."

I groan at the idea of being edged for that long but say, "Yes, Sir."

I'm not sure if it's this idea that tips Logan over the edge, but he gives one last thrust and comes inside me.

"Mmm, I love you, Lexi." Logan kisses my back before he pulls out of me.

We head to the bathroom, and as we pass Nate, he grumbles, "You two are way too fucking noisy for this time of the morning."

"Sorry, Nate," I laugh as I enter the bathroom.

"Not sorry, Nate. If you get your ass up, Lexi will suck your cock to apologize properly."

We've been in the shower for a few minutes, and Logan has washed me clean by the time Nate appears with his stiff cock jutting impressively in front of him.

"Hi, Sexy Lexi. I've been assured you'll sort this out for me."

He indicates to his erection, and I laugh.

"I think I can handle this." I drop to my knees in front of him and take him in my mouth.

As I suck him, Logan moves over to him, and they kiss each other. I groan around Nate's cock as I remember that I'm not allowed to orgasm until I fuck Ash at his place sometime, and my pussy aches at the thought.

I spend a long time sucking Nate's cock while he and Logan make out before Logan says, "I'll leave you two to it. She's not allowed to come, Nate."

Nate grins down at me. "Noted. Stand up and kiss me, Lexi."

I do as instructed, even though I don't need to follow instructions from Nate. He lifts his hand to my breast and thumbs my nipple as we kiss.

"So, you're not allowed to come, huh?" He grins at me.

"Not until I come on Ash's cock at his place sometime."

Nate's eyebrows raise. "Tonight?"

"Hopefully," I laugh. "If he's up for it. Otherwise, I'm fucked until he does."

Nate's hand drifts to the crest of my thighs, where he lazily draws a circle around the outside of my clit, which causes me to groan.

"And what if I make you come right now?" Nate teases me.

"I'll bear the punishment for you doing that. Do you really want me to suffer?"

Nate nips my bottom lip with my teeth and growls, "Maybe. I do like watching you get punished."

I shudder as he begins stroking my clit, unsure if he's going to go through with this or not, but then he stops and pushes my back against the shower wall. The tile is cold against my back as Nate pushes his cock into me, and he groans as he sheaths himself inside me.

"God, you feel good. As tempting as it is to make you come, I won't do that to you." He continues fucking me as he talks. "Plus, the thought of you fucking Ash tonight is hot. I might message him and get him to take a dirty pic of you to send me as proof it happened."

I moan at the thought of Ash showing me off to Nate instead of the other way around.

"Do you like that idea, Lexi?"

"Yes," I gasp as he thrusts roughly into me.

On some level, I find it strange that I'm so into the idea of fucking Ash tonight, especially considering we're meeting with Cassie. But at the same time, I've enjoyed the times we've played together over the past two weeks. He's good in bed, and we've all had a lot of fun.

Nate claims my lips with his and kisses me passionately as he finishes inside me. I wrap my arms around his neck and kiss him back as he moves me into the warm spray of the shower.

"I love you, sexy."

I smile at him. "I love you, too."

We clean ourselves up and kiss again, with Nate holding me tight for a long time before we get out of the shower. We dry ourselves off, and Nate puts on a pair of jeans and a shirt before we head out to the kitchen hand-in-hand.

"Morning, Angel," Dante says with a smile from the living room where he's sitting on the sofa drinking coffee with Logan.

I grin and walk over to climb into his lap. "Morning, Honey."

"I heard you've had a fun morning," he says.

"Yes. I didn't even get my coffee." I pout at him.

He laughs and offers me his cup. "Would you like a sip?"

"Yes. I would die for a hot cup of coffee," I groan.

As I drink some of the delicious brew, Logan shakes his head. "Funny, that. She told me she'd love to drink it ice cold."

The hot liquid runs down my throat, and I take another sip quickly before I hand the cup back to Dante as I say, "Really? I don't remember saying that at all."

"Would you like to be spanked properly this morning, Alexandra?" Logan asks with an eyebrow raised.

"Oh, now that I think about it. I might have said *something* like that." I feign an enlightened look.

"That's what I thought," he laughs.

Dante gently strokes my inner thigh, and as he moves tantalizingly close to my pussy, he says, "I've also been told you're not allowed to come unless it's around Ash's cock at his place."

"Yes," I groan.

"How does that make you feel?" Dante stops stroking my leg, which allows me to focus on the question as he looks into my eyes.

"I know I should feel bad about it, especially since we're going through all this shit with Cassie, but I'm mostly just worried that he won't want to fuck tonight, and I'll be edged for a week or something," I groan again at the thought.

"If you think Ash wouldn't happily fuck you any day of the week, you'd be sorely mistaken," Nate snorts with a laugh.

Dante has continued stroking my thigh, though, and I've lost my ability to focus as he toys with my pussy lips. I bite my lip and spread my legs a little wider, hopeful that I'll get to fuck him as well this morning.

"Don't you need to have breakfast before you leave for work, Angel?" Dante murmurs in my ear.

"I think today's a good day to start intermittent fasting," I laugh.

"I see," he says, his cock stiff against my ass, and I moan loudly as his fingers finally touch my drenched pussy. "You're not allowed to come, though. Do you really want this?"

"Yes, Honey," I answer, even though I know it's going to be torment.

"If you want to play with her, I'll make you guys breakfast, and it'll be ready when you're done," Logan offers.

"This is why we need you living with us full-time," Dante laughs and then kisses me. "I guess we have no reason not to, Angel."

It's still early, and the sun is rising on the horizon as Dante leads me by the hand to our bedroom. We lie in bed together and kiss for a long time.

"Are you really okay, Lexi?" he asks with a concerned look on his face.

I nod. "I am. I mean, I'm stressed as fuck about the meeting with Cassie, but everything else is fine. I really do want to fuck Ash tonight, even though I know I probably shouldn't want that."

Dante kisses me again, softly and tenderly, before he says, "Never be ashamed of what you want sexually, Angel. I'm glad Logan helped you through the shit Cassie said to you. I hope you know that if whatever she says tonight screws with your head again, we'll all be here for you, and we love you, and you have nothing to be ashamed of."

I smile at him and kiss him again as I wrap my arms around his neck and press my soft body against his hard, muscled one.

I break our kiss, and he gently strokes my back as I say, "I know, Dante. I love you, too"—I smile as I remember what I told Logan—"and I'm the happiest little slut in the world because you guys keep filling all my holes."

Dante chuckles and raises an eyebrow at me. "Is that so?"

"Yes, it is."

"Have all your holes been filled this morning, then?"

I bite my lip and shake my head. "No, Honey."

"Which holes haven't been filled?"

"Just one. My ass." I swallow, and my pussy clenches because I know he's going to take that now.

Sure enough, he reaches down and squeezes my ass cheek. "Then, I guess this is the one I'm having."

I moan into his mouth as he kisses me, and when he's done, he pulls back to grin at me.

"Especially since it doesn't matter if you come or not." Dante rubs my clit, and I moan. "You're mine to use. I get to take my pleasure from you, and you get no satisfaction from this." I moan softly, and he raises an eyebrow at me. "You're not going to come. Are you, Angel?"

"No, Honey," I moan.

"Good. Worship my cock."

I move down to take his cock in my mouth, and I groan when he reaches between my legs to rub my clit as I do. Dante keeps me on edge the whole time I'm sucking him. I'm dripping wet, and he uses his fingers to bring me to the brink of orgasm multiple times by the time he decides to fuck my ass.

I'm a shivering mess as he walks away to get the lube. My nerve endings are on fire, and every cell in my body is screaming for release. I know that I can't come, and even the thought of it threatens to tip me into the orgasm that is hovering so closely nearby.

I bite my lip and stare wide-eyed at Dante as he returns. He leans down and bites my nipple, causing a shock of arousal to dart there.

"You're not going to come, are you?"

"No, Honey," I gasp.

He moves between my legs, and I groan as he licks my pussy while he lubes up my asshole. I'm so close to orgasm, and I moan loudly as it threatens to crash over me. It's so close, and my body shakes as I struggle to keep it at bay.

Dante lifts his head but continues to push two fingers in and out of my ass as he says, "You're not going to come, Angel."

"No"—I gasp—"Honey."

"Good. Get on your hands and knees."

I pant for breath as I follow his instruction, and it's barely a second before Dante plunges his cock into my ass. He has hold of my hips, and he fucks me as I bite my lip to withhold a moan.

Dante holds himself deep inside me and reaches down to play with my breasts. "You can react, Angel."

I moan loudly as soon as he says this, his breath hot on my neck before he kisses it. He continues to play with my breasts as he uses his other hand to reach between my legs and stroke my clit.

"Honey," I moan loudly, and my orgasm comes rushing ever closer.

"You're not going to come, Angel," Dante growls.

"No, Honey," I answer, but I shudder because I'm perilously close to coming.

I pant for breath as I try to keep it at bay, and my mind clouds over with the pleasure Dante is building in me. He continues this onslaught for a while before he gives me relief by returning upright as he pulls his cock back and slams it into me again.

I gasp as I'm jolted forward, and my ass stretches around him, "Oh god, Honey. Yes. That's so good."

After some time, he leans forward and brings me to the edge of orgasm again. By the time he finally comes, I'm dizzy with ecstasy and lust, completely on edge, and desperate for release.

Dante pulls his cock out of my ass and unloads on my back. The squirts of hot cum land on my lower back and ass, and I'm glad he's avoided getting any in my hair since I don't really want to wash it this morning.

His cock is warm and hard where it sits on top of my ass, and Dante gently rubs my ass cheek with his hand as he says, "Mmm. Very nice, Angel. Your ass was a very enjoyable hole indeed. The guys missed out."

He takes me by the hand and leads me to the shower. Dante takes the cloth and washes me before he takes me in his arms and kisses me. I smile and relax into his embrace as his love washes over me like the spray from the shower.

"I love you, Honey," I tell him when our kiss ends.

He kisses the top of my head and says, "I love you, too, Angel. We should probably go have breakfast so you can go to work."

We walk into the kitchen to the smell of bacon and eggs being cooked.

"Mmm, that smells delicious," I say as I sniff the air.

"I figured you've expended a lot of energy this morning, so I started cooking as soon as I heard the shower turn on." Logan smiles at me and slides a plate of food across to me.

"Thank you," I say with a smile back at him.

I begin eating the food as Logan places a mug of steaming hot coffee in front of me.

"You didn't even have to die for it," he teases me.

"That's a relief." I take a sip. "It's good, too."

We sit and talk as we eat our food, but my nerves have returned in full force. The meeting tonight with Cassie is at the back of my mind the whole way through breakfast.

By the time I've dressed for work and collected up everything to leave, I feel mildly nauseated.

"I'm so nervous about seeing Cassie tonight," I complain to the guys as I slip my keys into my handbag.

"You'll be fine, Angel. Ash will be there. It'll be okay." Dante hugs me and gives me a kiss as he holds me tight.

"God, I hope so. I wish she were out of our lives for good."

"Hopefully, after tonight, she will be." Nate takes my hand and pulls me to him so he can kiss me.

Somehow, I don't think she'll be willing to give up on Ash that easily, but I just nod and kiss Nate before I hug Logan as well.

"I love you all. I'll call you to tell you how it went after Cassie leaves."

"Sounds good." Logan's hand drifts to my ass, and he squeezes it as he pulls me tighter against him. "Then maybe he'll let you come on his cock after that."

I groan, "God, I hope so."

Logan laughs and kisses me before he lets me go. I drive to the Beverly Center store and greet Sherry, who gives me an update on how it's going before I head to my office. I open my laptop and am looking through my emails when I get a text from Ash.

How are you feeling?

I smile and send him a quick reply.

I'm fine. Just shitting bricks. You?

My phone starts ringing, and I chuckle as I answer it, "Hi, Ash."

"It'll be fine. I'll be there to run interference, and I won't let her get away with insulting you."

"I appreciate that." I bite my lip and say in a husky voice, "I'm looking forward to seeing you, though."

"I was thinking we could order in some dinner afterward," he says, and I can tell that he's aroused.

My pussy aches as I remember Logan's instruction, but I decide not to reveal that to Ash just yet. "I've definitely got one or two ideas about something you could eat for dinner."

"Oh, really? What would that be?" Ash asks in an amused voice.

Before I can reply, the sound of beeping comes through the line, and I pull the phone away from my ear to see Heather Fletcher's name on the screen.

"Damn. I have to go. Heather Fletcher is calling me. I'll see you later."

"Bye, baby. I'll see your sexy ass later. We'll deal with my ex, and then I'll eat you for dinner."

"Bye, Ash," I groan as I press the button to hang up on him and answer the incoming call. "Hi, Heather. How are you?"

"I'm good, darling. I was just wondering how you're doing today?"

I can hear the concern in her voice, and I'm so embarrassed about the shit with Cassie causing me to act like an idiot in front of Heather.

"I'm okay. I'm sorry again about what happened yesterday."

"Not a concern. I'm just worried about you."

My jaw tightens as I think about what I have to do tonight, but I manage to say as casually as I can, "I appreciate that. It'll be fine. I just had something I needed to deal with."

"Well, the offer to talk is always there. I'm still in Los Angeles, though, so I was wondering if I could come and see the Orange County store today."

"Of course," I agree quickly. "What time?"

"In an hour or so?" Heather suggests.

Fuck.

I curse internally because it's a forty-minute drive for me, which means I need to leave ASAP to get there.

"Not a problem," I lie. "I'll see you then."

We end our call, and I groan as I hit my head on the desk. I close my laptop and put it in my laptop bag before I head out to see Sherry on my way out of the store.

"Heather wants to meet me at the Orange County store," I say as I give Sherry a tight smile.

"I thought you went with her yesterday?"

I shake my head. "No, something came up, so we ended up skipping it. I have to go right away, though. She wants to meet in an hour."

Sherry looks at her watch and cringes. "Good luck."

"Thanks. I'll see you on Wednesday."

Sherry nods, and I bid the other women working today farewell as I leave the store. On the way to Orange County, I call Vera and let her know that Heather and I are heading there.

"Thanks for letting me know. I wondered why you guys didn't come yesterday."

I wince and say, "Yeah, sorry. Something came up. I should've let you know we weren't going to make it."

I make good time to the store, and I arrive five minutes before Heather said she would be here. I greet Vera, who gives me a store update, and I rush around the store, trying to make sure that everything is absolutely perfect before Heather arrives.

Vera rushes into my office. "Yeah, I'm pretty sure Heather is here, Lexi."

"Thanks, Vee." I smile at her and follow her back into the store.

We stand behind the counter and watch the shitshow that's happening outside. Heather's presence has been heralded by a crowd of paparazzi who appeared first and gave Vera the clue to the fashion designer's arrival. They snap pictures with big cameras hanging around their necks, and they crowd around the door to Black Lilac. There seems to be far more of them bothering her today than yesterday.

I understand why when a bodyguard I haven't seen before enters the store. Heather comes through next, looking as cool and stylish as she always does. After that comes the person I'm sure has caused the multiplication of paparazzi, Harrison Fletcher.

The bass guitarist for Cruise Control is tall and handsome, with a friendly smile on his face as he catches the eye of one of the girls who works in the store. Finally, after Harrison, comes Heather's bodyguard, Callum.

The first bodyguard does a quick walk around the store while Callum stays at the entrance. Meanwhile, Heather comes over to where I'm standing behind the counter with Vera.

"Hi, darling," she says with a smile.

I step out around the counter to hug her. "Hi, Heather."

"Honey, this is Lexi Sullivan. She owns this store." Heather smiles up at her husband, and it's so obvious how in love they are as he smiles back at her before looking at me.

"Lexi, hi. I think we've met before. I know Dante, at least." He holds his hand out to shake mine.

"Probably," I laugh. "Though, I think Nate knows you guys better than Dante?"

Harrison nods. "Yeah, he's friends with Hayden. They've been to Vegas a few times to play poker."

Heather has drifted away while Harrison and I have been talking, and she's currently flicking through a rack of clothes nearby with a frown on her face.

She turns to look at me. "Are these from the same designer that made the jumpsuit?"

"Yeah, they are," I tell her with a smile on my face.

"I could tell," she says, and she looks satisfied with herself.

I raise an eyebrow at her. "I'm impressed, considering we've sold out of the jumpsuit at this store."

She shrugs. "I like their style, but I couldn't quite remember the label name. It also seemed familiar."

Harrison takes a seat on a bench in the center of the store and pulls out his phone as Heather walks around looking at clothes. A group of customers comes in, and they gasp when they see him.

They rush over to him, and I consider intervening, but he seems okay with them talking to him. At the very least, he's polite about taking photos with them, and he signs some autographs as well. As soon as they've gotten the autographs, they go on to look at clothes without continuing to harass him or bother Heather, so I let them be.

The other customers have been rung up and have left the store by the time I've shown Heather where I think her clothes will be displayed. She's also tried on five outfits and decided to purchase three of them.

Harrison gives her an amused smile. "Are you sure you don't want the other two outfits as well, Angel?"

"Don't tempt me," she laughs before turning to me. "He says that as if he doesn't moan all the time about how many clothes I buy."

"I wouldn't say that I 'moan,' per se. It's more that I think you have more clothes than you could possibly wear in a lifetime, but whatever makes you happy." He puts his arm around her and drops a kiss on her head as she smiles.

"Well, these clothes make me very happy. If you're ever in contact with the designer, definitely pass on my compliments on their designs."

"I will," I promise. "It was lovely to see you again, Harrison."

"You, too." He smiles at me.

The couple leaves the store amidst a flurry of activity from the paparazzi, who have been hanging around since they arrived.

Chapter Eleven

Meeting of the Minds

I spend the rest of the day at the Orange County store since there's not much point in going back to Beverly Center just for the afternoon. I leave the store just after five, and as I drive to Ash's, my nerves and arousal swirl together. By the time I arrive in the underground garage for his apartment, I'm completely on edge.

This is the first time I'll be playing with him on my own. We spent time together in the bedroom the first night, but it wasn't the same. None of the other guys will be here at all tonight. I know that I have their approval to play with Ash, but it's still strange.

That's without even getting into the Cassie issue, so the butterflies in my stomach are racing as I knock on his door.

"Hi, baby," he greets me with a smile as he opens it.

"Hey," I say as I walk past him and allow him to close the door behind me.

I set my bag on a table by the door before he hugs me, and I wrap my arms around his waist to hug him back. I have the urge to kiss him, so I turn my face up to his and instinctively seek his lips with mine. Ash kisses me back, and I part my lips to allow his tongue access to my mouth. Our tongues intertwine, and his hand slides down to my ass.

He grabs it and pulls me harder against his stiffening erection as we kiss. I pant for breath as our kiss ends, and we look into each other's eyes, our bodies still pressed against each other.

"You sure know how to greet a woman, Ashton Woodford," I tell him with a grin on my face.

He smirks at me. "Trust me when I tell you that Cassie won't be getting a greeting like that."

"God, I'd hope not." I wrinkle my nose at him, as well as at the reminder of Cassie.

"Hey"—Ash takes my chin in his hand and holds my face in place as he kisses me again—"I shouldn't have mentioned Cassie. Try not to think about her."

I sigh. "Easier said than done."

"I suppose you're right." Ash lets me go and nods. "What should we do for the next hour while we wait for her? Do you want a drink?"

I bite my lip because I kind of want to play, but I'm not sure if it's a good idea to do anything before Cassie arrives. Ash looks me over as he waits for a response, and his gaze lingers at my breasts.

"Do you want a drink, Lexi?" Ash asks again in a husky voice this time.

I shake my head in response, and he gives me a slow smile.

"Nobody else is here today, so I'm going to need you to tell me what you want."

"An orgasm," I say truthfully. "Logan banned me from having one unless it was here and I was coming around your cock."

Ash's eyebrows fly up on his face, and he asks, "Really?"

Even as he asks the question, his breathing rate increases and his cock is an obvious bulge in his jeans.

"Yes. Do we have time before Cassie gets here, or do you want to wait until after she's left?"

Ash steps back toward me and places a hand on my breast. He strokes my nipple through the fabric of my top with his thumb as he lowers his head to softly trail kisses from my shoulder up to my ear.

"I want to fuck you before she gets here as well as after she's left, and I will fucking make time stop if I need to in order to be able to fuck you right now," he growls, and I gasp.

He claims my lips with his again, and I wrap my arms around his neck as I press my body against his. When our kiss ends, Ash takes my hand and leads me to his bedroom. We stand at the end of the bed, and he pulls my top off over my head.

My nipples are stiff against the silk lace of my bra, and Ash groans when he sees them. He lowers his head to my right breast and takes it in his mouth. His tongue is warm and wet against my nipple as he sucks on my breast.

He removes his mouth but keeps his eyes level with my breasts as he murmurs, "Logan was right. Your breasts are so glorious that I couldn't wait until they were uncovered to get my mouth around them."

He takes my other breast in his mouth as he reaches his hand underneath my skirt and into my underwear to find my wet pussy, and I moan as he begins to rub my clit.

"I can't have an orgasm unless it's around your cock, or I'll be punished."

He moves up to kiss me as he continues to rub me, then asks, "Is that so?"

"Yes." I place my hands on his forearm and tug at it to get him to stop rubbing my clit, and he laughs.

"Okay, I won't make you come, then." He pulls his hand out of my pants.

"You can do whatever you like after I've come on your cock," I tell him.

He raises an eyebrow at me. "Is that a promise? Whatever I like?" He raises a hand to stroke my breast through my bra. "Because there are a lot of things I would like to do to you."

"What would you like to do?" I ask around a moan at the pleasure he's giving me.

He continues to stroke my nipple as he lowers his other hand to my ass and grabs it while he pulls me against his erection. "For a start, I haven't had your ass yet."

"Good thing Dante fucked my ass this morning in preparation for you to split me in half," I laugh.

Ash kisses me as he squeezes my ass with his hand. "Good thing he did. In the meantime, we should probably fuck if we're going to because time is getting away from us."

I reach between us to unbutton his jeans. "I guess we should."

I drop to my knees as I pull his pants and briefs to his ankles, freeing his erection. I wrap my hand around the base of his cock and take him in my mouth. Ash groans, and I delight in the sound of it.

He's so thick and hard. I love it. I reach my hand into my pants and stroke my clit slowly as I suck him. I know I can't come, but it's still enjoyable, and I moan onto Ash's cock while I blow him. I'm aware of the time limit we have, though, so I don't do it for long before I stop.

Ash kicks his shoes, jeans, and briefs off as he kisses me and reaches behind me to unclip my bra. He tosses it aside and lowers his head to my breast. I moan as the pleasure hits me, and I run my hands through his hair while I pant for breath.

"Fuck, Ash. That's good."

"I'm glad, baby," he murmurs.

He drops to his knees and pulls my skirt and thong down and off before he tosses them aside and buries his face in my pussy. Again, I can't resist running my hands through his hair while he eats me out.

I close my eyes and throw my head back as I moan, "Ash."

He pushes two fingers in and out of me as he licks and sucks my clit. My orgasm is rapidly approaching, and I gasp as it nears.

"I can't come this way," I manage to pant.

Ash pulls his head away from my clit, but keeps pushing his fingers in and out of me. "Damn. I forgot about that. I did promise I wouldn't give you an orgasm until you were on my cock, but fuck, your cunt is tasty."

I gasp and bite my lip as he gets a satisfied look in his eyes.

"Mmm, there it is. Okay, you can come on my cock, then."

He pulls his fingers out of me and pulls me to the bed. Ash lies on his back, and I climb onto him before I lower myself onto his cock. Relief from knowing that I can come any time now washes over me, and I enjoy the feeling of Ash filling me.

"God, you feel good," I groan.

"I'm not god. I'm Ash." He smirks at me, and I laugh.

I lower my head to kiss him passionately as I fuck him. "You're a god in bed. I can't believe we haven't been fucking for all the years we've known each other."

Ash reaches up to play with my breasts and smiles at me. "It's a damn shame, but at least we get to fuck now."

"Too fucking true." I kiss him again, then straighten up to ride him.

Ash reaches between us and rubs my clit, which causes me to moan his name, and he watches me through eyes that are dark with lust. "Come for me, Lexi."

I bite my lip and nod as I moan his name again. "Ashton."

I give in to the ecstasy that he's building in me and focus on the pleasure as he thrusts into me and rubs my clit. I'm lost in the feelings swirling around inside me, and it isn't long before my orgasm crashes over me. My pussy clenches around his cock as I gasp and pant for breath.

"Fuck, Ash. Oh, fuck, yes. Fucking hell, fuck, fuck, fuck." My body shakes, and I collapse forward on him, unable to remain upright for another second.

Ash kisses my head as he wraps his arms around my back. He cuddles me tightly to him as he continues to thrust into me, but he increases his speed, and I can barely breathe because it's so good and I'm so sensitive at the moment. When I kiss his neck and taste his salty sweat, I can't resist putting some suction against his skin. I do this for a few seconds before I trail my tongue up his neck, along his jaw, and to his lips.

I kiss him, and our tongues dance together as his cock jerks inside me and he orgasms. He hooks a leg around the back of mine, and his cock moves just that tiny bit further inside me while he releases himself in me.

"Yes, Lexi," he moans.

We lie together and pant for breath for a minute or so before we move to the bathroom to clean up.

"Fuck, that was good," Ash says with a smile as I wash myself in the shower.

"Shit, yes. So good." I grin at him.

Ash looks at his watch and cringes. "We've got, like, fifteen minutes before Cassie's meant to be here. We don't have time to cuddle. Is that okay?"

"Fuck." I speed up washing myself with the shower gel Ash has. "No, that's fine. That's for BDSM scenes with Dante and Logan." I hand him the washcloth. "I don't have to do that with you if we haven't done anything hardcore like that."

"Okay. I just want to make sure I'm doing everything right." He smiles at me.

He's in the middle of washing his stomach, but I lean over and kiss him. "You're fine. I'll go get dressed while you finish up."

I step out of the shower and grab a towel off the rack to dry myself.

There's only one, so I call to Ash, "I'm using this towel. I hope that's okay."

"Sure. I'll just dry myself with a damp towel. That's fine," he laughs.

"It's your fault. You knew I was coming over tonight."

"Wouldn't it be presumptuous to assume we'd have sex?"

I stick my head back in the shower and grin at him as he wrings out the washcloth.

"As if I wouldn't want that glorious cock of yours inside my pussy on any given day of the week. Enjoy your damp towel."

I blow a kiss to him with a laugh as I close the shower door, and I just finish drying myself when Ash gets out. I hand the towel to him, and he immediately twirls it around, then snaps my ass cheek with it.

I squeal at the stinging sensation as the towel makes a cracking sound in the air when it hits me.

"Ow! That hurt," I grumble as I rub my cheek, and Ash laughs.

"Sorry. I didn't actually mean to get you that good." He begins drying himself with the towel, and I glare at him while trying not to laugh myself.

"Payback is a bitch, and her name is Lexi Sullivan. I won't forget that, Ashton Woodford."

He places his hands on my hips and bends down to kiss the spot where the towel hit me. His lips are soft and warm against my burning ass.

"You can kiss my ass all you want, but it won't change anything," I warn him.

He stands up and kisses me quickly while he goes back to drying himself. "Oh well, it was worth a try, I guess."

I snort and walk into his bedroom, where I quickly pull my clothes back on before I check my reflection in the full-length mirror at the side of the room.

"Fuck. My makeup is ruined!"

I rush out to the entrance of his apartment and grab my bag before I head back.

"Can you fix it?" Ash asks with a concerned look as he pulls his t-shirt over his head.

I nod as I sit in front of the mirror and begin pulling my makeup back out of my handbag. "I can make it passable. More 'end of a long day at work' and less 'I just screwed your ex-boyfriend fifteen minutes ago,'" I joke.

Ash sits on the end of the bed and watches me as I powder my face and reapply my lipstick, eyeshadow, and blush.

"How are you feeling?" he asks as I work.

"Nervous as shit, but grateful you managed to keep my mind off my nerves for a little while, at least."

"Happy to help," he laughs.

The memory of the pictures Cassie sent comes to my mind, and I think I might be sick.

"I just don't know what she thinks she's going to achieve by coming here tonight. Surely, she doesn't think you're going to get back with her." I pat some glitter eyeshadow on my eye with my finger.

"I honestly don't know. I was tempted to unblock her just to see if she would send something through, but I figured it wasn't worth opening that can of worms."

I sigh as I put my makeup back in my bag. The end result is nowhere near perfect, but it looks decent enough for Cassie to not guess what we've been doing. I pull out a bottle of perfume and spray myself just in case Cassie happens to recognize the scent of Ash's shower gel.

"Well, I guess we'd better go face the firing squad." I wrinkle my nose at him in the mirror as I stand up.

He nods. "Yeah. Fuck. The sooner this is over, the better."

I follow him out of the room and back into the living room. I walk to the apartment door and pretend I've just arrived as I try to think about what I would've done back before having sex with Ash is the first thing I would do when I arrived here.

I mime hugging him and murmur, "Hey, Ash. How are you?"

"I'm good," he says with a laugh as he gives me a bemused look from over on the sofa.

"Me, too. Nervous." I walk toward the sofa and dump my bag on the dining table on the way toward him. I smile and exhale a deep breath with relief because it feels so familiar, and I turn my gaze to Ash. "Then, you offer me a drink. I say 'thank fuck' because I'm nervous, and we sit together and talk while we wait."

"Would you like a drink, Lexi?"

"Thank fuck. I'm so nervous. Yes, please." I take a seat on the sofa but away from Ash, and he laughs again as he gets up and gets us drinks.

It's less than a minute after Ash hands me the drink that Cassie lets us know she's arrived.

"I'm going to puke," I moan as Ash sets his drink aside.

"It'll be fine, baby," he murmurs and gives me a reassuring

smile as he stands and walks over to buzz her up.

I take a deep drink from the whiskey Ash has given me and cough as the fire hits my throat. When Cassie knocks on the door, my heart pounds even harder in my chest.

"Come in, Cassie." Ash's words echo around the room, and the nausea threatens to overwhelm me.

I take a smaller sip of the whiskey, and it goes down smoothly as Ash leads Cassie to the living room. I'm horrified when I notice a small, purple bruise on his neck.

I gave him a fucking hickey like we're goddamn teenagers.

I quickly look away from it, even though Cassie's behind him, and can't possibly see it right now. I don't want to draw attention to it. Ash takes a seat on the sofa next to me, but he sits a respectable distance from me as though he wasn't buried in me earlier.

The scent of his shower wash reaches me, mixed with the scent of him, and I'm grateful I had the forethought to spray some perfume on myself. Cassie takes a seat in an armchair opposite us and glares at me.

"Well, I'm here, Cassie. What do you want to discuss?" Ash asks in a cold voice.

She turns her gaze to him and frowns. "You're not even going to offer me a drink?"

"No."

His one-word reply is curt, and the hurt is evident in Cassie's expression before it closes over and she indicates to me. "You clearly got Lexi a drink."

"Lexi is a wanted guest in my home. You, however, have coerced me into meeting with you. So, what would you like to discuss?"

A flare of pleasure blooms within me that Ash wants me here and not Cassie. I knew it, but it's nice to hear him say it anyway.

There's a tense silence while Cassie looks between us. My body is angled slightly away from Ash, and I meet her gaze with my chin held high. I refuse to give any sign that there's anything more between Ash and me than there was when they were together.

"I'm not comfortable talking with Lexi here," Cassie says.

"Too bad. You brought her into this when you sent her photos and *heavily* implied that you would release them if she didn't convince me to see you," Ash growls at her.

"I didn't know what to do, Ashton," Cassie sighs. "You'd blocked me and refused to talk to me. I didn't know how else to convince you to see me."

"Blackmailing Lexi wasn't the way to do it, but I guess you were successful, so maybe it was. What do you want now that you're here?" He raises an eyebrow at her, and I grit my teeth as I wait for her reply.

"Can we just talk privately, please, Ash?" she begs.

"No, we can't. I have no desire to be anywhere private with you."

Cassie looks back and forth between us again, and she seems distressed. A part of me wants to offer to leave the room, but I don't do it because I don't want to overrule Ash like that.

She looks at me with a deep frown on her face, then turns back to Ash again. "I guess I want to know if there's any chance for us. I'm so sorry about what happened, and I love you. We should be together."

Ash doesn't hesitate in responding, and the moment Cassie stops speaking, he firmly says, "No."

"You won't even give me a chance?" A tear rolls down her cheek as she asks the question.

"No," he repeats.

Despite myself, I feel bad for her. I definitely don't want Ash to take her back, but this is a pretty depressing experience for me, so I can only imagine how she feels.

"Why not?"

"Because you have to ask that question, Cassandra. It was over when you insulted Lexi the way you did. An insult that you've doubled down on multiple times since then, I might add, which makes me think you're not sorry at all. You're just upset that I broke up with you."

There's an awkward silence before Cassie wipes away the tears streaming down her face. "You can't do this, Ashton."

She repeats her words from the night he broke up with her, and I shake my head because it's clear he's not going to take her back regardless of what she says.

"Yes, I can. Is there anything else, or would you like to leave now?" he asks in a surprisingly gentle voice.

I look over at him, and his jaw is tight. I know that he's not a cruel person, so this is probably difficult for him.

Cassie doesn't reply at once, though. She wipes at her tears again and turns to stare out the windows at Los Angeles below us. When she speaks, her voice has a strange and eerie quality to it.

"You can't do it, though."

She takes a deep breath and exhales it slowly. Something about her change of demeanor and the tone of her voice brings a knot of fear to my stomach.

"Because of the photos. I know you don't want the world to see *her* like that." Cassie turns her gaze to me as she finishes what she's saying, and her lip curls when she does.

I frown at her and do my best to give away none of my inner fear at the thought of Cassie having those photos, let alone her releasing them to the public.

"What exactly do you think Ash is going to do in exchange for the photos?"

I can barely breathe as I wait for Cassie's response. I'm dreading it because I don't know what she'll say when Ash inevitably denies whatever her request for him is.

"I thought that maybe he would be willing to at least try to make it work between us rather than so callously throwing away what we have." She turns her gaze to him, and I look at him as well.

His jaw is tight, and Cassie gasps softly as he shakes his head at her. "No. I've already told you that. I also warned Lexi that I would say no if that's what you wanted. I love Lexi and the guys, but I'm not going to be trapped in a loveless relationship to cover for them."

Cassie flinches when he says he loves me, and she glares at me, then turns back to him. Her eyes dart to his neck, and I work hard not to cringe as she takes in the obvious hickey I've given him.

"Are you fucking her?" she demands in a cool voice.

"Would it make a difference if I were? I didn't break up with you to fuck Lexi. I broke up with you because I didn't want to be with you anymore. Lexi wouldn't even be here tonight if you hadn't done what you did, so you're the reason she's even in my apartment. It's the first time she's ever been here without Dante, if that's what you're worried about."

My heart pounds in my chest, and I work hard to keep my face neutral. He's taunting her, and I'm concerned that it's going to push her over the edge. Sure enough, she looks between us again. I meet her gaze, and I can see that she's realized her mistake in bringing me to Ash's apartment.

I'm sure that she doesn't know what we did before she arrived, or she'd have lost her shit, but the fear that we might do something after she leaves is written all over her face.

So I'm unsurprised when Cassie asks quietly, "Are you going to fuck her when I leave?"

"It's literally none of your business what I do. You're not my girlfriend. You're here because you held those photos over Lexi's head to get me to see you, and that's it. I think that you should probably leave if you don't have anything else to say to us."

It aligns me with him as a team against her, and I can tell she doesn't like it one bit. I casually smooth out my skirt over my knee for something to do and then slowly blow out a breath of air as I try to calm my racing heart.

"Fine, then. You really won't reconsider being in a relationship with me?" Cassie's voice is cool and calm now.

"No." Ash returns to his monosyllabic answers for her.

"Okay. Well, I have those photos. If they're combined with me filling in the pieces for the media, they're quite the story. I think I could probably sell them for at least a hundred thousand dollars."

My mouth drops open, and I stare at her, certain of what I heard her say but completely disbelieving of it.

"Are you fucking serious?" Ash explodes.

He glares at her, but Cassie's jaw sets, and she shrugs. "I'm just telling you what I know. It's a *very* juicy story. Lexi Sullivan. The slut who sleeps with most of Wicked Stallion. Hell, it's probably a better story if I add you into the mix. I'll tell them I broke up with you when I caught you in bed with her."

I wish I were fucking recording this conversation. I can't believe we didn't think to do that, considering how she got herself here. I should've fucking known, but at the same time, nausea takes hold, and I can barely manage to excuse myself in time to rush to the kitchen sink to throw up because the bathroom is too far away.

It's embarrassing as hell for Cassie to get to see how this has affected me. I empty the contents of my stomach into Ash's sink and cringe as I keep retching. Tears stream down my face from a combination of the vomiting as well as the sheer fear of what will happen if Cassie goes public.

A hundred thousand dollars.

We can find it, but should we? I think we have to because she has the photos. She's right that she could sell her story along with the photos for a fucking fortune. Probably far more than she's asking us to pay her, to be honest.

"Are you okay, Lexi?" Ash asks from nearby as he gently rubs my back.

I stiffen because I don't want to risk Cassie figuring anything out, but at the same time, this is definitely something Ash would've done before we ever played together.

"Yeah," I manage to say as I splash my face with water. "Sorry about your sink." I cringe down at the remnants of my vomit that haven't been able to make it through the drain cover.

"I don't give a fuck about the sink." Ash waves away my concern. "Are you sure you're okay?"

I nod. "Yeah. Can I have a drink of water?"

"Of course." Ash gets me a water and wraps his arm around me before he kisses my head.

It's still nothing that he wouldn't have done in the past, but

I'm on edge because I'm aware that Cassie can still watch us from where she is. I duck out from under his arm and take the glass of water he got me back to my position on the sofa.

"I'll need to talk to Dante, Logan, and Nate," I tell her. "We'll discuss what you've asked and get back to you."

"Don't take too long. It's a hot story," she warns me.

I nod. "Of course. I'll call them straight away to talk and let you know what we decide."

"In the meantime, you can fuck off now," Ash growls from nearby. "I want you out of my fucking apartment."

Cassie shrugs and stands before she primly picks up her handbag and hangs it over her shoulder. I recognize it as one that Ash bought her when they were together, and something about that makes me hate her even more.

I didn't realize that I hated her until right now, but I do. I hate Cassandra Foster with every cell in my body.

Chapter Twelve

Let There Be Pizza

Ash doesn't say anything to Cassie as he escorts her to the door while I sit in numb shock where he left me on the sofa. He drops next to me and puts his arm around me to pull him into him for a hug.

"Are you okay, baby?"

I shake my head. "No. How could I possibly be okay?"

I look up into his beautiful blue eyes, and they're full of concern as he says, "You're right. It was a dumb question."

I sigh and rest my head on his chest as I wrap my arms around his waist. He wraps his other arm around me and holds me safe and secure in his arms. I draw strength from being here and breathe in the scent of my friend.

"No matter what happens, we'll get through it together, Lexi. Okay?"

He tilts my face up to look at him, and I give him a small nod. "Not okay, but we'll definitely all be together, at least."

"Precisely." Ash kisses my lips softly. "We should call the guys."

I video call Dante, and he's stretched out on our bed when our call connects.

Immediately, he frowns and asks, "Are you okay, Angel?"

"No," I squeak out around a lump in my throat. "Are Logan and Nate there?"

Dante's eyebrows raise, and he nods. "I think they're in Nate's room, but I'll go get them."

Despite the situation, I bite my lip at the thought of what Logan and Nate might be doing together, and I wish I were there with them to fuck as well, or even just to watch. I squeeze my thighs together against my arousal, and I wonder if they could send me a video sometime as Dante takes the phone with him to knock on Nate's door.

"Guys? Are you decent?" Dante calls.

There's a muffled reply that sounds like Nate's voice before Dante enters the room.

"Am I interrupting anything?" Dante asks.

"No, we were just watching a movie and waiting to hear from Lexi. Is she on the phone?" Logan's voice says.

"Yeah. Video call. Angel?"

Dante lifts the phone up to his face as he sits on the end of Nate's bed, and the other two men take seats on either side of him.

"Hi, guys," I say and give them a small smile.

"What happened, Lexi?" Nate asks with a frown on his face.

I take a deep breath and sigh as I look up at Ash. He squeezes me tightly with the arm he's still got around me and gives me a reassuring smile.

I turn back to the screen and say, "Cassie wants money not to leak the pictures."

"Dammit. I thought that might be the case," Dante says in a tight voice.

"How much?" Logan asks.

"A hundred thousand," Ash tells him.

"Fuck," Nate groans.

"She's threatening to sell the story with details, along with saying that she broke up with Ash because she found me in bed with him," I tell them, and I choke up on the last few words as fear grips me that Cassie might actually go through with it.

There's silence in the wake of my words, and I watch the men on the screen as they take in what I've said.

Nate is the first person to find anything to say. "What are we going to do?"

"Should we go to the police?" Ash asks.

Logan shakes his head, but it's Dante who replies, "We can't. You know it'll *definitely* leak if we do that."

"Should we tell Isaac, at least?" Nate asks the question this time.

Dante and Logan look at each other before Dante says, "I don't know how he would react. I think we should keep it to ourselves if we can." He looks at the screen and asks, "If we pay her, Ash, do you think she'll go away?"

Ash cringes. "I don't know. I'm not sure she would, but I don't see any other option. We'd need to make sure she deleted all copies of the photo and hope to fucking god that she does."

"I can't believe we're talking about whether or not to pay Cassie a hundred fucking thousand dollars because she's blackmailing us," I groan and shake my head.

Ash kisses me quickly and squeezes me tightly as he says, "It fucking sucks. I'm so sorry, Lexi. I wish I'd never even dated her."

"It's not your fault. Whatever happens, we're in this together," I remind him, and he smiles at me.

Dante blows out a breath of air and says, "Lexi, send her a message and tell her we'll give her a check tomorrow."

I whip my head around to look at the screen in front of me. "Are you sure?"

"No, I'm really not, but unless someone else has a better idea…" he trails off into silence as nobody volunteers any better solution. "Well, that's settled, I guess. We'll have to pay her."

Dante's words are greeted by more silence as the weight of the situation sinks in. Cassie is blackmailing us, and we, like the fools we are, will be giving her the money. I can't help but worry that this won't be the end of it as I flick away from the call and into my messages with Cassie.

Dante said to tell you that we'll pay. We'll give you a check tomorrow.

Her reply comes back quickly.

Why can't he just write me a check tonight?

"Fuck, she's annoying," I grumble as I roll my eyes at the screen.

The call is still connected even though I can't see the guys, and Nate asks, "What did she say?"

"She asked why we can't write a check tonight."

Dante scoffs, "We don't have a hundred grand sitting in our checking account. It's in investments. I'll break a term deposit early to get the cash."

"I have a hundred grand in my checking account," Logan says. "Don't break your term deposit for this shit."

As he's talking, I type out a response to Cassie.

We need to transfer some money to our checking account. When and where do you want to meet?

"I've told her we need the bank to do a check, anyway. I also asked where she wants to meet." I flick back into the video call to see the faces of the men I love, all fraught with tension as they look at Dante's phone.

"Good work, Angel."

Cassie's reply shows up, and I cringe as I see it.

I'll come to your place as soon as you've got the check.

"She's going to come to our place," I tell the guys.

"Oh, joy. Can't wait to have Cassie around," Nate says in a dry voice.

We talk for a few more minutes about the issue, and I message Cassie back that I'll see her at our place tomorrow before Logan's face breaks into a smile.

"I know it's probably not the time, but have you had an orgasm since I saw you last, Alexandra?"

I laugh and look up at Ash, who grins at the screen. "She came on my cock as instructed."

"Good to hear. It's nice to know that she follows my instructions so well."

Despite everything, my pussy aches at the turn this conversation has taken, and I bite my lip while I ask him, "Do you have any more instructions, Sir?"

"My only instruction is to try to forget this shit and just have fun with Ash tonight, Alexandra."

"Am I staying here tonight, Sir?"

The thought of spending the entire night playing with Ash on my own is both strange and exciting.

"If he wants you to, otherwise he can send you home, and I'll play with you," Logan murmurs in a husky voice.

Ash raises a hand to my breast and begins to stroke my hardening nipple through the soft fabric. "I doubt that will happen. You're offering her to me for the night, and there's no way I'm not taking her."

"As long as she comes back to us in working order," Nate laughs.

"I make no such promises." Ash turns to grin at the phone before he lowers his lips to my ear and murmurs, "I'm going to fuck your ass tonight."

"We'll leave you two to it. Love you, Angel. Have fun."

I'm already stuck in a haze of lust, but I manage to tell the guys I love them before Dante ends the call, and I moan, "Ash."

He drops his hand from my breast down to my waist. "As much as I'd love to just dine on you all night long, we should probably order dinner."

"*Or*"—I take his hand and place it back on my breast—"we could have sex again and *then* order dinner."

He chuckles and shakes his head as he thumbs my nipple. "Is that really what you want?"

"Yes," I moan and bite my lip as I look into his beautiful blue eyes.

Ash claims my lips with his, and I wrap my arms around his neck as I kiss him back. His cock is hard underneath me, and my pussy aches with my need to have him inside me again, even though I know he doesn't intend on fucking my pussy.

He breaks our kiss and grins at me. "Let's order pizza for dinner."

I narrow my eyes at him. "You did that on purpose."

"Of course I did." He laughs and places his hand over mine before he moves my hand back and forth on his stiff cock. "Don't think that I won't be suffering, too."

"Good," I say with a pout.

Ash removes his hand, but I continue to stroke his cock through his jeans as I kiss him again. He lowers his hand down my back to my ass and squeezes it.

"I'm going to enjoy fucking your ass, Lexi." He raises an eyebrow at me. "Didn't you say that you barely ever wear clothes?" He takes the hem of my top and shakes it as he says, "Don't you think you're wearing too many right now?"

I grin at him. "I definitely do."

I know I can spend the next hour or so teasing Ash, so I grin at him and stand, then turn to face him as I pull my top off over my head. Out of habit, I fold it neatly and set it aside before I raise an eyebrow at Ash.

"Better?"

"Hmm, I'm not sure. You still seem to be wearing quite a lot of clothes."

I spin to face away from him, unbutton my skirt and bend at the waist as I drop it to the floor.

"Such a nice ass. I can't wait to get my cock in it," Ash murmurs in a husky voice.

I step out of my skirt and fold it before I set it on my top as I turn to face Ash.

"I'm definitely looking forward to you fucking my ass. I believe you said we should eat dinner first, though?"

"Wait a second. You're still wearing underwear that you need to take off." Ash frowns at me.

I smirk at him as I straddle him and lower my lips to his ear.

"Sorry, Ash. You're not my Dom. You don't get to make demands of me. I only stripped to my underwear because *I* wanted to."

I nip his earlobe with my teeth, and he groans as I grind myself on his cock, which is hard underneath my pussy.

"Is it always going to be like this? You teasing me until I'm so painfully hard that I give in and fuck you?"

"Maybe," I laugh. "I never have the control during sex, and I've discovered it's a lot of fun."

Ash pushes me off him and onto my back on the sofa as he braces himself over me, and I gasp at the sudden movement.

"Do you think you've got the control here, Lexi?"

I nod as I grin at him. "Yup. I mean, what are you going to do? Fuck me? Don't threaten me with a good time."

"What if I don't fuck you tonight after all?"

I pull his head down to mine and kiss him. Our tongues intertwine, and all of my nerve endings are on fire with my desire to have sex with him again. He keeps himself braced above me, with his thick cock pressed against my pussy which is soaking my thong.

"As if you'd pass up the chance to fuck my ass tonight," I snicker. "But in answer to your question. If you don't fuck me tonight, I'll just drive to Logan's and give him the honor."

"I see. Well, if that's the case, you'd better call the pizza place and order our pizza. The sooner we eat, the sooner I can fuck you."

My eyebrows raise in surprise. "Who calls to order pizza? Wouldn't we just order online?"

"No. We can call and order from a place nearby. I'll grab the menu."

He climbs off me, and I exhale a massive breath of air because even with him bracing himself on me, it's a relief to breathe easily again. I miss the feeling of Ash's cock against me, though, and I can't wait for us to finish dinner.

He comes back with the menu for a pizza place, and I sit up as he hands me his phone along with the menu and says, "Pick what you want and call to order. I'll eat whatever you want."

"You know what I want you to eat," I tease him and spread my legs to allow him a view of my pussy covered only in the wet lace of my thong.

Ash sits on the coffee table in front of me and says, “I am very hungry.”

I look through the menu and decide on a pizza with broccoli, mushrooms, and cherry tomatoes, then look at Ash’s phone.

“It’s locked,” I tell him.

Ash stands and takes two big steps to stand between my legs. He looks down at me, amusement in his beautiful blue eyes as he holds his hand out for his phone.

I give it to him, and he unlocks it before handing it back to me. “Here you go.”

I open the phone app and type in the number on the menu, then press the green button to call and put the phone to my ear. As the phone starts ringing in my ear, Ash drops to his knees in front of me. He hooks his arms around my legs to pull my ass forward on the sofa, and I gasp as I fall against the back of it.

“You’d better be quiet while I eat you, Lexi.”

I don’t have time to respond before a voice in my ear says, “Valentino’s Pizza, can you hold please?”

“Uh, yes,” I say as Ash pulls my thong to the side and exposes my pussy.

Hold music comes through the line as I moan softly and bite my lip while Ash looks up at me with a wicked grin before he leans forward and flicks his tongue over my sensitive clit. I resist the urge to moan again, even though I’m still on hold, because I don’t know when the employee will come back.

Ash pushes two fingers into my pussy as he continues to eat me, and I’m in a daze of lust by the time the pizza shop employee says, “Sorry about the wait. How can I help you?”

“Yes, hi,” I say in a breathless voice. “I wanted to order a pizza.”

“Well, you’ve called the right place,” the employee says with a chuckle. “What do you want?”

“Errrm…”

I hesitate because I’ve completely forgotten what the pizza was called, and I'm lost in ecstasy as Ash swirls his tongue around my clit. I lift the menu up and blink a couple of times at it as I struggle to focus.

"Yes, I wanted a large Verdura with garlic bread." I spot the desserts on the menu and say, "Ooh." It's a half-moan because Ash reaches a hand up and into my bra to play with my nipple, but I play it off as though it's just from what I saw as I say, "Can I get two cannolis as well?"

"Sure. They're really good."

I swallow heavily and try not to pant because I'm ridiculously close to orgasm, and I manage to get out, "They sound it."

"Okay, so one large Verdura pizza, a garlic bread, and two cannolis. Is that right?"

"Yes," I breathe out.

"Is this for delivery?"

"Yes."

I've lost the ability to function, and Ash is driving me wild. My orgasm crashes over me, and I bite my lip hard to stop myself from screaming out. I clutch Ash's shoulder and dig my fingers into his skin to try and tether myself to something as my body shakes, and he continues to eat me out.

"And what address are we delivering to?" The voice in my ear sounds like it's coming from the end of a long tunnel.

I can't answer because I know if I open my mouth, I'm going to scream Ash's name instead of his address. I can't stop myself from grinding my hips against his mouth, and I wish it was his cock inside me instead of his fingers.

"Hello? Did you have the address?"

I draw on every reserve of strength that I have and the practice from years of Dante training me not to react to sexual pleasure, to utter a single word. "Yes."

"Great, what is it?"

I blow out a breath of air because Ash is not giving me any relief, and I grit my teeth as I manage to give Ash's address through stilted speech as another orgasm threatens to hit me.

"Excellent. We'll see you in half an hour."

"Thanks." I hit the red button to end the call, and I drop Ash's phone next to me as I give in to the pleasure he's giving me when my second orgasm hits. "Fuck, Ash. Yes, that's fucking good."

I thrust my fingers into his golden locks. He looks up at me, and his stunning blue eyes look into mine for a few seconds before I close my eyes, throw my head back, and ride out the last of my orgasm.

Once my body has stopped quaking, Ash pulls his fingers out of me and moves my thong back into place. I open my eyes and watch him do it, then he sits on the sofa next to me.

I take his hand and raise it to my mouth, where I clean the two fingers he fucked me with, and I'm satisfied as hell when he moans as I do.

I remember Logan doing this to Nate and the effect it had on him when he did. So I try to replicate that, sucking Ash's fingers as though they're his stiff erection, and I'm trying to get him to blow down my throat.

"Oh god, Lexi. I want your mouth on my cock."

I swirl my tongue around the tips of his fingers, then push them as far into my mouth as they'll go while I keep up my suction on them.

Finally, I pop his fingers out of my mouth and grin at him. "Do you?"

Ash takes my hand and places it on his rock-hard cock. "I definitely do."

"Too bad you got me to order pizza. We couldn't possibly risk me giving you a blow job in case it arrived early."

He stares at me for a few seconds, and the air around us crackles with sexual tension. I don't know what he's going to do, but I'm surprised when he bursts into laughter.

"Goddammit. I honestly can't tell who's teasing who anymore. You're driving me nuts, Lexi."

I can't help but laugh with him, and I climb onto his lap to straddle him. "You gave me a fucking orgasm while I ordered pizza."

"And you displayed your pussy for me after you refused to take off your underwear. Can you really blame me?"

I lower my head to kiss him, and he wraps his arms around me, holding me tight while we kiss. I'm still so incredibly turned on, and I'm having a great night with him.

"Okay, truce?" I ask him when our kiss ends. "We can watch a TV show or something while we wait for the pizza and no more tormenting each other until after we've eaten."

"Truce," Ash agrees with a grin.

"Let's kiss on it," I suggest, and Ash puts his hand on the back of my head and pulls me back down to kiss him again.

Our tongues intertwine, and Ash's cock is hard underneath me while my pussy aches for him to sheath himself inside me. I moan softly into his mouth as I think about how easy it would be for him to fuck me right now.

Ash breaks our kiss and places his hands around my waist before easily setting me down on the sofa next to him. "Okay, that's a deal. If we don't stop now, we'll be fucking when the pizza arrives."

I smirk as Ash turns on the TV. He starts a comedy show for us to watch as he puts his arm around my shoulders and pulls me into his embrace. I rest my head on his chest, and we laugh together as we watch it and wait for our food to arrive.

My senses are filled with Ash, and I can't help but remain aware of him as we laugh together. His scent is arousing, earthy, and masculine, along with the smell that I associate with sex now. When he laughs, it reverberates in his chest, and occasionally, he will squeeze me tightly or drop a kiss on my head. It's an enjoyable way to pass the time before our food arrives, and when it does, I'm saddened that I have to let Ash go to get it.

I remain hidden from sight as he goes to the apartment door to pay for the pizza after he buzzes the delivery guy up. I can't hear what they're saying, but heat rushes to my cheeks as Ash laughs with the man while he pays. I know it's unlikely this is the person I spoke to on the phone, but I'm still embarrassed at the memory of having an orgasm while I ordered. I wonder if they knew and told everyone about it, and the thought of it causes my pussy to ache.

Ash appears with the food, and I ask, "Oh my god, did he say something about my phone call?"

"What? No?" Ash raises his eyebrows at me, then grins. "Do you wish he had?"

My cheeks burn with heat, and I shake my head. "No. I just heard you laughing."

"Oh. He was a fan. When I paid, he asked if I could sign the receipt." Ash sets the food on the coffee table, then sits on the sofa and strokes my nipple through the lace of my bra. "I should've told him that whoever took our order was on the phone while I made Lexi Sullivan come for me."

My breathing is shallow, and I complain, "Hey, I thought we agreed on no teasing until after dinner."

"You're right."

Ash lowers his mouth to my breast and nips my taut nipple with his teeth through the fabric of my bra. I moan softly as a shock of arousal darts straight from my nipple to my pussy.

"I blame your glorious breasts. I can't help but touch them or get my mouth around them." He smirks at me, and I clench my thighs against my arousal.

"I see. Well, why don't you get us plates and drinks, so we can finish this meal and you can finish in me." I lean forward and reach a hand up to stroke his cock in his jeans.

Ash groans and repeats, "I thought we agreed on no teasing until after dinner."

I continue to stroke his cock and grin at him. "Did we? I'm having trouble remembering."

"I'm about five seconds from bending you over the back of that sofa and fucking you right here because pizza is better cold anyway," he growls.

"Mmm, sounds like fun. You should definitely do that." The pizza smells amazing, though, and my stomach chooses this moment to rumble.

Ash laughs, "Okay. You clearly need to eat before I fuck you."

I'm disappointed, but also not because Ash serves up the pizza, and it's just as good as it smells. We continue watching the comedy show, and after we've finished eating, we wait a little while before having our dessert, during which time I relax back into Ash's embrace again.

We watch another episode of the show after we finish our meal, and Ash gently strokes my arm with his hand. His fingers brush the swell of my breast, and I lower my hand to his thigh. I stroke it as well, coming closer and closer to the bulge in his jeans. The air around us is thick with sexual tension, and I can't focus on the show anymore. I'm constantly on edge as I wait for his next touch of my breast, and I'm filled with the desire for us to move on from this.

An entire episode passes with us doing this, but by the end of it, I'm rubbing his cock, and his hand is fully on my breast and stroking my nipple with his thumb. Ash kisses me as the episode ends, and his tongue dances with mine.

His hand drops to my waist, and his fingers slide beneath the waistband of my panties to find my wet clit. I spread my legs a little wider to give him better access, and he breaks our kiss before he lifts his head and watches me.

"Come for me, baby. You're so sexy when you orgasm."

"Yes, Ash," I moan as waves of pleasure flood through me.

When my orgasm hits, Ash watches me through hooded eyes while I moan his name over and over before he finally pulls his fingers out of my underwear and licks them clean before he kisses me. I can taste my juices on his tongue, and it's so erotic and sexy. I can't wait for him to finally fuck me.

He breaks our kiss and says, "Get on your knees and face the back of the sofa." I do as instructed and bite my lip as Ash says, "Such a fucking great view. I'll be back in a second. I just need to get lube."

I watch him walk away toward his bedroom and admire the view of his ass in his jeans. When he comes back, though, he's stark naked and holding a bottle of lube. I let out a low moan at the sight of him. He's gorgeous, with his golden hair and stunning blue eyes, every rippling muscle on display, and his thick erection ready to fuck me.

Ash stops at the back of the sofa, takes my chin between his forefinger and thumb, and explores my mouth with his tongue. "Do you like what you see, Lexi Sullivan?"

"Fuck, yes. You look like a Norse god, sent to Earth to fuck me stupid," I tell him honestly.

"I see. Well, I'd better fulfill my mission then."

He moves around behind me, and one of his hands strokes my ass cheek for a few seconds before he pulls my soaked underwear down. It drops to my knees, and I don't bother getting it off properly. I'm too eager for Ash to fuck me again.

He unclips my bra, and I do slide that off, which allows my breasts to hang free as I rest my elbows on the back of the sofa again. Ash reaches around to twist one of my nipples, and I gasp as my arousal heightens. My pussy is so wet that my juice drips down my thigh.

I gasp when Ash's tongue traces up my inner thigh the same way he did in the car at the airport. This time, he doesn't stop at my pussy and instead trails his tongue up to my clit, which causes me to moan his name.

He pulls his head back and murmurs, "You're so fucking tasty."

He places his hands on my hips, and I'm surprised when he slams his cock into me. I love the feeling of him filling my pussy, but he's told me repeatedly that he's taking my ass tonight.

"I thought we were going to do anal," I tell him around a moan as he pounds into me.

"We are, but I couldn't resist shoving my cock into that juicy cunt of yours," he growls.

I gasp loudly at his words, and my pussy clenches around his cock.

Ash chuckles and leans forward, his breath hot against my ear as he tells me, "There's that reaction I enjoy so much. Just think about the fact I'm going to be fucking your ass soon, too." My pussy clenches again, and Ash groans, "God, you're hot. I want you to come on my cock again before I do, though."

He reaches around to find my clit and rubs it again while he fucks me. It doesn't take long before I'm doing exactly that, and I come apart around his thick cock.

"Ashton," I moan loudly.

He leans forward and kisses my back before he straightens up again. Cold lube drops onto my asshole while Ash holds himself buried inside me. He pushes two fingers into my ass while he uses his other hand to rub my clit, and I moan in ecstasy. After a while, he drops more lube on my ass and pushes a third finger in.

He fucks me with three fingers for a while before he asks, "Are you ready for this, baby?"

"Yes. Fuck, yes," I moan.

I'm not at all ready for it, though, because as soon as he starts to push his cock into me, I can practically see how thick and hard it is. I panic, and my asshole tightens up.

Ash pulls himself back and says, "Relax, baby. You can take me. I know you can."

He rubs my clit again, and I force myself to relax as he puts pressure on my ass with his cock. I pant for breath and bite my lip as he enters me inch by inch. When I finally feel his muscled thighs pressed against the back of mine and my ass cheeks touch his stomach, I can barely believe I've managed to take him.

He rubs my ass with his right hand while he continues to stroke my clit with his left as he slowly pulls himself back out again. "Fuck yes. You're so tight, and fucking your ass is so hot."

I can't manage a response. All of my senses are aflame, and I'm focused on staying relaxed as he pushes himself in again. He fucks me slowly, pulling himself out and pushing in at a snail's pace while I become accustomed to his size and girth in my ass.

After quite a few slow thrusts, Ash picks up the pace. He holds my hips and begins to fuck me properly. He doesn't go too fast at first, but once he's successfully pumped into me a few times, he starts to thrust roughly into me much faster. I gasp, and I'm lost to the experience of him fucking my ass. It's mildly painful but far more pleasurable, and I rest my cheek on the back of the sofa as I reach between my legs to rub my clit while we fuck.

I rub myself to orgasm multiple times before Ash buries himself in my ass and empties his load in me. He collapses forward and kisses my back before he straightens up.

"God, that was so fucking good, Lexi." He squeezes my ass cheek. "Your ass is almost as good as your pussy."

He pulls out of me, and we head quickly to the bathroom to clean up. Ash and I spend a long time making out under the warm spray instead of cleaning ourselves. When we finally do, we get out and dry off before we head to his bed together.

I'm exhausted, and I curl up against Ash in his bed. I can't help but think of Cassie now that I'm not distracted by playing with him, and my body tenses up.

"Are you okay, baby?" Ash asks in the darkness.

"Yeah. Just thinking about Cassie."

Ash sighs and is silent for a moment before he says, "I know it's easier said than done, but try not to. Just be here with me and forget about her for now."

I nod my head. "Okay, I'll try."

I turn my face up to find Ashton Woodford's lips in the darkness and try my best to forget about his ex-girlfriend.

Chapter Thirteen

Dracula's Shot Glass

I wake on Saturday morning in Ash's arms, with a knot of fear in my stomach and nausea threatening to overwhelm me. All I can think of is the hundred grand that we're going to give Cassie today. I had nightmares last night about her taking the money and selling the story anyway.

I'm so distracted by thoughts of Cassie that it isn't until Ash stirs that I fully realize whose arms I'm wrapped in. He doesn't wake, so I take this moment to just look at his face, beautiful in repose. He's so handsome, and I love him so much. I'm glad we've added this new aspect to our friendship.

It's a little strange spending the entire night with him alone, but I had a good time. I want to get home to my men, though. I think Ash will probably come with me. He'll want to be there when we see Cassie. At least, and I hope he will. I want us all together as a team to face the opponent who's threatening us.

He opens his eyes and blinks at me a few times before he smiles and yawns. "Morning."

"Morning."

He puts his arm around me and pulls me over to rest my head on his chest before he closes his eyes again. I force myself to relax and enjoy the moment with my friend, despite the butterflies tumbling around my stomach. I try to reach for my phone on the side table without disturbing Ash, but it's out of my reach.

As I roll away to get it, he tightens his grip on me. "Don't go yet."

"I wasn't," I laugh. "I was just trying to get my phone."

He loosens his hold on me, and I swipe my phone open as I lie back down with him.

"What time is it?" he asks, his eyes closed again.

"Seven-thirty."

"There's a seven-thirty in the morning now?" Ash groans, and I laugh.

"Yes, there is."

He falls silent, and I open my messages to Dante.

Just woke up. Ash is still sleeping. I'll be home soon.

I scroll through my social media feed and like a picture that Heather has posted of Harrison and her at a club with April and Julia last night.

As I'm writing a comment, a message from Dante shows on the screen.

Okay. Will see you when you get here. Love you.

I smile at the message. I can't wait to get home to the three of them, but I can barely stand the nerves that seem to increase with every minute that passes.

I just want to be done with Cassandra Foster and never see her again. I hope to every higher power there might be that today is the last day I have to be in her presence.

I don't know what gives my feelings away, but Ash says, "Stop stressing, Lexi."

His eyes are still closed, and I chuckle. "How do you know I'm stressing?"

"I've known you for a long time. I would've guessed you would be stressing even if I couldn't feel that your body was wound as tight as a spring." He opens his eyes and gives me a reassuring smile.

"It's going to be okay."

I bite my lip and sigh. "What if it's not, though?"

"Then we'll work out how to get through it. We're all in this together." He wraps me tightly in his embrace and kisses the top of my head. "What time do you want to go home?"

"As soon as I can, please. I was kind of just waiting for you to wake up so I could leave."

"Ouch." He says it in a jovial tone, so I know he's not actually offended.

"Yeah, I just had such a terrible time with you last night." I lower my hand to his stiff morning erection and stroke his cock with my hand. "Which is obviously the reason I can't wait to leave."

Ash moans as he reaches between my legs to find my dripping wet pussy and starts to rub my clit. "I thought that went without saying."

I thumb the head of his cock as I reach the tip of it before I continue to stroke him. I'm satisfied by his moan, and I can't help but gasp when he uses the arm that's still around my shoulders to reach down and tweak my nipple.

"This is definitely terrible. You giving me a hand job first thing in the morning isn't amazing at all." Ash pants for breath as he says it.

He claims my lips with his as he continues to rub my clit and play with my nipple. Waves of pleasure roll through me, and I moan into his mouth as I stroke him faster. Ash matches my speed, and I break our kiss and flop back to look at the ceiling before I close my eyes and focus on the pleasure he's giving me.

My orgasm hits me, and I moan, "Fuck, yes, Ash."

I struggle to keep my rhythm as my body shakes, but I pick it up again as my orgasm passes. Ash doesn't stop playing with my breast, but he thrusts his fingers into my pussy, and I can't stop myself from thrusting my hips up to meet his fingers.

"God, you're so fucking hot."

I pump his cock faster and bite my lip as I look at him and say, "Come for me."

"I'm more than happy to do that for you."

He kisses me again, and he thrusts his tongue into my mouth roughly. He twists my nipple painfully at the same moment his cock jerks in my hand, and he grunts as he comes.

I break our kiss to pull my head back and watch him orgasm. He's beautiful, and it's so fucking erotic to see his 'O' face that another orgasm rips through me. His hand has stilled in its movement, so I use my spare one to take hold of his wrist and push his fingers deeper inside me.

I clench my thighs tight around his hand as my interior muscles do the same around his fingers, and I scream his name. My body shakes again, and when my orgasm ends, the room is filled with the sound of our pants for breath.

"Nothing like a little mutual masturbation in the morning," Ash chuckles.

I kiss him quickly and nod. "Fuck, yes. There's just one thing I need to do now."

I push him onto his back, and he pulls his fingers out of me. As I throw the covers off him, I lower my mouth toward his crotch.

"Someone has to clean up this mess, and I guess that someone has to be me." I grin at him.

"Me, as well," he laughs and makes a show of licking his fingers clean as I look up at him. "Tasty."

His cum has squirted across his taut stomach and up to in between his pectoral muscles. I can also see some glistening on the tip of his cock, so I start by swirling my tongue around that.

Ash groans and thrusts a hand into my hair as I do. I move on to the trail of salty cum where it starts at his pubic bone and follow it up to where it ends in a thick pool between his pecs. His skin is warm and smooth over his hard muscles, and when I've ensured he's been licked completely clean, I lift my head.

"Tasty."

"Have I mentioned how hot you are?" He raises an eyebrow at me.

"I'm not sure. How hot am I?" I try to keep a straight face, but

I can't stop the smile that plays on my lips.

"So hot that I can't believe I haven't fucked you sooner. It's so weird getting to fuck you now," he admits.

I laugh. "Yeah, it's kind of weird waking up in bed with you."

"Are you complaining?"

I sit up and take in his glorious body. His cock is softening now, but it's still thick, and I know how good it would feel inside me. His face is beautiful and having every inch of his muscular body exposed for me to look at is spectacular.

"Definitely not. I'll never complain about getting to play with you. As far as friendships go, I think this is the best kind of friendship." I grin at him.

Ash raises a hand to my breast to hold it as he softly thumbs my nipple, and a dart of arousal shoots to my pussy.

"You're one hell of a friend, Lexi." He pulls my face to his, and our tongues intertwine as we kiss for a minute or so before he ends it. "I'm sorry about all this shit that's happening, but I'll never be sorry for dumping Cassie."

At the sound of her name, everything comes rushing back, and my body stiffens again. Ash's body is stiff as well, though, and I realize how stressed he is about it. He's been so strong and supportive of me throughout the call on Thursday and the meeting yesterday that I hadn't noticed how concerned he was until now.

"It'll be okay, Ash. As you said, whatever happens, we'll all get through it together. We have each other, and that's what's important because no matter what happens, Cassie can't take that from us."

He swallows and nods. "You're right. Okay, let's get you home so we can deal with my fucking ex. I also need to call my bank manager about transferring a hundred thousand dollars to Logan."

"What? You're going to pay the money?" I gasp.

"She's my fucking ex. I should be the one that's out the cash she's extorting from us." He shrugs casually.

I frown at him and purse my lips as I shake my head. "I doubt Logan will agree to that."

"I don't plan on telling him until it's done." Ash shrugs, then narrows his eyes at me. "Don't you tell him, either."

I shake my head. "I don't agree to that. You need to discuss it with the guys. We're a team, remember?" I kiss him softly to take the sting out of my refusal to agree to what he's asked of me. "No team wants one member to burden the entire load, no matter how badly he feels about his ex being a complete shrew."

He sighs and looks away from me before he says quietly, "I do feel like it's all my fault. If I'd broken up with her when she first started trashing you guys, she wouldn't have been able to get those photos."

"She'd still have known, though, and we told her because we trusted her, too. At the end of the day, it's nobody's fault but Cassie's. Come on, let's get ready and go home. I feel like I need backup to convince you I'm right," I joke.

I'm relieved when Ash laughs and kisses me again. We shower, and I pull my clothes from yesterday back on, but I leave my underwear in my handbag as we head to the kitchen for breakfast.

Ash and I talk as we eat toast together. Neither of us mentions Cassie, but the topic hangs in the air around us, and I can't help but notice the signs of his stress now that I've realized he is. He shifts in his chair a lot, pushes his toast around on his plate, and stares out the window while he thrusts his fingers through his hair during lulls in the conversation.

I want to soothe his frustration, but I don't know how because I can't make Cassie *not* blackmail us. All I can do is try to distract him a little, so once we're in his car and are headed home, I smile at him.

"You told me about times you thought about fucking me. Want to know about some times I thought about fucking you?" I suggest.

Ash grips the steering wheel tighter, and his eyebrows fly up as he darts a glance at me. "Uh, yeah?"

I can already think clearly of a time I fantasized about it. "Do you remember your first tour? We were at a hotel in some city in Texas. Dallas, I think it was. Anyway, nobody else wanted to go swimming, so it was just you and me. We had a race from one end of the pool to the other."

He grins at me and nods. "I won, but you tried *so* hard to beat me. I didn't win by much."

"Right." I smile back at him. "So, we were hanging on to the edge of the pool and trying to catch our breath. All I could think about was wrapping my legs around your waist and fucking you."

"I had no idea," Ash gasps. "Were there any other times you can think of?"

"Remember the same holiday you told me about?" He nods, and I continue, "One night, Dante and Logan went to bed early while you, Nate, and I stayed up drinking. Nate passed out, and it was just the two of us talking and drinking for hours."

Ash pulls up at a set of lights and turns to look at me as he says in a voice thick with lust, "I remember that night."

"All I could think about was how much I wanted you to push me down on the sofa and fuck me. I went back to our room and fucked Dante while I pretended it was you."

I can remember fucking Dante in the dark and doing my best not to let Ash's name fall from my lips after I'd spent all evening with him.

"Fucking hell, Lexi," Ash whispers.

"I know. I felt terrible for it," I admit. "It was so hot, though."

Ash reaches across and pulls my skirt up to my hips, exposing my pussy to his view before he takes off from the lights.

"Have you told Dante about any of this?" Ash asks as he slowly rubs my wet clit in circles, and I moan softly.

I think about the night in question and the way I threw myself at Dante as soon as I got to bed. He'd asked me at the time, 'What's got you so worked up, Angel?' and I'd told him I was just horny.

"I think he knows. He's always known me better than I know myself."

I spread my legs wider and bite my lip as I look at Ash's profile while he fingers me. I've only told him two of the times I've thought about fucking him, but I've probably fantasized about him as much in the past as I've done it about Nate and Logan.

Ash pulls up at another light and leans over to kiss me passionately. When the light turns green, he ends our kiss and pulls my skirt back down to my knees.

"I'm sure the guys will appreciate you being horny when we get there." He looks over to smirk at me as I pant for breath.

"Not fucking fair," I groan.

"I'm led to believe you spend a large amount of your time waiting for orgasms," Ash teases me.

"Yes, I do." I pout, then remember something from yesterday. "Don't think I've forgotten that I need to pay you back for snapping me with the towel."

He chuckles and says, "Noted. I'll live in fear."

"As you should."

He's not my Dom, so I grin to myself and flip my skirt back up as I spread my legs again and lower my fingers to rub myself.

"Ash," I moan as I bite my lip.

He raises an eyebrow at me. "Are you trying to make me crash this car?"

"No," I gasp as I increase the tempo at which I stroke myself. "I'm trying to give myself the orgasm you so rudely refused to give me."

I reach into my top to pull and tweak my nipples as my ecstasy builds. Ash reaches his hand across to my pussy, and I swat it away before I continue masturbating.

"You've lost pussy privileges for the rest of this trip," I tease him, even though we're practically at the apartment. "If you're not careful, it'll be off-limits for the rest of the day."

"What about your cunt, though?" he growls in the sexiest voice I've ever heard from him, and I gasp.

I throw my head back and close my eyes as my orgasm hits. My body shakes, and I moan in ecstasy when I come. I pant for breath as I continue to stroke myself through my climax, and I only open my eyes when the car comes to a stop.

Ash asks, "Do I have pussy privileges again?"

"I suppose our trip has technically ended," I concede.

He unbuckles my seatbelt and pulls me over so I can straddle him. He undoes his jeans, and I lift myself as he also lifts his ass to shove them and his briefs down enough to release his cock.

He pulls me down to sheath himself inside me as he kisses me. Our tongues dance together as we fuck. The steering wheel is hard against my back in the cramped space, but I love that he couldn't wait until we got upstairs to do this.

I grind myself on his cock as he fills me completely and breaks my kiss before he yanks my top and bra down under my breasts.

Ash takes one in his mouth as he plays with the other, and it's my undoing. I tip into orgasm again, and my pussy clenches around his cock as waves of pleasure crash over me.

"Fuck, Ash. Oh, god."

"Mmm, yes. Come on my cock, baby."

He lifts his head to say this, and I don't know what takes me over, but I lean down and bite his bottom lip as I fuck him through my orgasm. Ash groans as his fingers dig into my hips. He pulls me roughly down onto him a final time and holds me down while his cock jerks, and he spills his seed inside me.

I smash my lips against his to kiss him, and the coppery taste of blood hits my tongue. I break our kiss to look at him, and, sure enough, his bottom lip is already starting to swell from my bite, with the inside of his lip bleeding.

"Fuck. I broke the skin." I cringe as I look at it.

Ash raises a hand to his lip and wipes it before he looks at the blood on his hand. He flips the car visor down and checks his lip in the mirror.

"Are you a fucking vampire or something?" He laughs and shakes his head as he flips the visor back up.

"I guess we'll find out soon," I joke. "Let's get upstairs so you can ice it and try to reduce the swelling."

I reach over and grab my bag to pull my panties out of it. I slide back to my seat and wriggle into them while trying my best not to make a mess.

Ash does his pants back up and wipes at some blood on his lip before he laughs. "Are we even for the towel now?"

"I think we probably are." I cringe as I look at it. "I'm so sorry. I didn't mean to bite so hard."

Ash leans over and reaches under my skirt. He cups my pussy with his hand while he looks into my eyes. His scent mixed with the smell of blood overwhelms me, but he's so sexy, and the warm touch of his hand on my pussy causes me to gasp.

"Well, if you keep my cum inside you while we meet with my ex, I might accept your apology." He smirks at me.

"Do you have any idea how fucked up that is?" I raise an eyebrow at him.

"That I'll be meeting her while my lip is swollen and bleeding from your bite and you're full of my cum? I have some idea. It's *kind of* funny, though. I mean, I'd literally never have fucked you if she hadn't been so paranoid that she started to try to poison me against you."

He falls silent for a second and looks out the car window at the parking garage. When he speaks again, his voice is strange.

"I don't know. I guess it's also a reminder that life is better even though this shit is happening and that we're all a team."

He turns back to look at me, and his crystal blue eyes pierce through me. I blink at him and nod before I swallow heavily.

"Okay. I'll do it."

Chapter Fourteen

Belonging

As soon as I enter the apartment, I know my men are all here. There's something in the air that tells me, along with the physical signs like Logan's car keys hanging with ours nearby.

Sure enough, as we near the living room, music starts playing. It's a new song that I haven't heard before, not even the one from the other week. The music is rougher, and I can tell they're taking out their frustration in the music they're writing.

I listen as I dump my bag near the door and head to the kitchen to take an ice block out of the freezer.

"Here you go," I say to Ash as I hand it to him after I wrap it in a wet tea towel.

"Thanks."

He presses it to his swollen lip, and I shift as I remember the cum inside me. His amused chuckle sounds out from behind me as I lead the way to the living room, and my cheeks heat as we walk into the room.

The three men are positioned around the room, and my heart swells at the sight of them. Nate sits in an armchair, and his dark hair has flopped into his eyes as he sings. Dante has leaned forward on the sofa, and the corded muscles in his forearms flex as he strums the guitar. Logan is relaxed on the other end and is tapping a beat on one leg and the arm of the sofa.

Ash strides into the room as he listens and picks up the sheet music from between Logan and Dante. He drops between them, sets the music on his lap, and reads it as the guys continue to sing.

I lean against the wall and watch them with a smile. Despite the clear anger in the tone and lyrics of the music, the men making the music are all so beautiful and magnificent.

They sing about some unknown threat circling them and binding them closer together. A part of me hates the idea of Cassie holding enough importance that she's inspired a song, but at least their feelings on her are clear.

When they reach the end of the song, I smile at them. "You guys have been busy."

"We had to do something while we waited for you, Sexy." Nate gives me a charming smile, then raises an eyebrow at Ash. "What the fuck happened to you?"

Ash lowers the ice pack to reveal his swollen lip. It's stopped bleeding, but it's puffed up badly, and there are two obvious teeth marks.

"Lexi happened."

Three heads whip toward me, and Nate bursts into laughter while both Dante and Logan frown at me.

"You bit Ash?" Logan's mouth is a tight, flat line as he asks the question.

I cringe and nod my confirmation, which causes Nate to laugh harder as he says, "That's hot."

"Right before we have a meeting with Cassie, Angel?"

Dante's voice is cold and harsh, his shoulders are tense, and his displeasure is obvious. Nate's laughter cuts off as he clearly realizes the impact this could have on what's about to happen.

"Shit," he breathes out. "Bad time to get freaky, Sexy."

"I know. I'm sorry, guys."

I look at the floor and wonder if either Dante or Logan will punish me for this. Nobody speaks, though, and there's a heavy silence in the room. I hate that I fucked up by biting Ash when we were fucking, and I know there's no way to fix it before Cassie comes over today.

Ash finally breaks the silence. "It's fine. I'll cover for Lexi."

"I had no doubt that you didn't plan to tell her who bit you," Dante scoffs.

Another silence falls, and I worry my bottom lip between my teeth before I look between Dante and Logan. "Am I going to be punished for this?"

Logan's eyebrows raise, and his gaze snaps to Dante's before he turns back to me. "I didn't plan on it. I told you to enjoy yourself, and what you do with Ash is between you two. I'm only mad because it might fuck things up with Cassie."

He opens his arms to me, and I take the unspoken invitation. I walk over to him and fall into his embrace. He wraps his arms around me and kisses the top of my head as he squeezes me tight.

"As Nate said, it was a bad time to get freaky, but I won't punish you for that."

Logan turns my face up to his and kisses me. Our tongues intertwine, and when our kiss ends, I smile at him as he pushes me off his lap and toward Dante. I head over to my husband, and when he takes me in my arms, I get the usual sense of being home that I get whenever I'm with him. His warm embrace is like a calming blanket being placed over me, and I look up into his chocolate brown eyes. His concern and frustration are obvious, though, and I'm unsure if he will punish me or not.

"My instinct is to punish you, Angel." Dante sighs deeply. "But Logan is right. I wasn't even the one who told you to stay the night. It would be unfair of me to punish you for this. As one of your partners, however, I am within my rights to be annoyed that you've risked Cassie guessing you're involved with Ash now."

"We're not involved. We just play together," I point out.

Dante's jaw immediately tightens, and he growls, "I don't want to argue semantics with you. You know what I mean, and I doubt that Cassie would care about the definition, either."

"You're right. I'm sorry." I frown at him, and there's an awkward silence in the room.

Dante hugs me and gives me a short kiss before he says in a low voice, "I love you, Lexi, but this wasn't smart. You can go see Nate now."

I'm mildly relieved to move over to Nate. The tension is rolling off Dante, and I'm glad I got away without punishment. Right now, though, Nate is the safest of the three of them. He can't punish me at all, plus he's sitting back in the armchair and looks relaxed, unlike Dante and Logan.

"Are you mad at me, too?" I ask as I take a seat on his lap.

Nate immediately snakes one arm around my waist while he slides the other up under my skirt to stroke my inner thigh as he pulls me back against him.

"Nah. God knows I'm the king of bad sexual decisions. It's just another example of how fucking hot you are."

His fingers glance against the edge of my underwear, and I gasp as he reaches underneath and skates them across my clit. His other hand slides up from my waist to pull and tweak my nipple through my top. Despite their moods, both Logan and Dante watch us from the sofa while Ash moves to sit in another armchair.

Nate lowers his fingers to push them into my pussy, and he falters. I turn my face to his, and he frowns at me for a second before he pushes his fingers in and out of me a few times. He moves his lips down to nip my earlobe with his teeth, and I moan loudly.

"Are you just wet, or are you full of cum?" Nate murmurs in a low tone in my ear.

I look over at my Doms, but I'm pretty sure they couldn't hear the question.

I turn my head to kiss Nate, and our tongues dance together for a few moments before I whisper back to him, "The latter, but now might not be the time for everyone to know."

Nate pulls his fingers out of me and pushes his fingers into my mouth as he says at a normal volume, "Taste yourself, Lexi."

I look at Ash as I suck his salty cum combined with my juices from Nate's fingers. Then Nate maneuvers me around to straddle him. The bulge in his jeans presses against my pussy and makes me ache for him to fill me.

From behind me, Logan growls, "Let's get Cassie here for me to pay her a hundred grand. Then she can fuck off so I can play with my toy."

I shudder at his words and the obvious desire in his voice. Nate lifts his hands to my breasts and thumbs my nipples through my top as he captures my lips with his again.

"About that. I think I should pay the money. She's my ex, so this is my fault," Ash says.

Nate pauses the movement of his thumbs and breaks our kiss before he turns to look at Ash. "What? No. You don't have to do that."

"Of course not," Dante agrees.

"Well, I should pay something," Ash objects.

"You can pay twenty-five grand if it makes you feel better. A quarter of it is fair, but I agree with the others that there's no way we can let you cover the whole amount," Logan tells him.

Nate presses his lips against mine again, and I lose the thread of the conversation as he starts playing with my breasts again. I wind my arms around his neck and kiss him back with an equal amount of passion. He moves one hand down to my ass and squeezes it as he pulls my top down under my breasts. He rolls my nipple between his fingers, and I moan into his mouth as waves of pleasure roll through me.

He breaks our kiss and lowers his head to take my other breast in his mouth. His tongue is warm and wet as he swirls it around my stiff nipple. I grind myself against his erection and close my eyes as I pant for breath. Nate squeezes my ass again, then trails his hand around to slide it between us and under the waistband of my panties.

I come apart when his fingers find my clit, and I grip onto his shoulders as my orgasm rips through me. "Nate, fuck yes."

Nat removes his mouth from my breast, and I whimper at the loss of contact as he says, "I love watching you come, Sexy."

I open my eyes to see him watching me, and I pant for breath as my body shakes. He kisses my neck and up along my jaw before he captures my lips with his again.

Nate ends our kiss and pulls his hand out of my underwear, then puts his fingers in his own mouth to clean them. I inhale sharply as he does because it's so fucking hot to know he's tasting Ash as well as me.

"Tasty," he murmurs with a smirk at me.

I blink at him a couple of times before I kiss him again. He tastes of my pussy juice, but there's also the salty tang of Ash's cum as well. I thrust my fingers into his hair as we kiss, and when I pull my lips away from him, we both pant for breath.

"That was hot," I murmur.

"You're welcome for the orgasm," he says with a grin.

I laugh and turn to face the others. All three have bulges in their pants, and I want to fuck them, but I told Ash I'd keep his cum inside me during the meeting, so I clear my throat.

"I guess someone has to call Cassie. Should it be me?"

"If you're finished with Nate, I guess it should," Dante says in an amused tone.

I stand up and wobble a little as I get to my feet.

Ash chuckles and says, "Lexi's orgasm-drunk."

"Fuck you," I laugh at him.

"Already did that in the car, but maybe later."

I head to the entry to get my phone out of my bag with the sound of the guys' laughter ringing out behind me. I unlock it as I walk back and take a seat on Nate's lap again. They're quiet, and I navigate to Cassie's name in my contacts and call her.

My heart pounds in my chest as the phone rings in my ear, and I can barely breathe as I wait for her to answer. A huge part of me hopes the call just rings out.

Unfortunately, after a few seconds, her voice comes through the line. "Hello?"

"Cassie. It's Lexi. We're ready for you to come over and get this check."

"Okay. I'll see you soon." Her voice is cool and even.

"Great," I manage to say before the line goes dead. "Fuuuuck," I breathe out as I lock my phone and set it aside. "I can't wait for this to be over."

The air in the room is thick with heavy tension, and Logan breathes out a slow breath of air before he nods. "Me, too."

My body is wound tight with tension, and it feels as though every minute that passes ratchets that tension up another notch. I go to my bedroom and change my outfit, so Cassie doesn't see me wearing the same clothes I wore to Ash's place yesterday.

I head back to the living room, sit on Nate's lap, and he strokes my thigh softly over the dress I've put on. It's comforting, but I still twist and untwist the hem of the dress. While I was out of the room, Logan went to get the check for Cassie. I can't stop my gaze from wandering to where it sits on the coffee table as we wait for her to arrive.

By the time Cassie knocks on the apartment door after she's buzzed up, I'm concerned that I might vomit in the middle of the living room. Dante goes to let her in, and when he walks into the living room with Cassie behind him, I drop my dress and smooth it out over my knees. I don't want her to see how she's managed to affect me.

"Hello, everyone," she says in a stiff voice.

Dante takes his seat back on the sofa, and nobody responds to Cassie. She scans the room and scowls when she sees me sitting on Nate's lap.

Logan stands and picks up the check, then walks over to Cassie. "You can have this as soon as you give me your phone."

Cassie's eyes widen before she glares at him. "What the fuck? No. You're not having my fucking phone."

"Then you're not having this check and we'll deal with the consequences. Or you can give me your phone and buy a new one with the hundred thousand dollars you're extorting from us."

His voice is ice-cold and his eyes are so dark that they're black. She stares at him for a few seconds before she pulls out her phone and hands it to Logan.

"Are there any copies anywhere?" he demands.

"No," she says in a sulky voice.

"You'd better not be lying," Logan growls as he glares at her. "Unlock it."

She does as instructed and he flicks through the phone for a minute or so before he holds it out to Cassie again.

"Put your password in so I can wipe the phone."

Cassie looks pissed, but she enters the password and hands the phone back to Logan. I'm completely numb as I watch this happen, I can't believe that this is happening right now.

Logan presses a button on the screen, then slips the phone into his pocket and holds the check out.

"Why can't I have it back if you've wiped it?" Cassie sulks.

"I don't trust you not to somehow restore it," he says, his jaw tight.

She takes the check and reads it before she frowns and looks up at him. "Why is this from you?"

"You got your hundred grand. Does it matter who pays it?"

She purses her lips and looks as though she might object, but instead, she says, "I suppose not."

Logan turns and walks back to the sofa, where he drops down next to Dante.

"Do you need someone to see you out?" Ash asks, his voice hard.

I turn to look at him at the same time that Cassie does. He has a scowl on his face, and his jaw is tight. The ice block is gone, but the swollen lip is obvious, and my gaze snaps to Cassie's to see her reaction.

She seems frozen as she stares at him. The hand holding the check drops to her side, and she strides over to stand in front of him. My breath catches in my throat, and Nate squeezes me tight. He presses his lips to my back in a kiss as I wait in horror to see how this plays out.

"What happened to you?" Cassie demands.

"I walked into a door."

Ash shrugs casually, and I have to hold back hysterical laughter because that excuse is not going to fly at all.

"Bullshit." Cassie turns her face to glare at me, and I keep my face neutral as she scrutinizes me before she looks back at Ash again. "Did you fuck her?"

"For fuck's sake, Cassandra," Ash growls. "This isn't cute. You're acting like a jealous girlfriend, but you're not my girlfriend, so you don't get to make demands of me. I'm single now, so I'll fuck whoever I want, whenever I want, and you don't get a say in it."

He turns to look at me, and I give him a tight smile. For a millisecond, the anger is gone as he looks at me, but then he turns back to glare at Cassie again.

"For the record, I was totally committed to you and probably would've married you if you hadn't shown me who you really are." Cassie gasps quietly when he says this before he considers, "But you did, so thanks for that. Anyway, you've successfully fucking blackmailed us for a hundred grand, and you've got your damn money, so do you need someone to see you out or not?"

There's silence for a few seconds before Cassie says in a quiet voice, "No, I know the way out. Goodbye, Ash."

We sit in silence as she turns and leaves. When the door to the apartment opens and slams shut, Dante holds his finger up to his lips and then walks out of the room.

When he comes back, he says, "Okay, I saw her waiting for the elevator. Given her behavior, I wouldn't have put it past her to hide and try to get more information."

"Good thinking," Logan says.

Another silence falls before Nate says, "Who wants to bet that's not the last we hear of her?"

I cringe at the words, but he's only voiced exactly what I've been worried about since Cassie sent me the pictures on Friday.

"Don't say that, Nate," I beg him. "I'm stressed enough as it is."

"Sorry, Sexy." He hugs me and kisses my cheek.

"Did we just make a big mistake?" Ash asks quietly.

I chew my bottom lip and shake my head at him. "If we did,

it's done now. Nothing we can do about it short of Logan canceling that check."

"If I did that, the story would be out before dinner." Logan sighs and shrugs. "I think that was our best shot at keeping her quiet. Now we have to hope she sticks to it."

I hate this so much. I hate that I have to rely on Cassandra Foster doing the right thing when I trust her about as far as I can throw her. I heave a deep sigh as I look out the windows to our right. As the guys talk about some apartments Anthony has sent through, my mind is full of worry. Nate starts massaging my shoulders, and I let out a soft sigh at the enjoyable feeling.

"You're so tense, Sexy. Let me help you relax," he murmurs.

He takes my hair and pushes it in front of my shoulders before he continues to massage them. He moves his hands down my back, kneading away the tension, and I close my eyes to focus on what he's doing. It's so good, and I let out a quiet moan.

"Is that good?" he chuckles.

"So good," I assure him.

"I'm glad."

He keeps going for another few minutes before he slides his hands around me and up to my breasts.

"You know. I'm led to believe that women hold a lot of tension in their breasts. So I should probably massage these, too."

I laugh, but it turns to a moan as he tweaks one of my nipples. I lean my head back on his shoulder and arch my back as I press my breasts into his hands. My nipples are hard pebbles and ache as he strokes and twists them.

Warm hands touch my knees, and I open my eyes to see Logan kneeling in front of me as he pulls my legs apart. "I'm ready to play with my toy now."

My pussy clenches, and I bite my lip as I realize Logan is soon going to know I'm filled with Ash's cum. He pushes my dress up to my hips as he moves forward in between my legs. Nate pushes my dress down under my breasts, and Logan looks up at us with lust-filled eyes.

"God, you're beautiful, Alexandra. I'm going to eat you out, and you can come if you want to."

I'm glad because I'm already close just from what Nate is doing to me. Logan leans forward and bites my clit through my panties. I squeal, and Nate twists my nipple painfully, making me moan. Logan pulls my panties to the side, and cool air hits my pussy before his warm, wet tongue is on it. He swirls his tongue around my clit, and I thrust my fingers into his hair as I pant for breath.

Logan pushes his tongue inside me and freezes for a second before he starts to thrust his tongue in and out of me as he rubs my clit with his fingers. I fist his hair in my fingers and hold on tight as waves of ecstasy crash over me, and I come with Logan's tongue buried deep in me.

He swipes his tongue over my clit a couple of times, and I shudder at the feeling before he moves up to kiss me. His tongue intertwines with mine, and the taste of Ash's cum is strong as we kiss.

He turns to face the others. "It seems somebody already played with my toy today."

"What can I say? She jumped on my cock in the parking garage. I was hardly about to push her off." Ash smirks at him.

"I see. Well, I was thinking that maybe we should tie Alexandra up, and we can take turns fucking her. What do you think, Dante?"

I shudder at the idea of it, and my pussy aches to be filled by all of them.

"That seems like a very good idea. Stand up, Angel."

Logan moves aside, and my skirt falls to my knees as I stand up. My breasts are still on full display, and my nipples are still painfully hard.

"Take your clothes off. You will be naked until you leave for work on Monday. Do you understand?"

"Yes, Honey."

I remove my dress and fold it carefully before I set it on the coffee table. Then I remove my panties and place them on top of the dress. All four men eye my body greedily, and my pussy aches as they take me in.

"Lead the way to our bedroom and take your clothes with you, Angel," Dante instructs.

I nod and pick up my clothes. "Yes, Honey."

When I get to the bedroom, Dante tells me to put my clothes in the hamper, which I do before I come back into the room. Ash walks over to me, unzips his jeans, then grabs my hand and places it on his cock. I stroke him through his briefs as he kisses me.

He pulls his head away and chuckles. "Be gentle, Lexi."

"Uhuh." It's all I manage to say through my lust before I kiss him again as carefully as I can.

I gasp into Ash's mouth when Logan spreads my ass cheeks apart and tongues my hole. He's the only one so far who's done this, so I know it's him. I reach into Ash's underwear and wrap my fingers around his thick cock. He groans as I stroke him, and our tongues dance together.

Nate wraps his fingers around my chin and breaks our kiss when he turns my face to his. He's stripped naked, and his erection juts forward impressively. It presses into my side as he moves closer to take my mouth with his. I continue to stroke Ash, and Nate takes my other hand and puts it on his cock.

Logan's tongue is thrusting in and out of my ass as he reaches between my legs to rub my clit as well. I alternate between kissing Ash and Nate as I keep up my rhythm, stroking their cocks. Nate's kisses are rough, while I try not to hurt Ash with my kisses.

When my orgasm hits, I throw my head back and moan, "Oh yes, yes, Sir. Fucking fuck yes."

Logan strokes my clit through my orgasm, and when my body stops shaking, Dante says, "Come here, Angel."

I blink a few times as the guys move away from me to reveal the bed where Dante has the ropes ready to go. I get on the bed, and Logan helps him tie me spread-eagle in front of them. When they're all naked, they stand around the bed as they slowly stroke their cocks.

"What are we going to do with you, Alexandra?" Logan raises an eyebrow at me.

I'm so aroused being totally exposed and completely at their whim, and I breathe, "Anything you want, Sir."

"That's right." He steps forward and trails his fingers over my breast. "We can do whatever we want, and you can't stop us."

I bite my lip at the hungry look in his eyes. I'm secure in the knowledge that I can always stop it if I need to, but I have no desire to stop anything. I want them to use me.

Nate climbs onto the bed, lies next to me, and captures my lips with his when I look at him. The bed moves as the other men climb onto it, and then hands and lips are all over my body. I break my kiss with Nate to look down when someone tongues my pussy, and it's Dante who's eating me out.

I moan his name, and Logan cuts me off by kissing me. Nate plays with one breast, and Ash plays with the other; they pull, tweak, lick, and suck them, and I'm lost in ecstasy. Logan ends our kiss and moves his cock near my face.

"Suck me, Alexandra."

I have to strain a little to get him in my mouth, but I manage to wrap my lips around him, and he fucks my mouth. Dante flicks his tongue back and forth across my clit, and I moan onto Logan's cock.

Logan pulls out of my mouth, but it's only a few seconds before Ash takes his place. I look up into his striking blue eyes as he fucks my mouth. When I come again, Dante removes his mouth from my pussy and pushes his cock into me. He fucks me roughly with quick, hard thrusts, and my body jerks with each movement from him.

Logan has moved down to my breast and takes it in his mouth. Nate is still playing with the other one, and he reaches down to rub my clit while Dante fucks me. It doesn't take long with this amount of stimulation for another orgasm to rock my body, and my pussy clenches around Dante's cock.

He thrusts into me a few more times before he pulls out and asks, "Who wants the next turn?"

I shudder at the knowledge that they really are using me

tonight. They're giving me plenty of attention, but they're also going to take turns with my body, and I love that.

"I'll go next," Nate says after removing my breast from his mouth.

He positions himself at my entrance and shoves his cock into me while Dante moves up to my head. Ash pulls his cock out of my mouth and turns my face to Dante, who wastes no time in pushing his cock into my mouth. Logan flicks my nipple, and I gasp at the stinging sensation.

Dante holds my face in his hands and fucks my mouth. I pull at the restraints without thinking because I want to hold onto him.

He chuckles above me and says in an amused tone, "Did you forget you're ours to do with what we want today, Angel? You don't get to touch us, but we can touch you however we want to."

Logan lifts his head before he twists my nipple painfully, and my body jerks as I squeal around Dante's cock. "Your body is ours tonight, Alexandra."

I moan, and Dante continues to fuck my mouth. Nate grips my thighs, and his fingers dig into my flesh as he thrusts into me. After some time, Ash takes his place.

I float into subspace and give in to the experience. Everything becomes a haze of love and lust as the men take turns fucking me and playing with my body.

I lose count of the orgasms they give me and watch as they move around me. I'm mildly aware of a dull ache in my arms and legs, but it's almost as though the pain can't touch me where I am.

Logan is the first to come, which he does down my throat. I swallow his offering in euphoric bliss and eagerly suck him dry. Ash is next, and he buries himself deep inside my pussy, refilling the deposit he left there earlier. When Nate orgasms, he pulls out of me and comes over my chest.

Dante takes his place as Logan scoops Nate's cum up and feeds it to me. "Taste Nate, Alexandra."

I should probably answer, but instead, I eagerly lap the cum off his fingers. Logan gives me an intense look and frowns at me.

"Are you okay, Alexandra?"

I blink at him, and it takes a moment to process his question. Dante is fucking me while he rubs my clit, and the taste of Nate's cum fills my mouth. All of my senses are full of these men and the pleasure they're giving me.

"Yes, Sir," I manage to moan as I nod my head.

Logan kisses me tenderly, and it tethers me to something when Dante finally comes. His cock jerks and swells inside me as he spills his seed there. He pants for breath as he looks down at me.

"Well done, Angel."

Nate appears next to me and kisses me as Logan and Dante untie me. As they release me, pain comes rushing in, and the ache in my wrists and ankles becomes a lot more noticeable.

I rotate my wrists and shake my arms as they move to my legs. Nate kisses me a final time, and then Ash leans over to kiss me as well before they leave the room. I'm bereft as I watch their retreating backs, and my body begins to shake.

Logan drops the rope he's just untied on the floor and moves next to me. He wraps me into his embrace as my emotions take hold and tears start to fall.

"You're beautiful, Lexi." He gently strokes my back. "Such a good girl. You did so well."

Dante's warm hand strokes my forehead, and he murmurs, "Yes, you did. Come with me to clean up, Angel."

Logan presses his lips to mine in a soft kiss before he pulls back from me. The same disappointment when Nate and Ash left hits me, but it's only a second before Dante scoops me into his arms, and I'm secure and safe again.

He carries me into our bathroom and holds me tight under the warm spray. It takes a long time for me to stop shaking, and he keeps murmuring words of comfort as he holds me before he washes me as well.

When we get out of the shower, he carefully dries me and then takes me to our bed, where he lies with me for what feels like hours as I adjust after the scene.

"Are you feeling better, Angel?"

I nod. "Yes."

We leave the room and find the guys in the living room playing video games. The four of us spend the rest of the day hanging out together. We get pizza and drink beers for dinner while we watch a movie. Every now and then, someone will play with my body, but it's fun teasing, and I'm more than ready to fuck when I go to bed with Nate.

Later, I lie in bed with him and try to forget my worries about Cassie, but it's difficult. I don't fall asleep until long after Nate goes quiet and his breathing has evened out. I focus on his strong arm holding me against him until my brain can no longer hold my concern that Cassie will ask us for more money in my head long enough to prevent me from sleeping.

Chapter Fifteen

Date Night

I smile at an email from Heather in my inbox. It's been two weeks since she was here in LA, and we've been emailing back and forth since. The Serenity clothes should be ready and shipped to the stores late next month, but we've started just talking in general, and it's nice to have a friend who gets the celebrity lifestyle.

I've missed having a friend like that since Cassie turned on me so viciously. It's a shame that Heather lives in Chicago, but she comes to Los Angeles regularly and plans to come over when the clothes are ready. We also have the shared sub experience, but I haven't mentioned it in email, and neither has she. On some level, I think we're both scared that we'll be hacked and our secrets will be shared with the world.

I reply to Heather's email, then close my laptop and walk into the store itself. Jasmine is folding some shirts and tidying up some of the displays.

"Are you okay to close up on your own tonight, Jazz?"

She looks up and smiles at me. "Of course. Big night planned?"

"Yup. Dante's planned a romantic night in for us."

I can't stop the grin that comes to my face. Apparently, Nate is spending the night at Logan's and Dante 'has plans for me.' I've been wet all day just thinking about it.

"Lucky girl."

"Tell me about it. I'll see you next week."

My excitement builds on the drive home, and when I get there, I put my bag away before I go to look for Dante. I find him in the office, and he looks up when I walk in. He pushes his chair back from the desk and turns it to face me.

"Hello, Angel. Did you have a good day at work?"

I nod my confirmation. "Yes, I did. We had a good day. What about you?"

"Good. We recorded a demo of your song. We still don't have a name for it, though. Personally, I think it should be called 'Naked Angel.'"

His eyes rove over my body from head to toe, and I can feel it as surely as if he's touching me. My nipples harden against my bra, and a dart of arousal shoots to my pussy.

"Take your dress off, Angel. You won't need any clothes for the rest of the night."

"Yes, Honey."

I pull the zipper of my dress down my side to where it stops at my hips.

"Slowly," Dante murmurs as I'm about to pull the dress off.

This instruction alone is enough to cause a dart of electricity to shoot through my body. I bite my lip as I push the straps off my shoulders one at a time. My chest heaves as I slowly pull the top of the dress down over my breasts, exposing them to Dante's view in my lace see-through bra.

His eyes darken, and there is an obvious bulge in his jeans, but he does nothing to adjust himself. He is, as always, a master of self-control. As much as I want to rip this dress off myself along with my underwear and jump onto his cock, I force myself to pull it down agonizingly slowly.

Once it makes its way over my hips, though, gravity takes control, and it drops to the floor. Dante hasn't instructed me to do anything else, so I stand in front of him with my dress pooled at my feet.

"Step forward."

I swallow and take a step out of my dress.

"Turn to face away from me." When I've done as instructed, he says, "Bend at the waist to pick up your dress."

I do as I'm told, and I can feel the wetness in my underwear, aware that there is a damp patch that Dante will be able to see right in front of his face. I grab the dress and straighten up again.

"Fold it and set it aside." He indicates to a spot on the desk for me to place the dress, and I do. "Turn to face me again."

I'm closer to him now, and I can smell his scent. His cock is hard in his jeans, and I want nothing more than to wrap my lips around it. I know that I don't get to choose if or when that happens, though.

"Remove your bra. Lift it up so I can watch your breasts drop."

I swallow and nod. "Yes, Honey."

I reach behind myself to unclip my bra and hold it tight as I pull it up and over my breasts. Gravity takes hold again, and they drop into Dante's view. He's always enjoyed this, and I'm drenched from putting on this display for him. I carefully set the bra down on my dress when Dante tells me to and await my next instruction.

"Come here, Angel."

I take a couple of steps forward so that I'm in front of him. Standing over a person would generally make someone feel as though they held the power, but Dante has a commanding presence, even sitting in a chair. Particularly for me. I'm eager for him to exercise his control, and I want to pant for breath, but I keep control of my reactions because it's just us tonight.

He reaches his hand forward and strokes back and forth along the damp patch that I've created in my panties. Every time his fingers touch my clit through the fabric, a spark of arousal floods through me. I work hard not to react, and Dante looks up at me through hooded eyes.

"This is one reaction you've never been able to control. Isn't it, Angel?"

"Yes, Honey."

I say it through shallow breaths but manage to sound relatively normal. He presses his thumb on my clit and rubs it in circles as he watches me.

"So wet. So much desire that you're hiding. No reactions, Angel," he reminds me.

"Yes, Honey," I repeat.

It's already becoming difficult, and my heart pounds in my chest as I try to breathe normally but struggle to do it. Dante slips his hand underneath the fabric of my underwear and rubs my clit directly. The skin-to-skin contact is so much better, and I bite the inner side of my lip to stop myself from reacting.

He reaches up to twist my nipple, and I can't help but moan, "Yes, Honey."

"Naughty, Angel." Dante pulls his hand out of my underwear and shakes his head. "I was just about to tell you that you could react. Now, you'll be counting instead."

He grabs my hand and pulls me down over his knee. I gasp even though I should've expected it, and Dante brings his palm down roughly on my ass cheek.

"Still being naughty. You know better." He pulls my panties down to the tops of my thighs and spanks my ass again. "I haven't held you to our rules much lately, so I'm very disappointed that you would break them on our night together." He hits the other ass cheek this time, so it doesn't sting too badly. "I want you to count, Angel. We're not counting to a specific number. I just want to see how many hits it takes before I feel your ass is sufficiently red enough for my liking. Start at four."

My pussy aches, and I work hard not to squirm on his lap. He hasn't given me a punishment like this in a long time, and I'm excited for it. I know that he is, too, because his hard cock presses into my belly as he brings his hand down on my ass again.

"Four," I gasp.

His hand comes down harder this time, and it smarts painfully. I squeak out the number five just before he spanks me again. When we reach number nine, my pussy is so wet that my juices drip down my lips, and I'm sure it's making a mess on Dante's jeans. The thought of there being a wet patch on them makes me even hotter.

"Ten," I tell him, and this is where most of my punishments would end, but he keeps going.

He alternates between my cheeks; they're both hot and sting more with each hit. He gives me no relief, and by the time we've reached the thirties, I'm pretty sure this is the most intense spanking he's ever given me. I writhe with each hit and make sure I call out the number as an excuse to move.

I desperately need him to fuck me, but I'm sure he's going to torment me before he does, and it isn't until I moan the number thirty-seven that he speaks again.

"Your ass is lit up like a Christmas tree, Angel. Or maybe Rudolph's nose. I'm not sure which, but I'm definitely feeling very festive when I look at it."

He leans down and kisses each of my burning cheeks, his lips soft against them as he does. Dante traces the line of my pussy with his hand, and I bite my lip to stop myself from gasping. He pushes two fingers into me, and it gets harder to stop myself from reacting.

"So wet and ready for me. Do you want my cock inside you, Angel?"

"More than anything, Honey."

He reaches over to thumb my nipple before he twists it, and I can barely breathe because I'm about to come, and I have no doubt that I'm not allowed to do that.

"Maybe if you're a good girl. Go put your clothes away, including your panties. Leave the heels on, Angel."

"Yes, Honey."

I struggle for balance as I stand, and the blood rushes away from my head, leaving me light-headed.

"Are you okay?"

I take a deep breath and nod. "Yes. I'm fine."

"Good."

Dante leans forward, tugs on my underwear, and pulls it down enough that it drops to the floor. I step out of it, and Dante swipes it off the floor before handing it to me. I smile at him as I take it and walk to the bedroom. My juices drip down my thighs as I walk back to the office, and I hope that Dante will be ready to fuck me soon. I'm more than ready.

When I enter the office, he stands. "Come with me, Angel." I follow him to the living room, and I'm unsurprised when he says, "Sit on the coffee table."

I take my place and spread my legs wide. Sure enough, he takes one look at my exposed pussy, then promptly sits on the far end of the sofa as he pulls his phone out of his pocket. He unlocks it and looks down at the screen without saying anything else.

I watch him and wait impatiently for him to play with me again. A couple of times, he moves his head in such a way that I think he's ready, but then he doesn't look at me. My whole body is itching for his touch, for him to set a spark to the tinderbox that I've become, ready to go up in flames.

His phone rings, and he answers without so much as looking my way. "Hello." He's silent for a second, then he nods. "Oh, I think she's busy working at the moment. It might be on Do Not Disturb." I assume whoever is on the phone asked about me as Dante listens again. "Of course, she's happy to bring her mashed potatoes to Thanksgiving, Mrs. Woodford."

I raise my eyebrows because the timing for Ash's mom to be calling Dante is awkward. Our families celebrate together every year, and I always bring my loaded mashed potatoes. We're celebrating at the Woodford household this year, and I'd kind of forgotten about it, so I'm grateful for the reminder.

"Anytime. We look forward to seeing you next Thursday."

Dante ends the call but still doesn't look at me, and immediately the interlude is over. My arousal comes back to me in full force, and I'm on edge, full of hope and desire as I wait again. When he finally puts his phone away and turns to look at me, his gaze alone sets me alight, and I'm pretty sure that I would come the second he touches me if I allowed myself to do it.

"On your knees, Angel." I drop to my knees, and he gives me a wicked grin. "Come here on your hands and knees."

I crawl toward him slowly because I have to work not to pant for breath. It's so hot to do this, and when I look up at him, I can see how turned on he is. I stop in front of him, and he removes his t-shirt, then unbuttons his jeans before shoving them and his briefs to his ankles.

"Worship my cock, Angel."

I take his length in my mouth and revel in finally getting to do some kind of actual sex act. He's been driving me wild since I got home, and I love that I get to suck his gorgeous cock. I lick and suck him while also playing with his balls. He places his hand on my head and strokes it as I blow him.

Eventually, he murmurs, "Very nice. I want to be inside you now, Angel. Straddle me."

I can barely contain my excitement as I take him out of my mouth and climb up to straddle him. Dante immediately wraps his fingers around my upper arms and grips them tightly as he holds them to my sides. He pulls me down roughly onto his cock, then begins to fuck me.

He keeps pressure on my arms, and it's clear that I'm not allowed to use my hands for anything. Dante uses his grip on me to pull my torso forward and take one of my breasts in his mouth. I pant for breath as he thrusts in and out of me.

Dante pulls his head back and looks me in the eyes. "React, Angel."

"Oh my fucking god, yes. Fucking hell. Shitting fuck, Dante. Yes!"

He chuckles but continues his rhythm, and my ecstasy explodes. As I tip into orgasm, I moan loudly, and my body shakes. He fucks me roughly and takes my breast into his mouth again. I grind my hips against him and lose myself as the pleasure overtakes me while he moves from breast to breast, constantly fucking me roughly.

When I come again, my pussy clenches hard around him as his cock jerks inside me. He releases my arms but uses a hand to pull my face to his as he thrusts his tongue into my mouth and takes possession of that as surely as he possesses every other part of me right now.

He reaches between us with his other hand to rub my clit while he fucks me through his own orgasm, and when he stops moving inside me, he continues to rub my clit while he kisses me. He brings me to orgasm again before he finally stops, and I drop my head on his shoulder as I try to catch my breath, the remnants of my orgasm still flooding through me. Dante holds me in his arms as I rest my head on his shoulder. He gently strokes my back as he pants heavily in my ear.

He kisses my neck and asks, "Can you stand up, Angel?"

"Yes, Honey."

I climb off him and squeeze my pussy tight as I clench my legs together to try and stop myself from making a mess. Dante quickly picks me up and carries me to our bathroom. I wrap my arms around his neck as my post-orgasm glow fades and the world feels a little colder and darker again.

I'm shaking by the time we reach the shower, and Dante quickly turns it on. He sets me down, and I sigh as the warm spray hits me. He kisses me all over before he runs the washcloth over my skin to clean me.

When he reaches my pussy, he sets the washcloth aside and holds my hips with his hands as his tongue flits across my clit. I rest my hands on his shoulders as he licks and sucks my clit. Pleasure rolls over me, but in a calming way, and there's no intensity to the orgasm he gives me. My body still shakes again when it hits, though, and Dante swirls his tongue around my clit a final time. He picks up the washcloth and continues to wash me with it.

I smile down at his beautiful face when he looks up at me. "Thank you, Honey."

"You're welcome, Angel."

I step out of the spray when he's done, and he quickly washes himself before we get out of the shower. He wraps the towel around me from behind and holds me tight in his arms as he kisses my head.

"I love you," he murmurs.

"I love you, too," I say with a contented sigh.

Once he's dried and gotten dressed, Dante takes me out to the living room. We sit and watch a TV show together on Netflix. I curl into Dante's lap, and he pulls a blanket over us. Underneath it, he gently strokes my stomach with his thumb as we watch the show.

Dante had ordered Thai food, and when our dinner arrives, it smells amazing. He accepts the delivery while I remain hidden under the blanket. When he appears in the living room again, he smiles at me.

"You can serve me now, Angel. The food is in the kitchen."

Arousal floods through me at being told to serve him as I nod, then stand, fold the blanket, and throw it over the back of the sofa. Dante takes a seat at the dining table while I get cutlery, napkins, and glasses. I set them out on the table, and his eyes rove over my body as I do. My nipples are painfully hard, and I ache for Dante to touch me. I dish up our food and take the plates out to the table.

I place Dante's in front of him first, then set mine down in my place opposite him as I ask, "What would you like to drink, Honey?"

"White wine."

I take my seat after I've poured us both a wine, and Dante smiles as he picks up his glass. "Thank you, Angel."

"You're welcome, Honey."

I wait until Dante begins to eat before I take a bite of my food. It's so delicious that I can't help but groan as the flavors hit my taste buds, and Dante chuckles.

"Tasty?"

I swallow my bite and gush, "Yes. Oh my god, so good."

"I'm glad. Anthony has an apartment for us to visit tomorrow, by the way. I doubt you'll have seen the email. It came through after you left Black Lilac."

"Oh, really?"

We still haven't come across anything suitable, and I've started to lose hope that we'll ever find something to fit our needs. Nights here without Logan have a tinge of melancholy to them from the knowledge that he's alone in his apartment without us. Nights with Logan at his place have the same melancholy from knowing that I won't get to see Dante or Nate until the next evening. I just want us to all be together as the family we are.

Dante takes a sip of his wine as he nods. "Yes. There's no listing yet. Apparently, it's quite unique and fits our needs, so he wants to show it to us before he puts it on the market."

"That sounds promising." I smile at him as a flicker of hope passes through me that we might actually find somewhere new to call 'home' together. "I won't get my hopes up, though."

After dinner, Dante says, "Clean the table, Angel. I'll be in the bedroom when you're done."

My heart thrums in my chest as I follow Dante's instruction. I make sure there's not a single crumb left on the dining table, and the kitchen is spotless by the time I make my way to our bedroom. I find him relaxed on the bed, looking devastatingly handsome as he reads something on his phone.

He looks up and says, "Come here, Angel." I climb onto the bed, and he sets his phone aside. "What am I going to do with you?"

Dante pushes me onto my back as I stare up into his chocolate-brown eyes. He's resting on his side next to me, and he begins to trail a path around my body with his hand, but he avoids my breasts and pussy as he does.

"I very much enjoyed dinner, but I think it's time for dessert."

He lowers his head and pulls my nipple into his mouth. His warm, wet tongue swirls around my hard nipple as Dante reaches between my legs. My pussy is drenched, and he easily pushes two fingers inside me before he begins to rub my clit. Ecstasy builds inside me, and I have to pant for breath.

When Dante bites my nipple, I can't stop the low moan that escapes me, and Dante raises an eyebrow at me. "Again, Angel? Do

I need to retrain you?"

"I'm sorry, Honey."

I cringe as I say it because he hasn't stopped stroking my clit, and I'm lost to the pleasure he's giving me but aware that I broke a rule.

"So you should be. No orgasm for you now." He gives my clit a light tap with his hand, and I jump at the stinging sensation in my most sensitive area. "It appears I do need to spend some time tonight retraining you. Luckily, we have all night."

Dante moves down so that his face is hovering above my pussy. He strokes my outer lips with his pointer fingers, and it takes everything in me not to moan again.

"I'm going to eat my dessert now. No orgasm and no reactions, Angel."

His breath is hot on me as he speaks, and my pussy aches as he pushes my legs further apart. He buries his face between my legs, and I focus hard on my breathing to try and control my reaction to it. The pleasure is overwhelming, though, and it's intensified even more so by the fact that I can't just give in to it.

I want to thrust my fingers through Dante's hair and pull his face harder against my clit. I want to squirm and writhe and moan and scream obscenities as I come, but I push my orgasm away as it nears. I close my eyes to focus because the sight of Dante's face buried in my pussy is turning me on too much.

My pussy clenches and unclenches over and over as I come perilously close to the orgasm Dante is threatening to give me. I give a tiny pant, but I manage to withhold every other reaction and lie as still as possible despite the lust taking over every cell in my body.

By the time Dante stops his onslaught against my clit, my eyes have rolled back in my head, and I'm at his mercy. He stands up and strips off his clothes as I watch. He's beautiful and sexy, and mine, and I'm floating on a high as his cock is exposed. It juts out in front of him, and a part of me wants to suck him, but I'm traveling along on this ride right now.

He grabs my legs and pulls me further down the bed so my ass is at the edge. Then he pushes his cock into me, and I can't prevent the mewling noise of pleasure that I make.

Dante immediately taps my clit again. "No, Angel."

The sharp, stinging sensation only serves to heighten my ecstasy, though. When he grabs my ankles and puts each of them on his shoulders as he begins to fuck me, I'm not sure if I can hold off much longer.

"You're not going to come, are you?"

"No, Honey," I manage to say.

He reaches between us and rubs my clit. "Good. I need to teach you a lesson. Do you know what that might be, Angel?"

I can't think straight with this amount of stimulation, but I manage to murmur, "I'm yours."

"Well, that is a good lesson." Dante chuckles. "What else might I be teaching you?"

His cock is so hard, and I'm so full as he continues to fuck me while he quizzes me. I want to wrap my legs around his waist and fuck him back, but not being able to makes it even better. It's suddenly illuminated for me.

"No reactions because then, when I have permission, it's better."

Dante leans now and captures my lips with his. He thrusts his tongue into my mouth and explores it for a few seconds before he pulls back, all the while fucking me into sweet oblivion.

"Precisely, Angel. It's what's going to make the orgasm you get tomorrow even better because you'll have waited for it. *Earned* it. You're not going to come. Are you, Angel?"

"No, Honey."

A part of me clicks that he just said I won't be getting an orgasm until tomorrow, but I'm so far gone in my ecstasy that it's all I can do to prevent it from crashing over me. Dante gives me some relief by finally stopping rubbing my clit. He grabs hold of my hips, and I'm grateful because I can tell he's seeking his orgasm now.

When he grips my hips tighter and buries himself inside me, then unleashes his load, I don't think I've ever been more relieved. Dante and I go to clean up in the bathroom, and my level of arousal dips to a simmer. The need to come is hovering in the background as I snuggle into Dante's embrace.

He kisses my head and hugs me tighter. "Good night, Angel." He reaches between my legs and rubs my clit. "I look forward to seeing you come tomorrow when Logan and Nate are home."

I want to groan at the knowledge that I have to wait for them to get home to have an orgasm. At the same time, I'm also horny as hell and excited for Dante to play with me until they do.

Dante pulls his hand away from me and pushes his fingers into my mouth. "Taste yourself."

I suck his fingers clean before he pulls me back into his embrace, and my tiredness finally outweighs my arousal, so I drift off to sleep.

Chapter Sixteen

Two for the Price of One

Dante spends Saturday morning teasing me because Nate and Logan will be meeting us at the apartment Anthony is showing us today. So it'll be many hours before I can get any relief, and by the time we're getting ready to go, I'm aching to be fucked.

Dante strides over to me after I've pulled on a robin-egg blue dress that falls to my mid-thigh. "You look beautiful."

He reaches underneath the hem to find my dripping wet pussy and slowly rubs my clit in circles. I work hard to keep my reaction under control as he watches me.

"So wet. I'm sure that Logan and Nate will have a lot of fun with you this afternoon." He pushes his fingers into my pussy and begins to fuck me with them. "Do you want that, Angel?"

"Yes, Honey," I breathe.

Dante returns to rubbing my clit and nods at me. "I'm sure you do." He raises his hand to thumb my nipple, which is hard against the top of my dress, and murmurs, "As much as I want to stay here and play with you some more, Anthony will be here soon."

He turns and walks out of the closet. I blow out a breath of air and bite my lip as a shudder rolls through me. I'm on edge, and as excited as I am to see the apartment, I'm desperate for release. I quickly pull on a pair of silver heels and head out to find Dante putting on the Breitling watch Ash gave him for his birthday.

He looks up and smiles. "Ready to go?"

"In more ways than one," I joke.

Dante chuckles and comes over to take me in his arms before he kisses me. "I love you."

"I love you, too."

He takes my hand, and we head to the living room, where I sit on the coffee table until Anthony arrives to take us to the apartment.

"I think you'll really like this one," he assures us. "I've never seen anything like it. It's a little bit more than the top of the price range you gave, but I immediately thought of you when I got the listing."

"Do you have any more information to give us?" I ask because his email didn't tell us a lot other than the fact it met our requirements.

"I could, but I think you should experience it for yourself. If you really want to know, I'll tell you, of course." He gives me a grin in the rearview mirror, looking very satisfied with himself.

I'm about to say that I want him to tell us, but Dante says, "Seems like it'll be a fun surprise. We wouldn't want to ruin that, would we, Angel?"

He raises an eyebrow at me and toys with the hem of my dress. Cool air hits my pussy, and his fingers brush my outer thigh.

My arousal outweighs my curiosity, and I force myself to nod and answer his question. "Of course not, Honey."

Dante leans across and kisses me before he sits up and faces the front of the car again. "That's settled, then."

When we reach the apartment building, we enter the underground parking garage with a code and park in one of the assigned spots next to Logan's AMG. Nate and Logan are both sitting in the car waiting for us.

My heart swells at the sight of them, and I can't resist the urge to give each of them a hug and kiss on the cheek as we greet them.

I wish I could do more, but I dutifully return to Dante's side to keep up appearances.

As Anthony swipes a card across a receiver at the elevator, he says, "This is a private elevator that goes to the penthouse we'll be looking at today."

"Score one for privacy and security," Nate says with a grin.

We get into the elevator as Anthony presses a button that says 'PH1,' and the doors close before it starts to move. When the doors slide open, we're in an entry area that leads into a massive living space. Everything is fresh and modern, with lots of sparkling marble, and the smell of fresh flowers comes from a vase sitting on a table nearby.

We follow Anthony into the room, and he says, "I'll let you have a look around unless you'd like a tour this time?"

After the first couple of trips, we've started looking through the places on our own. I definitely prefer being able to discuss our thoughts and plans without having the agent hovering around.

"I think we'll be fine, but we'll let you know if we need you."

"Of course." Anthony nods and takes a seat at a dining table nearby.

We look through the kitchen first, then walk back out past Anthony as we look through the living room.

"Fuck, yes. I love this theater room," Nate says as he pushes open a heavy door.

It has a plush dark gray carpet and three tiers of seating with four armchairs in each row that face the big screen on the wall at the front of the room. As Nate and Dante walk across the room to look at the equipment, Logan enters the room behind me and closes the door.

He wraps his arms around my waist, pulls me back against him, and kisses my neck. "I missed you last night, Alexandra."

"I missed you, too, Sir." I shudder as he nips my earlobe with his teeth.

He lowers his hand to grab my dress and pulls it up to expose my pussy. I pant for breath as he uses one hand to hold my dress up and the other to reach between my legs. My pussy is wet and throbs with my ache for an orgasm. I gasp when Logan's fingers make contact with my clit, and he begins to stroke me. I look up into his beautiful face. His eyes are hooded, and his cock is hard against my ass.

As much as I'm desperate for release, I manage to tell him, "I can't come until we're home."

"Is that so?" He strokes me faster, and I bite my lip as I nod. "Well, I guess you'd better not come, then."

He lowers his head and captures my lips with his, his tongue invading my mouth as he kisses me. Arousal flows through me, and I'm so wrapped up with Logan that it comes as a shock when someone tugs my dress down under my breasts.

I break our kiss to turn and face Nate as he takes one of my breasts in his mouth. Dante is leaning against the wall on the other side of the room as he watches us. Nate's tongue is wet and hot against one nipple as he uses his hand to twist and pull the other.

My orgasm is so close now, and I bite my lip as I do my best to keep it at bay. I succeed, and I'm high on ecstasy as the guys continue what they're doing. I moan their names quietly, and when Logan begins to toy with my earlobe again, I almost lose all control.

"I can't come until we're home."

It comes out in a pleading tone this time. I'm begging them not to make me come because I know that I can't hold it off much longer. Logan is the first to stop. He nips my earlobe a final time as he removes his hand from under my skirt.

Nate keeps going a little longer. He looks up at me through long, dark lashes as he swirls his tongue around my nipple and twists the other one a final time before he stands up.

He pulls me away from Logan and against his hard body as he smashes his lips against mine. Our tongues intertwine, and I wrap my arms around his neck as my pussy throbs, but my orgasm recedes and becomes less threatening.

Nate breaks our kiss but keeps me in his arms. "Hi, Sexy."

"Hi, Nate."

"Do you know how badly I want to fuck you right now?" He raises an eyebrow at me as he pushes his crotch against me, his cock hard under his jeans.

"Not as badly as I want it, trust me," I groan.

Nate laughs and releases me. "I'm sure."

Nate and I make our way over to Dante, where we look at the theater equipment. My breathing rate is still fast as we leave the room and continue to look at the rest of the apartment. There's another big living area with some rooms off it, but this one also has a spiral staircase at the side of it.

"What the fuck?" I ask when I catch sight of it and stretch my neck to try and see what the opening is at the top of it, but I can't see anything. "Where does that go?"

"Do you want to look at the rest of the rooms before we see?" Dante asks.

I shrug, and we all follow him into a room that's set up as an office with high-tech equipment in it. There are three smaller bedrooms with their own bathrooms and through a hallway is a large master suite.

"Whoa. I love this room," I say as I walk into it.

There are floor-to-ceiling windows and two large walk-in closets. The bathroom is a display of marble and glass with a big spa bath at the corner of the room up a set of steps. There's a double shower and through a door next to it is a toilet and bidet.

"This is my room," Nate declares with a grin.

Dante, Logan, and I look at him, and I realize that we hadn't discussed who would get the master room. I guess I'd assumed it would be Dante's and my room, but I realize now that it doesn't necessarily have to be.

"If you want the master, I'm okay with that." Dante shrugs.

I turn to blink at him. He's got a pleasant smile on his face, and I can't see any sign that he's not genuinely okay with the idea.

"I was joking, but I'm not going to say no," Nate laughs.

"You won't even have to share a closet with Lexi like I've had to. You'll get your own." Dante winks at me.

I take his hand in mine and stretch up on my toes to kiss him. "I love you, Honey."

"I love you, too, Angel. It's not like the other rooms aren't more than fine."

I'm so happy with my three men, and I can actually see a future for us living here, which is a lot more than I could say for some of the places we've seen.

I smile at him, then turn to the others. "So, do we like this place, then?"

"We should check out where that staircase goes, but definitely. It has a spare room left for the sex room, which was my biggest requirement." Logan gives me a grin. "After all, Lexi has to have a room."

A dart of arousal shoots to my pussy at the thought of all the things these men will do to me in 'my room' if we buy this apartment.

"Hey, if I'm getting this room, it's definitely a yes from me," Nate laughs.

"Let's go check out the mystery staircase, then," Logan says.

We walk back to the living room, and Logan leads the way upstairs, followed by Nate, while Dante and I walk hand-in-hand up the stairs behind them.

"I love this view," I tease as I look at Nate's ass.

He looks back over his shoulder at me and smirks as he says, "I bet you do."

We come out in another living room, and I frown as I look around at what seems to be a whole other apartment connected to the first one. There are doors coming off this area in a similar way to the ones in the room below, and through a big hallway, I can see another big living room which would be above the one we arrived in from the elevator.

"Is this a two for the price of one kind of deal or something?" Nate asks, and he sounds as astounded as I feel.

"I'm not sure," Dante says.

We find three more bedrooms like the ones below and another master bedroom and study. The layout is slightly different, but it's basically the same. Where the theater is below, there's gym equipment on the tiered area that has seats in the other apartment.

There's another dining area near the elevator, and instead of a kitchen, there's another massive bedroom and en suite bathroom. I'm blown away, and I can't understand what the fuck is going on.

"I can't believe this," I say for about the thousandth time as we walk back through the apartment toward the staircase.

"I need answers," Logan says with a shake of his head.

"This definitely meets our needs, and Anthony did say it was a unique listing," Dante says. "He didn't say it was two apartments, though."

Anthony grins at us as we approach him. "Did you like the apartment?"

"Don't you mean *apartments*?" Nate asks.

Anthony chuckles. "I suppose I do. This place has everything you want. I don't think it will last long when I list it, but if you want to put an offer in before I do so, the owner is open to taking offers prior to listing."

I want this place more than I want to keep breathing. It's absolutely perfect. It's everything that we wanted in an apartment and more.

I look up at Dante and say, "I think we'd be interested in putting an offer in. What do you think, Honey?"

"If you're happy with it, I'm happy with it." He smiles down at me. "Yes, we'll put an offer on the place."

"Excellent. Congratulations, Mr. and Mrs. Sullivan. If you can take a seat, we'll do up the paperwork." Anthony looks over at Logan and Nate. "This will take us about twenty to thirty minutes. I know you came here together, so it's up to you if you want to stick around or not."

I hadn't thought about this part. Nate and Logan look back at us—the other two men I love, but nobody can know about it. This is so momentous for all of us, our first home together as a family.

I want them to officially be a part of it, so I smile at Anthony. "Logan and Nate are actually going to be co-owners."

The guys both look surprised but quickly compose their features as Dante squeezes my hand under the table, and I look up to see him smiling at me.

I turn back to Anthony and pull a suitable explanation out of my ass. "This place is even more perfect than you could've guessed. The guys spend a lot of time on tour, so they won't have to worry about leaving their apartments empty because I'll be here. There are basically three master bedrooms, and we can split the cost three ways. I assume the guys will be able to take the elevator directly to the upstairs apartment?"

"Yes. Initially, the swipe cards only worked for the relevant floor, but the previous owner had them changed so they can go to either floor."

Nate takes a seat next to me, and Logan sits next to him as he asks, "What *is* the deal with this place? Why is it two apartments joined together?"

"The previous owner is a billionaire who has seven children. He bought the two apartments and had the staircase installed to join them. He also had the upstairs kitchen converted into a bedroom for his guests."

My mouth drops open, and I gasp because it's crazy, but it also makes sense. I would never have thought of connecting two penthouse apartments together, but I'm glad that guy did. My phone starts buzzing as we're in the midst of completing the paperwork, and Ash's name is displayed on the screen.

I raise my eyebrow at Dante, but answer the call as I stand and take a few steps away from the table. "Hey, Ash. What's up?"

"Do you have a moment to talk?"

My blood runs cold, and I immediately think he's heard from Cassie.

"Um, we're filling out paperwork to put an offer in on a place at the moment. Is it important?"

He's quiet for a few seconds, then says, "Kind of. Do you need to call me back?"

My heart pounds in my chest, and I know that I can't wait to hear what he has to say. I need to know whatever it is that Cassie's done now.

"No. Give me a second." I look up at Anthony and ask, "Can I have a moment, please? I have to take this call."

"Of course. Take all the time you need."

I walk swiftly to the theater room and close the door behind me before I ask, "What's Cassie done now?"

"Huh? What? Oh, no. It's not about Cassie," Ash says quickly.

I let out my breath in a whoosh of air as relief floods through me. I was sure she'd somehow contacted him and wanted more money from us.

"Fucking hell, you scared me," I scold him as I walk over and drop into the nearest plush armchair.

It's comfy with buttery leather, and I wonder if these come with the place or if we can include them in the deal somehow if they don't.

"Sorry. I didn't mean to scare you. I guess I just felt like I should tell you that I've got a date next Friday."

Ash's words come through the line as I'm testing the recline on the chair and I sit bolt upright as they do.

A date.

"Oh."

I don't really know what else to say about it, and I frown ahead at the blank screen in front of me.

"Is that okay? I mean, I assumed it was okay, but I sort of thought I should tell you."

Is it okay? I feel a little bit weird about the idea of Ash going on a date with someone, but we're just friends who have sex.

I'm not sure what to say, so I go with something practical. "We'll have to use condoms if you're sleeping with other people."

"I'm not. I mean, I haven't been. I suppose if things go well with Štěpánka, I will. Yeah, I don't mind wearing condoms with you if it comes to it."

"Is that her name? Where's she from?" I ask out of curiosity.

"Yeah, it is. She's a model from Czechia. I met her at a party last night, and we've been talking today."

"I'm not going to be 'the other woman,' Ash. You can't tell her you're sleeping with me specifically, but I don't want to sleep with you if she thinks you're exclusive."

I've been with Dante since I was a teenager, so this is an incredibly weird conversation to have.

"I've told her that I'm seeing someone, but it's not exclusive." He snorts and half-laughs. "I didn't really know how else to explain it. I just said you were seeing other people as well."

I can't help myself, and I burst into laughter. "That's one way of putting it."

I sigh and decide to figure out how I feel about this later. I have no right to stop Ash from going on a date if he wants to. We agreed there would be no hard feelings whenever he wanted to move on from Cassie.

"Look, I'm happy for you. It sounds like you're being upfront with her, which is all I ask. If you do end up becoming exclusive, we'll stop playing together. No hard feelings."

Ash blows out a breath of air and sounds relieved when he says, "Cool. Thanks, Lexi. I love you, and I've been freaking out for the last hour that you'd be angry with me."

"Of course not. I love you, too. I should probably go back because we're putting an offer in on this place."

"Oh yeah, you said that. It's good?"

I nod, even though he can't see it. "It's perfect. I'll tell you about it later. We'll see you on Thursday at your mom's place for Thanksgiving, too."

"Okay." He's silent for a second, and I think he might say something else, but he says, "I guess I'll see you then."

I kind of want to invite him around to play with us tonight or tomorrow. We've done it most weekends, but I'm not sure how I feel about playing with him, despite our conversation. If he's going on a date, maybe I should just let him move on from Cassie without the complication of us playing as well.

"Bye, Ash."

I hang up the call before I give in and invite him to play. When I walk back into the dining room where the guys are sitting, they all have worried looks on their faces.

"Everything okay?" Dante asks.

I force a smile at him. "Yeah, everything's fine—no emergency or anything. I'll tell you guys about it later. Let's finish this paperwork."

The guys shoot me concerned looks as we finish signing the offer on the apartment, and when we get down to the parking garage, Dante tells Anthony that he's free to go because Logan and Nate will give us a lift home. He gives us a cheery wave as he congratulates us again, and he gets into his car.

As soon as he's gone and we're seated in Logan's AMG, he looks at me in the rearview mirror. "What did Ash want? Was it about Cassie?"

"No, it wasn't. He just wanted to tell me he's got a date on Friday."

The three men exchange glances before Dante says, "I see. Are you okay?"

"Yes." I shrug a shoulder. "We're just friends who play together sometimes. Why wouldn't I be okay?"

"Do you want to talk about it?" Logan asks as his eyes search my face.

"Not really. It's what it is, and I can't change that. Plus, I've been waiting to have an orgasm for about eighteen hours, so the sooner you drive us home, the better."

Dante looks at me for a few seconds, then says, "Move to the middle seat, Angel."

I do as instructed, and he pulls the skirt of my dress up before he spreads my legs wide. Logan turns to look out the windscreen as he puts the car into gear.

"Hang on a second," Nate says. "I want to sit in the back, too."

"Of course you do," Logan laughs.

He leans across and kisses Nate. As I watch them, a shock of arousal shoots to my pussy, and I'm very aware of the fact I'm on display. When their kiss ends, Logan turns to look at me as Nate gets out of the car to join us in the back.

"Your pussy looks like it needs a good pounding," Logan murmurs in a husky voice.

Nate slides onto the seat next to me and closes the door as he says, "It definitely does."

Logan pulls out of the garage as Nate reaches between my legs to stroke my clit. My breathing is shallow, and my heart pounds in my chest.

"Pull your dress down and show us your breasts, Alexandra," Logan says as he pulls up to a set of lights.

I catch his gaze in the rearview mirror as I pull my dress down under my breasts.

My nipples are taut and painful as Dante plays with one while Nate lifts his hand from my pussy to play with the other one.

"I want you to rub yourself, Alexandra. Bring yourself as close to orgasm as you can, then stop."

"Yes, Sir," I pant.

I do as Logan instructed and stop rubbing my clit right when I'm about to come. Dante and Nate are still playing with my breasts. Dante strokes one with his thumb in a maddeningly slow way. Meanwhile, Nate has his lips clamped around the other one and sucks on it as I pant for breath.

"Again, Alexandra," Logan says when he notices I've stopped rubbing myself.

"Yes, Sir."

I repeat the process and stop myself from coming when I get too close to my orgasm.

"Again."

"Yes, Sir," I moan.

Logan has done this five more times by the time we pull into the garage under our building, and I'm delirious with lust. Every cell in my body is on fire, and I'm more than desperate to come now. It's the only thing I can think about, and I think that the pleasure from Dante and Nate might tip me over the edge as Logan parks the car. I need an orgasm so badly that I'm ready to take any punishment I'm given if it happens.

"Cover yourself up, Angel," Dante says as he lowers his hand. "We can't exactly have you walking through the parking garage like that."

I give a low moan at the thought of it, even though I know he's right. The guys stand a respectable distance from me in the elevator because of the cameras, but as soon as we're in our apartment, hands are all over me.

We're still standing in the entry of the apartment when Logan pulls my dress down under my breasts as Nate disappears under my skirt and tongues my clit. I alternate between kissing Dante and kissing Logan while they play with my breasts, and it's barely thirty seconds before I moan into Logan's mouth when my orgasm rips through me.

My whole body shakes as I succumb to the pleasure I've been denied for so long. Nate continues to flick his tongue back and forth over my clit while I ride out my orgasm. I break my kiss with Logan, bite my lip as I throw my head back, and moan loudly. Logan kisses my neck and up my jaw to my lips before he claims them again.

Dante bites my nipple, then lifts his head to say, "Take your dress off, Angel."

Logan steps back from me, and I pull my dress off over my head to reveal Nate with his face still buried in my pussy. He has his fingers in me now, too, and he pushes them in and out as he pulls his head back to look up at me.

"I want my cock inside you right this fucking second, Sexy."

He pulls his fingers out of me and licks them as he stands. Dante takes my dress off me while Nate leads me to his bedroom. When we get there, Logan steps in front of me and looks me over from head to toe.

He places his hand around the back of my neck and looks into my eyes. "I instructed you to do something in the car, and you didn't respond appropriately. What should my toy say when I ask it to do something?"

I can barely focus enough through my arousal to answer, "Yes, Sir."

"Correct."

He puts pressure on the back of my neck to push me over to the bed. When my knees hit it, Logan pushes me down, so I'm bent over it. My pussy juice runs down my thigh as he bends down to put his face near mine.

"You're going to be punished now, Alexandra. Then, that pussy will get pounded the way it needs to be. I want you to count."

"Yes, Sir," I manage to pant.

He moves away, and it's only a second before he brings a hand down on my ass. I count aloud to ten, and Logan kisses each cheek and rubs them gently before he moves away. My ass burns, and my need to be fucked is intense. I don't move from my position, and I groan in satisfaction when Nate finally pushes his cock into my aching pussy.

"Oh god, yes," I moan.

Dante appears at my side and lies on the bed in front of me. "Worship my cock, Angel."

I take him into my mouth while Nate keeps fucking me. I trail my tongue up Dante's cock and swirl it around the head before I begin to suck him. I'm not sure how long I've been doing it when I notice Logan move to stand at the edge of the bed.

I remove Dante from my mouth and continue to stroke him as I turn to look at Logan. Nate has wrapped his lips around Logan's cock while he pounds into me, and I groan at the glorious sight of Nate giving Logan a blow job. I watch them, and it's so hot that it tips me into orgasm.

I ride the waves of ecstasy, but pain cuts through it as Dante twists my nipple while he glares at me. "Did I tell you to stop worshiping my cock, Angel?"

"No, Honey," I gasp.

He tugs my nipple a little harder and growls, "No, I didn't. Don't fucking stop until I blow down your throat."

I drop my head again, and he lets go of my breast as soon as he's back in my mouth. The pain from my nipple travels a direct path to my pussy, though, and I'm in ecstasy as I worship Dante's cock. I can't see Logan and Nate, but I can imagine what they're doing as I watch Dante's reaction to my blow job, and it makes me even hotter.

Nate comes inside me with a groan as he grips my hips tight, and he thrusts into me a few more times before he pulls out. I'm filled again when Logan pushes himself into me a few seconds later. I moan onto Dante's cock, and he strokes my head as he watches me.

Logan really does pound me, and I struggle to focus on the blow job I'm giving Dante. I have to try to find a rhythm while I'm lost in the ecstasy, and I'm grateful when his cock jerks in my mouth and he shoots his load into my mouth. I'm careful to make sure I swallow everything and clean his cock entirely before I remove him from my mouth.

"Thank you, Angel," Dante murmurs.

I collapse onto the bed again as Logan thrusts into me. I'm shoved forward every time he does, with the edge of the bed digging into my shins in a pleasurably painful way. I reach up and grab hold of the bedsheets to try and get purchase of something, but Dante reaches over and tickles under my arm.

"Holy shit," Logan says from behind me as he pauses in his movements.

"What?" Nate asks.

"When Dante tickled her. Fucking hell, her pussy clenched me so tight I thought she might cut my dick off."

"Really?" Dante asks in a surprised tone.

"Do it again."

"No," I gasp.

Logan's hand comes down in a stinging hit to my still-burning ass cheek. "What have I told you about that word, Alexandra?"

"Don't use it. Ever. It means nothing unless I use my safeword."

He smacks my ass cheek again, and I jerk as the pain comes,

followed by the pleasure of it.

"That's right. Do it again, Dante," Logan growls.

Dante grabs my hand and pulls it up. It takes everything in me to resist the urge to pull it back down again. When he tickles me, though, I can't stop myself, and I yank my hand down as I squeal loudly.

Logan groans from behind me as my pussy clenches around him. "Fuck, that's so fucking good. Again?"

Nate is the one who does it this time, so I have no warning because he tickles under the arm that's still clutching the bedsheets above my head. I squeal and jerk as I pull my arm down to stop him.

Logan groans behind me as his cock jerks inside me, and he buries himself deep when he comes a second later. I come apart around him, and we ride the waves of our orgasms together.

As we pant for breath, Dante says, "Well, that was interesting. I've tickled Lexi when she's been tied up before, but I've never been inside her when I did it."

"I think this is definitely something we should play with again," Logan says. "You should feel it. Amazing."

He leans down and kisses my back before he pulls out of me. We go to the bathroom, where Dante begins to wash me while I kiss both Logan and Nate before Nate washes himself and leaves the bathroom. I'm enveloped in Dante's embrace and then Logan's in turn as they finish washing and drying me.

"How are you feeling, Angel?"

I smile at Dante, full of peace, calm, and with a sense of happiness around me. "Perfect."

"Good."

The men dry themselves, and then Dante disappears while Logan grabs some of his clothes from the closet and gets dressed. He carries me back to the living room, where he kisses me before depositing me on Nate's lap for a cuddle.

"Hopefully, we'll all be living in the same place soon," Nate says.

"I don't want to get my hopes up, though. I'll get excited when our offer is actually accepted," Logan says with a sigh.

I move over to climb into his lap and smile at him. "The sooner you're living with us, the better. I'm taking Monday off work for my doctor's appointment, so I'll be able to come over earlier than usual."

"Well, that's something." He kisses me, and I sink into his embrace.

The conversation moves on, and it's not until I'm lying in bed with Logan and Nate later that night that I allow myself to think about Ash. I still don't like the idea of him going on a date, and I'm not sure why. I was fine with it when we discussed it, and it was just an abstract concept that might happen in the future.

Now that it's actually going to happen, I feel conflicted about it. He's said multiple times that he's not interested in being a fully-fledged member of this alternate relationship we have, though, and I need to respect that.

Ashton Woodford is free to be with anyone he wants to be with. No hard feelings.

Chapter Seventeen

Give Thanks for Cock

"Alexandra, it's lovely to see you again." Dr. Leland smiles as she holds the door to her office open and indicates to the chair in front of her desk.

She's been my gynecologist for years, and I'm comfortable with her, even when I have my legs in stirrups.

"It's great to see you, too, Dr. Leland." I return her smile and take my seat.

The doctor takes a seat at her desk and looks at her computer for a few seconds before she turns to me. "Okay, so we're going to replace your IUD today."

"Yup. It's going to expire soon, and I don't want to have any accidents."

Considering I frequently have four different men come inside me, I doubt I could go long without getting pregnant if I didn't have my IUD in. I get a weird pang when I realize that it's three guys now.

Dr. Leland chuckles. "They actually remain relatively effective for a year or two after they expire, but I wouldn't recommend leaving it in past expiry."

"I got my period last night. Is that going to be a problem?" I cringe.

"Not at all. I'll still get you to do a pregnancy test to be sure you're not pregnant, but it makes it easier to insert the IUD if you're on your period."

Unsurprisingly, the pregnancy test comes back negative, and the doctor removes my old IUD before putting the new one in. Afterward, I sit back in front of her desk, and she hands me some paperwork about the IUD.

"You shouldn't have sex in the next twenty-four hours. It should be effective immediately because it's been inserted within seven days of your period starting. However, I always advise my patients to use protection for seven days after insertion to be safe."

I nod as I read something similar on the piece of paper in front of me. "Makes sense."

"After your period each month, just check that you can feel the strings to make sure it hasn't moved."

"I will do. Thanks so much for everything."

"Not a problem. Do you have any other questions?"

"Nope. I think you've covered everything."

"And you feel okay?"

I nod my head as I stand to shake her hand, then put the paperwork in the big tote bag I'm using today. I sling the bag over my shoulder then head out to the reception area to pay for my appointment. Once I'm in my Tesla, I smile as I put Logan's address into the GPS.

I'm excited to spend the evening with him, even if we can't have sex. I cringe as a cramp hits me, and I take some painkillers before I start driving. The cramps are still painful when I get there, and I want to get out of my tight jeans and into the comfy sweatpants I brought with me.

Logan is in the office with his door open as I pass him on the way to the bedroom. "Hi, Logan. Bye, Logan."

When I get to his room, I dump my bag on his bed and rummage in it to pull out my clothes.

"Everything okay?" Logan asks as he wraps his arms around me from behind.

I lean back against him as I place my hands over his and smile. "Yeah. I just had my IUD changed, and I have my period. My painkillers haven't kicked in yet, and I want to get into something more comfortable."

"Makes sense." He kisses my neck and lets go of me. "I'll just enjoy the show, I guess."

He lies on the bed and relaxes with his hands behind his head, one ankle crossed over the other. He indeed watches me as I pull off my jeans and blouse.

"God, that feels so good," I say as I take off my bra.

"It *looks* so good," Logan says with a wicked grin at me.

"Hey, you. No sex for twenty-four hours."

"I think you'll find that I'm perfectly capable of enjoying the view without having sex."

"Good to know," I laugh as I pull on the sweatpants.

I climb onto the bed next to him, and he wraps his arms around me before he kisses me. His tongue dances expertly with mine, and we're both breathless when he ends our kiss.

"So, what would you like tonight, Lexi? I'll get you anything you want, and we can do whatever you want."

"I'm the boss?" I raise an eyebrow at him.

He laughs and playfully swats my ass. "I wouldn't go that far. I'm just choosing not to exercise my control over you for now."

Despite the fact that I can't have sex with him, I'm overcome with desire at his words.

"I see. Well, I want to stay in this bed and not go anywhere. I want to eat pizza and ice cream while we watch romantic comedies on Netflix."

He kisses me again and says, "Okay. Deal. I'll order the pizza in about an hour." He reaches into his nightstand and pulls out the remote control for his TV. "I have control over you, but I'll allow you to have control over the TV."

"So kind."

I put a movie on, and we laugh together as we watch it. When it's almost finished, he orders the pizza, and it arrives a short way into our second film.

I head to the bathroom while he goes to greet the delivery driver. I can't use my menstrual cup because of the IUD insertion, so I'm relying on my trusty period underwear today. I rinse it and wring it out before I drape it over the edge of Logan's bath. I'll have to wash it later, but for now, I pull on another pair and wash my hands before I head back into the bedroom.

"All good?" Logan asks from the bed where he has the pizza boxes sitting next to him.

"Yeah, I do have some laundry to do, though."

"I'll do a load later if you want."

Heat rushes to my cheeks, and I say, "You might not want to. It's my period underwear."

"Lexi, I'm quite aware that you bleed once a month. I've even fucked you while you've been on your period. I'm not sure why you would think I'd have a problem including your underwear in a load of laundry," he says in an amused tone.

My cheeks get hotter, and I point out, "I don't know. Some guys don't even like buying tampons or pads for people."

"Yeah, and some guys need to buy tampons and pads for themselves, but I know the type of guys you mean. They're scared to go down the period aisle as if it'll make their penis fall off or something."

He rolls his eyes, and I burst into laughter as I say, "You never know. It could happen."

"I know a few trans people who wish it worked that way," he chuckles. "Well, I'm willing to take the risk that handling your period underwear might cause me to lose my penis. At least I'll have lost it for a good cause, I guess."

I'm still laughing as I climb onto the bed next to him. He moves the pizza boxes to his other side, and we turn the movie back on as we eat. It's only been about twenty minutes when my phone rings, and I see Dante's name on the screen.

"Hi, Honey. Is everything okay?"

"Yes, it is. Is Logan there?" he asks, and it sounds as though he's smiling.

Dante asks me to put the call on speaker when I confirm he is. "Okay, he can hear you. What's up?"

"Nate's here with me, and we just got a call from Anthony. Our offer was accepted, and we've got the apartment."

"Oh my god!" I yell, and Logan laughs.

We talk for a few more minutes before we end the call. Logan gets us glasses of champagne to celebrate. We finish the pizza and a tub of ice cream between us as we watch the rest of the movie.

When it finishes, I ask, "Do you want to watch another one?"

"If you want to, we can."

I shake my head and turn the TV off before I hand him the remote. "No, I'm fine."

"What do you want to do, then?" He asks as he sets it aside.

I can't wipe the smile off my face at the knowledge that he's going to be living with us soon.

I look into his beautiful face and tell him, "I want you to tell me something I don't know about you."

Logan raises his eyebrows and looks surprised. "That's a tough one. We've known each other a long time."

"I know, but I bet there's something."

I rest my head on his chest, and he wraps his arms around me as he kisses the top of my head. I listen to his heart beat as I wait for him to answer my question.

"When I was eight, we went on a trip, and I saw the Grand Canyon for the first time. It was the most amazing thing I'd ever seen, but I was too scared to go near the edge of the viewing area. My mom had to hold my hand the whole time we were there, so she couldn't go look properly, either. Poor Mom," he laughs.

"Poor Baby Logan," I say with a laugh as well. "I want to go back in time and give you a cuddle."

"What about you? Tell me something I don't know about you."

I don't want Ash to go on a date with someone else.

The thought comes to my mind far too quickly. I can't tell Logan, and I know it's not fair to Ash to stop him from dating, so I come up with something else to say.

"Whenever I go over a set of railway tracks, I lift my feet a tiny bit."

He laughs and shakes his head. "Why?"

"When I was a kid, one of my friends told me it's bad luck to have your feet on the floor when you drive over railway tracks."

"Why do you still do it, then?"

I shrug, and heat rushes to my cheeks as I realize how stupid it is. "I don't know. I kind of just got in the habit of doing it and never stopped."

"That's pretty cute." He's silent for a few moments, then he asks, "Are you nervous about Thursday?"

"Huh? Why would I be nervous?"

It'll be the first time I've seen Ash in person since he told me he's going on a date, and I am kind of nervous about it, but I don't want to admit it.

"We haven't been around our families since we got together," he points out.

"Oh, shit."

I hadn't thought about that. Hiding our relationships from the public is one thing, but our family members are the people who know us the best. After what happened with Cassie, I have zero desire for anyone else to find out about us.

I sigh and cringe. "Well, I wasn't that nervous about Thursday, but now I am. I guess I'll just have to work really hard to resist the temptation to fuck you on the Thanksgiving dinner table."

Logan turns my face up to his and gives me a wicked grin. "Do you think you have that kind of willpower?"

"I'm resisting the urge tonight, aren't I?" I raise an eyebrow at him.

"You do seem to be." He raises a hand to cup my breast and slowly brushes my nipple with his thumb. "Is there anything you want to do, Lexi?"

My pussy clenches, and arousal floods through me. We'll be celebrating Thanksgiving on what's supposed to be my next night with Logan. I also know there are plenty of ways for us to enjoy ourselves tonight, so I nod.

"What would that be?"

"I want you to use me. We just can't do vaginal sex. Anything else is fine."

Logan kisses me, and his tongue explores my mouth for a few seconds before he asks, "If you need to safeword for any reason at all, you will?"

"Yes, Sir."

"Take your top off, Alexandra, then sit on me as if you were fucking me."

I pull my sweatshirt up and off over my head, exposing my breasts to his view before I straddle him. His cock is hard against my pussy, and I wish he were inside me.

"I love your breasts." He reaches up and, as he twists one nipple, a shock of arousal shoots to my pussy. "They're so much fun to play with."

He reaches his other hand down to rub my clit through my panties. I moan as he continues his assault on my senses. I rub myself back and forth on his hard cock while he pleasures me, and I close my eyes to focus on the sensations he's giving me.

"Look at me, Alexandra."

I open my eyes and look into his chocolate brown eyes, full of lust as he watches me. I succumb to the feelings building inside me and tip into orgasm as I moan his name. He continues what he's doing as my body shakes and my orgasm passes. I realize he's going to give me a second orgasm, though, when he keeps going while watching me.

I'm lost to the pleasure, and my orgasm builds in the background of it. I can sense it coming close as I moan and writhe on Logan. It's about to crash over me when Logan pushes me off him and onto my back.

I gasp in surprise as he climbs onto me, his bodyweight heavy on me as he pulls one of my nipples roughly. "My turn, Alexandra. Did you think you were going to get two orgasms when I've had none?"

"Um, yes, Sir," I answer honestly.

"Seems foolish to think that I wouldn't want my toy to give me pleasure. You only got an orgasm because it pleased me to do so. You aren't going to come again until it pleases me. Understand?"

The knowledge that he controls when I get to come is so fucking hot, and my breathing is shallow as I nod. "Yes, Sir."

Logan unzips his jeans and pushes them and his underwear down enough to pull his cock out. It's thick and hard in his hand as he grips it and begins to stroke it slowly.

"How best to use my toy, I wonder." His cock is so close, and I can't help but lick my lips as I look at it. Logan chuckles, "Maybe I'll let you suck it for a little while, my beautiful slut toy." I groan at his use of the word slut, and he raises an eyebrow at me. "Do you like being reminded that you're my slut?"

"Yes, Sir." My blood is on fire, and every cell in my body is on edge as I give myself to him.

"Noted."

He moves forward, and the rough denim of his jeans rubs my nipples as he pushes his cock between my lips. I swallow him eagerly, and when he begins to thrust his hips against my mouth, fucking me, I float away with the ecstasy. I'm his, and this is everything.

I can barely stay aware enough to keep myself from coming as the stimulation of everything brings another orgasm toward me. Logan thrusts roughly in and out of my mouth, gagging me with his cock, and nothing has ever felt this good. I'm eager to swallow his cum, but he pulls his cock out and pants for breath as he looks down at me.

He grabs one of my hands and holds it up above my head. I realize what he's about to do at the last second, and I squeal as he tickles me. I try to yank my hand away, but he grips my wrist tightly while my body writhes, and I laugh.

"No! No!" I screech.

Logan lets go of my hand and twists my nipple roughly. "Don't fucking say that word, slut. I'm going to tickle you if I want to tickle you because you're my toy."

I'm so fucking close to coming at his reminder that I belong to him. The threat of him tickling me more. The pain of him twisting my nipple. I'm enjoying this experience too much, and my pussy aches with desire as I pant while I look up into his beautiful face.

He grabs my other hand and pulls it up. I know what's coming, but I can't stop my reaction as he tickles me. I laugh, and my pussy clenches, but I bite my lip and don't tell him no, even as I wriggle underneath him.

"I can't wait to do that to you when I'm fucking you again," he murmurs in a husky voice after he stops. "Actually, wait here."

He climbs off me, and I watch as he strips naked, his cock jutting in front of him before he walks away into the bathroom. He comes back with a towel and pulls a bottle of lube from his bedside table. He lays the towel out next to me and rolls me onto it face down.

Logan pulls my sweatpants and underwear down and off before he tosses them aside, and I swallow heavily as I realize he's got the towel to protect the bedsheets. He spreads my cheeks apart and thrusts his tongue into my ass. I moan as I rub my crotch against the towel.

"You're not allowed to come, Alexandra."

I moan and say, "Yes, Sir."

He keeps eating my ass, then drips cold lube onto it. He fucks my ass with two fingers and drips more lube onto it before adding a third. Finally, he grips my hips and pushes his cock into my ass. He leans forward and kisses my back as he begins to fuck me. His weight pushes me into the bed, and I turn my head to the side as I pant for breath.

Logan thrusts roughly into my ass and holds himself there. Without warning, he tickles me again, and I squeal and pull my arm down.

He groans behind me, "Fuck. It works in your ass, too."

I'm subjected to him tickling me over and over for the next few minutes. He tries it in different ways. The short burst of him just tickling me before I yank my arm down. The longer times of him holding my arm up with one hand while he tickles me with the other. Tickling under both arms and continuing to do so once I pull my arms down. I writhe and squeal and laugh under his heavy bodyweight, with his cock sometimes pumping into my ass and other times just held deep inside me.

He thrusts his hand around me and reaches down to rub my clit. His thighs rest against mine, his cock is deep in my ass, and his breath is hot against my neck as he pants, too.

"Come on my cock, Alexandra."

He tickles me again, and I squeal, but pulling my arm tight against my body doesn't stop him. His fingers of one hand continue to torture me while the fingers on his other hand pleasure my clit. I laugh hysterically while my orgasm comes close, despite the tickling. My pussy repeatedly clenches along with my ass around Logan's cock.

I've lost control of my body, and I writhe underneath him, even while I seek his fingers harder against my clit with my hips. I have tears in my eyes from laughter as a powerful orgasm hits me. My entire body seizes as it hits, and I scream in ecstasy. My vision blurs, and I shake as the orgasm continues for a long time, so pleasurable that I barely recognize when Logan's cock jerks in my ass, and he comes inside me.

He collapses on top of me and pants against my back. He lies there for a few seconds before he drops hot kisses on me.

"You're so beautiful, Alexandra. Thank you for that."

"You're welcome, Sir."

Logan pulls his softening cock out of me and climbs off the bed before he scoops me up, towel and all, to carry me to the bathroom. He cleans me off and helps me get dressed before he puts on a load of laundry and joins me back in bed. I fall asleep utterly satisfied and wrapped in his arms.

*****

"Hi, Mrs. Woodford." I smile at Ash's mom as she opens the door for us.

"Lexi, it's lovely to see you, dear." She gives me a hug.

I thrust the heavy container of mashed potato at her as we pull apart, my stomach full of approximately a million butterflies. "Here. I brought my mashed potato."

"Excellent. Dante, it's good to see you."

"Happy Thanksgiving, Mrs. Woodford." He smiles and hugs her as well before we move past her.

"Ash is in the sitting room with his sisters. You two are the first to arrive," she tells us. "Let me take your coats, and you can go join them."

We thank her as she takes our outerwear, then we head toward where she said Ash was. Nate and Logan are coming together. We figured it would be less obvious if we weren't all together. Usually, Dante and I arrive at Thanksgiving dinner together, not with the others.

When we get to the sitting room, Ash has a drink and is talking to his sisters, Ella and Vivian. He looks as gorgeous as ever, relaxed in an armchair, wearing black trousers and a collared blue shirt that matches his eyes.

He looks up at us and smiles. "Lexi. Dante. Hi, guys."

We greet everyone, and I walk over to give Ash a hug because it's what I would normally do. When I hug him, his body is as stiff as mine, and I give him an awkward smile before I hug his sisters.

I take a seat on Dante's lap as we talk to Ash and his sisters. I avoid Ash's gaze and talk enthusiastically with Ella and Vivian about Black Lilac and Heather Fletcher, plus her clothes and the deal I've done with Serenity. When Nate and Logan arrive, I get up and hug them as though I haven't fucked either of them today.

"Hey, Sexy Lexi," Nate says. "How have you been?"

I laugh and nudge him. "Pretty good. What about you?"

"Yeah, good. Logan and I played some pool at my place."

It feels as though we're putting on a show, and I'm sure everyone's watching us and analyzing our every move. When I look around, though, they're not. Ash's sisters talk to Logan and his brother, Samuel, who arrived about ten minutes ago with their parents.

Dante's parents arrive next and say hello to all of us kids before they join the other parents. When my dad arrives with my stepmom, I give them both a big hug before they head to the other room.

After everyone has arrived, we all get drinks and gather in the dining room, where Ash's mom says a few words about what she's thankful for. We go around the room saying what we're each thankful for this year and when it's my turn, my eyes flicker from Dante to Nate and Logan, then to Ash, before I quickly look away again.

"I'm thankful for relationships with people who I know will always be there for me, no matter what."

I get a plate of food from the table and take it to the living room, where a big dining table has been set up for the kids to sit and eat. I take a seat in between Dante and Nate. The food is delicious, and Ella smiles at me.

"Your mashed potato is as tasty as ever, Lexi."

"Thanks." I smile back at her.

Nate puts his knife and fork down before he casually lowers one hand below the table and picks up his glass of wine with the other. As he takes a sip, he slips his hand up under my dress and rubs my bare pussy. Dante instructed me to wear no underwear since my period finished last night.

I spread my legs a little wider and cut some meat off a slice of turkey as I resist the urge to moan.

"So, the music video you two were in was something," Sam says as he looks at us.

Nate and I both freeze in our movements. He snatches his hand back, and I snap my legs shut as heat rushes to my cheeks.

"Yeah. That was a fun video shoot," Nate laughs casually.

"I've gotta say, it was weird seeing you two together." Vivian shakes her head.

"Hey, try being me." I force a laugh as well.

My pussy is wet from what Nate was doing, and I squirm from the discomfort of both that and the topic of conversation.

"If you'll excuse me, I need to use the bathroom."

I smile politely at everyone and push back my chair. When I get to the downstairs bathroom, it's occupied, so I head upstairs instead. I use the toilet before I wash my hands and stare at my flushed face in the mirror. Being here is so uncomfortable. As is hiding my relationships with Nate and Logan from everyone.

On top of that, I'm so aware of Ash's presence and the fact he's going on his date tomorrow night. When I open the door to the bathroom, I'm surprised to find myself staring into his ice-blue eyes.

"Can we talk, Lexi?" he asks.

I shrug my shoulders and say, "Sure."

I follow him across the hallway and into his childhood room. It bears all the hallmarks of a teen boy's occupancy. There are posters of sports cars and scantily clad women on the walls amidst pictures of rock star heroes. In the corner of the room is an old electric guitar. There's a dresser against the wall next to the wardrobe and a bed underneath the window.

"What's up?" I ask casually.

"I don't know. I guess I just wanted to make sure you're okay with tomorrow."

He scrutinizes my face, so I walk away from him and take a seat on his bed for something to do.

"Of course I am. Why?"

"You haven't talked to me since I told you about it and…"

I raise an eyebrow at him. "And what?"

"We haven't played together since then, either."

My heart pounds in my chest, and I avoid his gaze. I'm not sure what I should say because if he wants to go on a date, that's his choice.

"I've been busy," I say.

He walks over and sits on the bed next to me before he takes my chin in his hand. He turns my face to his and forces me to look at him.

"Are you sure that's all it is?"

"Yes."

"And you're fine with me going on my date with Štěpánka?"

His eyes search my face, and I work hard to keep any of my concern out of my expression as I nod.

"And the only reason we haven't played is because you've been busy?"

I nod again, and he looks at me for a few seconds before he presses his lips against mine. I stiffen at first but then give in to the kiss. Our tongues dance together, and I wrap my arms around his neck. Ash pulls me down on the bed as we continue our kiss.

He reaches under my dress and groans when his fingers find my bare pussy, "I should've known when I saw Nate fingering you under the table."

"You could tell?"

Heat floods to my cheeks, and he nods. "It helps that I know what I'm looking for."

He pushes me onto my back and pulls my skirt up to my hips as he moves between my legs. He spreads my legs wide, and I bite my lip as I look down at him. I told myself I would let him move on from Cassie without us playing together, but I'm so turned on, and he's as sexy as ever. I don't want to stop this…so I don't.

"I'm going to eat the best Thanksgiving meal I'll ever have," he growls. "You'd better come quietly if you don't want everyone downstairs to hear us."

I gasp as he buries his face in my pussy. I grab hold of the sheets and buck against his mouth as he pleasures me. I pant for breath and watch him in blissful ecstasy as he uses his tongue and fingers to bring me to orgasm. When I come, I thrust my fingers into his hair and pull his mouth harder against my clit.

Ash stands up and unbuckles his belt as he says, "You're going to need to be equally quiet when I fuck you."

All I can manage to do is pant for breath as I nod, even though my brain is screaming at me that this is a terrible idea and I'll regret it. My body wants it, though. Needs it, even. I have to have Ashton Woodford buried deep inside me right now, and I groan when he pushes his thick, hard cock into me.

"Tell me how good that feels, Lexi," he murmurs.

"*So* fucking good."

"Tell me how much you like my cock in your wet cunt," he growls as he stares deep into my eyes.

I gasp, and heat floods to my cheeks as I admit, "I love it. You feel amazing when you fuck me."

He pulls his cock back so the head is right at my entrance before he thrusts forward and slams it back into me. "You're damn right, I do."

He reaches up and pulls my breasts out of my dress. It's got a tight bodice, and it's slightly painful when he does. My breasts are barely able to be pulled out, and I pant for breath.

"Play with your tits while I fuck you."

I place my hands on my breasts, desperate to please Ash. Something deep and visceral in me wants to give him an amazing experience. I want to be everything he wants, and I tweak and pull my nipples while I bite my lip as he fucks me.

"God, you're fucking sexy." He lowers his head to one breast while he reaches between us to rub my clit again. "Come for me, Lexi."

He straightens up again and thrusts in and out of me while he rubs my clit. I play with both my breasts as I stare into his eyes. He's beautiful, and I still have that need to do anything he asks of me, so I focus on how good his cock is inside me. I let the pleasure build, and when my orgasm approaches, I do nothing to stop it.

I look right in his eyes as I moan, "Ash, oh fuck yes."

My body shudders, and I wrap my legs around his waist as I come on his cock. He makes a guttural growl as he leans down and covers my lips with his. His kiss is deep and passionate as he thrusts into me roughly. I meet his thrusts with my own. I want him harder, faster, and deeper. I want him inside every part of me, and

I give everything I have to him.

When he comes, his cock swells and fills me with his cum. I squeeze his waist with my legs as I come again on him. I put my hand on the back of his head and hold his face against mine as I kiss him as passionately as I can.

Eventually, he pulls out of me, and I groan. "Fuck. I don't have any panties."

Ash laughs and kicks off his shoes, then pulls off his trousers and briefs, which he tosses to me. "Wear these. It'll be hot to know you're filled with my cum at the Thanksgiving dinner table."

My cheeks flush with heat, and my pussy clenches as I pull his underwear on. I stand up as Ash buckles his belt, and he looks at me and grins.

"Sexy." He strides over to me and places his hands on my breasts as he thumbs my nipples. "You should go downstairs like this."

"Uh, no. Hard pass." I laugh.

Ash lowers his mouth to one and swirls his tongue around my stiff nipple. "Are you sure? I quite like being able to do this to you." I moan softly as he tweaks and pulls my nipples. "Goddammit, you make me want to stay up here and play with you all night, and we really can't. Someone might come looking for us soon."

He pulls my dress back over my breasts, and I flinch at the pain. "Ouch."

"Are you okay?"

"Yeah, this dress wasn't exactly designed to be under bust," I laugh.

"Sorry. Let me kiss it better." He kisses each of my breasts over my dress and then kisses me on the mouth as he rubs them with his thumbs before he asks in a husky voice, "Is that better?"

"Much," I murmur as I reach between us to rub his cock through his trousers.

He grabs my wrist and pulls my hand away. "Yeah, you're going to need to stop that right now."

"Or what?" I smirk at him.

"Or I'll take a page out of Dante's and Logan's books and spank you," he taunts me.

"You can't threaten me with a good time."

Ash kisses me again and says, "Let's go."

I check my reflection in the mirror of his dresser, smooth down my hair and dress, then nod. "Okay."

I feel strange as I follow Ash downstairs, and we take our seats back at the table. Nobody pays much attention to us, but Dante, Nate, and Logan all give us meaningful looks that tell me they know what just happened. I know they'll be okay with it, but I'm not sure if I am.

It's not until we're eating dessert and I shift in my seat that some of Ash's cum seeps out of me. As it does, I remember with horror that I wasn't meant to have unprotected sex this week.

Chapter Eighteen

Home Sweet Home

I take a look around the empty apartment, and I'm hit with a pang of sadness. "I can't believe this is the last time we'll be here."

"We've made some good memories in this place." Dante slips his arms around my waist and pulls me into his embrace. "It's time to move on and make memories in our new apartment, though."

It took the movers a surprisingly short amount of time to pack all of our things into their trucks and leave the apartment completely bare.

Logan's and Nate's apartments were emptied earlier in the week, and they're there today to greet the movers when they arrive at the new place.

"I know. I didn't expect to be sad about leaving this place behind at all. It just feels like we're closing the door on a chapter of our lives."

Dante kisses the top of my head. "Because we are. Come on, let's get over to the new place. I think you'll feel better as soon as you're there."

He's right, of course. The man knows me better than I know myself, and by the time we're pulling into the underground garage,

I'm bubbling over with excitement.

The movers are still bringing some of our furniture in, so I'm careful to keep my distance from Logan and Nate. When Dante comes back from seeing the movers out to the elevator, I squeal with excitement.

"We officially live together!" I announce.

I'm wearing a strapless dress, and Logan strides over to me, then yanks it down and to the floor in one swift movement.

"Correct. Which means you shouldn't be wearing clothes in my apartment."

I gasp as I'm suddenly exposed to three hungry sets of eyes. Their gazes rove over my body, and I'm more than ready to christen this new apartment.

Dante moves over to me and spanks my ass, then grabs a handful of my ass cheek as he growls, "Does your dress belong on the floor, Angel?"

"No, Honey."

I bend over to pick it up, and my ass presses against Dante's stiff cock. He doesn't move to give me any room, so I step out of the dress while I remain pressed against him, and I snatch it into my grasp as I stand up.

"Go put it away and then meet us in your room, Alexandra," Logan says in a low, sexy voice.

"Yes, Sir."

I take the dress to the room that will be Dante's. In the end, he took the master in the downstairs apartment after all. The one upstairs is just as glorious, and Logan has the second master up there, so Nate decided to have the upstairs one.

As part of keeping up appearances, my clothes were all set up in Dante's room, so I deposit my dress in the hamper and head back out.

I arrive at the staircase as the guys get there, so I lead the way upstairs, and as he walks behind me, Nate announces, "I love this view."

I grin back at him, and my pussy aches with arousal. I know

what's coming, and I can't wait. I lead the way to the sex room and step aside so Logan can unlock the door.

He brought all the equipment here himself in a U-Haul with the help of Nate before any of the movers did anything. He also changed the door handle to a keyed lock so that no one would come in here during the move.

Dante leads me over to the St Andrew's Cross and shackles my wrists while Logan shackles my ankles. I stand spread-eagled against the padded, X-shaped piece of furniture. I'm so wet already that when my pussy clenches, my juices run down my thigh. I love being so completely vulnerable to anything they want to do to me.

Logan grabs a pair of nipple clamps and puts them on my nipples. I gasp at the pain when he tugs on the chain between them, and he grins at me.

He pushes two fingers into my pussy and pumps them in and out as he says, "My toy is wet and ready to be filled, I think."

"Her ass can't be used with her tied like this." Dante appears with a new butt plug, bigger than the biggest plugs we've used before. "So we might as well fill it with this."

Logan steps aside, and Dante pushes the plug into my pussy. It's thick and long. I can't stop the gasp that escapes me when he brushes my clit with his thumb, and Dante glares at me.

"Naughty, Angel. You know better."

He tightens the nipple clamps and gives the chain a painful tug. I resist the urge to moan, but I have to pant for breath. Dante fucks me with the butt plug as he watches me intently. I manage to withhold my reactions, but it's a struggle. I want to moan and scream and wail. The need builds inside me, especially when Dante begins to rub my clit while he fucks me.

As my orgasm builds, I keep my body still. I allow the pleasure to build around me and maintain my position until Dante smiles at me.

"Very good, Angel. You can react now."

At once, I give in to the feelings and allow my body to respond. "Oh my god, yes."

I moan, and my body shakes as I bite my lip. Dante continues, and my orgasm crashes over me in waves of ecstasy that flood into my very being. A finger rubs lube around my ass before pushing its way inside, and I look down to see Logan preparing me to take the butt plug Dante is currently using to fuck me.

After another minute or so, Logan moves away, and Dante pulls the butt plug out of my pussy and pushes it into my ass. I groan as it stretches me wide before slipping inside. Dante steps away again, and it's strange to have no hands on me after the last few minutes.

I'm left standing tied in front of the three men, nipples clamped, pussy dripping, and with my ass full of the plug. They all have obvious erections in their jeans as they look at me.

"God, that's hot," Nate murmurs. "You guys do good work."

"Thanks," Dante laughs.

Logan looks at me and smirks, then moves over to stand at Nate's side. He reaches down to rub his cock through his jeans, and Nate turns his head to kiss him. Logan deftly unbuttons Nate's jeans with one hand, and it's only a few moments before he's pulled his cock out and is stroking it in his fist as they kiss.

I give a low moan as desire floods through me at the sight of it. I want to suck Nate, but I also love watching Logan giving him pleasure. I catch sight of their tongues intertwined with one another as they kiss, and it's so erotic that I can barely stand it.

"Mmm, Logan. That's good," Nate tells him when their kiss ends.

"You like that, huh? Let me show you what I like."

Logan drops to his knees in front of him and wraps his lips around Nate's cock. The pure ecstasy on Nate's face as Logan blows him drives me wild. I love watching this, and Logan knows it. He knows that I want to be closer. That I want to be involved. That being tied up and unable to participate is torture.

I ache to be a part of it, and I can do nothing but watch as Logan brings Nate right to the edge of orgasm before he takes him out of his mouth. "Go fuck Lexi if you want to."

Nate blinks at Logan for a few seconds, and I think he might tell him he doesn't want to before he nods and grins at him. He steps around Logan as he looks up at me, and the desire is obvious in his eyes.

"I'm not going to last long," he warns me as he approaches.

He shoves his cock into me, and I moan as I finally get the satisfaction of having one of them inside me. My pussy tightens around his thick cock, and he thrusts in and out of me. Nate kisses me as he holds my waist while he fucks me. It isn't long at all before he buries himself in me and blows his load.

He kisses me again as he pulls out. I'm left feeling utterly unsatisfied, but when I look at Logan, I know this was his plan from the wicked grin on his face.

"How was that for you, Alexandra? Did you enjoy having Nate fuck you?" He raises an eyebrow at me.

"Yes, but I need more, Sir."

"You'll get plenty more when we're ready to give it to you," Dante says.

Nate's cum is dripping out of me, but neither Logan nor Dante say anything about it, and Nate relaxes on the bed nearby as he watches us. Logan comes forward with a vibrator that he switches on low and places on my clit. The pleasure reverberates through me as Logan pulls the nipple clamps off one by one and then tosses the set aside. He clamps his lips around one of my nipples and swirls his tongue around the tight bud. My body begins to shake, and I'm about to come when he swiftly pulls the vibrator away and bites my nipple hard.

I gasp in surprise and disappointment as he steps away from me again. "Oh, no. You don't get to come yet, Alexandra. What good is a toy if it isn't wound up and ready to play with?"

Dante steps forward next. He trails a riding crop softly over my body, then taps my nipples with it. I jump at the stinging sensation. He does this over and over again on different parts of my body. He even hits my clit a few times, and I come painfully close to orgasm.

It feels as though they spend hours tormenting me. Dante and Logan take turns to use different tools on me and drive me wild with lust. Even though I haven't been told not to come, it doesn't matter. Neither of them allows me to get close enough to tip over the edge.

Finally, Dante thrusts his cock into me instead of any of the many implements he's pushed inside me so far this evening. It's warm and hard as it stretches my pussy, and his breath is hot on my neck as he grunts while he fucks me.

"Hold still for a second," Logan says, and Dante turns to look at him in surprise.

"Huh? Why?"

"You'll see. Just do it."

Dante turns to look at me and pushes his cock deep inside me before he holds himself there. I'm looking into his chocolate-brown eyes, lids heavy with lust, when Logan tickles me. I have no recourse tonight, so I can't stop him in any way.

I squeal loudly, though, and Dante's eyes widen as he gasps and his mouth drops open. "Holy fucking shit, Logan."

"It's good, isn't it?" Logan says. He stops tickling me and twists my nipple instead. "I've done it a few times now. It's hot as fuck every time."

"Damn. I had no idea. I feel like I've been missing out for years," Dante says in awe.

He tickles me a few times while he fucks me. Logan plays with my breasts, and occasionally he kisses me as well. Finally, Dante buries his cock in me and empties himself there. He kisses me and rubs my clit until I'm just on the brink of orgasm, then he pulls himself out of me and quickly steps away.

My body shakes as my orgasm ebbs away, and Logan smirks at me. "Did my little slut not get to come?" I shake my head as my pussy clenches, and Dante's cum seeps out of me. "What a shame. Maybe, if you're a good, little slut toy, I'll let you come on my cock. Would you like that, Alexandra?"

"Yes, Sir," I moan.

Logan steps forward and says, "We'll see. I might just leave you tied up in this room to be used whenever we want to use you. Don't you think that twenty-four hours spent here would do you good?"

I inhale sharply at the thought and swallow heavily. It would be way too much, but I think Logan knows that. He's teasing me, torturing me with the thought of it, and I'm wildly aroused by the idea.

"I'm not sure I could handle it, Sir," I answer honestly.

Logan nods. "I don't think you could, either. Now that we live together, I'll have plenty of opportunities to test you and see how you do. What do you think, Dante? You know her the best."

He turns to look at him, where he's taken a seat on a chair nearby and is watching us with interest. Dante tilts his head to the side as he assesses me.

"I think you'd be surprised at what our angel is capable of. We could work her up to it."

Logan turns back to me. "Not tonight." He trails his hand over my body before his fingers come to rest on my clit. "Soon, though."

He rubs my clit unbearably slowly, and I pant for breath. He takes a breast in his mouth and begins to lick and suck it, sending sparks of electricity shooting throughout my body. When I'm close to orgasm, he stops, and I moan as I'm once again denied my release.

"You know the one thing I don't like about the cross?" Logan says in a thoughtful voice. "It's that I can't have you suck my cock." He sticks two fingers in my mouth, and I suck them as though I'm trying to have him blow down my throat.

"If only you had someone else in the room who was willing to do that," Dante says in an amused tone as he smirks at me.

Logan laughs and says, "Nate, what do you think?"

"Well, I actually meant me, but if Nate wants to do it…" Dante trails off into a shocked silence.

I can barely breathe because the thought of it drives me to a level of arousal that is nearing insanity. My husband, sexy as fuck, who once had a blow job from Logan as a gift to me, is willing to return the favor. I know he'll be doing it as part of my torture tonight, but that almost makes it hotter.

Nate and Logan both stare at Dante in obvious shock, and Dante looks over at Nate. "Obviously, I'd only do it if you're okay with it. I'd clear it with Lexi, but she doesn't get a say anyway, and from the looks of her, she'd love to see it."

Nate blinks at him, then looks between him and Logan. "I'm not sure."

"That's totally fine. It doesn't have to happen. I just wanted to tease Lexi, but I wouldn't want to do it at all if you're not a hundred percent okay with it." Dante smiles at him.

"No. I kind of want to see it," Nate admits. "Just…if I'm not okay when it's happening…"

Logan strides over to him and kisses him. "We'll stop, of course. If you're not sure, though."

Nate looks between them again, then at me, and nods at Logan. "Do it. I probably want to see it as much as Lexi does."

He stands and walks over to me, and my pussy clenches at the sight of the stiff cock that gives away his arousal. He sticks three fingers in me and roughly fucks me with them.

"She's full of cum, and still wet as fuck."

He pulls them out of me and pushes his cum-covered fingers into my mouth. The taste of my juices is right there with the taste of Nate and Dante's cum. Nate uses his hand to play with my breasts and pussy as Dante drags the chair over, sets it sideways in front of me, and indicates for Logan to take a seat.

"Don't make me come. I still want to fuck Lexi," Logan murmurs, and Dante nods as he gets on his knees in front of him.

Dante wraps his lips around Logan's cock, and I groan at the sight. Logan catches my gaze and keeps it while Dante blows him. Logan thrusts his fingers into Dante's hair, and my pussy aches as I watch them.

Logan gives a low moan and asks, "Are you sure you haven't done this before?"

Dante pulls him out of his mouth and pumps Logan's cock

with his fist as he shrugs. "I can assure you I haven't, but I know what I like having done to me."

He puts him in his mouth again, and Nate has returned to playing with my breasts, but I'm sure that any contact with my clit right now would send me right over the edge of the abyss. Nate slowly strokes his cock with his hand as he watches them as well before he turns to take my breast in his mouth. His tongue is hot and wet as he swipes it across my nipple, and I moan as I close my eyes.

"Look at me, Alexandra," Logan growls.

I open my eyes and blink as I force myself to keep them open despite the pleasure flooding through me. My body begins to shake, and my orgasm nears, but Nate notices and stops what he's doing.

Logan groans and thrusts his hips up to meet Dante's mouth. It's obvious how much he's enjoying this, and I look at Nate to check on him. He's stroking himself faster now, and his eyes are hooded with lust as he stares at the two men in front of us.

"Okay, that's enough, Dante," Logan says, and Dante pulls him out of his mouth at once.

Dante moves over to the side of the room, and I'm surprised to see that he's not rock hard like Nate. His cock is semi-erect, and it's clear that show was just to torture me.

"Come here, Nate," Logan says.

He walks over and into Logan's embrace. They kiss passionately, and Logan reaches between them to stroke Nate's cock while Nate does the same to him. My body is aflame with desire and the desperate need to have an orgasm. Watching them together is as hot as it always is, and I can barely breathe as I watch them pleasure each other.

Logan breaks their kiss and murmurs, "I want you to fuck me."

"Anytime," Nate says with a laugh.

Logan gets the bottle of lube from where it was left underneath me, and he raises his eyebrows as he does. "You've made a mess of this floor, Lexi." He scoops up some cum on his fingers and stands up again. "Open wide."

I open my mouth and allow him to push his fingers into my mouth. The salty cum hits my tongue, and I swallow it as I suck Logan's fingers before he pulls them out of my mouth.

He walks back over to Nate and kneels on the chair in front of him. Nate opens the lube and squirts some on Logan's ass. He rubs it around Logan's hole then pushes a finger into him. I pant for breath, just from this. Nate adds more lube and is soon fucking Logan's ass with his fingers while he strokes his cock with his other hand before he pulls his fingers out and positions himself behind Logan.

My pussy clenches, and my nipples are so stiff they hurt as I watch Nate grab hold of Logan's hips and thrust his cock into him. Both men groan as Nate buries himself in Logan. I lick my lips and wish more than anything that I had my mouth around Logan's stiff cock right now.

As they fuck, it's all I can think about as I watch it jerk with each of Nate's thrusts. I can imagine it pushing down my throat, and the ache in my pussy increases. It takes Nate a long time to come this time, and I'm delirious with lust by the time that he does. When Nate buries himself deep in Logan and lets himself go, I moan in ecstasy with them, participating in the act from the sidelines.

Nate pulls his cock out of Logan, and I groan as I watch cum drip from the head of his cock. Logan turns and kisses Nate as he wraps his fist around Nate's cock and thumbs the head, and Nate moans into his mouth.

"I love you," Logan murmurs as he lets go of Nate's cock.

"I love you, too." Nate kisses him again, and it's almost a minute before they break apart.

Finally, Logan turns to me, his eyes dark with lust as he stalks toward me. Without a word, he pushes his hard cock into my dripping pussy, and I gasp in delight as I'm filled again. The sensations overwhelm me as Logan thrusts roughly in and out of me.

My eyes roll back in my head, and I float away into blackness with nothing but the pleasure surrounding me until Logan's hand wraps around my jaw, and he asks, "Safety light check."

I force myself to open my eyes into what feels like much too bright a light and blink at him. His cock is still in me, and the world is still a sea of pleasure, but I know I need to answer, or it will all end.

"Green," I decide.

Nothing is wrong. Everything is just far too right. I'm in ecstasy and being carried away into sweet oblivion. I give in to the sensations when Logan starts moving again.

"Dante, come watch her," he says in a faraway voice.

Logan fucks me, and I realize Dante has come to stand next to me when he gently strokes my side. He keeps giving me gentle touches, even occasionally stroking my nipples, and orgasms roll over me multiple times. Whenever Logan checks on me, I assure him that I'm green, but he seems less sure than I am.

When he finally buries himself deep inside me, Dante reaches down and rubs my clit to give me a final orgasm around Logan's cock. My body shudders, and the intense climax to our scene takes me over. I make a sound I don't even recognize as being my own, and my pussy clenches around Logan's cock as though it's trying to ensure he never leaves it. He grunts as his cock spasms inside me, and his own orgasm leaves him panting for breath.

He kisses me while his cock is still emptying its load in me. It's gentle, sweet, and his tongue toys with mine as he strokes my head gently. It's soothing, and I slowly meet his kiss as I come back to my senses.

"Good girl, Alexandra."

When he pulls out of me, it's as though reality hits me at once. I hurt all over. My arms ache from being up for so long. My ass is sore from being stretched by the butt plug that's still in it. My nipples sting from the treatment they received. Meanwhile, my pussy aches from the amount of use it's seen over the last few hours. I gasp at the pain and writhe a little in my restraints.

Logan notices and says, "We'll get you out right now, Lexi."

He quickly releases one arm while Dante does the other, and I groan at the pins and needles when my arms drop to my sides. Logan takes one of my arms and shakes it while Dante repeats the movement on my other side. I can barely stay upright now that I've been released, and I droop onto Dante, who holds me up while Logan releases my legs and removes the butt plug.

"I think you should go shower her since your room is up here. I don't think she can make it downstairs," Dante says. "I'll clean the toys and come see her when you're done."

Logan nods and picks me up to carry me to his new room. My body has started to shake as I come down, and Logan squeezes me tight as he takes me into his bathroom. He sets me down, and I immediately slump to the floor, my legs unable to hold me up.

He turns the water on and then frowns at me where I sit on the floor. He strides out of the shower, and the sound of the water running in the bath as well comes to me.

Logan gets down on the floor and pulls me into his lap, so my legs are in the spray as he kisses me. "We're going to have a bath. I think you need it." He gently rubs my arm with his hand. "You did so well, Lexi."

He kisses me and holds me tighter as my body shakes. He washes me under the water before he turns off the shower and carries me into the bath when it's ready. The water is hot and soothing as I sit on Logan's muscled thighs.

I relax back against him and close my eyes as my exhaustion takes me over. I don't know how long I sleep, but I wake to the sound of low, quiet voices.

"Is she okay?" Dante asks.

"I think so. It just took a lot out of her." Logan strokes my stomach with his thumb.

"How long has she been sleeping?"

"Almost thirty minutes. I plan to wake her when the water gets cold." Logan kisses my head softly.

"Just make sure she's okay. I was definitely worried about her."

"Me, too," Logan says and kisses my head again.

"I'm fine," I tell them with my eyes still closed. "This is very nice. I love you, Honey."

Dante chuckles, and I can hear the relief in his voice when he says, "I love you, too, Angel."

By the time we get out of the bath, I'm feeling relatively normal. Logan still dries me and holds my hand as we head downstairs to find the other guys. I'm naked, as usual, but it would almost be weird to wear clothes at home. Especially now that Logan is living with us.

We find the guys talking in the living room as they drink whisky. I sit on Nate's lap and kiss him while Logan gets himself and me a drink.

"Ash is coming over," Dante says, and my head snaps around to look at him.

"Why?" My heart beats a little faster in my chest, and I suddenly wish I *were* wearing clothes.

"We're not sure, but he said it was important."

"Is he bringing anyone with him?" I ask in a meaningful tone.

Ash has been seeing Štěpánka for four weeks now. We've met her a couple of times, and it was awkward as fuck both times. I've basically avoided playing with Ash, and I'm sure it's been noticed. Luckily, as my doctor said, the IUD was effective immediately, so my little slip-up at Thanksgiving didn't result in any accidents.

"I asked if he was going to be alone, and he said yes."

There's an awkward silence for a few moments, and I ask, "Should I get clothes on?"

"Do you want to get clothes on, Angel?" Dante raises an eyebrow at me.

"Well, he has a girlfriend now. I'm not sure if it's appropriate."

The three men exchange glances, and I look ahead at the empty coffee table in front of us while I keep my expression neutral.

"If Ash is uncomfortable when he gets here, you can put clothes on," Dante tells me.

My nerves multiply as we wait for Ash to get here, and by the time he arrives, I think I might be sick. I haven't been exposed to him since Thanksgiving, and when he walks into the living room with Dante, his eyes immediately snap to me. His eyes widen slightly and his gaze roves over my body before he looks away.

"Hi, everyone," he says as he takes a seat in an armchair nearby, where he sits stiffly.

"Hey, Ash. What's up? You apparently said you had something important to tell us?" Logan asks.

Ash nods. "Yeah." He sighs, and his jaw tightens before he says, "Cassie contacted me."

My stomach drops, and I suddenly forget about being naked and my attraction to the man who just dropped this bombshell on us.

"Fuck," I breathe out.

"'Fuck' is right." Ash turns his beautiful blue eyes to meet mine, and despite the topic of conversation, his eyes dart down to my body, and I can tell he's aroused. He swallows as he looks back into my eyes and says, "She saw pictures of Štěpánka and me on a date. Now she's threatening to go to the media again. She says the story is even juicier now, and she thinks she could get more money. I think she's bitter that I'm moving on."

I can't stop the tears that fall from my eyes as I realize we're never going to be free from her. She's going to keep holding the knowledge she has over our heads, and we can't stop her. Nate wraps his arms tightly around me and holds me while I cry.

"I watched her delete those photos, though," Logan says in a flat voice.

"She had copies, of course. She told me with great delight that she still had the photos to use against us," Ash growls.

"How much does she want now?" Dante asks.

"The same again. She swears this will be the last time, and she'll really delete the photos." He sighs again. "I don't know that I believe her."

It takes us almost two hours to come to the conclusion that we'll pay Cassie again. I feel sick even just thinking about it, but we've talked through every possible option, and we can't find anything else to do. Ash messages Cassie and tells her to meet him tomorrow at his apartment so he can give her the check.

"I guess that's that, then," he says as he locks his phone. "I don't feel good about it."

"Neither do any of us, I don't think," Dante says quietly.

Ash gives us a small smile. "So, this is your new place, though?"

"Yeah, it is." Dante smiles back at him. "Want to have a look around?"

"Sure."

We show Ash through the apartment, and he's clearly stunned by the second apartment, even though we'd told him about it before.

"I know you said it was a whole other apartment, but it really is," he says as he shakes his head when we get to the top of the staircase.

"Imagine our surprise, given we had no clue when we first came here," Logan laughs.

When Ash opens the door to the sex room, I get hot all over as he stares into it. Despite the intense scene we did earlier, a large part of me wants to fuck Ash right now.

"Well, this place looks like fun," Ash murmurs.

"It is," Nate chuckles. "You missed out, Ash. A few hours ago, Lexi was tied up to that cross while we fucked her."

Ash turns to face me and steps forward, so he's directly in front of me. He raises a hand to my breast, and I gasp as he rubs his thumb over my nipple.

"It's been a long time since I got to fuck Lexi," he says as arousal floods through me.

I want it. So badly. The guys don't say anything, and it's clear this is between Ash and me. Dante may have prompted it by leaving me naked, but I'm not sure it wouldn't have come to this if he hadn't anyway.

"We'll need to use a condom," I say with a swallow.

"No, we won't."

I blink at him and then frown. "It's not safe to have

unprotected sex if you're sleeping with someone else."

"I haven't slept with Štěpánka." Ash shrugs, his hands still on my breasts, his thumbs rubbing circles around my hard nipples.

My stomach flips, and I ask, "Why not?"

He looks away into the bedroom, then back to me. "We're taking it slow."

He lowers his mouth to one breast and sucks it before he lifts his head and kisses me. His tongue intertwines with mine, and I wind my arms around his neck as we kiss, and he continues to play with my breasts.

He takes my hand in his and leads me to the bed in the corner of the room. The door clicks shut behind us, and my heart pounds in my chest as I realize we've been left alone.

Ash stops next to the bed and strips off his clothes. His cock is already hard, and I can't resist the urge to drop to my knees and take him in my mouth. He groans, and I look up at him as I suck him. I love the noises he makes, and he looks like a Norse god as he watches me. Blonde hair, ice-blue eyes staring down at me, and with his square jaw tensed as I pleasure him.

I stand and push him onto the bed. His eyes are hooded as he moves back to rest his head on the pillows while he watches me climb on after him. I straddle him and lower myself onto his cock, allowing a moan to escape my lips as he stretches my sore pussy.

"God, you're beautiful," he murmurs as he reaches up to take my breasts in his hands while I begin to ride him.

"I could say the same thing," I reply as I look down at the stunning man I'm fucking.

I grind myself on him, and it isn't long before I'm coming on his thick cock. He takes hold of my hips and pulls me down on him as I come apart around him, then he fucks me until he reaches his own orgasm, and I collapse on him.

We pant for breath as we lie there in bliss, and Ash says quietly, "I missed you, Lexi."

"I missed you, too."

Chapter Nineteen

No Hard Feelings

We settle into a routine in our new apartment, and I flit from bed to bed each night, satisfied with the three men I love. The only fly in the ointment is Ash and the women he's involved with.

He gave Cassie the check the day after we moved into the apartment, and she assured him this was the last time. We're all on edge, though, sure that she's going to rear her ugly head again when we least expect it.

He's been out with Štěpánka a few times since then, and I try not to analyze how that makes me feel too much. I keep thinking about the fact he's not sleeping with her and wondering why that is.

I'm at the Orange County Black Lilac store, and I'm staring blankly at my laptop screen, just thinking about everything, when an email from Heather shows up on my screen.

To: Lexi Sullivan
From: Heather Fletcher
Subject: Serenity clothes arrival

Hey Lexi,
Monday's the day. Are you excited? I can't wait to see you again.
It'll be good to catch up in person.
Heather

I smile and type back a reply, assuring her that I'm definitely excited and that I can't wait to see her, too. We're going to have dinner together on Sunday night, and it'll hopefully go better than our lunch date did on her last visit to LA.

I'm still in a weird mood, though, so I head into the store only to find the girls crowded around the computer we use to run our billing software.

"Oh, hey, Lexi." Vera looks up and smiles at me. "We're just looking at pics of your gorgeous friend on a date with that model on the weekend."

My stomach drops, and I growl, "Is this what I pay you to do? Read gossip sites about celebrities?"

"Uh, no. Of course not," Vera stammers. The sales associates all scatter to the winds, and Vera says, "I'm sorry, Lexi. We're up to date with everything, and the girls were telling me about it, so we searched the pics online so I could see. Is everything okay?"

I blow out a breath of air and shake my head. "I'm sorry. I shouldn't have snapped. You guys all work hard. I guess I'm just a bit sensitive about paparazzi stuff. They follow the guys around a bit more now, and I hate it."

Another Wicked Stallion single was released recently, though I wasn't in the music video this time. It shot to the top of the charts, and there's a lot more attention on us as a result of that. I'm on edge whenever I see the paparazzi, and I have to be a lot more careful about my interactions with the guys in public, especially Nate.

"I get it. I'm sorry."

"It's all good. I'll be in my office if you need me."

I spin on my heel and head back to my office, my mood not having improved from this interaction. I feel like shit for snapping at the girls, and I decide to order lunch to apologize. I make the order and message Vera to tell her we're having lunch on me, but it doesn't clear my mood.

I pull out my phone, open my messages with Ash, and type one out.

Can we talk?

I shake my head and delete the message before I write another one.

Why aren't you sleeping with Stepanka?

I delete that as well and drop my phone on my desk a little too hard. Ashton Woodford is free to do whoever he wants. If that's a model from Czechia, that's a model from Czechia. Fuck, he can even get back together with Cassie if he wants to. It doesn't matter to me.

I repeat this mantra to myself all afternoon and apologize profusely to my employees for snapping at them. They very graciously accept both my apology and the token of my gratitude for their hard work.

My stomach is still twisted up in knots by the time I leave work, though. I write about ten messages to Ash that I delete, then lock my phone and put his address into the GPS. I need to speak to him in person, but I'm nervous as hell about it.

I write a message to the group chat I have with Dante, Nate, and Logan.

I'm going to be home late tonight. Love you.

Dante's the first to respond.

Thanks for letting us know. Love you, too, Angel.

Nate's and Logan's replies come through as I'm nearing Ash's place.

Not a problem. Love you, Lexi.

And I love you, too, Sexy Lexi.

I pull into the underground garage of Ash's apartment using the keycard he gave me, and my heart pounds as I approach his parking spaces. A part of me is worried that there will be an unknown car in one of them. Luckily, there isn't, and the presence of Ash's car tells me that he's likely to be home.

By the time I get upstairs and knock on his door, I want to puke. As I wait for him to answer, I alternate between wanting to run away and being certain that this is a conversation we need to have. I'm pretty sure my heart is beating so loudly that they can hear it on the floor below, though.

When Ash opens the door and raises his eyebrows at me, I still have to fight the urge to run like the wind. "Lexi. What are you doing here?"

"I came to see you," I manage to choke out. "Are you alone?"

"Yes." His surprise disappears, and he looks concerned as he steps aside to let me in. "Has Cassie contacted you?"

"No. No, it's not that," I tell him as he closes the door.

"Okay. Do you want a drink or something?"

I shake my head. "No. It's fine."

I drop my bag on his dining table as we pass it on the way to the living room. Losing this feels like losing a chunk of armor, and I fiddle with the hem of my dress as he sits on the sofa next to me.

"What's up?" he asks, his blue eyes piercing into mine.

I can't stand it, so I look away from him and out the windows at Los Angeles below us as I ask, "Have you slept with Štěpánka yet?"

I hold my breath while I wait for his reply, and I think that I might die if he says that he has. I don't know why, but it'll feel like a betrayal. Even though I know, logically, that he's free to do it.

"No."

I don't think a word has ever sounded sweeter to my ears, and I wipe away a tear that's rolling down my cheek as I turn to look at him again.

"Why not?"

He swallows heavily and says, "We're taking it slow."

"You were taking it slow three weeks ago. You've been seeing her for almost two months…" I trail off because I can't bring myself to ask if it's because of me.

This time, he looks away and says quietly, "I don't know, Lexi. She wants to. I know I should want to as well, but it doesn't feel right. Whenever we start to do more than kiss, I just…can't bring myself to do it."

My heart pounds in my chest, and I don't know why this is so scary. I don't want to put myself out there, but Ash is one of my closest friends, and I've loved him for a long, long time. I know that I'll regret it if I don't tell him what I want to tell him before he actually goes through with it.

I let out a heavy sigh and say, "Look at me, Ash."

He turns to me, his beautiful face forlorn, and he looks as conflicted as I feel.

"I don't want you to sleep with her."

The words ricochet through the air around us, shattering the illusion I'd built that I was okay with any of this from the beginning.

"Why not?" His eyes pierce through me again, but I don't look away this time.

"Probably the same reason you can't seem to bring yourself to do it." I sigh and shrug my shoulders. "I didn't want you to go on a date in the first place."

"Why didn't you tell me that?"

I snort and shake my head. "We made a deal. We'd play together, and you'd be free to sleep with someone if you found them. No hard feelings. I couldn't go back on that and prevent you from finding happiness because I wanted to keep you to myself."

He slides closer to me on the sofa and places his palm on my cheek as he gently strokes my bottom lip with his thumb.

"You want to keep me for yourself?" I nod and kiss his thumb. His eyes are hooded, and his voice is low and full of lust as he asks, "What do you want to do with me?"

I move his hand aside and climb onto his lap as I look deep into his eyes, even though I'm not sure what I'm searching for yet. "Everything."

I press my lips to his and thrust my tongue into his mouth. He wraps his arms around me and strokes my back as we kiss. We both pant for breath as we break away and look at one another.

"Tell me what you want me to do, Lexi. Ask me to do anything, and I will."

My heart swells, and I bite my lip before I say the thing I want more than anything else. "I want you to stop seeing Štěpánka and only sleep with me. I know it's not fair because I sleep with Dante, Nate, and Logan as well, but it's what I want."

I have no qualms about asking this because I'm so sure it's what I want, and I'm equally certain that he will do it for me.

"Done," Ash says, and he pulls me back to kiss him again.

He pushes me down, so I'm lying on my back on the sofa as he continues to kiss me. His body is hot against mine, and I feel as though I'm burning up with my desire for him. I wrap my legs around his waist and my arms around his neck as we kiss for a long time.

"Do you know how many nights I've masturbated while imagining you were here with me, Lexi?" he murmurs.

"How many?" I ask and gently nip his bottom lip with my teeth.

"Nearly every fucking night since Napa," he admits, and my pussy aches with desire. "Then, I'd get to play with you, and it was only fuel for my fantasies. I've absolutely defiled you in my mind in probably every way imaginable since I first made you come."

The knowledge that he's been here, fantasizing about me, drives me wild. I thrust my pelvis against him, pushing his hard cock against my wet slit even though we're both still fully clothed.

"The number of times I've watched the 'Heavenly Promises' music video is ridiculous. I had the thirty seconds before the bridge on repeat, and I've masturbated to it so many times just watching you come over and over and wishing you were here for me to make it happen in person."

"Well, I'm here now," I point out. "You said that you would do anything I asked you to do. I'm offering you the same. I said you couldn't be my Dom, and I meant it, but tonight I'll give you control over me. Take me and use me in any way you want to. Make your fantasies come true."

He groans and asks, "Are you serious?"

"Deadly." I grin at him. "There's nothing you can't make me do. I'm yours, Ash."

His cock is rock hard against me now, and I can't wait for him to fuck me with it, but I'm also curious about what he'll do with my offer.

"Take your clothes off, then." He grins at me.

I take my dress off and, out of habit, begin to fold it before I set it aside.

"Drop it on the floor. None of that folding shit. I want to think you're so desperate to fuck me that you can't be bothered with it."

I drop the dress immediately and grin at him as I stand in front of him wearing a bra and heels. "I am desperate to fuck you. That's why I'm here."

I unclip the bra and drop it on the dress. My pussy is drenched, and my juices drip down my thigh as I stand in front of him.

He places his hand on my legs and strokes up and down my outer thighs. "Tell me how much you want me."

"Let me show you." I take a step to the side, spreading my pussy and offering a view of how wet I am.

Ash reaches behind me and spanks my ass, his big hand leaving a painful sting behind. "I said to tell me. I didn't say to show me your cunt. Are you doing everything I say or not?"

I pant for breath, and I swear to god that I might just fucking come right now. I know I said Ash couldn't Dom me, but fucking hell was that hot.

"I want you more than I want to keep breathing. I want you to fuck me so hard that you turn me inside out. I want your fat cock in my pussy, filling me with your cum as you split me in half. I want to be so sore tomorrow that I can barely walk."

His fingers flex on my thigh, and he says, "Is that so?"

I nod, and he leans forward and runs his tongue through my wet slit. When it hits my clit, I come apart and moan his name as my body shakes. He swirls his tongue around my clit as he licks and sucks it until my orgasm passes.

When it does, he pulls his head back and looks at me. "Tonight, you can only call this your cunt." He cups my cunt in his hand and squeezes it as it clenches, and my juices drip onto him. "Got it?"

"Yes, Ash," I moan.

"What am I holding right now?" he asks with a wicked grin on his face.

"My cunt," I gasp, and it clenches again as I unwittingly try to rub my clit against his hand.

"Where do you want me to bury my cock?"

"In my cunt."

I struggle to breathe as the eroticism of this experience takes me over. It feels dirty to call it that, and it makes me hotter than ever.

"Put your left leg on the back of the sofa behind my head," he tells me.

I do as instructed, and it spreads my cunt wide in front of his face. I balance on my right leg as Ash strokes up and down my inner thighs. His fingers come close to my cunt, but he doesn't touch it, and he looks up at me as he gets closer and closer.

"What do you want me to touch, Lexi?" he murmurs as he watches me.

"My cunt. Please touch my cunt."

"Only because you asked so nicely," he laughs.

His fingers brush ever-so-softly against my clit, and I moan in satisfaction. He keeps up this torturous barely there contact for a long time, and I'm delirious with lust by the time he rubs me to an orgasm.

It's barely passed before he says, "Now give yourself one. I want to watch *you* do it."

My jaw drops, and I blink before I lower my hands and do what he's asked. I watch him watching me, and it's fucking hot as shit to put this display on for him. I push the fingers of one hand in and out of my cunt roughly because I need a good fucking right now, and with my other hand, I rub my clit until I come so hard that my juice squirts out and onto Ash's lap.

"Mmm, so you're a squirter," he says.

"I, uh, no. I've never done that before," I tell him.

He chuckles. "So I get one of your firsts. Nice."

He pulls my hands away and buries his face in my cunt. I'm lost again to the pleasure he gives, and he eats me until I've had two more orgasms, his face glistening with my cunt juice when he finally comes up for air.

"Get on your knees," he growls.

I lower my leg, stumble a little before I get my bearings, and fall to my knees. Ash stands and drops his jeans and briefs to the floor before he unceremoniously stuffs his cock into my mouth.

He holds my face in his hands and fucks me with reckless abandon. My jaw aches from his thick cock, which hits the back of my throat and restricts my access to oxygen. He grabs a fistful of my hair and uses it to pull my head down on his cock. When I gag, he pulls my head back with my hair, and the pain on my scalp sends a shock of arousal straight to my cunt.

He does it repeatedly, gagging me over and over before he pulls me back by my hair as my cunt aches with desire. Finally, he pulls out of my mouth and pushes me over. I instinctively shoot my hands out to catch myself, so I end up on my hands and knees.

Ash drops behind me and puts a knee between my legs before he shoves my right leg over. He puts his other leg down and shoves my left leg over with it, so I'm spread wide in front of him.

He rubs my ass with one hand and strokes my cunt with the other. "Such a nice fucking ass. I'm going to spank it for no reason other than I can. What do you think about that, baby?"

I bite my lip and moan. There's something about it not being a punishment. It really does make this night about him just using me for whatever takes his fancy, and that is so hot that I almost come just from the thought.

He smacks my ass, and I jump at the stinging sensation. "I

asked you a question."

"It's fucking hot," I tell him.

"That's my baby," he murmurs.

He spanks my ass cheeks over and over. There's no rhyme or reason to how hard or which ass cheek he hits. By the time he's finished, though, every hit sends fiery pain throughout my body, and I'm in ecstasy as he grabs my hips and thrusts his cock deep into my cunt.

I groan aloud and meet his thrusts with my own. He reaches around to rub my clit as we fuck. It takes approximately five seconds before my orgasm rips through me, and I'm screaming his name.

"Yes, baby. Come for me. Make that cunt milk me dry when you do."

My cunt squeezes his cock with every wave of my orgasm, and Ash's groans of pleasure are utterly satisfying. He pulls out and plunges his fingers into my cunt instead. He swirls them around, and I roll my hips against him to seek more pleasure, but I'm left empty after a few seconds.

His cock is back in me again almost immediately as he pushes his fingers into my ass, and I realize that he's using my own cunt juice as lube. He repeats this over and over until he's fucking my ass with his fingers in time with his cock fucking my cunt. Finally, he pulls out of my cunt and plunges his cock into my ass instead.

I squeal as he pushes himself inside me. I don't have time to adjust tonight, and he buries himself to the hilt, then holds himself there. I pant for breath as I try to accommodate him, but I'm a ball of painful ecstasy.

Ash reaches around and rubs my clit again as he murmurs, "You can do it, baby. You can take my fucking cock in your ass. You're doing it right now. Relax and let it feel good."

As the sensations of what he's doing roll over me, my asshole loosens up, and Ash starts moving in and out of me. He keeps rubbing my clit until I come again while he fucks me. He spanks my ass, and the pain shoots straight to my cunt. Everything about this night is more perfect than I could ever have imagined. When Ash dumps his load in my ass, I scream in ecstasy, and his cock jerks inside me as he rubs my clit until I come one final time for him.

He keeps his cock in my ass and grabs two handfuls of my ass cheeks which he squeezes and lets go, massaging the hot flesh. I moan softly, and he leans down and kisses my back.

"Fuck, that was good," he tells me.

I mumble some incoherent response, arousal still flooding through every cell of my body, and I'm high with ecstasy. He pulls out of me and reaches out a hand to help me to a stand.

"Let's go clean up," he says.

I take a single shaky step before he scoops me into his arms and strides toward his bedroom. When we get in the shower, I start to shake, and Ash looks at me in concern.

"Are you okay, baby?" he asks as he wraps his arms around me.

"Yeah. It's the comedown. What we did was very much like a BDSM scene, so I'm probably going to need you to take care of me."

"Anything you need." He kisses the top of my head and strokes my back gently with his hand. "Tell me what to do."

"Wash me, dry me, cuddle me in bed."

He presses his lips softly against mine, then says, "I'm more than happy to do that."

Ash does a good enough job of washing and drying me, but it's not quite like being with Dante or Logan. I appreciate the effort, though. When we're lying naked in bed together, and I'm cuddled up against him, everything is perfect, and I've never felt happier.

"I love you, Ash."

The words come from my lips unbidden, but in the glow and warmth surrounding me, I don't even have time to be concerned that he might not return the sentiment before he does.

"I love you, too, Lexi. I think I've been resisting it for a while."

I turn my face up to his, and he kisses me. Our tongues dance together as the world glows gold around me.

"I didn't want to admit it, either. I kept telling myself that I was okay with you dating someone else, but I really wasn't."

His ice-blue eyes pierce through me again as he says solemnly, "Whenever I was with her, I wanted it to be you. When you were avoiding me, I could barely stand being away from you, but I told myself that I didn't want to be a part of this whole thing, so I needed to date someone else."

I bite my lip and frown at him as the glow fades a little. "Does 'this whole thing' still bother you?"

"No." He shakes his head, and the world glows brighter again. "You guys are all my best friends. Sharing the woman I love with the guys I love as well doesn't bother me. It's far better than forcing myself to be with someone I don't love the way I love you."

"And how do you love me, Ashton Woodford?"

He kisses me passionately before he ends it and says, "With every part of my heart and soul."

Chapter Twenty

You Have the Power Over Me

I'm a little nervous as Ash and I drive to the apartment on Saturday morning. I sent the guys another message last night explaining that I was spending the night at his place, and we're going to tell them about us today.

I'm sure they'll be happy for us, but we need to decide what this will mean going forward. I don't want to push Ash too far too fast, but I only just got my family under one roof, and I'm not looking forward to splitting my time between two houses again.

I look over at Ash, the sunlight gleaming off his golden hair as he drives, and I smile to myself. I'll do whatever it takes to be with him. I've never been happier than I was last night, knowing that he loves me, too.

He lifts my hand to his lips and kisses the back of it. "I love you, baby."

"I love you, too," I assure him.

We enter through the bottom apartment and eventually find Dante in the office on the computer. He looks up and smiles when he sees us.

"It's good to see you two. Did you have fun last night, Angel?"

I look up at Ash and smile as I look into his beautiful blue eyes.

"I really did. We wanted to talk to you guys about something if that's okay?"

"Sure. Logan and Nate are upstairs if you want to go get them. We'll head to the living room."

I nod and make my way upstairs. I check Nate's room to no avail. The sex room is quiet when I pass by, but when I reach Logan's room, moans are coming from inside as I knock on the door.

It falls silent, and Logan calls out, "Hello?"

"It's me. If you're busy, that's fine. Can you come downstairs when you're ready?"

There's a moment of silence before he calls back, "Come in, Alexandra."

"Yes, Sir," I respond dutifully.

I push open the door, and my pussy clenches immediately at the image presented to me. Nate and Logan are lying on their sides with each of their mouths around the other's cock. The distinctive sucking sound of a blow job is multiplied as they pleasure one another, and they look spectacular with smooth, tanned muscles on display and hard, thick cocks wrapped in big, soft lips.

Logan swirls his tongue around Nate's head, and Nate groans as he moves back and forth on Logan's cock while he pumps it with his fist.

I reach between my legs and rub my soaking wet clit as I watch them. I don't know how long I stand there pleasuring myself as they pleasure each other before a moan escapes me, and Logan finally halts in his movements before he turns to look at me.

"Do you like watching us, Alexandra?"

"Yes, Sir," I say with a nod.

Nate is still enthusiastically sucking Logan's cock, and Logan is leisurely stroking Nate's as he talks to me.

"Hey, Nate, do you want Lexi's mouth on your cock or your mouth on her pussy?"

Nate slowly pulls Logan's cock out of his mouth and swirls his tongue around the head before he groans, "I want her to suck me dry so I can blow down her throat."

He immediately puts Logan's cock back in his mouth and swallows him as deep as he can. Logan moans and looks down at him with hooded eyes for a few seconds before he turns back to me.

"You heard the man, Alexandra. Get your fucking mouth on his cock now, or you'll be punished."

I bite my lip and nod as I stride across the room and climb onto the bed so I can suck Nate. Logan moves back, so I have room to lie down and put Nate's cock in my mouth.

Logan immediately shoves my dress up to my waist and smacks my ass roughly.

I jump and gasp at the stinging sensation as Logan growls, "This is for wearing clothes in my apartment."

My pussy clenches as I realize my error, and by the time Logan has finished spanking me, my pussy juices are dripping from me while I suck Nate, and I'm heady with lust.

Logan spreads my legs and buries his face in my pussy. His tongue flicks across my clit, and he pushes two fingers inside me as he eats me out.

I'm lost in the giving and receiving of pleasure. The air is filled with our hot moans as I blow Nate, who's blowing Logan, who's eating me. I clamp my hands on Nate's muscled thighs as an orgasm rolls over me, and I hold him deep in my mouth as my body shudders.

Logan doesn't stop, and he nips my clit with his teeth as my orgasm passes. It heightens my pleasure, and I continue to move on Nate as my ecstasy builds again.

Logan's skilled tongue brings me to orgasm twice more before Nate's cock jerks in my mouth, and his hot, salty cum pours down my throat. I suck every last drop with pleasure and am rewarded with his entire body shaking as I lick the tip of his head and flick my tongue into the slit there to taste his final offering.

Logan is still eating me, and I turn my gaze to the sight of Nate blowing him. I thrust the fingers of one hand through Logan's thick hair as I pull him harder against my clit and slide my other hand to

Nate's ass. I massage his muscular cheek a few times, then slip my finger to his hole.

I don't have any lube, so I just toy with it, pressing my finger against it and putting a little pressure on it. He moans around Logan's cock, and I'm surprised.

I reposition myself, so my face is at his hole, and his legs are on either side of my head. I've never done this before, and I'm a little nervous about what it'll be like as I dart my tongue out to slide along his perineum.

Nate jolts, and his legs squeeze my head for a second before he relaxes. I flick my tongue around his hole, and it doesn't taste any different from licking any other skin, but the knowledge that I'm eating Nate's ass makes me feel dirty, and I'm so turned on by it that I come on Logan's face again.

My clit is so sensitive now that when he continues to flick his tongue across it, I can barely stand it. In this heightened level of pleasure, I thrust my tongue into Nate and almost come again immediately when he groans.

"Fucking hell, Lexi. Yes. Fuck my ass. That's so fucking good."

His words spur me on, and I alternate between thrusting my tongue inside him and pushing a finger into him now that I have some lubrication to do it with. I grind my pussy on Logan's face and lose track of the orgasms he gives me.

By the time Nate swallows his load, though, I can barely think straight. I moan softly when Nate moves, and his ass disappears from my view at the same time as Logan takes his mouth off my pussy.

It's only a second before Nate's mouth is on mine, though, and his cock is thrust inside me. I'd barely even noticed that he'd gotten hard again while I was tonguing his hole, but I groan as he stretches my aching pussy.

His tongue intertwines with mine as he thrusts his cock in and out of me. I wrap my arms around his neck as we fuck, and I kiss him back in complete ecstasy.

He breaks our kiss and groans, "Oh, fuck yes, Logan."

I look down and notice that Logan has taken my place eating Nate's ass. He's pulled Nate's ass cheeks apart, and his tongue is buried in him. The sight is enough to make me come apart around Nate's cock, and he grins at me as I squeeze him tight.

"Fuck yes, Sexy. Come on me. Do you like seeing Logan eat my ass?"

"Mmhmm," I moan.

Nate kisses me as he thrusts roughly into me again. "I like it, too. It's good. Just like it was when you had your tongue in me." I bite my lip at the memory of it, and he chuckles. "Who knew you'd like eating ass, Lexi?"

"Who knew you'd like having it done?" I counter and bite my lip.

Nate reaches between us and rubs my clit while he thrusts in and out of me as he moans. "Well, it feels fucking good, and if there's one thing I've learned, it's that there's no shame in enjoying things that feel good." He looks deep into my eyes and murmurs, "Come for me, Lexi."

Another few thrusts and I'm coming again on his cock, but this time, it jerks inside me, and he comes in me as my pussy clenches around him.

He smashes his lips against mine, and our tongues dance together in ecstasy. When our kiss ends, we pant heavily as we look into one another's eyes.

"I love you, Lexi," he murmurs.

"I love you, too."

"And I love you both," Logan laughs as his face appears near ours.

He kisses us both in turn and then smiles at me as he lifts me up to carry me to the bathroom. He pulls my dress off over my head and tosses it aside.

"As punishment for wearing clothes in my apartment, you're not allowed to wear that dress for a month," he growls.

I nod, even as I sulk a little internally because it's one of my favorite Serenity dresses. Logan washes me in the shower, and I sigh in contentment as he does.

When he holds me under the spray and kisses me, I relax into the feeling of being his and smile as our kiss ends.

Logan places his fingers under my chin and turns my face up to look at him. “Did you enjoy eating Nate’s ass?” A shot of arousal heads to my pussy, and I nod. “I did not expect that,” he chuckles.

“Neither did I.” I grin at him. “I know I like it when you do it to me, and his ass was just *right there.*”

“I haven’t even done it to him before. I didn’t think he was ready for anal play, so thanks for opening that door.”

I bite my lip as I imagine the possibilities, and Logan trails his finger around my areola as I murmur, “You’re welcome.”

He tweaks my nipple as he kisses me again and, while we kiss, a rush of cold air hits me before Nate’s warm body presses against my back. Nate kisses my neck while I kiss Logan, and then he spins me to face him before he kisses me as well.

We spend a long time kissing and cuddling under the warm spray before we get out, and Logan dries me off. The guys get jeans and shirts on while I’m left to walk naked with them to the staircase to go downstairs.

We find Dante and Ash sitting on the sofa in the living room, and both men’s eyes darken when they see me.

I kiss Dante as I make my way to sit on Ash’s lap. He smiles at me and kisses me passionately before I turn to face the others. I’m sure that my heart is going to explode with how much love I have for the men in this room.

“What’s going on?” Nate asks.

I look at Ash and then back at the guys. It’s kind of funny being on the opposite side of this with Ash now. Twice, I told him about bringing someone into my marriage, and now it’s him.

I turn back to Ash and grin at him. “Not it.”

He laughs and shakes his head. “I see how it is.” He turns to the others and says, “You’ve probably guessed, but Lexi and I are together.”

“Finally!” Nate exclaims. “It’s taken you long enough.”

"Yeah, yeah. I just wasn't sure if I wanted to be stuck sharing a woman with your sorry ass," Ash teases him.

Ash kisses my neck, and I look to Logan and Dante for their reactions.

"I'm happy for you, Angel," Dante assures me. "I expected it the first time you had sex."

I lean over and kiss him before I relax back with Ash again. "You know me better than I know myself."

I look at Logan, and he smiles at me. "I hope you don't think I'd have a problem with it."

I heave a sigh of relief even though I wasn't really concerned they wouldn't accept Ash as one of my partners. I finally feel as though our family is truly complete and everything is right with the world.

"I guess there's just one other thing to discuss." I bite my lip and look at Ash. "How are we going to do this?"

"What do you mean?" He raises an eyebrow at me.

"Well, when Logan was living in his own apartment, I spent Mondays and Thursdays with him. He'd also come to stay at our apartment on the weekend. Should we do the same thing?"

Ash frowns and nods. "I suppose so. It's not like there's not plenty of room here for me to stay on the weekend."

There's a heavy silence in the room when he finishes speaking. My heart pounds in my chest, and I'm scared to ask the question because I don't want him to say no. I also know that I should clear it with the guys first, but their eyes are on me as if they're waiting for me to make the call.

"There's also plenty of room for you to have a permanent room here if you want it." I swallow heavily and hold my breath as I wait for his response.

"Are you asking me to move in?" Ash asks, and I can't gauge from the way he says it what his answer would be if I ask him.

"I mean, it would make sense, wouldn't it?"

My heart beats faster, and Ash holds my gaze with his as he asks, "Are you asking me to move in, Lexi?"

"Yes. I want you to move in with us."

He kisses me and says, "I feel very much loved and wanted. I've been thinking about it since last night. If the guys are okay with it, then, of course, I want to be here with you. I decided that I would wait to be asked because I didn't want to assume."

He turns to look at the guys who all agree to Ash moving in with us.

"I thought you'd be unsure about it," I tell him.

"Once I got past my hang-ups about what it means to be with you, I knew that I don't want to be apart from you anymore."

"Well, I don't know about these guys, but you're not making *me* feel very much loved and wanted, Ash," Nate smirks at him.

"Shut up," Ash laughs. "Dante's been with Lexi for ten years, and you're fucking Logan. Excuse me if I was a bit worried that I'd be some kind of fifth wheel."

"As if you'd be a fifth wheel. With a dirty mouth like yours, you fit right in with these guys." I smirk at him as I recall him forcing me to call my pussy my 'cunt' last night.

He slides his hand between my legs and cups my pussy as he growls quietly in my ear, "Just because I like calling this your cunt?"

"Exactly."

I claim his lips with mine and slide my tongue into his mouth to dance with his as he rubs my clit. Dante takes hold of my leg and places my foot in his lap on his hard cock. He strokes up and down my leg as he watches Ash play with me.

"We've just had her, so we'll leave you two to it," Logan says.

I look over to see him and Nate standing near the entrance to the room. Dante nods, and they walk away. I realize that, on some level, they might still feel as though he gets the final say. It's a notion I'll need to disabuse them of in the future because they're just as important to me as Dante is.

Today, though, I suppose they could see it as Dante welcoming Ash into our marriage. I think he did that months ago, though.

Ash's erection digs into my ass, and Dante's cock is firm underneath my foot. Ash plays with one of my breasts while he rubs my clit, and I moan as he brings me to orgasm.

"Let's take this somewhere a little more comfortable," Dante suggests.

"Sure," Ash says.

Ash pushes me off his lap, and Dante takes my hand as he leads me toward his room.

"Stand by the bed, Angel."

I do as instructed, and the two men eye me greedily as I stand naked in front of them.

"Link your arms behind your back," Dante says.

When I do this, my breasts are pushed further forward, and Ash bites his lip as he looks at them.

"Isn't she beautiful?" Dante murmurs to him.

"Sexy as fuck," Ash agrees.

Dante looks at Ash and raises an eyebrow at him. "Well, what should we do with her?"

"Anything we want." Ash stalks toward me as he says it.

He traces a figure eight around the outside of my breasts. On each circuit, he tightens the path, so it travels closer and closer to my nipples.

I pant for breath and grasp my arms tighter behind my back as I resist the urge to grab him and smash my lips against his. When his finger brushes my nipple, I gasp, and Ash grins at me.

He steps back from me to stand next to Dante again. "I bet her pussy is wet."

"Probably. Sit on the bed and spread your legs, Angel."

I'm thrilled to do this as I take a seat and spread my legs wide. Both men eye my pussy, and Ash strokes his hard cock in his jeans while Dante ignores his but steps forward to me.

He crouches down in front of me, so he's eye-level with my pussy. He moves so close that his breath is hot on my aching center. I think he might be about to eat me, but he doesn't. He traces around the outside of my pussy before he draws a line down the middle, straight over my clit, and I force myself to withhold the moan I want to release.

Dante looks up at me with a satisfied smile on his face. "Good girl, Angel."

He pushes two fingers into me then rubs his wet fingers back and forth over my clit. My pussy aches, but I hold still despite the arousal flowing through my body.

"She's definitely wet," Dante confirms with a look back at Ash before he stands up and turns his face to mine. "Clean my fingers, Angel."

I suck my juices off him and swirl my tongue around the tips before he pulls his hand away from my mouth and steps back.

"I should probably check, too," Ash says in a husky voice.

He crouches in front of me and inspects my pussy as well. I pant for breath, and my pussy clenches as he looks at it.

"This is one very wet cunt," he murmurs, and I gasp as my juices drip down my inner thigh that Ash licks away.

He stands up and steps back again. I'm heady with desire, and I look at Dante.

"What do you want, Angel?"

"To come, Honey," I say in a pleading tone.

He looks at me and gives me a wicked grin. "Play with yourself, Angel. Bring yourself to the edge of orgasm, but *don't* come. No reactions."

I nod and groan internally because I know this is going to be torture. I watch them watching me as I stroke my clit. It's fucking hot, and when Ash unzips his jeans and pulls out his cock, I almost moan but manage to stop myself.

As I masturbate, Dante strips as well, so when I get to the edge of orgasm, they're both standing naked in front of me. Their cocks are stiff, and Ash slowly strokes his, but Dante doesn't touch his erection and leaves it jutting in front of him.

I imagine my lips wrapped around it as I stroke my clit, and the thought of worshipping his cock tips me over the edge. I gasp and moan as I come, my pussy clenching over and over as my orgasm rips through me.

Dante is in front of me at once, and he yanks my hand away

from my pussy as he growls, "I fucking told you not to come."

He pulls me off the bed and takes my place in one swift movement. Still holding my wrist, he pulls me down and over his knee. His stiff cock presses against my stomach, and I gasp for breath.

"Count, Angel. It's twenty for that."

He brings his hand down hard on my ass cheek. It stings painfully, but my pussy drips juice onto his thigh as it does.

"One," I moan.

He spanks the same ass cheek even harder the second time, and I can barely manage to get out the number. By the time he's reached ten, both ass cheeks are on fire, and my pussy needs filling more than ever.

"Do you want to do the next ten?" Dante offers.

I snap my head around to look at Ash, and he stares open-mouthed at me.

"Really?"

"Sure." Dante rubs and massages my hot cheeks. "She should know better than to come when she's been told not to. If she doesn't, then she needs to be taught what happens."

I'm mortified when Ash steps forward. Nate has never spanked me, even though Dante has offered a few times. Logan has taken over punishments from Dante before.

Allowing Ash to punish me is humiliating. I know he enjoyed spanking me last night, though, so I shouldn't be surprised he took Dante up on the offer.

Ash crouches down next to me and takes my chin in his hand to force me to look at him. "You've been a bad girl. I watched you come right in front of our faces when you were told not to. Is that okay?"

"No," I answer dutifully.

"Do you want me to spank you now?"

"No," I manage to say.

Ash kisses me, and he thrusts his tongue in and out of my mouth a few times before he ends the kiss. "Too fucking bad. I'm going to do it. I'm going to tan your hide, and you're going to learn to do as you're told."

Fucking hell.

Maybe I *do* want Ash to Dom me after all. He smacks my ass harder than Dante or Logan ever has, and I gasp at the pain. He brings his hand down again, and I'm in ecstasy.

When he does it a third time to the same ass cheek, Dante says, "You seem to have lost count, Angel. Start from one."

I groan in time with Ash's next hit and manage to say, "One."

It's a relief when he switches ass cheeks, but he goes just as hard on that one. When he reaches ten again, he pushes his fingers unceremoniously into my pussy.

"Her cunt is so fucking wet. She loves this shit, doesn't she?"

I writhe on Dante as I seek contact with my clit, and he traps my hips and pushes me down roughly. "Stay still, Angel. Let Ash fuck you and finish your spanking."

I force myself to stop moving, and it's as though the movement still happens internally. My insides writhe beneath my skin, and everything in my body is set on fire with the next orgasm.

I'm so lost to it all that I barely remember to count when Ash unexpectedly pulls his fingers from my pussy and smacks my ass.

"Eleven," I say just before he hits me again.

By twenty, I'm pretty sure I won't be able to sit tomorrow, and I'm wild with lust. Dante pushes me off his lap, and my legs can barely keep me upright. He moves off the bed and over to where Ash has stood near where he was before my spanking.

"Sit on the bed again, Angel."

I whimper as I take a seat on my hot ass, and a tear rolls down my cheek.

"Safety light check?" Dante says at once.

"Yellow, Honey."

He nods. "Noted. Is it the pain from your ass?"

"Yes," I tell him.

"Kneel in a position that's comfortable for you."

I find a way to kneel with my legs in a kind of 'V' so my ass cheeks aren't touching anything and look up at Dante.

"Now, where were we before you so rudely interrupted us with your orgasm?" he asks in a thoughtful voice.

"Appreciating her body," Ash tells him as he steps forward and cups one of my breasts in his hand.

He strokes his thumb over my nipple, and I moan softly. He juxtaposes this with a painful twist of my other nipple, and I cry out in pain.

Ash crouches down and looks into my eyes as he plays with my breasts. He's gentle for the most part but intersperses it with rough twists and bites.

By the time he decides he's done, I'm gone. I've floated away on the waves of ecstasy and have no thoughts other than when I will be touched next. Dante steps forward, and when he pushes his cock past my lips, I moan in satisfaction.

He twists my nipple roughly and says, "No reactions."

I can't help it, though, and I moan so often and get so many twists of my nipples that Dante frowns at me.

"Safety light check?"

"Green, Honey."

I simply don't care about the punishments. The ecstasy I'm in is too high, and I'm enjoying this too much.

When I stay silent for the next minute or so of Dante fucking my mouth, though, he says, "React, Angel."

I moan onto his cock at once, and he continues to fuck my mouth for a long time. Pressure on my legs parts my knees and exposes my pussy to Ash.

He leans forward and manages to get his tongue to my clit. I lift myself up a little, and he swipes his tongue across it with more pressure while I make mewling noises of ecstasy.

He pushes three fingers in and out of me while he eats me out, and it sends me over the edge. I moan his name around Dante's cock, and my body shakes as I come.

"Get on your hands and knees, Angel."

We move position, and I get on my hands and knees facing

away from them with my knees at the edge of the bed. A cock is pushed into me, and I know it's Dante. After years of fucking me, he's so familiar, and I'd know the hands on my hips anywhere. He pulls me back onto him while he thrusts into me and Ash appears in front of me to kiss me.

He plays with my breasts and rubs my clit while Dante slams into me over and over. I come on Dante's cock multiple times before he pulls out and moves onto the bed.

Dante hasn't even reached my mouth before Ash pushes his thick, hard cock inside me. I gasp in surprise, and Dante stuffs his cock into my mouth.

"Drink my cum, Angel," he growls as he pumps his cock with his fist.

I'm pushed further onto his cock by Ash's thrust from behind, and I suck hard as I am. A few more thrusts like this, and Dante's hot, salty cum pours over my tongue and down my throat.

He groans as his cock spurts the liquid into me, and I swallow it gratefully. I balance on one hand so I can wrap my fingers around his cock and pump it a few more times to ensure he's empty. Then I suck and lick his head as well. I dip my tongue into the slit at the top and revel in the shudder from Dante.

He collapses back on the bed, his head resting against the pillows as he watches Ash and me through lust-filled eyes.

"I like watching you fuck my wife, Ash."

Ash's cock jerks inside me, and my pussy clenches tightly around him at the words.

"Trust me, fucking your wife's tight, wet cunt is basically my favorite thing to do ever." I gasp and grip him tighter with my pussy. "That's right, baby. Milk my cock. Make me cum deep in your cunt." The word again sends a thrill of arousal through me.

"Do you want that, Angel?" Dante murmurs, and I nod. "Beg him for it, then, and maybe he'll give you what you want."

"Please, Ash. I want you to come in me," I moan.

Ash swats my ass cheek, and I jump at the pain as he thrusts roughly into me again.

"Where do you want me to come, Lexi?"

"Inside me," I say.

He smacks my ass again and growls, "Where?"

"In my cunt." I give in because my ass actually hurts now, and I don't want to safeword to stop this. "Please come in my cunt, Ash."

His cock jerks, and he groans, but Dante says, "*Beg* for it, Angel. I don't believe you want it."

I lose myself as an orgasm hits me with his words. The humiliation of being told my begging wasn't good enough. The spanking. The fucking. It's all amazing, and my orgasm rocks my body.

When it passes, I open my eyes and lock my gaze with Dante's as I beg, "Pleeeeease, Ash. Please, please come in my cunt. It's all I want more than anything else. I need you to come in my cunt. It's wet and ready for you to dump your load in me like the slut I am. I'm yours to use, and I'm begging you to fill my slut cunt with cum."

I've barely finished speaking when Ash does just that. His hot cum pours into me as his cock spasms in my pussy. I love it, and my body comes around him as the sheer bliss I'm in tips me into the abyss again.

Ash thrusts into me over and over, fucking me hard through his orgasm, and I clench his cock as tight as I can while he does. When he holds himself inside me and rubs my clit, I lose all control as another orgasm hits.

"Fucking hell, Ash. Yes! Fuck!"

He keeps rubbing through my orgasm and to another one. I can barely hold myself up as he does, and my arms shake along with the rest of my body, threatening to give way.

I catch Dante's eye, and he says, "You will take however many orgasms Ash wants to give you, Angel."

It's painful, though, and my clit is so sensitive now that it feels like one big orgasm that never ends. I moan and wail, and my body shakes even more. Dante moves forward and lifts me upright, holding me up as Ash continues to rub me. His cock is still inside me, and my ass is pressed against his stomach.

Tears roll down my cheeks from the pleasure that completely overwhelms me, and Ash doesn't stop. Dante keeps his gaze trained on my face, but I know I'm nowhere near my safeword because this experience is exquisite.

Dante kisses me, and his tongue dances with mine as I moan into our kiss. After another orgasm, though, I break our kiss to scream in ecstasy. Ash's cock jerks in me, and he rubs me through the orgasm, then finally stops.

The room is silent except for the loud pants for breath that all three of us are making. My body is jelly, and I can't move.

"Fucking hell," Ash says into the silence. "You're amazing, Lexi."

"Mmm," I murmur.

He pulls out of me, but I can't move, and cum drips out of my pussy onto the duvet.

"Oh, dear," Dante laughs. "That's definitely a sign that Lexi's spent."

He carries me to the bathroom, and Ash follows him. I can't stand, so Ash holds me up while Dante starts the shower.

Ash kisses me gently and murmurs words of comfort to me before he hands me over to Dante. Ash washes himself then leaves the shower.

I'm still exhausted when Dante has finished washing and drying me, but at least I can manage to stand. Only just, though, so Dante picks me up and carries me back to bed.

He lies me down under the top sheet while he removes the dirty duvet and retrieves another one. He spreads it out over the bed and climbs in next to me. He pulls me into his embrace and kisses me gently.

"How was that for you, Angel?"

"Amazing," I assure him.

"Do you want Ash to Dom you?"

I shake my head as I think about last night. "No. He's fucking amazing when I let him have full control, but it's not something I need or want from him all the time. I still like to have power over him sometimes."

Dante chuckles and shakes his head. "Lexi, if you don't think you have power over all of us, you're sorely mistaken."

I form a reply in my head, but my exhaustion takes me over, and I never get to speak the words aloud before I drift into sleep.

Chapter Twenty-One

Steak and Blowjob Day

Dante hands me a green dress with a tight bodice that has a sweetheart neckline and a skirt that flares out from the waist and falls to a couple of inches above my knee.

"No underwear, Angel. We want access to you all evening." His eyes are dark as they travel my naked form.

"Yes, Honey."

Harrison has come over to Los Angeles with Heather, so our dinner out tonight is now going to include the guys. We're going to a popular restaurant downtown, and I'm nervous because I know the paparazzi like to hang out and catch celebrities as they arrive and leave.

I pull the dress on, and once the zip is done up, I turn to face Dante. My breasts are pushed high by the tight bodice with plenty of cleavage on display. He places his hands on my breasts and runs his thumbs back and forth over my nipples. They're stiff and obvious against the soft fabric.

"I like this dress on you. What will you do if the paparazzi take your picture, though?" I shudder at the thought, and he smiles. "Everyone in the world will know how turned on you are when they see your stiff nipples. Unless you think you can control your body, Angel?"

"I can try, Honey," I breathe, certain that I can't.

The thought of everyone around the world seeing me like this is hot. I know that people will take the pictures and add them to galleries of celebrities with hard nipples. The thought of strangers masturbating to photos of me heats my blood, and Dante's cock is stiff in his trousers.

He raises my skirt to my hips and exposes my pussy to his view. "What if there's a gust of wind and your skirt flies up?" He spins me away from him to face the mirror. "I want you to look and see what would be on display." He runs his hand down my stomach to rub my wet clit. "You like that idea, don't you?"

"Yes, Honey," I breathe, even though I don't think I could survive the humiliation if it actually happened.

"Maybe I'll lift your dress myself, just to make sure it happens."

I gasp at the thought of Dante purposely exposing me to the world, even though the thought is wildly erotic. He continues to rub me as I pant for breath, but he doesn't bring me anywhere near orgasm before he stops.

"Come out to the living room when you've finished getting ready. I'm not done with you."

"Yes, Honey."

I pull on a pair of silver heels, finish doing my hair and makeup, then toss my powder and lipstick in a silver clutch before I head out to the living room. I find the guys all there and sitting next to one another in a line on the sofa, even though we don't need to leave for another two hours. I wondered why Dante insisted I get ready so early, but it appears he has something planned.

"You look good, Sexy Lexi," Nate says as his eyes rove over my body.

"Lift your dress, Alexandra."

I do as Logan asks and pull the skirt of my dress up to my waist for them to see.

"Mmm…her cunt looks as wet and juicy as ever," Ash says as he licks his lips.

My pussy clenches, and Dante says, "On your knees, Angel."

I drop to my knees, where I'm standing about twenty feet away from them. Dante looks at me as he unbuckles his belt, and, in unison, the other guys follow suit. I watch as they stand in sync and drop their trousers and briefs to the floor before sitting down again. It reminds me of watching them perform together as a band, and it's, categorically, one of the best shows I've ever seen.

"Come here, Angel." I start to stand and walk over to them, but as I do, Dante says, "No. Come here on your hands and knees."

My cheeks burn with heat as I crawl to Dante and the guys. They watch me with hunger in their expressions, their cocks rock hard as I make my way toward them. Cool air hits my heated pussy as I arrive in front of Dante, and my breathing is shallow as I look up at him.

"Worship my cock, Angel."

I take him in my mouth, and he places a hand on my head as I sink onto him. I revel in the feeling of blowing him, and I can sense when he's about to come.

"Stop, Angel," Dante says and pulls my head off his cock. I look up into his chocolate-brown eyes and blink at him as I try to understand his request. "Blow Ash."

"Yes, Honey."

I move across on my knees so that I'm in front of Ash and take his thick cock in my mouth. Some movement catches my eye from next to me, and I glance over to see what it is. Nate's fist is wrapped around Logan's cock, and he pumps it up and down as I blow Ash.

I let out a low groan at the sight of them because I love watching them pleasure each other. Ash strokes my head while I suck him and play with his balls. When I think he's about to come, he grabs my hair to pull me off his cock with it, and the pain in my scalp sends a shock of arousal straight to my pussy.

He still has his fist in my hair as he holds my face up to look at him. "Go suck Logan."

I realize the plan as I move across again. Logan and Nate are slowly stroking each other as they look at me, and I bite my lip as I watch them.

"What do you want, Alexandra?"

"To suck your cock, Sir," I say as arousal floods through my body.

He leans across and kisses Nate, their tongues intertwining as they stroke one another. Nate rubs his thumb around the head of Logan's cock, and Logan gives a low groan that sends me wild. Finally, they break apart, and Logan turns to look at me.

"Okay, go ahead."

Nate pulls his hand back, and I sink onto Logan's cock. I take him as deep as I can for as long as I can, and the small thrusts of his hips tell me he's enjoying himself. My hands rest on his thighs for balance, and Logan wraps his fingers around my wrists.

"She's not putting these to good use," he murmurs.

He takes my hands and places each of them on Ash's and Nate's cocks, and I groan around Logan's erection. Ash guides my hand on him and places his over mine as he strokes up and down while Nate's cock fills my other fist, and I pump him.

Logan's cock jerks in my mouth, but he's the king of orgasm denial, even for himself, so I know he won't come. My dress is lifted over my hips, and when Dante thrusts his cock into me, I gasp in shock. He fucks me slowly, nowhere near the kind of rhythm to make me come. I suck Logan for a long time while I stroke the others, but I don't have any chance of getting Ash or Nate to orgasm with my hands because I'm too focused on the sensations in my mouth and pussy.

"Go suck Nate, Alexandra," Logan eventually growls.

My jaw has a throbbing ache as Dante pulls out of me, and I move on to Nate. I wrap my lips around his thick cock while Dante rubs my clit, and I moan in ecstasy. He brings me to the edge of orgasm before he stops and pulls my dress back down over my ass.

I groan in disappointment, and it's less than a second before he rips my dress back over my hips, and he growls, "Don't you dare complain if I decide you're not ready for an orgasm, Angel."

He smacks my ass hard, and my pussy clenches as juice drips down my thigh. I gasp onto Nate's cock and continue my blow job while Dante punishes me. I'm in complete ecstasy, and when he finishes spanking me, Dante rubs my clit until my body shakes, and I'm on the precipice of orgasm before he stops again.

I don't dare make a sound as he pulls my dress down, but Nate does. He thrusts into my mouth and makes a guttural groan as he holds his cock down my throat.

"I'm going to come. Get the fuck off my cock right now," he growls.

I blink at him as I remove my mouth from him, and he smirks back at me.

"Go blow Dante."

I turn toward him, and he's sitting back next to Ash again. I don't bother trying to stand. Instead, I just crawl over to him. Both Logan and Ash rub my hot ass cheeks as I pass them.

This continues for so long that I lose track of how many times I blow them. Occasionally, one will fuck me while I blow another, or they get me to give them a hand job while I suck someone else. Nobody lets me orgasm, and they move me on before they come. My jaw is in agony by the time Nate is the first one to blow in my mouth. I swallow his load, and he thrusts into my mouth a few more times before he smiles down at me.

"Thank you, Sexy. You can go blow Dante now."

I crawl back over to Dante and put him in my mouth as Ash positions himself behind me to fuck me. My pussy clenches around his cock, and he groans.

"Mmm…I fucking love being in your cunt, Lexi."

I'm at such a heightened state of ecstasy that it almost tips me over the edge, but Dante notices and reaches down to twist my nipple in the dress.

"No. Do *not* come, Angel," he growls.

I suffer through Ash fucking me as he rubs my clit, and when Dante has me move on to Ash, I can taste my pussy juice on his cock. He places his hand on the back of my head and forces my mouth to the base of his thick, hard cock. It makes its way down the back of my throat, and I gag on him, my jaw throbbing with pain.

Ash fists his hand in my hair and pulls me back by it before he shoves me down again the second I catch my breath. He gags me with his cock over and over, and my eyes roll back in my head as my pussy clenches repeatedly. I want to come, and I'm so, so close, but the pain in my jaw seems to be preventing me from really getting there.

It doesn't stop Ash, though, who pulls me all the way down on him, my nose to his stomach, as he comes down my throat. I gag, and he pulls my head back as cum drips out of my mouth, over my lips, and onto Ash's thigh.

"Clean me up, baby," he murmurs as he looks at me.

I start by licking his thigh, then around his cock, and finally up his shaft to the head. I take him in my mouth and suck him a few times before I pop him out of my mouth.

"Come finish me off, Alexandra," Logan tells me.

I look over, and he's in an embrace with Nate, who is stroking his cock. Logan kisses him again as I take my place in front of him and wrap my lips around his erection. Nate strokes him while I blow him but pulls his hand off Logan's cock after about a minute. It feels like it takes hours for Logan to blow.

Whenever he comes close, I can sense him holding back from it, which drives me mad. I'm in complete agony, and Dante has been rubbing my clit on and off to bring me to the brink of orgasm over and over. I'm wild with lust, and I desperately need release, but I know I won't get it.

Logan holds off longer than I could ever have expected. He grunts and moans as he keeps his orgasm at bay.

Finally, Dante says, "You have a time limit, Logan."

"Fine," he murmurs.

He places a hand on either side of my head and fucks my mouth roughly. His cock thrusts in and out of me while Ash reaches a hand down and strokes my breast through my dress. I moan onto Logan's cock, and he fucks me harder. Finally, he holds himself deep in my mouth as he comes down my throat. He pushes his cock in and out a few more times as his cock jerks, and he spills his seed in me.

Finally, he pulls me off him, and I can't hold myself up anymore. I collapse on my back on the floor and gasp for breath as the ache in my jaw intensifies now that there's no sexual pleasure to combat it.

Ash reaches down and flips my skirt up to my hips. "There. I like this view."

"Me, too," Logan agrees, and a few seconds later, I hear the telltale sound of his phone taking a picture of me.

"Oooh, we get to take pictures of her?" Ash asks.

"I do," Logan laughs.

After another few seconds, Ash takes a picture of me. Then, he moves around to take one from another angle. He pushes my legs apart to spread me before he takes another one. He kneels over me, pulls my dress down under my breasts, and takes yet another picture.

"You're so fucking hot, baby," he murmurs as he rolls my nipple between his forefinger and thumb while he snaps more pics.

"Thank you," I say, in total bliss despite my painful jaw and the desire to be fucked to orgasm.

"We have to go," Dante says. "The limo will be here soon."

Ash pulls my dress back up and climbs off me.

"Come here, Angel," Dante says, and I go to sit in his lap. He holds me tight and strokes my arms gently as he asks, "How are you?"

"In desperate need of an orgasm, thank you for asking," I groan.

Dante chuckles. "Naturally. But are you okay?"

I have a slight comedown, but I know we don't have time for full aftercare, so I say, "I should be fine as long as I get to be with you and Logan in the limo."

Dante kisses me softly. "Of course."

When the limo arrives, I catch sight of myself in the window of the car as we climb inside. "Holy fucking shit. I'm a fucking mess," I gasp.

Nate pulls me hard against him and bites my earlobe with his teeth. "Yes, you fucking are, and you're going to stay that way."

He swipes a smudge of lipstick away from my lips, but I pull out my compact and check my reflection to see that the rest of my lipstick is clearly worn away. There are tear tracks on my face from where they ran down my cheeks a few of the times I was gagged. My hair is a disaster and sticking out in all directions.

"The paparazzi will take photos," I breathe.

"And the whole world will see our slut looking beautifully used by her men," Logan says from my other side as he slides his hand up my inner thigh to rub my clit.

"Isn't this a bad idea?" I ask with a gasp.

"Is it, Angel? Don't you like the idea of everyone seeing you after you've blown four men one after the other and swallowed their loads?" Dante twists a clearly obvious nipple in my dress. "Because I think you do."

I pant for breath as Logan strokes me faster, and I moan, "Yes, Logan. Oh god, yes."

He yanks his hand away, and I blink at him for a few seconds as my orgasm rapidly recedes.

"I can't do it," I moan, and I'm not sure if I'm talking about walking the paparazzi looking as used as I do or surviving the torture of Logan's orgasm denial.

"Yes, you can, Angel." Dante kisses me with a slow, loving kiss. "We'll crowd around you, and they'll barely be able to see you."

Relief floods through me, and I nod. "Okay."

Logan and Dante keep me on edge throughout the rest of the ride to the restaurant. When we get there, the paparazzi are indeed there to take our pictures, but the guys crowd around me, and I keep my head down. In all honesty, it's probably not much different from the usual pictures they get of me.

When we get inside, though, it's a different matter entirely. I'm suddenly aware that everyone here can get a very good look at me. It's only when I'm around other people that I remember the guys are famous, like, *really* famous now.

This latest single has put them into the next level of celebrity, and people whisper and stare as we speak to the hostess, who stammers over her words. She takes us to a table where Heather and Harrison are seated and talking casually despite the people around them all gawking at them.

They stand and hug us as we greet them, then I take a seat between Heather and Dante.

"I'm so excited about tomorrow," I tell her with a grin.

"Me, too." She smiles back at me.

We talk while we order appetizers, and when they arrive, the ache in my jaw intensifies when I try to chew. I do my best to keep the pain from showing in my expression, but Dante looks at me and gently strokes my leg.

When we're ordering our mains, I'm about to order a salad for something nice and easy to chew when Dante says, "You should have the steak, Angel. It sounds delicious."

I blink at him, then turn up to look at the waiter and force a smile at him as I say, "I'll have the filet mignon steak, medium rare, thank you."

Dante squeezes my leg and kisses my cheek before he whispers in my ear, "Good girl. With every chew, you can think of us."

I shudder, and he's absolutely right. Eating the steak is pure agony. Every chew forces me to work my aching jaw, but it equally causes my pussy to throb with pleasure at the memory of them using me.

Halfway through, though, I think I'm going to cry, so I say, "If you'll excuse me, I need to use the bathroom."

I've been in there for a couple of minutes when Heather appears with a concerned look on her face as I dab at my eyes with a tissue. "Are you okay, darling?"

I glance around the bathroom to make sure it's empty, then nod. "Yes. It's probably TMI, but I swear to god I spent, like, two hours giving head before we came here, and Dante made me order steak."

"Oh my fucking god." Heather bursts into laughter. "What an asshole. It's totally something Harrison would do to me, though."

"It huuuuurts," I moan as I stretch my jaw.

Heather pulls out a compact and steps next to me in the front of the mirror to powder her nose. "Pro-tip. Cut *much* smaller bites than you usually would. If it's a good steak, it should break up pretty easily in your mouth. I'd suggest shredding it on your plate, but if Dante's anything like Harrison, that would get me punished before we even left the restaurant."

I laugh and nod. "Without a doubt. Fuck, I'm so glad we're friends. I've never had someone that I could tell this shit to."

"Yeah, until the guys got partners, I was pretty short on lady friends and nobody who was a sub. It's also hard when your closest friends are guys who are all hot as fuck and in a band. Every woman I knew just wanted to fuck my friends." She shrugs and puts her compact back in her dress pocket.

I snort. "Sounds about right. I got burned pretty badly by the last friend I had."

Heather puts an arm around me to give me a hug and smiles down at me. "Well, you've got me now. Ummm, is this look something you were planning?" She raises an eyebrow at me.

"No. 'Freshly facefucked' wasn't actually the look I was going for tonight," I tell her in a dry tone.

She bursts into laughter and nods. "I figured. Let me help you out."

She pulls out her powder again, a small comb, and a lipstick. By the time she's finished, I look a lot better. At the very least, I don't look like I've just had my mouth around multiple cocks.

"Thank you so much," I say as I breathe a sigh of relief.

We walk back to the table together, and as we take our seats, Harrison says, "You two took your time."

"I gave Lexi a makeover. The poor thing said the wind was terrible and caused her eyes to water. I figured it was probably best to fix her up before we have to walk through the paparazzi when we leave." She says it all very casually with a smile at him before she picks up her wine glass to take a sip.

Dante and Logan both give me looks, but I keep my face

neutral. They don't know that Heather is a sub, so they have no reason to think that I would have told her why I looked like a mess.

I follow her advice, and, sure enough, cutting the steak into much tinier portions does make it easier to manage, even though my jaw is still painful as hell.

When we finish dinner, we decide to go to Tempest, a club in downtown Los Angeles, and both Heather and Harrison come with us. The paparazzi take our photographs leaving the restaurant, but the interest gets even more intense when we arrive at one of the hottest clubs in town.

"Wicked Stallion! Are you guys looking forward to going on tour soon?" someone calls out.

"We sure are," Nate says with a smile.

"Is it true you're having an affair with Lexi?" another person asks.

Nate looks at me and laughs. "No. Lexi and I aren't having an affair."

Heather scoffs quietly next to me, "They still ask that about Seb and me *all* the time, even now he's with Lita."

She doesn't know that there are a shitload more valid reasons behind them asking about Nate and me than there is about her and her friend, so I just smile.

"How do you guys know each other?"

To my surprise, this question is directed at Heather and me. She puts an arm around my shoulders and gives the paparazzi member a beautiful smile.

"Lexi has an *amazing* line of stores called Black Lilac, and they're going to be stocking Serenity from tomorrow."

This news sends them wild. They snap tons of photos of us and call out more questions as we head into the club.

"Well, that's probably going to do more to promote the store than any of the ads I've paid for," I laugh at her.

"You're welcome." She grins at me as we head to the bar to get drinks.

We have a great night at the club and don't leave until almost three in the morning. The limo drives Heather and Harrison back to their hotel, and she promises to see me bright and early in the morning.

"You know…a few hours from now," she laughs.

I cringe as I hug her back. "Shoot me now and put me out of my misery."

As soon as the limousine is on its way to our apartment, Ash reaches under my skirt and thrusts his fingers into my pussy. I moan as I turn my face to look into his ice-blue eyes.

"Do you like that, baby?" he murmurs.

"Yes," I gasp.

Nate pulls my dress under my breasts and says, "I'm going to shove my cock into your pussy as soon as we get home."

"She's definitely ready for it," Ash assures him as he kisses me.

I alternate between kissing Ash and kissing Nate while Dante and Logan watch on for the rest of the drive home. When we get inside, Ash leads me to the room he's decided will be his. He pulls my dress off and tosses it aside as I lie on the bed with my head on the pillows.

The guys all stand around the bed in various states of undress, but all with stiff cocks. Nate fucks me first, and Ash climbs onto the bed next to me and rubs my clit until I come around Nate's cock.

He clamps his lips around my breast as Dante pushes his cock into me after Nate pulls out. He grabs my legs and puts them over his shoulders as he pounds into me. Ash straddles my chest and stuffs his cock into my mouth. My jaw still hurts so badly, but the pain is pleasurable as Dante fucks me roughly.

Nate moves over to play with my breasts as Dante dumps his load in my pussy, and it's only a moment before Logan takes his place. Dante moves to my sides and rubs my clit. Waves of pleasure roll through me as I come on Logan's cock, but the ecstasy doesn't end as I'm subjected to the sensations even as my clit becomes incredibly sensitive.

My body shakes, and Ash pulls his cock out of my mouth and

claims my lips with his. Nate has his lips around one breast, and Ash tweaks the other nipple as he kisses me. Another orgasm rips through me, and I come on Logan's cock as he buries himself in me and comes while he thrusts in and out of me. He pulls out of me, and Ash wastes no time in ending our kiss so he can push his cock into my pussy.

Logan moves up to lie next to me and kisses me gently while Ash fucks me. I'm floating away, and he tethers me to Earth amidst all the pleasure.

Ash thrusts into me a final time and grips my thighs tight as he comes with a loud groan. I'm treated to cuddles and cleaning from Logan before I end up tucked into bed with Ash, exhausted, satisfied, and painfully aware that my alarm is going to go off in three hours.

Chapter Twenty-Two

Pool Time III

"I'm pretty sure I'm dying," I groan to Heather as I let her in the back door of Black Lilac's Rodeo Drive store.

The front of the store is crowded with paparazzi after last night's announcement, despite the fact that I've already called the police once today to move them along.

"I know the feeling." She scrunches her nose up at me. "My head is pounding, and I didn't want to stop for painkillers since we were being followed."

"Come with me," I laugh as I head to my office.

I pull out a box of headache tablets, and Heather thanks me as she takes them off me.

"We played for over an hour when we got home," I say with a yawn. "It was good, but I'm tired as hell."

"God, no wonder you're wrecked. Harrison at least waited until this morning to be my alarm cock—" she cuts herself off and bursts into laughter. "I meant to say 'clock,' but considering he woke me up with his cock in my mouth, it's pretty accurate."

I laugh as well, then stop and groan, "Don't make me laugh. My head hurts."

"I'll just have a little look around the store while we wait for the delivery." The glee is obvious in Heather's expression as she says it.

"Is Harrison going to want to have words with me later, Heather?"

She smirks at me. "Probably. I have to keep on top of good fashion, you know."

"No doubt. I'll just check my emails while you have a look around."

There's nothing overly important in my email, but I reply to a few and clear the unread ones before I head into the store. We order coffees to drink, and they arrive about fifteen minutes before the delivery of the clothes comes in.

"Oh my god, I'm so excited!" I jump and clap my hands as the first boxes are brought through and into the storeroom at the back.

We start going through the clothes with Jasmine, the store manager, who stares at Heather in awe occasionally, but Heather ignores it. Everything is checked off against the packing list and the order before it's added into our inventory system.

By the time we take the clothes into the store to set them up, it's packed with customers, and I kind of wish Heather hadn't announced it last night. We'd normally wait until the day after a delivery to set up a new shipment of clothes in the store, but the customers have been harassing my staff all morning about wanting the Serenity clothes they were promised.

We work as quickly as possible, and Heather signs a few autographs for people, which blows my mind. I'm so grateful nobody sees me as that kind of celebrity, though a few Wicked Stallion fans do casually mention Dante and the "Heavenly Promises" music video to me.

By lunchtime, I'm dead on my feet. I call Vera and Sherry, who report that the other stores are having the same experience. For once, I'm actually grateful to leave the store when Callum drives Heather and me to The Henry for our lunch reservation.

When we've received our meals and are eating, Heather asks, "How's your jaw today?"

"Still fucking painful. That's why I ordered soup."

It's an absolutely delicious chicken tortilla soup. It's thick and creamy, and the chicken is soft enough not to require too much chewing.

"Solid choice," she laughs as she spears a piece of tortelloni on her fork, then groans as she chews it. "This is good. I bet even Seb and Lita would like it."

"They're picky about their pasta, are they?"

Heather rolls her eyes. "That's an understatement. But they'd like this, I think."

We're silent for a minute, and I'm aware that we'll have to face the paparazzi again when we leave the restaurant. We've been seated in a booth at the back of the restaurant, so we have a little privacy, though I'm very aware of the other patrons close by.

"Do you mind if I ask what happened the last time we were here?" Heather asks as she picks up her wine glass to take a sip.

My heart pounds in my chest as I remember Cassie's text and phone call. It feels like so long ago. Heather's clear blue eyes are looking at me with interest, and I consider how much to tell her. I decide to go with a version of the truth.

"Remember when I said last night that I got burned pretty badly by the last friend I had?"

Heather's eyebrows raise, and she nods her head. "Yes."

"She contacted me that day and threatened to go to the media with a story about Dante and me."

"Wow. That's fucked up." I wonder if Heather is going to ask what the story is, but she doesn't pry, and I'm grateful for that. "No wonder celebrities have trust issues. It feels like people see us as dollar signs."

I snort because Heather has no idea exactly how close to the truth she's gotten right now. "Basically. Anyway, let's not ruin our day talking about her."

"Of course not. Well, I promise never to sell a story about you, if that helps?" Heather gives me a grin.

"You know what?"

"What?"

"It really does, thanks. I'm so glad we met." I smile back at her.

We finish up our meal and make our way to a big, black SUV with the assistance of Heather's bodyguard. We answer questions from the paparazzi about Black Lilac and Serenity, but we both ignore questions thrown at us about our personal relationships with the bands.

When we get back to the store, Heather and I hang out together in the staff room for most of the day. A cake I ordered in the shape of the Serenity logo is delivered late in the afternoon, and Heather gasps when she sees it.

"This is amazing! Did you do this?"

I nod. "Yup. Cakes are going to the two other stores as well."

Heather takes a picture, and she tags me in it when she posts it online. I get the notification that @officialheatheryork has tagged me in a post, and I smile when I see it.

I've had a great day at @blacklilacfashion with @lexirosesullivan. Check out this cake she had made! Her stores are officially stocking @serenityclothesofficial, so make sure you go to any of her three locations to see my designs.

I press the little heart button to like the photo and write a comment amidst the ones that are already flying in.

It's absolutely been my pleasure, @officialheatheryork. I'm so honored to be working with your brand, and the clothes are gorgeous!

I punctuate it with the heart-eyes emoji, and Heather laughs as she likes my comment. "It's been a great day."

I couldn't agree more, and I'm still standing there with Heather, eating blessedly soft cake and talking when my phone starts vibrating in my pocket.

I pull it out of my pocket, and my stomach drops as I see the name Casandra Foster on the screen. On some level, I feel like I should've known she would call me today.

"Excuse me. I need to take a call," I say to Heather as I force a smile at her.

I rush to my office and slam the door behind me as I answer Cassie's call with my heart pounding in my chest.

"What do you want?" I demand.

"So aggressive, Alexandra. I just called to talk."

"Let me guess. You still have the photos, and you want more money."

I think I might be sick, and my jaw tightens as the nausea increases when Cassie's sickening laugh comes through the line.

"It's funny you should say that. Here's the thing, Lexi. It was *my* idea for you to stock Serenity, and here you are online, acting like it was some brilliant thing you came up with. I feel like I deserve some compensation for that, don't you think?"

Hot tears streak down my cheeks, and I want to throw my phone across the room because I'm so angry and frustrated.

"You've *been* compensated. Twice. We've paid you *two hundred thousand dollars*, Cassandra. You can't keep doing this."

"Can't I? The way I see it, I have all the power here. You don't want the world to know what a slut you are. I have pictures to show the world what a slut you are. If you pay me another two hundred thousand, I'll be set financially, and I'll leave you alone."

I snort in derision. "Bullshit. Why should I believe you this time when you've lied twice before?"

"Put it this way, Alexandra. What choice do you have? I'm happy to take this story to the highest bidder. I would've thought that would be you."

"Fuck you. I have to speak to the guys, though. You know that."

"I thought you would. Will you be on your back with your legs spread when you do?"

The vitriol in her voice turns the blood in my veins to fire.

"Maybe. Are you jealous, Cassie? Do you wish it was you

getting fucked by the gorgeous men of Wicked Stallion?" I snarl.

There's an awful moment where I realize I didn't exclude Ash, and my heart pounds in my chest.

"*All* of the men, Lexi? Because I thought Ash was dating some model from Russia."

"Czechia," I correct her as casually as I can. "Štěpánka is from Czechia."

I can't breathe, and I don't want to give her any more information than that.

"I see. She wasn't with Ash in those pictures of you from last night. Where was she?" Cassie asks casually.

"I have no clue. I'm not her keeper, and this conversation is done. I'll get back to you once I've spoken to the guys."

I hang up the call and drop my head in my hands. I'm so close to sinking into despair. I can't handle this and having Cassie holding those photos over our heads. I call the guys and tell them what happened, then promise to be home as soon as I can to discuss it.

When I get back to Heather, she takes one look at my face and asks, "What's wrong?"

"Remember that friend I told you about? She's basically obsessed and doesn't like seeing me happy. She saw your post and called me to threaten to go to the press again."

"Shit," Heather breathes out. "I'm so sorry. Do you want me to take the post down?"

I shake my head. "No point. She's seen it, and it's triggered her to come at us again."

"What are you going to do?"

"I don't know." I sigh. "We'll probably meet with her to—" I don't want to admit we've been paying her off, so I continue, "—try and talk her out of it again."

"Sounds crazy. I'm sorry you're going through this. If there's anything you need me to do, I'm always here for you."

"Thanks," I tell her, truly grateful for her support.

I don't stay much longer at Black Lilac. I'm so stressed, and

Heather gives me a big hug as she leaves as well, once again putting out the offer of her support. I thank her and drive to the apartment with my body wound tighter than a spring.

When I arrive, the guys are sitting in the living room with somber looks on their faces as they talk. I take them in before I announce my presence. They're so beautiful, and I love them all so much. I remind myself that I would do all of it again to be with these men, no matter what happens.

"Hi, guys," I say with a tight smile at them.

I greet Dante and Logan with a kiss each before I take a seat between Nate and Ash on the sofa. I press my lips against Nate's, and he pulls me against him before I end our kiss and turn to Ash to kiss him as well.

"We think we've come up with a solution," Logan says, and I raise my eyebrows at him.

"What is it?"

"We've spoken to a lawyer, and he's going to draw up an NDA for Cassie to sign. He'll email it through tonight to print out and give to her. She won't be able to talk about us to anyone at all, let alone the paparazzi."

I blow out a breath of air as the simplicity of it hits me. "Fuck. We should've thought of this before we paid her two hundred grand."

"That's what I said," Ash tells me with a bitter laugh.

It's as though a massive weight has been removed from my shoulders. It's so clear that this is a real solution to the problem of Cassie. We discuss it for another fifteen minutes and decide how best to go about it before I call her back.

"Alexandra," she answers the phone in a curt voice.

"I'll see you tomorrow at Ash's place. Two p.m."

"Why are you going to Ash's place?" she asks, sounding suspicious.

"To be frank, I don't want you in my home, and he's graciously offered to let me meet you there."

The truth is that we don't want her to come to our new place.

Ever. After tomorrow she'll be out of our lives, and this place won't be tainted at all by her presence.

"Fine. I'll see you there."

"There's one more thing," I say before she can hang up.

"What?" she asks, sounding annoyed.

"We'll only pay you if you sign a non-disclosure agreement." My heart pounds as the line goes silent, and I wait for her response.

"That's bullshit," she finally says.

I sigh and say honestly, "Cassie, this will be the third time we've paid you off to keep quiet. We're all tired and stressed, and we just want this to end."

"I'll have to think about it. I'll call you back."

We're all on edge for about half an hour before Cassie calls me back.

"Fine. I'll sign the agreement. I'll see you at Ash's tomorrow at two."

The call cuts out, and I sigh as I hang up and look at the guys. "She'll meet us there. I fucking hate this, but I'm glad it's almost over. I'll take tomorrow off work because I'll be useless."

"I can go over with you." Ash puts his arm around me and pulls me against him before he kisses my head. "I'll keep you distracted."

"I bet you will," I say with a laugh as I look up at him.

The heavy mood is broken, and Logan raises an eyebrow at me. "Are you wearing clothes in my apartment, Alexandra?"

Arousal floods through me, and I nod. "I am. Sorry, Sir."

"I'll give you a pass because of the situation, but I'd like you to remove them immediately."

I dutifully remove my clothing, and Dante has me take it and put it away. By the time I walk back into the living room, I'm wet with desire.

"Sit on my lap, Angel," Dante says.

I do as I'm told, and the guys talk while he gently strokes my body. In usual Dante fashion, he avoids my erogenous zones, and it drives me wild. Nate and Ash both spend a lot of their time staring at me, but Dante and Logan are both relaxed and casual while paying me no attention. All four men are obviously turned on, though.

"Let's play pool," Nate suggests.

We head to the upstairs living room where Nate's pool table now resides, and the guys play a few games. I sit on a stool at the side of the room with my legs spread as per Dante's instruction while I watch them. One of them will come over and play with me every few minutes, and I drip juice on the leather stool whenever they do.

"How about you play Nate next, Angel?" Dante suggests after Nate beats him.

"Of course, Honey. You know I love a good beating."

Nate stalks over to me and pulls my body roughly against his as I stand up. "I want you to beat me," he says with a smirk. "If I win, you have to spend the night with me."

"Deal. If I win, you have to spend the night with me, and if it's a tie, we have to spend the night together," I joke.

"I agree to those terms. Let's shake on it." He holds his hand out, and I laugh as I shake his hand.

Nate breaks and sinks two balls. He's got four down before I even get to take a shot. I bend over to do it and gasp when something hard runs up my slit. I look over my shoulder to see Dante with a pool cue in his hand and a wicked grin on his face.

"What's wrong, Angel? Shouldn't you be taking your turn?" He raises an eyebrow at me.

I turn back to the table, and as I take aim for my shot, Dante pushes the pool cue between my folds, teasing me with it as he puts pressure on it at my entrance. I hit the white ball as Dante pushes the cue into me a small way, but he pulls it out again as I stand up.

When I turn to look at him, he's holding the cue upright and looks totally innocently at me, but Logan also has a cue in his hands despite not being a part of this match.

"Your turn, Lexi," Nate says after he gets another ball down, leaving him with only one colored ball and the black eight-ball to go.

I move around the table, and Logan follows me. He wastes no time once I've bent over to push his pool cue into me, and I gasp. I try to focus on my shot, but I hold my position as the thick end of the cue stretches me. Logan pushes it in and out slowly, and I pant for breath as I hit the white ball and somehow manage to sink a ball.

I move again for another shot, and when I bend over, there's immediate pressure on my asshole, and I gasp loudly. I have no lube, and I know there's no way my ass can take a pool cue without it, but the pressure persists.

"Take your turn, Angel," Dante murmurs from behind me.

"Yes, Honey," I pant.

The pressure increases and, as the pool cue slips into my ass, I realize it's the shooting end, so it's small enough to fit. I scramble together enough focus to take my turn, but I don't get anything down.

Nate sinks his final ball, but when he shoots at the eight ball, he clearly doesn't even attempt to get it down. Instead, he shoots it at the side of the table, so it ricochets from side to side without going anywhere near the pocket.

"Whoops. What a terrible shot. Your turn, Lexi."

I blink at him a couple of times, then head to the other side of the table for my turn. As I pass him on my way, Ash reaches down and slides his fingers through my slit.

"Your cunt is so wet, Lexi. Do you like being fucked with pool cues?" He raises an eyebrow at me.

Heat rushes to my cheek at the humiliation of being fucked with something like a pool cue, and I shrug at him as I say as casually as I can, "I guess so."

The guys all laugh, and my cheeks burn hotter as I bend over the table. This time, Logan pushes the thick end of the cue into my pussy again, and I pant for breath as I take another terrible shot. My clit aches to be touched, and I need an orgasm.

Nate shoots the eight ball into the pocket this time but

immediately walks over and pulls it out again before he walks over to me. He places it on the table next to me as Logan removes the cue from my pussy. Nate spins me to face Logan, then picks me up and sets me on the edge of the table. The rubber bumper is cold and hard under my ass.

He hands me the black pool ball and murmurs, "Rub your clit with this."

I gasp as I take it off him. Dante and Ash have both joined Logan to stand in front of me. I lean back and balance on one arm as I spread my legs. My cheeks burn as I rub my clit with the cold pool ball against my hot, wet clit.

"What a pretty little pool slut," Logan says when I catch his gaze.

My orgasm rolls over me at his words. I don't know why, but being called a slut has become the hottest thing ever. I moan, and my body shakes while I come.

I close my eyes and throw my head back, so I'm surprised when a pool cue is pushed into my pussy again. Logan thrusts it in and out of me as I continue to rub my clit with the pool ball. He hands the pool cue off to Ash, who thrusts it further into me and causes me to gasp.

Ash fucks me with it for a few minutes before Nate takes over. I'm in complete ecstasy and lightheaded from how erotic it is to be used like this. There's something about being fucked by an implement that is hot as fucking shit. Dante takes over, and then Logan has another turn while I come again, and my pussy clenches around the thick pool cue.

Logan takes the cue out and puts the end near my mouth. "This needs cleaning, Alexandra."

I take the cue in my mouth as heat floods through me at the further humiliation of being made to clean it with my tongue. I can taste my juices on it, and I suck it as though I'm giving it a blow job.

"Very good." Logan pulls the cue away. "So, whose turn is it now?"

I blink at him. "But, I thought…"

"What did you think, Alexandra? We're playing pool. Is something about that confusing you?" He raises an eyebrow at me.

"Go sit on your stool, Angel. You lost your game, so I guess you're spending the night with Nate."

I can barely walk as I hop off the pool table and walk to the stool. I spread my legs, and my pussy repeatedly clenches while the need to be fucked overwhelms me. This time, Nate plays Logan and Ash comes over to me while they do.

"Let me eat this cunt. It looks tasty."

He buries his face in me, and Dante says casually, "Don't come, Angel."

I almost lose my mind trying to keep myself from having an orgasm while Ash uses his tongue skillfully to torment me. This goes on for two more hours. The guys play pool while I'm forced to sit where I am and be subjected to sexual torture whenever they see fit.

"On your knees, Angel," Dante finally says. "I think Logan, Ash, and I need to use your mouth before you go to Nate's bed. Don't come."

They crowd around me, and I slip off the stool and drop to my knees. They take turns fucking my mouth, and I use my hands to stroke whoever isn't in my mouth at the time. Nate crouches behind me and plays with my breasts. When he reaches between my legs and rubs my aching clit, I squeak in alarm around Logan's cock.

Logan grips my chin in his hand, shoves his cock all the way down my throat, and gags me with it. "Nate can do whatever the fuck he wants to do to you. It's up to you not to come, Alexandra."

He pulls his cock out when he finishes speaking and then thrusts it back in, fucking my mouth until his cum gushes into my mouth. Ash comes next, and by the time I've swallowed his load, I can barely hold off the orgasm that threatens to overwhelm me. Dante holds my face in his hands and facefucks me roughly until he achieves orgasm, and I have tears running down my face when I swallow his load.

He pulls me up to stand and kisses me gently before he pushes me toward Ash. I kiss Ash as well, then move on to Logan.

"Can you take care of her after you fuck her?" Dante asks Nate.

"Sure," he agrees.

"Nate is going to give you care, but we'll be here if you need us, Angel." Dante pulls me against him and rubs my clit in a maddening way. "You can come with him."

"Thank you, Honey."

The second the door is closed behind Nate, I throw myself at him and thrust my tongue into his mouth as I frantically attempt to undo his jeans.

Nate breaks our kiss and laughs. "Do you need something, Lexi?"

"Yes," I growl. "A fucking orgasm. Like, two hours ago."

Nate picks me up and throws me over his shoulder as I squeal and laugh. He walks toward the bed, tosses me onto it, and dives between my legs. I scream when his tongue hits my clit, and my body explodes into orgasm.

Nate lifts his head but keeps rubbing my clit as I come. "That's it. Come for me, Sexy. God, you're fucking hot when they work you up like this."

I buck against his fingers, and he leans down again to clamp his lips around my clit. I writhe and moan as two more orgasms hit me, one after the other. I pant for breath as Nate stands up and strips off his clothes, and I groan as I look at him. He's so fucking beautiful with his angular jaw, high cheekbones, a six-pack above the hard cock on display for me, and muscular thighs that I want wrapped around me.

He climbs over me and thrusts his cock into me before letting out a guttural moan before he fucks me harder than he ever has before. I realize he's been on edge probably as long as I have. It takes all the strength I have to roll him over and onto his back.

"Wrap your legs around me," I tell him as he looks at me in surprise.

Nate laughs. "Okay, then."

He does as I ask, and I love the feeling of his thick cock filling me while his thighs squeeze tight around me. We fuck like this for a while before I sit up and ride him. He grabs my breasts and twists and pulls them while we fuck. When he reaches one hand between us to rub my clit, I lose myself again. I clench his cock tight with my pussy as I scream his name, and my vision blurs around me.

His cock jerks inside me, and he fills me with his hot cum. I grind myself on him, fucking him through both of our orgasms before I collapse on top of him as I try to catch my breath. Nate wraps his arms around me and kisses my head.

"I love you, Lexi."

"I love you, too," I pant.

He washes me in the shower and then dries me before we head to bed, and I fall asleep wrapped in Nate's warm and loving embrace. I can't wait for tomorrow to be over and that contract to be signed so Cassie will officially be out of our lives.

Chapter Twenty-Three

Power Struggle

I carefully fold some of Ash's clothes and place them in a suitcase. We came to his place after breakfast so we could pack some of his stuff up to move to the apartment.

"Thank fuck I booked the movers for next month. I have so much shit to get rid of before I move."

I laugh and nod. "Yeah, combining four households into one means we do have a lot of extra things we don't need. Maybe we can find a good charity to donate them to."

"Good idea," he agrees.

We're both tired of packing by lunchtime, and we take a break for an early lunch. I go to a local café and get us toasted Turkish bread sandwiches with coffees to drink while Ash puts the boxes into one of the spare rooms that we've started piling things in.

Once we've cleaned up from our meal, I turn to Ash and walk backward out of the kitchen as I pull my t-shirt over my head to reveal my breasts to his gaze. "So, what should we do now?" I place my hands on my breasts and squeeze them as his gaze darkens. "I mean, we have two hours before Cassie gets here. We should do some more packing..."

"I'm definitely thinking about packing something of mine into you," he murmurs as he stalks toward me.

"What would that be?" I ask as I tilt my head up to look into his ice-blue eyes as he stops in front of me.

"My cock into your wet cunt for a start."

I gasp, and my pussy aches as he says it. He gets a look of deep satisfaction on his face as he lifts his hands to my breasts, but I wrap my fingers around his wrists and pull them away.

"Did I say you could touch my breasts?" I raise an eyebrow at him.

"It's like that, is it?" He laughs, and I nod.

I step back from him as I unbutton my jeans while I kick off my shoes. "Indeed, it is."

My heart pounds in my chest, my nipples are painfully hard, and my pussy aches as well. Ash's cock is stiff in his jeans, and I can't wait to fuck him.

I drop my jeans and step out of them as I continue my path to his bedroom. Ash pulls his t-shirt off and drops it on my jeans. My panties come next, and when I drop them, Ash groans.

He struggles to get his jeans unzipped, and I laugh, "Come on, Ash. Get it together. Do you want to fuck me or not?"

His eyebrows raise, and he strides forward to shove me against the wall that's next to the hallway opening I was about to walk through. He presses his body against mine. His stiff cock pushes into my thigh, and my breasts are squashed against his chest as he stares down at me with his hand on the wall above my head, so I'm pinned in.

"Yes. I want to fuck you. Today. Tomorrow. Every day for the rest of our lives."

He lowers his head and claims my lips with his. He pushes his tongue into my mouth forcefully, the taste of coffee strong in his kiss. I thrust my fingers into his hair and kiss him back with an equal amount of fervor. We kiss for a few minutes before I duck out of his embrace and under his arm.

I continue my path to his bedroom and taunt him, "I'm not sure you do want to fuck me. Your jeans are still on."

Ash growls as I turn to walk toward his room. I've only taken about five steps when I'm shoved against the hallway wall and find myself looking into Ash's beautiful face. His jeans are gone, and his cock is a stiff bulge against his light blue briefs.

He pushes it against my wet slit and rubs it up and down. "Still unclear on if I want to fuck you, Lexi?"

I reach behind him and grab his ass to pull him harder against my clit. "You're sending mixed signals, I think. It's super hard to tell."

"I'm about to fuck you right here and now to prove it to you," he says.

He lowers his head to my breast, and I moan as he takes it in his mouth. I allow him to suck my breast for a few seconds before I push him away from me.

"I don't know. You still have underwear on. Obviously, you don't want to fuck me," I taunt him as I finally make it to his bedroom.

I open the door and walk inside. I've only made it halfway to Ash's bed when he snakes his arm around my waist and pulls me back against him. His cock is thick, hard, and warm against my ass. His skin feels exquisite against mine, and my pussy clenches as he pushes his cock against me. He uses his spare hand to tweak and squeeze my nipples. At the same time, the hand around my waist moves down to my pussy, where he rubs my clit.

I allow the sensations to roll through me as my orgasm builds, and I moan, "Ash."

"Yes, baby. Come for me," he murmurs before he nips my earlobe with his teeth, and I gasp.

My body shakes as I come in his arms. "Fuck, yes. Shit, Ash. Oh my god, yes. Fucking hell."

He strokes me through my orgasm, and I spin in his embrace to kiss him before I drop to my knees in front of him. I take his cock in my mouth and revel in the groan of satisfaction he makes when I do.

I look up into his eyes as I suck him, and he bites his lip as he watches me. I groan onto his cock and raise my hand to play with his balls. He inhales sharply, and I sink onto his cock, so my nose touches his stomach. I hold him there as long as I can before I pull my head back and swirl my tongue around his head.

I do this repeatedly, and the air is filled with the sound of Ash's pants for breath and moans of satisfaction. I continue until he's about to come and pull him out of my mouth before I stand and press my body against him as I kiss him. Our tongues intertwine, and I thrust my hands in Ash's hair as he wraps one arm around my waist to pull me closer to him and places the other on the back of my head.

My pussy aches to be filled by the hard cock that's pressing against my stomach, and I break our kiss to say through panting breaths, "Let's get in bed."

I take his hand as I lead him to the bed, and he murmurs, "Sounds like a plan. I want my cock in your cunt." We stop next to it, and he reaches between my legs to push two fingers into me. "Mmm, just as hot and wet as ever."

He kisses me again while he fingers me, and I moan as our kiss ends, "I want to ride you."

"Your wish is my command."

He climbs onto the bed and lies with his head on the pillow. His legs are stretched out, and his cock points toward his stomach. I groan at the sight of him and bite my lip.

"You're so fucking hot. I can't believe I get to fuck you now," I admit.

I can practically feel it when his eyes rove over my body from head to toe, and he says, "Trust me when I say that I feel the same way. Now come here and let me do exactly that."

I laugh and climb onto the bed to straddle him. I hover my pussy above his cock and look into his eyes as I move down just enough for his cock to push between my folds but not actually enter me.

"Do you want this, Ash?" I raise an eyebrow at him.

"I think you know I do," he says with a laugh and thrusts his hips upward.

I move up, too, so that he doesn't get to enter me. I lie on him instead and press his cock between my pussy lips. I capture his lips with mine as I rub him up and down through my wet slit. His cock feels amazing as it rubs my clit, and I break our kiss to moan as I look down at him.

Ash angles his hips when I reach the head of his cock to try and slip it inside me, but I move so that he can't.

"Tell me what you want, Ash," I tell him.

A thrill of excitement runs through me at the opportunity to torment him this way. After all, I've learned from the best. I can see why Dante and Logan enjoy teasing me because seeing the pure need in Ash's eyes drives me wild.

"I want to fuck your cunt," he murmurs.

"My what?" I raise an eyebrow at him as I slip him the tiniest bit into me.

"Your cunt," he growls as he grips my hips to hold me still and thrusts into me.

I fuck him just long enough for him to relax his grip on my hips and then pull myself off him. My blood pumps through my veins, and my pussy aches as I do the thing that is the complete opposite of what my body tells me to do.

"Sorry, what did you say you want to fuck?" I give him a wicked grin.

Ash pants for breath, and he narrows his eyes at me. "I could easily overpower you, you know."

A dart of arousal heads to my crotch, and a low moan escapes me at the thought. I kind of want to roleplay that.

"Could you?" I rub my slit along his cock again. "All you need to do is tell me what you want to fuck."

This is a win-win situation for me. He either gives me the satisfaction of conceding to my control, or he overpowers me and fucks me on his terms.

I have no clue which route he'll take in the moments before he responds, but I'm in next-level ecstasy at the possibilities I'm presented with.

"I want to fuck your pussy," he groans.

A slow smile comes to my face, and I rub my clit on his cock again. "Do you? Is this what you want, Ash?" I move so he's the tiniest bit inside my pussy again.

"Fuck yes, Lexi. I want to fuck you."

I sink onto him once, then pull off, and he groans in obvious displeasure as I do.

"I will fuck you, but first, I want to sit on your face," I declare.

I move over to kneel above him, and my pussy clenches just from knowing that he's looking at my pussy and that I'm about to ride him.

"Do you like this view, Ash?" I ask as I look down at him.

"Very much so."

He reaches up and rubs my clit with his thumb while he pushes two fingers inside me. I allow him to do this to me until I moan his name when I reach orgasm.

"Thanks for that." I reach down and pull his hands away from my pussy. "Now, eat me until I come again."

I sit on his face, and he immediately starts to lick and suck my clit. I grind my pussy on his mouth as I writhe in ecstasy. He clamps his hands around my thighs and holds me firmly on him as he eats me out.

"Fucking hell, Ash. Fuck, yes. Oh, fuck."

My body shakes as he sends me over the abyss, and he holds me on his mouth as he continues to use his tongue to pleasure me. I come over and over, and after a while, I reach back to stroke Ash's cock in my fist while I ride his face.

I don't know how long we've been doing this when an icy cold voice says from behind me, "I fucking knew it. You goddamn fucking *whore*."

Ash and I both freeze in place at the sound of Cassie's voice. My heart has stopped beating, and I'm cold all over. I climb off Ash and spin to face her where she's standing in the doorway.

Ash quickly yanks the bedcovers over us, and I clutch his arm for comfort as I look at the woman who has tormented us for months.

"What the fuck are you doing in my apartment?" Ash growls.

"I knocked on the door, and nobody answered. Gee, I wonder why that was? Maybe because you were here fucking that slut. I should've known she'd be all over you. Does your *girlfriend* know?"

Ash doesn't answer her question, and instead, he asks one of his own. "How did you get in?"

"Well, since I was going to sign that NDA, I figured I'd give back the key I still had to your apartment."

"You already gave me back the key to my apartment." Ash narrows his eyes at her.

Cassie's cheeks flush red, and she says in a haughty tone. "I took a copy once when I lost my other key, remember? I couldn't find the second one initially, but I found it the other day, and so I thought I should return it."

Bullshit.

I don't say it aloud because I don't want to antagonize her, but I glare at Cassie in hatred.

Ash seems to think it's bullshit, too, because he asks, "By entering my apartment unannounced?"

"As I said, you didn't answer when I knocked because you were in here with this whore. I felt like an idiot standing in the hallway, so I decided to come inside to wait for you."

"You could've called," Ash snarls. "Instead, you saw fit to enter my apartment unannounced and come into my bedroom. That's breaking and entering."

"You're the one who gave me the key." She shrugs. "Anyway, I think I've seen enough."

She turns to leave, and I blink at Ash before I spring up from the bed. "Wait. Where are you going?"

She turns back to me and snorts, "You can keep your fucking money. I don't want it." She looks me over in disdain as I stand naked in front of her, and I hate that I didn't think to bring the bedsheet with me. "If Ashton wants to fuck three other men's sloppy seconds, that's his choice." She looks at Ash. "Enjoy fucking a used-up whore like her."

Ash launches out of bed and is in front of Cassie in a flash. His cock is semi-soft now, but he still looks glorious despite his anger as he towers over Cassie, his hands balled into fists.

"Get the fuck out of my apartment, you bitch," he snarls at her. "Lexi is a thousand times the woman you could ever hope to be. I should thank you for pushing me into her arms. If it weren't for you, I never would've gotten together with Lexi, and she makes me happier than you ever did."

There's a second before Cassie responds, where her face goes slack, and she looks between us before she composes herself. The look on her face is an evil mix of anger and satisfaction.

"Go fuck yourselves." She throws the key to Ash's apartment on the floor, then turns to storm out of the room and slams the door behind her.

I stare at the closed door in shock. "I can't believe that shit happened."

"Hang on," Ash says and rips open the door to rush out of the room.

I start to shake as the enormity of what just happened hits me. Cassie saw Ash and me having sex, and I doubt she's going to sign the NDA now. The sound of loud voices comes to me, and I rush to the door to listen.

"Of course I'm not going to fucking sign it now. You're fucking *her*!" Cassie snarls.

"You blackmailed us, and you broke into my apartment. You're signing the fucking contract." Ash sounds angrier than I've ever heard him in my life.

"Fuck off! Move out of the way and let me out of your stupid apartment. Also, get some goddamn clothes on. You're disgusting. I know where that cock has been."

I hate her.

I hate her so damn much that my blood boils in my veins. I want to run into that room and tear her to pieces. I'm not sure if I would like to do it metaphorically or literally. The way I feel right now, it could be either.

"You're not leaving until you sign that contract," Ash growls.

There's silence for a few seconds, and Ash asks, "What are you doing?"

"Sending myself the file so you can't make me delete it." Cassie sounds supremely satisfied with herself. "I'm not signing the contract, and you can't make me."

After another second, tinny voices come from what I assume is her phone.

"—disgusting. I know where that cock has been."

"You're not leaving until you sign that contract."

Cassie's sickening laugh rings out. "It won't hold up in court even if I sign it now. I suggest you let me go, or I'll have you charged with kidnapping."

"You wouldn't," Ash says, but he doesn't sound a hundred percent sure, and neither am I. "I'll tell them you blackmailed us and broke into my apartment."

"Okay, but that recording doesn't sound very good, does it?" She laughs again, and bile rises in my throat.

No further words are exchanged, but there's the loud sound of a door slamming before it falls quiet again. I walk back to the bed and sit on the edge of it in complete despair. I have no idea what Cassie will do, but I'm pretty certain we're going to be worldwide news before the day is done.

Hot tears roll down my cheeks, and I drop my head into my hands. It's only a few seconds before Ash sits on the bed next to me and pulls me into his arms.

"Hey, it's okay. It's going to be okay," he murmurs.

"It's not," I object. "How could it be? We fucked up so badly by having sex."

I realize with horror that this is my doing. I initiated the sex today. I'm the one who started this. I'm the one who Cassie couldn't handle being friends with Ash.

"This is all my fault," I whisper as I slash at the tears on my face.

Ash takes my chin in his hand and turns his face to mine. "No, Lexi. It's not your fault. It's nobody's fault but Cassie's. She's the one who blackmailed us. She's the one who broke into my apartment. I call complete bullshit on her just happening to have a spare key, and I don't remember her ever getting a copy because she lost it. I would bet my bank balance she took a copy before she gave me her key back."

His words don't make it any better. Knowing I should blame Cassie and that she likely took a copy of the key so that she could sneak into his apartment doesn't make me feel any less shit.

"What are we going to do?" I moan.

Ash kisses my lips gently and says, "We're going to call the guys and tell them what happened. Then we'll see what Cassie does, and we'll deal with whatever happens together because I love you, and that's all that matters."

"I hate this. We've spent all this time with her holding what she knows over our heads. Now we just have to wait and see what she decides to do. She has all the power, and we're just at her whim." Nausea threatens to overwhelm me just from saying it.

"Look at me, Lexi." I turn my gaze to his, and he smiles at me. "She has no power over us. The only important thing is our family. Together, we can do anything. So, let's call the guys and talk to them. I think you'll feel better if you do."

We make the call immediately and tell them what happened. I want to cry because I'm so upset, but I do my best to keep it together. I know there's no point in crying about it since it won't change anything.

"You couldn't have known that she would break into the apartment, Angel. It's not the fault of you two that she did what she did," Dante assures me.

"Thanks, Honey," I reply automatically, even though it hasn't assuaged my guilt.

"I know that if I'd been there, I probably would've been fucking your sexy ass when she broke in, too," Nate says with a laugh.

"Specifically her ass?" Logan asks in a cheeky voice, and it makes me smile.

"Ass. Pussy. Mouth. It's hard to say, really. The point is that my cock would've been somewhere in Lexi, as it should be."

Despite myself, I can't help but laugh. I love them so much, and it's obvious they're trying to distract me from my worries.

"I love you guys. Ash and I will be home soon. We just need to grab the suitcases and boxes we packed before lunch."

"Okay, Angel. We'll see you then."

We end the call, and I drop it next to me on the bed with a sigh.

"Are you feeling better?" Ash asks.

"I think I'll feel best when we get home, and I have you all with me."

Ash drapes his arm around my shoulders and pulls me close to him. "Of course. I think I'll feel better when I'm home with the guys, too."

He drops his lips to mine and gives me a loving, tender kiss. A sense of peace and well-being comes over me as I kiss him back.

Things with Cassie might have gone to complete shit, but everything has been worth it because Ashton Woodford is mine now. I have four men who I love more than life itself, and nothing that Cassandra Foster can say or do will change that.

I'm still worried about the things she can affect. The band. Black Lilac. Our families. My friendship with Heather. If this comes out, I don't know how those things will be affected by the news of our relationship.

"Is that everything?" I ask Ash as he picks up what I'm pretty sure is the final box.

"Yup, this is it. I still have a shitload of packing and sorting to do, but not today." He presses his lips to mine. "Let's go home, baby."

"You don't have to ask me twice." I smile at him.

Ash sets the box down again and pulls me into his arms. He presses his hard body against mine and claims my lips with his. We kiss for a long time, and we both pant for breath as our kiss ends.

"Maybe, when we get home, we could finish what we started

earlier." He dips his head to gently bite my lower lip.

A shot of arousal darts to my crotch, and I raise an eyebrow at him. "Well, that depends. What do you want to fuck, Ash?"

He gives me a slow, seductive smile as he slides his hands into my jeans to find my pussy. He strokes my clit a few times until I have to pant for breath.

He places his lips next to my ear and murmurs, "Tonight, I'll fuck your pussy. Tomorrow, I'll fuck your cunt."

I shudder at his words, and he pulls his hand out of my pants with a wicked grin at me before he picks up the box. We head downstairs and get into Ash's car to drive home. I still don't know what's going to happen with Cassie, but I do know that I'll have my four men by my side through it all.

Epilogue

We spend the evening refreshing online searches for the guys' names as well as mine and Black Lilac, but nothing appears.

"She's probably trying to get the best offer for the story," Nate says in a voice dripping with acid.

Dante locks his phone and leans forward to drop it on the coffee table. "Look, there's nothing. I'm *sure* we'll know the second there is."

"Should we tell Isaac?" Logan asks.

Dante nods. "I think we'll have to. We can call him in the morning."

"I think I'm going to be sick," I moan. "It's all I can think about."

Dante takes my phone out of my hand and sets it on the coffee table next to his. "I know how to get your mind off it." He looks at Logan. "What's your opinion on our angel wearing clothes, Logan?"

Logan gives him a wicked grin. "I've got to say, I'm not a fan. Especially not in my apartment."

My pussy clenches, and Dante's right that this finally distracts me from the Cassie situation.

"What do you want to do about it?" Dante asks him.

Logan looks at me as he replies to Dante. "I think she should get those clothes off if she doesn't want me to get a pair of scissors and cut them off her."

I know exactly what I want to do, so I quickly strip but drop my clothes on the floor at my feet before I sit on the sofa again and leave them where they are.

Dante hisses through his teeth, "Is that where your clothes belong, Angel?"

"No, Honey," I tell him with glee.

He takes my chin in his hands and searches my face for a few seconds. "Go put them the fuck away and come back here at once."

I'm dripping wet by the time I get back to the living room and stand in front of Dante.

"Spanking alone doesn't seem like quite enough punishment for being so wilfully disobedient," Dante says. "What do you think, Logan?"

There's a gleam in Logan's eyes as he looks me over. "It definitely doesn't.

"What do you think we should do to her?"

Nate and Ash are watching this show with stiff cocks, and I'm pretty sure I know what Logan will suggest as a punishment.

"Forty-eight hours without an orgasm will probably teach her what happens to slut toys who seek punishments."

Desire floods through me, and I inhale sharply as I blink at him. It's the longest I'll ever have been denied an orgasm. We've done half-days, but never two days, especially not with the way these guys use my body.

"If you want to complain, Angel, I'll make it a week," Dante says in a stern voice. "Bend over and put your hands on the coffee table."

I do as instructed and get a thrill of arousal, knowing the view I present to the guys sitting on the sofa. Dante comes to stand behind me, and he runs his hand over my ass.

"It just seems like not enough to spank you with my hand today." I hear the sound of his belt being unbuckled, and I inhale sharply. "I need to use something else."

He pulls his belt off, and it dangles below my face. It jerks and raises as he wraps it around his fist, and I can barely breathe. My pussy aches, and the knowledge that he's going to strap me while I can't orgasm for two full days has me in ecstasy.

"Count, Angel."

He brings the belt down over my ass cheek, and I jolt at the pain of the leather hitting my skin as a loud smacking sound rings out around the room.

"One."

"Good girl. Keep counting to fifteen."

I want to moan because fifteen is a lot, but I keep it in and say, "Yes, Honey."

He stops after seven and runs his hands over my cheeks. "So red and hot."

"Hot is fucking right," Ash says.

"Want to come look, Ash?" Dante asks.

There's the sound of movement as Ash gets up before another hand rubs my ass cheek as well. "Very hot."

He gets down below me, and his breath is hot on my pussy as he inspects it. I pant for breath as he does, and my pussy clenches.

"Her cunt is as wet as always." He pushes two fingers into me as I bite my lip and moan. "So ready to be fucked after her punishment."

He uses his other hand to rub my clit, and I pant for breath as he brings me to the edge of orgasm.

I'm just about to come when Dante says, "Enough, Ash. I should finish strapping her."

"Fine, fine. But I want my cock in her soon." Ash laughs and pulls his fingers out of me.

"I'd let you fuck her while I strap her, but I don't want to risk hitting you accidentally."

"Yeah, a belt to the cock isn't exactly an experience I want to have," Ash jokes.

The guys all laugh, and Ash leans down to kiss my burning ass cheeks before he steps away. It's only a few seconds before Dante's belt hits my ass again.

I can barely manage to get through to fifteen, and by the time I do, I'm lost to the pain and ecstasy of my punishment. I hold my position and wait for my next instruction.

"Her ass looks amazing. You can see the belt strokes," Logan murmurs from directly behind me, and I'm surprised because I didn't hear him get up.

He rubs his hand over my ass before I hear the telltale sound of his phone taking pictures of me. I'm wildly aroused at the knowledge that there will be photographic evidence of me in this position.

"Can you send those to me, Logan?" Ash asks.

"Take your own, you lazy asshole," Logan laughs.

"Good idea." There's clear amusement in Ash's voice.

After about fifteen seconds, he pushes his cock into my pussy and holds it there. When I hear the sound of his phone taking pics, I realize that he's taking ones of himself inside me, and I moan as my pussy clenches around him.

Ash drops his phone on the coffee table in front of me with it unlocked, and the picture of his thick cock buried in my pussy is displayed on it. It's so fucking erotic that I almost come around him immediately.

Nate appears in front of me and picks up the phone to look at the picture. "Hot."

"Let me see?" Logan asks, and Nate hands the phone to him.

Logan hands it to Dante, who is hard as a rock in his jeans. I lick my lips, and Nate laughs next to me.

"You want something to suck, Lexi?"

He kneels on the coffee table in front of me, and I watch him pull his jeans down. I look up into his beautiful blue eyes as he shoves his cock into my mouth.

It doesn't matter what Cassie does tomorrow tonight. I'm in pure bliss with the men I love, and that's all I care about right now.

Sneak Peek for Wicked Freedom

"We're here today with Cassandra Foster, the source behind the absolutely *shocking* story about Wicked Stallion. Cassandra, thanks for being with us today."

The interviewer smiles at Cassie, and I feel sick to my stomach. I clutch Dante's and Ash's hands as I sit in between them on the sofa to watch the interview that's been hyped up all week. Nate and Logan are sitting next to one another on the other side of the L-shaped sofa.

She's sitting in an armchair across from the interviewer, who's also in an armchair as though they're having some casual conversation and not blowing up our lives.

"Thanks for having me," Cassie says with a simpering smile.

The hair and makeup artists at the TV station have done a good job. Cassie looks stunning. Her black hair is in loose waves, and she's wearing a baby blue dress with soft, pink hues to her makeup. All in all, she looks innocent and not at all like a woman who would blackmail someone for two hundred thousand dollars and attempt to get another two hundred thousand as well.

"Now, let's start at the beginning. How did you meet Ashton Woodford?"

He squeezes my hand as she begins telling the interviewer about how they met at a coffee shop. She makes it sound as though

Ash chased her pretty hard at the beginning of their relationship, and he scoffs next to me.

"Bullshit. She initiated all those calls and texts. I should've known she was too needy from the get-go."

The interviewer leans forward in his seat when they've gone through Ash's relationship with Cassie. I can see the eagerness in his eyes as he practically salivates over what's to come.

"So, Cassandra. Tell us about the 'Heavenly Promises' music video. You've said that's when Nathaniel Walker first started sleeping with Alexandra Sullivan, as most of us suspected."

Cassie nods and looks somber with a slight frown on her face. "Yes, it was. I didn't know about it at first. They hid it from us. Her, Dante, and Nate, that is."

"How did you find out?"

This was all in the print article Cassie did that has since been chopped up, rewritten, and distributed worldwide.

"They called us over to their house and told us that Lexi and Nate were together and that Nate was living with them."

The interviewer steeples his fingers under his chin and says, "I see. How did you take this news?"

"I was confused at first. I mean, who does that? But Dante was fine with it, can you imagine? Anyway, everyone seemed okay, and they said Nate had been in love with Lexi for years, so that made it okay."

"Interesting. So, tell us what happened next?"

Cassie flips her hair behind her and says, "So, I accepted this alternate relationship they wanted to have. I was trying to be a supportive friend, but look where that got me!"

The interviewer gives a laugh with Cassie, and I want to vomit. She's putting on a good show and seems so hard done by. Ash puts his arm around me and kisses the top of my head as I sigh loudly.

"Anyway, it was a few months after that when Ash and I got called to come to Logan's apartment. Then they tell us that Logan and Lexi were in a relationship as well."

"So, let me get this straight. You were dating Ashton

Woodford, the lead guitarist for Wicked Stallion. You're saying that at this point, Lexi Sullivan is married to Dante Sullivan, who's the bassist. However, you've been told that she's also dating both Nathaniel Walker, the lead singer, and Logan Ballantine, the drummer, at the same time?"

Cassie nods her head and purses her lips. "That's correct."

"So, what happened next? Tell me about the demise of your relationship with Ashton Woodford and how that came about."

"I knew she wanted Ashton as well. She told me how she loved him as much as she loved the others, and I could see it in her eyes when she looked at him. I thought that he was committed to me. I really did."

She gives a bitter laugh, looking every bit the hard-done-by ex-girlfriend betrayed by her boyfriend as a pained expression crosses her face.

"Technically, the truth," I snort. "I did say I loved you as much as the other guys, but it wasn't romantic." I look up into his beautiful blue eyes and kiss his lips quickly before I turn back to the television.

"Then I found them in bed together."

The timeline she's given makes it sound as though it happened while they were still dating, and I seethe internally at the way she's spinning it.

The interviewer gives a shocked gasp as though he hasn't read this in every magazine or online article already this week. "He cheated on you with her?"

"I feel so stupid. I should've known he would do this from the very moment Lexi set her sights on getting the entire band into her bed." Cassie drops her eyes to the floor, and a single tear falls down her cheek.

The interviewer hands her a tissue and says, "It's not your fault. Nobody could expect their partner to do this to them."

There's a moment of silence while Cassie wipes her face, and she gives a solemn nod before the interviewer clears his throat.

"So, you came with plenty of 'receipts,' as they say. You had photographs of Lexi with both Nate and Logan, as well as voice recordings of Lexi admitting that she's sleeping with the band and Ashton talking about sleeping with her as well. What do you say to the Wicked Stallion fans who have accused you of taking advantage of the situation?"

Cassie recorded our phone conversation, where she baited me into talking about sleeping with them. She also got Ash to talk about sleeping with me before she left the apartment, and I overheard them arguing over her not signing the contract. She took snippets of things we said, totally out of context, to prove her story.

"I would say that if you'd been lied to and cheated on and betrayed like I have, you might start tallying your receipts as well."

"The band has been tight-lipped this week, but photos are coming out of Lexi in close embraces with the band members who aren't her husband. What do you say to the rumors that this has been going on for a long time?"

Cassie shakes her head. "No. That's not true. Though, I wouldn't be surprised if Lexi wasn't trying to get them all in her bed for years. We've all seen how close she was to the band, and I saw it in person. She probably wanted this all along."

The interview continues, and I watch in horror as Cassie displays every aspect of our lives for the world to see. By the time it ends and the TV is turned off, I sit and stare at the blank screen in shock.

I blink a few times and announce into the silent room, "So, that happened."

Acknowledgments

This book wouldn't be what it is if it weren't for the people that supported me along the way.

Mum – You actually get to hear these books read by a real human! I'm sure you're going to love hearing Michelle basically orgasm as she reads the book to you. This thank you *isn't awkward at all!*

Beate – Only one more reverse harem before I go back to contemporary romances for a little while. Sorry I have you reading a genre you hate!

Julia – It's almost time for your book, just Wicked Freedom to go! Thanks for being amazing and always giving me feedback when I need it.

Béné – I'm so glad you're along for this ride and, like Julia, I know that I can always count on you to give feedback whenever I need it. I really enjoy our middle-of-the-night conversations!

Štěpánka – Thank you for reading each chapter as I wrote and giving me your thoughts. I also really appreciate you lending me your name for a certain Czechian model. Thanks for not being freaked out when I asked you where you lived!

Daena – I've thanked you so many times now, I'm running out of things to say. Thanks for always listening and for having a smutty mind.

Ally – When this stupid pandemic fucks off, I'm going to come over and meet your babies! I love you. I can't believe you've made two wholeass humans since I saw you last!

Michelle – I cannot *wait* for you to read this book. You're currently busy narrating Wicked Opportunity but there's so much in this book that I'm excited for you to read. Especially the pool cues. *snorts*

Melissa – HAPPY BIRTHDAY!!!!!!!!!!!! I'm writing these acknowledgements on the 7th of March, but this book comes out on the 14th of March, so it works ABSOLUTELY PERFECTLY FOR THIS TO BE YOUR BIRTHDAY WHEN YOU READ THIS!!!!!!!! ;)

You're my oldest friend…well…not my *oldest* friend but my oldest friend, you know? Anyway, I love your guts. <3

All my advance readers – Thank you so, so, so much to all of my wonderful advance readers. I love that you're willing to read my work and give me your honest thoughts on it. I love the messages I get to discuss the books and how many of you are willing to spread the love by sharing my teasers and stuff. Team Cruise Control rocks!

Mark and Lorna Reid – I'm so grateful to you both for everything you do to make my books far more amazing than I could ever manage.

Damien – Thanks for everything. The boys and I love you. I couldn't get these books written without your support.

My readers – If you're reading this, thank you for being here on this author journey with me. I hope that you enjoyed this book. Even though it had more smut than Wicked Opportunity, I tried to balance the plot a little more, so hopefully it's enjoyable. I'm really excited for you guys to read the final book in the series…I'd better go write that. Today is the 7th of March, so I only have a month to write it!

About the Author

Siân Ceinwen lives in Western Australia with her husband and two sons. She grew up with a love of telling or writing stories for her friends to read and enjoy.

Wicked Betrayal is the second book of the trilogy about the members of Wicked Stallion.

If you enjoyed this, please share it with your friends, and please write a review on Amazon or Goodreads.

It would really be appreciated, as this helps more people to discover the book. Reviews assist with the algorithms used by these platforms to display books, so every little bit helps indie authors to get noticed.

You can also join Siân on Facebook, TikTok, or Twitter for all the latest news on the Something Wicked series of novels.

Printed in Great Britain
by Amazon

83276066R00200